The James Tiptree Award Anthology 1

The James Tiptree Award Anthology I

EDITED BY

Karen Joy Fowler · Pat Murphy · Debbie Notkin · Jeffrey D. Smith

TACHYON PUBLICATIONS · SAN FRANCISCO

Book design & composition by John D. Berry. The typeface is MVB *Verdigris.*

contents

vii Introduction | *Pat Murphy and Karen Joy Fowler*

3 BIRTH DAYS | *Geoff Ryman*

19 EVERYTHING BUT THE SIGNATURE IS ME | *James Tiptree, Jr.*

29 THE GHOST GIRLS OF RUMNEY MILL | *Sandra McDonald*

45 BOYS | *Carol Emshwiller*

61 GENRE: A WORD ONLY THE FRENCH COULD LOVE | *Ursula K. Le Guin*

71 *excerpts from* SET THIS HOUSE IN ORDER | *Matt Ruff*

93 JUDGING THE TIPTREE | *Suzy McKee Charnas*

105 THE CATGIRL MANIFESTO: AN INTRODUCTION | *Richard Calder*

131 LOOKING THROUGH LACE | *Ruth Nestvold*

187 "TIPTREE" AND HISTORY | *Joanna Russ*

191 WHAT I DIDN'T SEE | *Karen Joy Fowler*

211 THE SNOW QUEEN | *Hans Christian Andersen*

241 THE LADY OF THE ICE GARDEN | *Kara Dalkey*

263 TRAVELS WITH THE SNOW QUEEN | *Kelly Link*

283 Winners and short lists

293 Acknowledgements

295 About the authors

301 About the editors

introduction

1 | FIRST, SOME JOKES · *Pat Murphy*

What do sex, the future, and chocolate chip cookies have in common? That's what you probably want to know — I'll get to that. But first I have to tell you a couple of jokes.

Maybe joke isn't the right word. When I say "joke," maybe you think you're going to hear something like: "Two guys walk into a bar, and the first guy says...."

That's not the kind of joke I mean. I like jokes — but the jokes I like are not neat and tidy with a clever punch line. The kind of jokes I like are something subversive that takes you by surprise and makes you blink and turns the world into a different place, much stranger and more wonderful than you ever thought possible.

The James Tiptree, Jr. Award strives to be that kind of joke. And it really does relate to sex, the future, and chocolate chip cookies. But to understand the award, you need to know a little about James Tiptree, Jr. So I'll start there.

In the late 1960s, James Tiptree's science fiction short stories first appeared in the pages of science fiction magazines — and immediately caught the attention of science fiction readers. Tiptree's stories were nominated for science fiction's most prestigious awards, winning Hugo Awards in 1974 and 1977, and Nebula Awards in 1974, 1977, and 1978.

Though Tiptree's work was well known and widely admired, the author was reclusive, never appearing in public. In 1975, Robert Silverberg, in an introduction to a collection of Tiptree's stories, commented on this. He wrote: "Inflamed by Tiptree's obstinate insistence on personal obscurity, science fictionists have indulged themselves in the wildest sort of speculation about him.... It has been suggested that Tiptree is a female, a theory I find absurd, for there is to me something ineluctably male about Tiptree's writing. I don't think the novels of Jane Austen could have been written by a man nor the stories of Ernest Hemingway by a woman, and in the same way I believe the author of the James Tiptree stories is male."

Silverberg continued at some length, comparing Tiptree's work to that of Hemingway: "And there is, too, that prevailing masculinity about both of them – that preoccupation with questions of courage, with absolute values, with the mysteries and passions of life and death as revealed by extreme physical tests, by pain and suffering and loss."

One must be careful what one writes. Words can come back to haunt an author. Two years after Silverberg's introduction saw print, Tiptree's identity was revealed. James Tiptree, Jr. was a pseudonym of Alice Sheldon.

Daughter of a prolific author and an African explorer, Alice Sheldon had accompanied her parents on their travels around the world. She had been an artist, a painter, an art critic for the *Chicago Sun*. She joined the army in 1942 and became one of the first women to go through U.S. Army Air Force Intelligence School. Later, she was involved in setting up the CIA's photointelligence section, and after resigning from the CIA, received her doctorate in experimental psychology in 1967. By all accounts, she was a remarkable woman. That's the first joke – a joke on science fiction readers and a joke on Robert Silverberg.

Silverberg has been, I must say, a very good sport about all this. He's a smart guy, and he knows when to laugh at himself, a very good trait. When the world sneaks up behind you and gooses you, you have to laugh. In talking about the "masculinity" of James Tiptree's fiction, Silverberg was falling into a cunning trap – the trap of thinking that people are necessarily constrained by the gender roles assigned by our society. He read Tiptree's writing and recognized that this author had a deep understanding of some very "masculine" subject matter – something you would expect of a person who had served in Army intelligence, in the CIA. So of course, Tiptree was male.

That assumption leads us to the second joke. In 1991, four years after Alice Sheldon's death, Karen Fowler and I created the James Tiptree, Jr. Award. We did it to make trouble. To shake things up. To make people examine the fiction they read a little more carefully. And to honor the woman who startled the science fiction world by making people suddenly rethink their assumptions about what women and men could do.

The Tiptree Award is presented annually to a short story or novel which explores and expands gender roles in speculative fiction. The judges don't look for work that falls into some narrow definition of political correctness. Instead, they seek out work that is thought-provoking, imaginative, and perhaps even infuriating. To change the way that our society thinks about women and men, we need to see people in different roles. The Tiptree Award is intended to reward those women and men who are bold enough to contemplate shifts and changes in gender roles, a fundamental aspect of any society.

The James Tiptree, Jr. Award is devoted to those rare stories and books that challenge the norm, question our hidden assumptions, confront the expectations that we don't even think about, and tweak the unconscious prejudices that influence our perceptions. It takes a great effort to see beyond the technological limitations of our current world – and it takes an even greater effort to see beyond our current social limitations.

Since its inception, the Tiptree Award has been an award with an attitude. In the speech where I announced the creation of the award, I said – half in jest – that the award would be financed with bake sales. It seemed like such a perfect irony: women's work turned to a feminist cause.

One day after the speech, a group of Wisconsin science fiction fans began planning the publication of *The Bakery Men Don't See*, a cookbook that would feed mind as well as body. (The title is derived from James Tiptree's story "The Women Men Don't See.") Over the next year, heroic bakers all over the U.S. held bake sales that doubled as propaganda stations. (They lured you in with chocolate chip cookies, and then told you about authors you may have overlooked.) Work began on a Tiptree quilt, a project for those who would rather sew than cook. And the energetic creators of the first Tiptree cookbook (the only cookbook ever to be nominated for a Hugo Award) got to work on a second Tiptree cookbook, titled *Her Smoke Rose Up From Supper*, after the Tiptree story "Her Smoke Rose Up Forever."

Freddie Baer, a wonderful collage artist, began making spectacular T-shirts for each year of the award. Ellen Klages, writer and improvisational comedian, began conducting a fund-raising auction that people attend for its amusement value, as well as to support the award.

The Tiptree Award itself has expanded beyond the annual award. In its fifth year, the Tiptree organization decided that it was time to put together a list of stories and novels that might have won the Tiptree Award, back before the Tiptree Award existed. The "Retrospective James Tiptree, Jr. Award" effort, which involved all the judges from earlier years, resulted in a list of books and stories that anyone interested in gender exploration should read – and three winners: *Motherlines* and *Walk to the End of the World* by Suzy McKee Charnas; *The Left Hand of Darkness* by Ursula K. Le Guin; and "When It Changed" and *The Female Man* by Joanna Russ. The astute reader will, of course, note that essays by all three Retrospective Tiptree winners are included in this volume.

And of course the bake sales continue – as a political statement, as a means of involving people at the grassroots level, as an excuse to eat cookies, and as an attempt to strike the proper ironic note.

And that is, I suppose, the third joke. In the first year of the Award's existence, an old friend of Alice Sheldon's commented on the bake sales with a touch of disapproval. Alice Sheldon was not, this person said, a bake sale sort of person.

I am not a bake sale sort of person. I am not the sort of person who stitches quilt squares or submits recipes to cookbooks. Yet I have found myself whipping up batches of chocolate chip cookies, stitching a careful seam, and passing along a recipe for chicken casserole — all in the name of the Tiptree Award. It is a strange world where I make a joke — then find that the irony is on me.

But I will happily bake cookies to support this award. The James Tiptree, Jr. Award is dedicated to changing the world by changing our view of gender roles. And if you can't change the world with chocolate chip cookies, how can you change the world?

II | TRANSFORMATIONS IN READING · *Karen Joy Fowler*

I once listened in while some people reminisced about that moment when they first learned that James Tiptree, Jr. was a woman. Their responses ranged from disappointment to delight, but what struck me most was how vivid the memory was. They all remembered who had told them and where and what they were doing and what the time of day was and if they had a cup of coffee in their hand.

I myself never had the experience of reading the work of James Tiptree, Jr. without knowing. I found her stories first in anthologies with introductions (like this one) that unmasked her. Perhaps the editors felt that her femaleness was an important key to decoding her work. Perhaps the exterior story of her pen name was simply too good not to share. I never wondered and I never noticed that I might, as a result, not be reading her in the way she intended. If anything, I probably felt pleased to be in on the joke.

Her stories made a powerful and uncomfortable impression on me. I noted how often she linked male sexuality with violence, how often she dreamed of female solidarity, but never here and now, always in far away times and places. I sensed in her work, some time before I articulated it, that death held for her some awful allure. Which of these things would have changed if I'd believed she were a man?

Or would they all have remained, unchanged, but also unnoticed, in favor of other things — her refusal to comfort herself or anyone else, her toughness, her anger? These are questions about myself, the reader, that I can't answer.

Even harder are the questions I now have about her, the writer.

Could she have written the same stories under her own name? Would Alice Sheldon have felt as free to express herself as angrily, as despairingly, as James Tiptree, Jr. often did? What, if anything, is different about the stories she wrote as Tiptree and those she wrote under the female pen name of Raccoona Sheldon?

I once heard Diane Wakowski begin a lecture on poetry writing with the words, "First you have to create the person who'll write the poem." So the more I think about it, the more of a conundrum it becomes. Is James Tiptree, Jr. a woman? Or is James Tiptree, Jr. a man made up by a woman? And if so which one of them, the man or the woman, wrote the stories?

Does it make a difference? Why?

Of course, if anyone here is going to talk to you about pen names it ought to be Pat Murphy, whose recent mind-spinning three-book project had her writing first as Max Merriwell (a pen name of Pat's) and second as Mary Maxwell (a pen name of Max's (a pen name of Pat's)).

But talking with Pat can be dangerous. I had a conversation with her one day and when it was all over, I was helping administer a new award. I was a policy-maker. I was a troublemaker. I was a fund-raiser.

To be honest (or at least more honest), until I began to write myself, I never paid much attention to the writer's name at all. I can never remember which stories are Tiptree's and which Raccoona Sheldon's, because I rarely bothered to look. So if there were an obvious difference between the two, you'd think I might have noticed, but that, too, might overestimate me. Who knows what I might have been paying attention to. I have been so many readers. I can scarcely be expected to remember them all.

I was a reader long before I was a writer. And for many years, I was not a female reader. Many women share this past with me. Were the books we read growing up mostly about boys? It didn't matter to us.

We were boys ourselves (or a particular boy – the hero of the book) when we read them.

I don't mean to suggest that because we didn't notice, it didn't matter. If it hadn't mattered, we wouldn't have been so profoundly effected when, as older readers, we picked up that first novel – for me it was *The Golden Notebook* by Doris Lessing – and finally saw ourselves.

It's a wonderful thing to find yourself in a book. "That's exactly what I've always felt," you think and you are pleased by the author's thoughtful inclusion of you. You! You! Are worthy of literature. Are pretty damned faceted and fascinating.

Losing yourself in a book is equally wonderful. Sometimes you put the book down and, just for a moment, you've forgotten where and who you are. It takes you just that moment to be you again. Who were you in between? Someone fictional. Someone magical. Someone under a spell.

But then. Then – there are those times, rare and always to be remembered, when you finish a story and are not quite the same person you were when you started it. These stories, if specifically about gender, are the stories the Tiptree Award hopes to find.

The Tiptree Award is looking for stories that seduce or repel you. Instruct and surprise you. Push you around a bit. Take no prisoners. Make no apologies. The Tiptree Award is looking for stories for women.

And stories for men.

And stories for the rest of us, too.

The James Tiptree Award Anthology 1

Birth Days

Geoff Ryman

As Suzy McKee Charnas notes in her essay following this story, from the very beginning of the Tiptree Award the founding mothers didn't want a women's award. "Expanding and exploring gender roles" is larger than "expanding and exploring women's roles" – although, of course, men's roles have been explored for thousands of years.

All along, Tiptree judges have found stories about men's roles. This one, which starts as a contemporary (or near-contemporary) coming-out story, continues in stages thirty years into the future, as scientific discoveries turn out to have enormous implications for the narrator, for gay men, for all men, and for the human race.

Today's my 16th birthday, so I gave myself a present.

I came out to my Mom.

Sort of. By accident. I left out a mail from Billy, which I could just have left on the machine, but no, I had to go and print it out and leave it on my night table, looking like a huge white flag.

I get up this morning and I kinda half-notice it's not there. I lump into the kitchen and I can see where it went. The letter is in Mom's hand and the look on her face tells me, yup, she's read it. She has these gray lines down either side of her mouth. She holds it up to me, and says, "Can you tell me why you wouldn't have the courage to tell me this directly?"

And I'm thinking how could I be so dumb? Did I do this to myself deliberately? And I'm also thinking wait a second, where do you get off reading my letters?

So I say to her, "Did you like the part where he says my dick is beautiful?"

She says, "Not much, no." She's already looking at me like I'm an alien. And I'm like: Mom, this is what you get for being NeoChristian — your son turns out to be homo. What the Neos call a Darwinian anomaly.

Mom sighs and says, "Well I suppose we're stuck with it now."

Yeah Mom, you kinda are. Aren't you supposed to say something mimsy like, Ron honey you know we still love you? Not my Mom. Oh no. Saying exactly what she thinks is Mom's way of being real, and her being real is more important to her than anything else. Like what I might be feeling.

So I dig back at her. "That's a shame, Mom. A few years later and I would have been embryo-screened and you could have just aborted me."

Mom just sniffs. "That was a cheap shot."

Yeah, it was. NeoChristians are about the only people who *don't* abort homosexual fetuses. Everybody else does. What do they call it? Parental choice.

So Mom looks at me with this real tough face and says, "I hope you think you've given yourself a happy birthday." And that's all the conversation we have about it.

My little brother is pretending he isn't there and that he isn't happy. My little brother is shaped like a pineapple. He's fat and he has asthma and he's really good at being sneaky and not playing by the rules. I was always the big brother who tolerated stuff and tried to help Mom along. Her good little boy. Only now I'm samesex. Which to a NeoChristian Mom is like finding out your son likes dressing up as a baby and being jerked off by animals. Sometimes I think Neo is just a way to find new reasons to hate the same old things.

What really dents my paintwork is that Mom is smart. What she likes about Neo is that it's Darwinian. Last summer she's reading this article "Samesex Gene Planted by Aliens?" And she's rolling her eyes at it. "The least they could do is get the science straight," she says. "It's not one gene and it's not one part of the brain." But then she said, "But you gotta wonder, why is there a gene like that in the first place?"

My Mom really does think that there's a chance that homos are an alien plot. Please do not fall over laughing, it hurts too much.

Ever since the Artefacts were found, people have been imagining little green men landing on this beautiful blue planet and just going off again. So people scare themselves wondering if the aliens are about to come back with a nice big army.

Then about five years ago, it turned out that the genes that control sexual orientation have some very unusual sugars, and all of a sudden there's this conspiracy theory that the aliens created the samesex gene as some kind of weapon. Undermine our reproductive capacity. Even though when they landed we were all triblodites or whatever. Maybe having homos is supposed to soften us up for conquest. Hey, if the aliens invade, I promise, I'll fight too OK?

On my way to school I ring Billy and tell him "Mom found out. She read your mail."

Billy sounds stripped for action, "Did she go crazy?"

"She went laconic. You could just hear her thinking: you gotta own this, Ronald, you did this to yourself, Ronald."

"It's better than crying."

Billy's in Comportment class. He believes all that shit. To be fair to him, that "you gotta own this" was me digging at some of the stuff he comes out with. That stuff pisses me off. In fact right now, everything pisses me off. Right now, it's like my guts are twisting and I want to go break something.

Comportment says you've got to own the fact people don't like you, own the fact you got fat hips, own the fact you're no good in math, own the fact that glacial lakes are collapsing onto Tibetan monasteries. Comportment says hey, you're complaining about the Chinese treatment of Tibet, but what have you personally done about it?

It's like: we'll make everybody who has no power feel it's their fault if stuff goes wrong, so the big people don't have to do anything about it.

My Mom hates me being a homo. She likes being a big tough lady even more. So, she like, doesn't get all upset or cry or even say much about it. Being a tough lady is her way of feeling good about her son being an alien plot.

Billy is too focused on being Joe Cool-and-Out to cut me any slack. His stab at being sympathetic is "You should have just told her straight up, like I told you."

I say back to him in this Minnie-Mouse voice, "I acknowledge that you are absolutely right." That's another line he's used on me.

He's silent for a sec and then says, "Well, don't be a bitch with me about it."

"It's my authentic response to an emotionally charged situation." Still sounding like Minnie Mouse.

I'm mad at him. I'm mad at him because he just won't unbend. Nobody unbends. It's bad comportment.

Billy comes back at me. "This is just you going back to being a baby. Only you don't have tantrums, you just whine."

"Billy. My NeoChristian Mom now knows I'm samesex. Could I have some sympathy?"

"Who's died, Ron? Anybody dead around here? Did you lose any limbs in the detonation? Or are you just getting all significant on my ass?"

"No. I'm looking for a friend. I'll try and find one, you know, someone who likes me and not my dick?"

And I hang up.

Like I said, I'm so mad.

I'm mad sitting here right now. I got my stupid kid brother who's been giggling all day, like it's such an achievement he likes pussy. I got my Mom doing the household accounts and her shares and her rollovers, and she's bellowing into the voice recognition and it's like: look at me having to do all the work around here. I'm realizing that I've probably screwed up my relationship with Billy and wondering if I really am the incredible wimp he thinks I am.

It's like everything all around me is Jell-O and it's setting into lemon-lime, which I hate. I'm out. My brother knows and will try to give me a hard time, and if he does I'll slug his fat face. My Mom is being hard ass, and so I'm going to be hard ass back. I'm not an athlete, I'm not Joe Cool-and-Out, and I'll never go to Mom's Neo seminars.

I'm just sitting here all alone thinking: how can I win? What can I do?

I'll never be able to be a good little boy again. That is not an option. I'm not interested in being political about who I sleep with. I don't sign up to anything, I don't believe anything, and I don't like anybody, and I don't think anybody likes me.

Hey. A fresh start. Happy birthday.

So, 26 today!

I got up at 3:00 A.M. and holoed over to the Amazon to say hi to João. He looked so happy to see me, his little face was just one huge smile. He'd organized getting some of his sisters to line up behind him. They all waved and smiled and downloaded me a smart diary for my present. In Brazil, they still sing Happy Birthday.

Love conquers all. With a bit of work.

I called João later and we did our usual daily download. His testosterone levels were through the roof, he's getting so stimulated by his new job in the Indian Devolved Areas. He's about to go off to Eden to start his diplomatic work. He looks so sweet in a penis sheath and a parrot's feather through his nose. Standard diplomatic dress for a member of the Brazilian Consular Team.

I love him I love him I love him I love him.

I am so god damned lucky. They didn't have embryo-screening on the Amazon. Hey! A fellow sodomite. We're an endangered species everywhere else. Must eliminate those nasty alien genes.

Then I had to go and tell him about how my project was going. And he looked glum.

"I know you don't like it," I told him.

"It feels wrong. Like genocide." He pronounces it jenoseed. "Soon they will be no more."

"But it's not genocide. The babies come out hetero, that's all. No more samesex, no more screening, just happy babies. And the adults who are left can decide for themselves if they want to be cured or not. Anyway, the Neos say that we're the genocide."

"You don't need to help them."

"João. Baby. It won't affect us. We'll still have each other."

"The Indians say it is unwise."

"Do they? That's interesting. How come?"

"They say it is good to have other ways. They think it is like what almost happened to them."

That rang true. So me and João have this really great conversation about it, very neutral, very scientific. He's just so smart.

Before the alien gene thing, they used to say that homos were a pool of altruistic non-reproducing labor. It's like, we baby-sit for our siblings' kids and that increases the survival potential of our family's genes. Because a gene that makes it unlikely that you'll have kids should have died out. So why was it still here?

João tells his usual joke about all the singers in Brazil being samesex, which is just about true. So I say, wow, the human race couldn't reproduce without Dança do Brasil, huh? Which was a joke. And he says, maybe so.

I say like I always do, "You know, don't you, baby?"

His voice goes soft and warm. "I know. Do you know?"

Yes. Oh yes, I know.

That you love me. We love each other.

We've been saying that every day now for five years. It still gives me a buzz.

It was a big day at the lab too. The lights finally went on inside Flat Man.

Flat Man is pretty horrible, to tell you the truth. He's a culture, only the organs are differentiated and the bones are wafer-thin and spread out in a support structure. He looks like a cross between a spider's web and somebody who's been hit by a truck. And he covers an entire wall.

His brain works, but we know for a fact that it performs physical functions only. No consciousness, no narrative-of-the-self. He's like a particularly useful bacterial culture. You get to map all his processes, test the drugs, maybe fool around with his endomorphins. They got this microscope that can trail over every part of his body. You can see life inside him, pumping away.

Soon as I saw him, I got this flash. I knew what to do with him. I went to my mentor, wrote it up, got it out and the company gave me the funding.

People think of cells as these undifferentiated little bags. In fact, they're more like a city with a good freeway system. The proteins get shipped in, they move into warehouses, they're distributed when needed, used up and then shipped out.

We used to track proteins by fusing them with fluorescent jellyfish protein. They lit up. Which was just brilliant really since every single molecule of that protein was lit up all the time. You sure could see where all of it was, but you just couldn't see where it was going to.

We got a different tag now, one that fluoresces only once it's been hit by a blue laser. We can paint individual protein molecules and track them one by one.

Today we lit up the proteins produced by the samesex markers. I'm tracking them in different parts of the brain. Then I'll track how genetic surgery affects the brain cells. How long it takes to stimulate the growth of new structures. How long it takes to turn off production of other proteins and churn the last of them out through the lysosomes.

How long it takes to cure being homo.

It's a brilliantly simple project and it will produce a cheap reliable treatment. It means that all of João's friends who are fed up being hassled by Evangelicals can decide to go hetero.

That's my argument. They can decide. Guys who want to stay samesex like me...well, we can. And after us maybe there won't be any more homosexuals. I really don't know what the problem with that is. Who'll miss us? Other samesexers looking for partners? Uh, hello, there won't be any.

And yes, part of me thinks it will be a shame that nobody else will get to meet their João. But they'll meet their Joanna instead.

Mom rang up and talked for like seventeen hours. I'm not scared that I don't love her anymore. I do love her, a lot, but in my own exasperated way. She's such a character. She volunteered for our stem cell regime. She came in and nearly took the whole damn program over, everybody loved her. So now she's doing weights, and is telling me about this California toy boy she's picked up. She does a lot of neat stuff for the Church, I gotta say, she's really in there helping. She does future therapy, the Church just saw how good she is with people, so they sent her in to help people change and keep up and not be frightened of science.

She tells me, "God is Science. It really is and I just show people that." She gets them using their Personalized Identity for the first time, she gets them excited by stuff. Then she makes peanut butter sandwiches for the homeless.

We talk a bit about my showbiz kid brother. He's a famous sex symbol. I can't get over it. I still think he looks like a pineapple.

"Both my kids turned out great," says Mom. "Love you."

I got to work and the guys had pasted a little card to the glass. *Happy Birthday Ron, from Flat Man.*

And at lunchtime, they did this really great thing. They set up a colluminated lens in front of the display screen. The image isn't any bigger, but the lens makes your eyes focus as if you are looking at stuff that's ten kilometers away.

Then they set up a mini-cam, and flew it over Flat Man. I swear to God, it was like being a test pilot over a planet made of flesh. You fly over the bones and they look like salt flats. You zoom up and over muscle tissue that looks like rope mountains. The veins look like tubular trampolines.

Then we flew into the brain, right down into the cortex creases and out over the amygdala, seat of sexual orientation. It looked like savannah.

"We call this Flanneryland," said Greg. So they all took turns trying to think of a name for our new continent. I guess you could say I have their buy-in. The project cooks.

I got back home and found João had sent me a couple of sweet little extra emails. One of them was a list of all his family's addresses ... *but my best address is in the heart of Ronald Flannery.*

And I suppose I ought to tell you that I also got an encryption from Billy.

Billy was my first boyfriend back in high school and it wasn't until I saw his signature that I realized who it was and that I'd forgotten his last name. Wow, was this mail out of line.

I'll read it to you. *Ron*, it starts out, *long time no see. I seem to recall that you were a Libra, so your birthday must be about now, so, happy birthday. You may have heard that I'm running for public office here in Palm Springs* — well actually, Billy, no I haven't, I don't exactly scan the press for news about you or Palm Springs.

He goes on to say how he's running on a Save Samesex ticket. I mean, what are we, whales? And who's going to vote for that? How about dealing with some other people's issues as well, Billy? You will get like 200 votes at most. But hey, Billy doesn't want to actually win or achieve anything, he just wants to be right. So listen to this —

I understand that you are still working for Lumiere Laboratories. According to this week's LegitSci News they're the people that are doing a cure for homosexuality that will work on adults. Can this possibly be true? If so could you give me some more details? I am assuming that you personally have absolutely nothing to do with such a project. To be direct, we need to know about this treatment: how it works, how long a test regime it's on, when it might be available. Otherwise it could be the last straw for an orientation that has produced oh,...and listen to this, virtue by association, the same old tired list...*Shakespeare, Michelangelo, da Vinci, Melville, James, Wittgenstein, Turing*...still no women, I see.

I mean, this guy is asking me to spy on my own company. Right? He hasn't got in touch since high school, how exploitative is that? And then he says, and this is the best bit, *or are you just being a good little boy again?*

No, I'm being a brilliant scientist, and I could just as easily produce a list of great heterosexuals, but thanks for getting in a personal dig right at the end of the letter. Very effective, Billy, a timely reminder of why I didn't even like you by the end and why we haven't been in touch.

And why you are not going to get even a glimmer of a reply. Why in fact, I'm going to turn this letter in to my mentor. Just to show I don't do this shit and that somebody else has blabbed to the media.

Happy effin birthday.

And now I'm back here, sitting on my bed, talking to my diary, wondering who it's for. Who I am accountable to? Why do I read other people's letters to it?

And why do I feel that when this project is finished I'm going to do something to give something back. To whom?

To, and this is a bit of a surprise for me, to my people.

I'm about to go to sleep, and I'm lying here, hugging the shape of João's absence.

Today's my birthday and we all went to the beach.

You haven't lived until you body surf freshwater waves, on a river that's so wide you can't see the other bank, with an island in the middle that's the size of Belgium and Switzerland combined.

We went to Mosquerio, lounged on hammocks, drank beer, and had cupu-açu ice cream. You don't get cupu-açu fruit anywhere else and it makes the best ice cream in the world.

Because of the babies I had to drink coconut milk straight from the coconut...what a penance...and I lay on my tummy on the sand. I still wore my sexy green trunks.

Nilson spiked me. "João! Our husband's got an arse like a baboon!"

It is kind of ballooning out. My whole lower bowel is stretched like an oversized condom, which actually feels surprisingly sexy. I roll over to show off my packet. That always inspires comment. This time from Guillerme. "João! Nilson, his dick is as big as you are! Where do you put it?"

"I don't love him for his dick," says João. Which can have a multitude of meanings if you're the first pregnant man in history, and your bottom is the seat of both desire and rebirth.

Like João told me before I came out here, I have rarity value on the Amazon. A tall *branco* in Brazil...I keep getting dragged by guys, and if I'm not actually being dragged then all I have to do is follow people's eye lines to see what's snagged their attention. It's flattering and depersonalizing all at one and the same time.

The only person who doesn't do it is João. He just looks into my eyes. I look away and when I look back, he's still looking into my eyes.

He's proud of me.

In fact, all those guys, they're all proud of me. They all feel I've done something for them.

What I did was grow a thick pad in Flat Man's bowel. Thick enough for the hooks of a placenta to attach to safely.

I found a way to overcome the resistance in sperm to being penetrated by other sperm. The half pairs of chromosomes line up and join.

The project-plan people insisted we test it on animals. I thought that was disgusting, I don't know why, I just hated it. What a thing to do to a chimp. And anyway, it would still need testing on people, afterward.

And anyway, I didn't want to wait.

So I quit the company and came to live in Brazil. João got me a job at the university. I teach Experimental Methods in very bad Portuguese. I help out explaining why Science is God.

It's funny seeing the Evangelicals trying to come to terms. The police have told me, watch out, there are people saying the child should not be born. The police themselves, maybe. I look into their tiny dark eyes and they don't look too friendly.

João is going to take me to Eden to have the baby. It is Indian territory, and the Indians want it to be born. There is something about some story they have, about how the world began again, and keeps re-birthing.

Agosto and Guillinho roasted the chicken. Adalberto, Kawé, Jorge and Carlos sat around in a circle shelling the dried prawns. The waiter kept coming back and asking if we wanted more beer. He was this skinny kid from Marajo with nothing to his name but shorts, flip-flops and a big grin in his dark face. Suddenly we realize that he's dragging us. Nilson starts singing, "*Moreno, Moreno …*" which means sexy brown man. Nilson got the kid to sit on his knee.

This place is paradise for gays. We must be around 4 per cent of the population. It's the untouched natural samesex demographic, about the same as for left-handedness. It's like being in a country where they make clothes in your size or speak your maternal language, or where you'd consider allowing the President into your house for dinner.

It's home.

We got back and all and I mean all of João's huge family had a party for my birthday. His nine sisters, his four brothers and their spouses and their kids. That's something else you don't get in our big bright world. Huge tumbling families. It's like being in a 19th-century novel every day. Umberto gets a job, Maria comes off the booze, Latitia gets over fancying her cousin, João helps his nephew get into university. Hills of children roll and giggle on the carpet. You can't sort out what niece belongs to which sister, and it doesn't matter. They all just sleep over where they like.

Senhora da Souza's house was too small for them all, so we hauled the furniture out into the street and we all sat outside in a circle, drinking and dancing and telling jokes I couldn't understand. The Senhora sat next to me and held my hand. She made this huge cupuaçu cream, because she knows I love it so much.

People here get up at five A.M. when it's cool, so they tend to leave early. By ten o'clock, it was all over. João's sisters lined up to give me a kiss, all those children tumbled into cars, and suddenly, it was just us. I have to be careful about sitting on the babies too much, so I decided not to drive back. I'm going to sleep out in the courtyard on a mattress with João and Nilson.

We washed up for the Senhora, and I came out here onto this unpaved Brazilian street to do my diary.

Mom hates that I'm here. She worries about malaria, she worries that I don't have a good job. She's bewildered by my being pregnant. "I don't know baby, if it happens, and it works, who's to say?"

"It means the aliens' plot's backfired, right?"

"Aliens," she says back real scornful. "If they wanted the planet, they could just have burned off the native life forms, planted a few of their own and come back. Even our padre thinks that's a dumb idea now. You be careful, babe. You survive. OK?"

OK. I'm 36 and still good looking. I'm 36 and finally I'm some kind of a rebel.

I worry though, about the Nilson thing.

OK, João and I had to be apart for five years. It's natural he'd shack up with somebody in my absence and I do believe he loves me, and I was a little bit jealous at first...sorry, I'm only human. But hey – heaps of children on the floor, right? Never know who's sleeping with whom? I moved in with them, and I quite fancy Nilson, but I don't love him, and I wouldn't want to have his baby.

Only...maybe I am.

You are supposed to have to treat the sperm first to make them receptive to each other, and I am just not sure, there is no way to identify, when I became pregnant. But OK, we're all one big family, they've both ...been down there. And I started to feel strange and sick before João's and my sperm were...um...planted.

Thing is, we only planted one embryo. And now there's twins.

I mean, it would be wild wouldn't it if one of the babies were Nilson and João's? And I was just carrying it, like a pod?

Oh man. Happy birthday.

Happy birthday, moon. Happy birthday, sounds of TVs, flip-flop sandals from feet you can't see, distant dogs way off on the next street, insects creaking away. Happy birthday, night. Which is as warm and sweet as hot honeyed milk.

Tomorrow, I'm off to Eden, to give birth.

46 years old. What a day to lose a baby.

They had to fly me back out in a helicopter. There was blood gushing out, and João said he could see the placenta. Chefe said it was OK to send in the helicopter. João was still in Consular garb. He looked so tiny and defenseless in just a penis sheath. He has a little pot belly now. He was so terrified, his whole body had gone yellow. We took off, and I feel like I'm melting into a swamp, all brown mud, and we look out and there's Nilson with the kids, looking forlorn and waving goodbye. And I feel this horrible grinding milling in my belly.

I'm so fucking grateful for this hospital. The Devolved Areas are great when you're well and pumped up, and you can take huts and mud and mosquitoes and snake for dinner. But you do not want to have a miscarriage in Eden. A miscarriage in the bowel is about five times more serious than one in the womb. A centimeter or two more of tearing and most of the blood in my body would have blown out in two minutes.

I am one very lucky guy.

The Doctor was João's friend Nadia, and she was just fantastic with me. She told me what was wrong with the baby.

"It's a good thing you lost it," she told me. "It would not have had much of a life."

I just told her the truth. I knew this one felt different from the start; it just didn't feel right.

It's what I get for trying to have another baby at forty-five. I was just being greedy. I told her. *É a ultima vez.* This is the last time.

Chega, she said, Enough. But she was smiling. *É o trabalho do João.* From now on, it's João's job.

Then we had a serious conversation, and I'm not sure I understood all her Portuguese. But I got the gist of it.

She said: it's not like you don't have enough children.

When João and I first met, it was like the world was a flower that had bloomed. We used to lie in each other's arms and he, being from a huge family, would ask, "How many babies?" and I'd say "Six," thinking that was a lot. It was just a fantasy then, some way of echoing the feeling we had of being a union. And he would say no, no, ten. Ten babies. Ten babies would be enough.

We have fifteen.

People used to wonder what reproductive advantage homosexuality conferred.

Imagine you sail iceberg-oceans in sealskin boats with crews of twenty men, and that your skiff gets shipwrecked on an island, no women anywhere. Statistically, one of those twenty men would be samesex-orientated, and if receptive, he would nest the sperm of many men inside him. Until one day, like with Nilson and João, two sperm interpenetrated. Maybe more. The bearer probably died, but at least there was a chance of a new generation. And they all carried the genes.

Homosexuality was a fallback reproductive system.

Once we knew that, historians started finding myths of male pregnancy all over the place. Adam giving birth to Eve, Vishnu on the serpent Anata giving birth to Brahma. And there were all the virgin births as well, with no men necessary.

Now we don't have to wait for accidents.

I think Nadia said, *You and João, you're pregnant in turns or both of you are pregnant at the same time. You keep having twins. Heterosexual couples don't do that. And if you count husband no 3, Nilson, that's another five children. Twenty babies in ten years?*

"*Chega*," I said again.

"*Chega*," she said, but it wasn't a joke. *Of course the women, the lesbians are doing the same thing now too. Ten years ago, everybody thought that homosexuality was dead and that you guys were on the endangered list. But you know, any reproductive advantage over time leads to extinction of rivals.*

Nadia paused and smiled. *I think we are the endangered species now.*

Happy birthday.

Everything but the Signature Is Me

James Tiptree, Jr.

Most of Alice Sheldon's "essays" were written as letters, usually to Jeff Smith – who in the 1970s was editing mimeographed fanzines and today is a co-editor of this volume. She would write him long letters containing both personal and non-personal elements and ask him to extract the general material for publication.

In 1976 Tiptree wrote Smith a letter about the death of his (Tiptree's) mother, asking that it be published so that Tip's friends would know why he hadn't been corresponding lately. Afraid that the letter held too many clues to Tip's true identity, Smith used it to look for the mother's obituary. When he found it, he decided not to run the letter. Other people were getting clued in, though, and when he received a message from a friend asking "Is it true that James Tiptree is Alice Sheldon?" he wrote to Tip spelling out everything that was happening.

Alli Sheldon immediately wrote to Smith and to Ursula Le Guin confirming who she was, and then started telling all of Tip's friends, though still not saying anything publicly. A year later, in November 1977, she wrote Smith a long letter from Mexico that forms the bulk of the following essay, which also contains sections from the first "Alli" letter and some clarification lines from a few others written throughout the year.

Here is Alice Sheldon introducing herself.

How great. At last it's out, and you're the first to know, as I promised long ago you would – although I didn't expect it to happen through your own initiative. But at least you're the first I can write to in my own persona.

Yeah. Alice Sheldon. Five-feet-eight, sixty-one years, remains of good-looking girl vaguely visible, grins a lot in a depressed way, very active in spurts. Also, Raccoona.

I live in a kind of big wooden box in the woods like an adult play-pen, full of slightly mangy plants, fireplace, minimal old "modern teak" furniture strewn with papers, hobbies, unidentifiable and unfileable objects; the toolroom opens off the bedroom, there are six doors to the outside, and it's colder than a brass monkey's brains in winter, except when the sun comes out and shoots through all the glass skylights. We've added on porches (which turned into libraries), other excrescences – as somebody said, all it needs is a windmill on top. Not so ridiculous now. Ting (short for Huntington, my *very nice* more aged husband of thirty years who doesn't read what I write but is happy I'm having fun) used to raise thousands of orchids before he retired and started traveling; he gave them to the nation, i.e., the National Botanic Gardens, who wanted hybrids. So now in the middle of the living room sticks this big untended greenhouse I am supposed to be growing things in. What I'm growing is mealy bugs – must get at it. We built the place very modestly in 1959, when it was all woods here. Now houses, subdivisions, are creeping toward us. No more stags on the lawn – real ones. But lots of raccoons. Still private enough so you can sneak out and get the mail or slip a cookie to a raccoon in the buff if you want to.

If you'd asked me any time from age three to twenty-six, I'd have told you, "I'm a painter." (Note, not "artist" – painter. Snobbism there.) And I was. Oh my, did I draw, sketch, model, smear oils, build gesso, paint-paint-paint. (Age three I drew pictures of our bulldog, with lollipop legs.) I worked daily, whether I was supposed to be listening to lectures on Chateaubriand, whether my then-husband was shooting at me (he was a beautiful alcoholic poet), whether the sheriff was carrying our furniture out, whether Father was having a heart attack, whatever. And I wasn't too bad; I illustrated a couple of books in my early teens, I had a one-man show at sixteen, I exhibited in the All-American then at the Corcoran – and the painting, which used me as model, sold. Somewhere my naked form is hanging in a bedroom in North Carolina, if it hasn't been junked. I bought a shotgun, a Fox C-E double-barrel 12-gauge full choke, with the money. (Those were the three years when I was a crazy duck hunter, before I shot one too many cripples and gave it up never to kill another living thing, bugs excluded.) I believe the Fox is now far more valuable than anything I ever did.

The trouble was, you see, I was just good enough to understand the difference between my talent and that rare thing, *real* ability. It was as though I had climbed the foothills high enough to see the snow-clad peaks beyond, which I could never scale. This doesn't stop some people; it did me. What's the use of adding to the world's scrap heap? The reason people thought me innovative was that I was good enough to steal mannerisms and tricks they had never climbed high enough to study. But I knew where it was coming from.

And then came the dreadful steady unstoppable rise of Hitler – a great spreading black loin chop on the map – and I found out something else. There are painters who go on painting when a million voices are screaming in terminal agonies. And there are those who feel they have to Do Something about it, however little.

So I came back to Chicago – I'd been living in San Angel, near Mexico City, mucking around on the fringes of the Diego Rivera/Orozco/Siqueres crowd – and took a job as the *Chicago Sun*'s first art editor, while waiting for the Army to open female enlistments. (I wasn't one of the famous first group of female potential officers; for some reason it was important to me to go in as an ordinary G.I. with *women officers*.) Besides, I was having a great time discovering that Chicago was full of artists, who had to exhibit in NYC before they could sell to their Chicago neighbors. Chicago then had two art critics; one was a lethal, totally politicized Marxist (female), and the other was an elderly gent who knew art had died with Cezanne, and whose feet hurt. So when people sent works to Chicago shows they didn't get reviewed – or it was worse when they did. Anyway, I rooted out about forty producing groups, started what was then a new thing, a *New Yorker*–type calendar, told people interesting things to look for in shows. (One Art Institute guard, coping with a host of people with my "guide" clipped out, demanding to know which was the east room, asked me, "Did *you* do this?" Nobody had asked him anything but "Where is the toilet?" for twenty years.)

But this was all waiting, while the paper shortage cut me from a page to a half and then to a quarter. And then the great day came, and I trotted down to U.S. Army Recruitment Station Number 27 in three-inch heels and my little chartreuse crepe-de-chine designer thing by Claire somebody, and my pale fox fur jacket, and found a drunken second lieutenant with his feet on the desk. And when I said I wished to enlist in the Army, he caught an imaginary fly and said, "Ah, hell, you don't want to go in *that* goddamn thing." And I said if it was all the same to him, I did. And so – but that's another, five-year-long, fairly hilarious story.

People tell me I've had an exciting or glamorous or whatnot life; it didn't feel like much but work and a few adventures. A few, *ah oui*... All I write is really from life, even that crazy duck-shooting boy breaking the ice naked at ten degrees below zero on the Apache reservation was me, once ("Her Smoke Rose Up Forever").

As to science fiction: Well, you see, I had all these uncles, who are no relation at all, but merely stray or bereaved or otherwise unhappy bachelors whom my parents adopted in the course of their wanderings. (That sort of thing happened much more in the old, old days. The fact that Father was an intensely lovable man of bewildering varied capabilities, and that Mother was a blazing-blue-eyed redhead of great literacy and gaiety didn't hurt, of course; and in their odd way they were both secretly lonesome – having nothing but peculiar me for family.) This particular uncle was what used to be called a Boston Brahmin, dean of a major law school and author of a text on torts so densely horrible that I still meet lawyers who shudder at its name. In short, he was dignified and respectable to an extreme – on the surface, as it turned out.

The summer when I was nine we were up in the woods of Wisconsin as usual, and Uncle Harry returned from an expedition to the metropolis of one thousand souls thirty miles away with his usual collection of *The New York Times*, *The Kenyon Review*, etc. (There was a funny little bookshop-hole there that ordered things for you.) Out of his bundle slipped a seven-by-nine magazine with a wonderful cover depicting, if I recollect, a large green octopus removing a young lady's golden brassiere. We all stared. The title was *Weird Tales*.

"*Ah*," said Uncle Harry. "Oh. Oh yes. I, ah, picked this up for the child."

"Uncle Harry," I said, my eyes bulging, "I am the child. May I have it, please?"

"Uh," said Uncle Harry. And, slowly, handed it over.

And so it all began. He would slip them to me and I would slip them back to him. Lovecraft — Oh, God. And more and more and more; we soon discovered *Amazing* and *Wonder Stories* and others that are long forgotten. We never discussed them; it was just Our Secret. But I'll tell you one thing: You haven't read fantasy or SF unless you have retired, with a single candle, to your lonely little cabin in the woods, far from the gaslights of the adult world, and set your candle stub up in a brass basin and huddled under about sixteen quilts — the nights were cold and drafty, the candlelight jumped and guttered, shadows everywhere. And then, just as you get to where the nameless *Thing* starts to emerge, the last shred of candle gutters out, leaving you in the dark forest. And a screech owl, who has silently taken up position on the roof above, lets loose with a nerve-curdling shriek.

That's Tales of Wonder as they should be read, man.

Well, of course I was hooked, from then on, permanently. By the time World War II came along, I had about 1300 mags and paperbacks stacked in that cabin alone. (I gave them all to the county library, despite the sneers of the librarian, who doubtless used them for doorstops. Alas, alas; rubies, pearls, emeralds gone to the gravel crusher.)

With the war came a break, after which I started all over again (having discovered the magic of subscriptions). I now have about forty running feet of them double-stacked, plus head-high shelves bulging in all bathrooms, plus miscellaneous deposits. In addition, there's another forty feet of philosophy and politics and history, sixty feet of my old professional specialty (experimental psychology), twenty feet of math, astronomy, and miscellaneous, twenty feet of fiction by dead authors and another twenty of same by live ones (horrible how quickly one seems to have to shift them), twenty feet of women's studies and related material, and twenty feet of mostly poetry. And *something* has got to give. (Oh well, who needs *Das Kapital* anyway?)

The painful part of starting like that is that you read, read, read —

without, in most cases, noticing dull stuff like the author's name. Until I started to write it myself, of course; then names become acutely important. But I am still in the embarrassing position of not knowing who wrote some fantastic scene that is forever engraved on my liver. And then finding out, Oh my god, yes of course – *he* or *she* did that! (Worse yet, finding it out in his or her presence, whether in the flesh or in one of my Victorian correspondences.)

Now maybe this is the best place to lay to rest one last ghost – the business of the anonymity and the male pseudonym. First, the important part: *Everything I've ever told you or anyone else is true*, with one exception. David Gerrold came looking for me and I told him he was on a different street. If he'd waited before ringing the bell he would have seen through the glass a solitary figure staring at a *Star Trek* rerun in the dark, and I'm sure the jig would have been up. Other than that I have never told a lie or modulated my natural voice – I was very careful about pronouns, things like "child" instead of "boy," etc., etc. But it wasn't calculated. (I'm lousy at that.) All my letters have been just first draft typed as fast as I can go with my one finger. I can't help what people think sounds male or female.

You see, when I started, I was in rather a stuffy job atmosphere. A university. And I was something of a maverick; I kept having ideas that didn't jibe with the official academic outlook at my department. And when I started my own research it got worse. ("In this department we do feel rather strongly that recent PhDs do best when their work fits in with or amplifies some of the ongoing lines of research here.") Well, I wasn't about to fit in with or amplify anybody else's line; I had my own long-held desires, and I kept citing research nobody else had read, or had read and dismissed, and with great pain and struggle I set off on a totally independent tack, which had the ill grace, after four agonizing years, to pay off. (I still keep getting requests for it from obscure European universities, or behind the Iron Curtain.) With this background, the news that I was writing *science fiction* would have destroyed my last shreds of respectability and relegated me to the freak department, possibly even to the freak-whose-grant-funds-should-be-stopped division; those familiar with older academe will get the picture. Anonymity seemed highly desirable. The name "Tiptree" started by seeing it on a can of marmalade in the Giant; I was looking for a forgettable name so editors wouldn't remember rejecting my manuscripts. The "James" was one more bit of cover – and my husband threw in "Jr." for whimsy's sake. I was shocked when the stories all sold and I was stuck with the name. What started as a prank dreamed its way into reality.

You have to realize, this never was run as a real clandestine operation with cutouts and drops and sanitizing and so on. The only "assets" were one P.O. box, a little luck, and the delicacy and decency of some people who decided not to pry. Namely and chiefly one Jeff Smith.

When you wrote asking for the *Phantasmicom* interview was the first time I was approached personally by anyone, and I told myself, Dammit, say no. But then this business of really loving the SF world and wanting to say so welled up, and I thought I could kind of race over the bio bit without telling lies and start waving Hello. You'll note what I put in there about masks... So that's how it all started.

Then, from about the second year, when things began to get serious, "James" started to feel more and more constrictive. It was as if there were things I wanted to write as me, or at least a woman. (I still don't know exactly what they are, that's the odd part.) Meanwhile Tiptree kept taking on a stronger and stronger life of his own; if I were superstitious I'd say Something was waiting for incarnation there in the Giant Foods import section...maybe I do anyway. This voice would speak up from behind my pancreas somewhere. *He* insisted on the nickname, he would not be "Jim." And as to "Uncle" Tip – maybe I'm a natural uncle. See, I have no family, nobody ever called me Sis or Mom or even Aunt Alice.

And his persona wasn't too constricting; I wrote as me. Maybe my peculiar upbringing – where values like Don't-be-a-coward and Achieve! and Find-out-how-it-works and Fight-on-the-underdog's-side were stamped in before they got to the You're-a-young-lady stuff (which was awful) – maybe this resulted in a large part of me being kind of a generalized Human being rather than specifically female.

(I am very pro-woman, though; once when dabbling in NY politics I had the opportunity to personally thank one of the original suffragettes, then a frail but vital eighty, for the privilege of the vote. It was a beautiful moment.) But still I wanted to write as a woman. By this point it became obvious that killing Tiptree off, say by drowning him out on the reef here, wasn't going to be that simple. He – we – had all these friends, see. So all I did was rather feebly set up Raccoona Sheldon with a Wisconsin P.O. box and bank, and I confess to giving her some of Tip's weaker tales to peddle. (Except for the one called "Your Faces, O My Sisters! Your Faces Filled of Light!" in the anthology *Aurora* by McIntyre and Anderson. Nobody much mentions that one, but I consider it as good as I can do.) Anyway, the upshot of all this was that where I lived I wasn't, and I didn't live where I was, and things were reaching some kind of crescendo of confusion. Frankly, I had no real plan. So I was really relieved as well as traumatized to have Mother's ghost do Tiptree in. But it left me with an extraordinary eerie empty feeling for a while; maybe still does.

One problem caused by having a male pseudonym was that there was the desire to rush (by mail) up to many female writers and give them a straight sisterly hug. (And to some male writers, too; especially those I knew were feeling down. I guess I wrote some fairly peculiar letters here and there.) Another problem that may seem trivial, wasn't to me; people kept saying how lifelike my female characters were, while all the time I was perishing to find out if the *male* characters were living!

Things like being hooted at in the Women in SF Symposium really didn't bother me at all, because I doubtless would have done the same myself. And also I am used to being hooted at for unpopular ideas – the struggle I mentioned in the university was just one of a lifelong series. And then, too, I'm a feminist of a far earlier vintage, where we worked through a lot of the first stages all by our lonesomes. There are stages in all revolutions of consciousness where certain things are unsayable, because they sound too much like the enemy's line. Then after some years, when everybody is feeling more secure about unity on the facts and the wrongs, those "unsayable" things can be looked at objectively again, and new insight gained. I refer, of course, to my real interest in why people are mothers. (I just saw an article in *Psychology Today* that triumphantly claims that Fathers Do It Too – but turns out on reading the data that what they "do" is quite different. They play with baby; mother takes care of it.) There were, of course, a lot more things I felt like saying in the Symposium, but I thought that one was safe for Tip. As indeed it was – typical "male" nonsense.

I've been amazed at the warm, kind, friendly reaction I've been getting, even from the most unlikely people. I worried deeply about what had unwittingly become a major deception. I wrote at once to everyone I could think of who might feel I'd let them go out on a cracked limb. They couldn't have been nicer. If someone does feel griped, they haven't gotten it to me. The only problem seems to be that now I'm expected to produce something somehow grander, more insightful, more "real." Well, if I knew how, I would – the trouble is that the Tip did all I could in that line. If there is something – other than "Sisters" – which is going to burst forth from my liberated gonads, it hasn't peeped yet. In fact, I may be written out for a while. With each story I dug deeper and deeper into more emotional stuff, and some of it started to hurt pretty bad. "Slow Music" reads like a musical fadeout or coda to Tiptree's group of work.

Now, I've got one more thing to add to this terrible monologue. In a funny way, I found that as Tip I could be useful to my fellow female writers. There were times when Tiptree (male) queried anthology editors on why nothing from this or that female writer was being used. And as an old gent I may have been more helpful to sisters who were fighting depression than another woman could. They had to brace up and respond to my courtly compliments – Tip was quite a flirt – and they knew somebody quite different valued them. Whereas just another woman coming in with sympathy and admiration tends to dissolve in a mutual embrace of woe.

Now, adieu, dear Jeff and Ann. Outside the Caribbean is in roaring high tide, storms are chasing themselves overhead, the palm trees lit up olive and white by great bursts of lightning. And the generator is, as usual, failing. May you never be the same.

The Ghost Girls of Rumney Mill

Sandra McDonald

Sometimes, even in science fiction or fantasy, the way to examine something is to *not* change it. Here, traditional gender roles persist even after death, as the ghosts of some children, tied to one geographic location, separate themselves into a boys' club and a girls' club.

Dead girls in Rumney hang out at the old mill behind the oil farms that line the creek. Dead boys haunt the abandoned paint factory down where the water widens and circles the airport. Come down to the mill or the factory and you might feel the squeeze of our fingers on your hand or hear the wind sigh as we argue over who cheated at hopscotch or rock-paper-scissors or hide-and-seek. Come when the tide is high or the moon is full, and maybe you'll even see faint shadows in the shapes of our profiles.

To the living, the mill is a decrepit old dump with blood-colored paint flaking off the sides. To us it's a dreamy maze of secrets. Sunlight and moonlight stream through windows that are sometimes broken and sometimes intact. The grindstone never moves, except on the nights when the mill itself travels back in time and workers with long beards appear out of nowhere. They barrel up spices, load up their wagons and drive off into dark mists. Sometimes the city of Rumney disappears entirely, leaving behind skittering crabs, red-tailed hawks and the occasional rustle of Pawtucket Indians in the grass. And us, of course.

My name is Pauline. I was thirteen when my asthma got so bad that I stopped breathing right in the middle of history class. Sheila's fourteen and she likes to pester the night watchman over at the oil farm by moving his keys or rustling his newspaper. Eight-year-old Lisa accompanies her sometimes, always carrying the doll her parents gave her when she got sick with diabetes. The twins, Wendy and Peggy, died a year apart back when measles used to kill a lot of children. (Peggy will often scratch at her face and neck until we make her stop.) Younger than the twins is the Silent Girl, who wears a hair cap, keeps to the shadows and never speaks.

One summer night I was trying to pretend I was back in my old bedroom, which had posters of Australia on the walls and a blue quilt on the bed. With the door open I could see across the hall to my parents' room. If ghosts pretend hard enough it's like falling asleep and having a nice dream, and I had just about drifted off when the sound of Rachel singing "You Light Up My Life" broke my concentration. Rachel is sixteen and sang soprano in the Winnisemmit High School choir back when everyone liked music by the Carpenters and Olivia Newton-John.

I went to her and said, "You're singing too loud."

Rachel stopped. "I am not. Go back upstairs."

"Make me," I said. She can't because I'm the strongest girl in the mill. I can move heavy objects and pull hair and do mean things if I want. Nobody remembers more than I do about being alive, and when the wind howls the youngest girls turn to me for comfort.

Rachel scowled. "Everyone likes my singing but you."

Lisa jumped down from her perch on the grindstone. "Listen! Someone's coming."

We went outside. Sometimes homeless people cross over the bridge in search of a place to sleep. If a man tries to stay with us we tickle his feet until he goes away, but women are welcome as long as they don't make a mess or try to light fires. Tonight's visitor was Rita, an old lady with no teeth and coat pockets bulging with plastic bags. We watched in the dying light of day as she picked her way along the weeds.

"Rita, Rita, do you have any chocolate?" Lisa asked. Chocolate is what Lisa misses most from the world of the living. "Just a little?"

Rita shuffled toward the water to go pee, and we saw that her urine was dark and her inner thighs were covered with weeping sores. She muttered something crazy and pulled her pants back up. Seeing Rita always reminds me that it's better to be a ghost who makes sense then a living person who doesn't, but I'd still rather be alive. Oblivious to us, Rita came up to the mill and settled into a musty corner on the first floor. She displaced our resident litter of ghost kittens as she did, but they only meowed and scampered off into the shadows.

Back upstairs I tried again to imagine myself home, in bed, a yellow nightlight on the wall and my terrier Roscoe curled up beside me. Just as I thought I could smell Roscoe's stinky breath, Sheila breezed in with a smile on her face.

"There's a new boy at the factory who wants to come live with us," she said. "What do you think?"

Sheila likes boys but I don't. They were rough and mean when alive and they're rough and mean now that they're dead. Their leader is Mike, who used to be Rachel's boyfriend until he accidentally killed them both by smashing his car into a concrete barrier. Sammy got hit by a bus the same day the first astronauts landed on the moon. Richard died when someone shot at his brother, little David died of AIDS and Sean hanged himself in his dad's basement. (An accident, supposedly, but I don't know how someone accidentally hangs himself.) Sheila hopes to lose her virginity to Sean or Mike, but that's not easy to do when you don't really have a body.

Annoyed at the interruption, I said, "Only girls can stay here."

"He's a special case. Come look."

She pulled me to the window. In the wild grass below stood a thin boy just a little younger than me. He had wispy blond hair and might have been wearing a blue dress. (It's not always easy to tell what ghosts are wearing because most of the time we see each other only as blurry, watercolored outlines.) The boy looked unbearably sad, as if he'd had a dog like Roscoe and someone had just killed it.

Sheila said, "His name is Matthew, but he wants to be Michelle. The boys make fun of him because he thinks he's a girl."

"Of course they do. They would've beat him up at school." This Matthew person needed to learn that the dead aren't any more tolerant than the living. "He's as crazy as Rita."

"No, he's just like Boy George. I think it's kind of fun. Someone new to play with."

"Tell him to go away, Sheila."

Matthew went away but came back one day while the twins and I were tracing shapes in the dust on windows. We sketched letters of the alphabet and then Wendy drew a tree and Peggy drew a flower. Wendy said Peggy's flower looked stupid and Peggy said Wendy's tree looked more stupid, and so we gave up on the artwork and went outside to see Matthew and Lisa hosting a tea party for their dolls.

"More milk?" Lisa asked.

"Yes, please," Matthew said.

Wendy put her hands on her hips. "Why are you dressed like a girl?"

Matthew pretended to pour the milk for the doll he had fashioned out of newspaper, twigs and a beer can. The way his hair appeared to ruffle in the breeze annoyed me. My own hair was thick and curly and the hairdresser had cut it wrong the week before I died, so I was stuck being a ghost with a bad haircut.

Matthew said, "I was supposed to be a girl, but God got it wrong and I was born a boy."

"God doesn't make people wrong," I said.

"He makes mistakes, like babies born with part of their skulls missing or without arms or legs." Matthew's eyes got all squinty. "I knew I was supposed to be a girl ever since I was born. My mom's doctor said I could have an operation when I grew up. They can do that. Turn men into women."

"They can't do it when you're dead."

"Don't be mean, Pauline," Lisa said.

Matthew gave me a cold look. "I'm used to people who don't understand."

"I bet you are," I said.

"I want to have tea," Wendy said, and sat down to play with them. I waited for Matthew to argue some more but he didn't, so Peggy and I went down the creek looking for treasure to add to our collection. So far we've found a WHS class ring, a broken watch, three mismatched earrings, several muddy coins and dozens of pieces of glass worn smooth by the water. Yellow butterflies flitted overhead and police sirens wailed in the distance while we hunted around in the mud and reeds.

"Did God make Matthew wrong?" Peggy asked.

"No."

"But babies born without arms — "

"Everybody's born the way God wants. Sometimes we just don't understand why."

God is a touchy subject. If He's real than heaven probably is too, but if Heaven's real why aren't we in it? I don't remember ever going to church so maybe I'm damned, but Lisa once told us about her first communion (she got twenty-five dollars from her grandmother) and Rachel made her bat mitzvah (that's a Jewish thing). Babies are born with birth defects because of problems with their DNA or something, but I didn't explain that to Peggy because I didn't want her asking more questions. Matthew had been born a boy and died a boy and would forever be a boy.

"Matthew's just playing a joke," I assured her.

That night the smell of nutmeg became very strong. When we looked out the windows we saw a fine layer of white blanketing everything. Two sweating horses pulled a black sled past and kept going with the faint jingle of bells. The little ones wanted to make angels, but no matter how hard we tried we could only make faint indentations in the snow. The water in the creek rushed black and icy and the sky was a deep velvety black. When the novelty of winter wore off we huddled inside the mill owner's old office.

"Pauline, is Matthew a girl or a boy?" Lisa asked from where she nestled against my side.

"He's just trying to trick us. Remember the time Richard gave you a box and told you it was full of chocolates?"

Lisa sighed. "It was just tar and rocks."

Peggy scratched her neck. "Sammy used to hide in the grass and scare us."

"And Mike hung that dead rat up outside the door just to be gross," Sheila said.

"It wasn't a rat, it was a vole," Rachel said.

Sheila shook her head. "It was a rat."

"A vole," I said. "Rats have long tails and voles don't. Anyway, don't you see? Whenever they're bored, the boys try to think up ways to annoy us. If we just ignore Matthew he'll give up and go do something else."

The next day I wandered too far down the creek in search of treasure and found myself in the boys' territory. The factory is a long, low brick building with boarded up windows and a parking lot full of trash. When it slips back into time, the boys get to watch machines mix and can paint. The sounds of cheering rose over the din of car traffic and when I crept closer I saw Mike beating up Matthew.

"You want to be a homo fag forever?" Mike asked. "Fight back!"

Curled up on the ground, Matthew wasn't moving. Being hit when you're dead doesn't hurt as much it does when you're alive, but Mike had hit him a lot. The other boys stood around watching with various degrees of interest.

"Hey!" I yelled. "Stop that!"

They all ignored me. Before Mike could kick Matthew again, I picked up a rock and threw it as hard as I could. It struck the back of Mike's head, deflected as if bouncing off something soft and then dropped down to the dirt. He whirled around angrily.

"What the hell — " he started. "What's wrong with you, Queen Bee?"

He knows I hate that nickname. I said, "Leave him alone and stop being a bully."

"Pauline!" Little David dashed toward my legs and wrapped himself around my knees. Although this wasn't the best time for hugs and kisses I lifted him up. He smelled like talcum powder and slightly sour milk, but I liked the way his arms tightened around my neck.

"What are you going to do if I don't?" Mike asked with a cruel little smile. I don't know what Rachel ever saw in him. "Go back to your beehive, Queenie."

Tall, sad-faced Richard said, "Yeah, Pauline. We'll handle this."

"By fighting?" I shifted Little David's weight from one hip to the other and put scorn in my voice. "You can't think of anything better to do?"

Sean juggled a cigarette butt between his hands. "What's there to do that we haven't done a thousand times before?"

"You don't have to hurt him," I said. "Get up, Matthew."

He pulled himself up and wiped at his mouth as if there were blood there. Maybe it was just the memory of blood from other fights. He shot me an angry look, probably embarrassed because I'd seen him lose so badly, and backed away from Mike with a little limp.

"He's a homo sissy." Mike glared at first Matthew and then me. "I told him to go live with you girls and not come back."

I said, "You're just prejudiced and narrow-minded. Violence doesn't help anything."

Mike flexed his fist. "Punching you would help. I'd feel good about that all day long."

Sean threw his cigarette butt to the ground and stepped on it as if he'd really been smoking. "This is stupid. Let's go throw rocks at ducks or something."

Most of the boys drifted off. Without an audience Mike lost all his bluster, so he just muttered a threat or two and went inside the factory. I took Little David down to the creek, which widened at that point to join the river. Tankers and freighters unloaded at a half-dozen docks. Airplanes roared over our heads, some of them so low we could see the landing gear retract. We waved at the passengers, but of course they didn't see us.

Little David curled up in my lap. "When can I go home, Pauline?"

I didn't have an answer so I said nothing. Matthew stepped out of the bushes — I hadn't even heard him follow us — and said, "Don't worry, David. One day we'll all get to heaven, and it'll be just like home." To me he said, "I didn't need your help."

"You weren't doing so good on your own."

"What's the point?" Matthew shielded his eyes against the sun and watched another plane take off. "He'll just do it again someday."

"The point is you should fight back. You're a boy, too."

Matthew jerked as if I'd touched him with a live electrical wire. "I'm not a boy! Can't you see that's why he hates me? They all do."

He ran off to go sulk. I felt a little bad and waited for him to come to the mill again, but a week passed before he appeared in a dinghy that must have drifted away from one of the boat clubs near the airport. He didn't have any oars, but the incoming tide pushed him along and made the boat spin in circles.

"Anybody want a ride?" he asked. "It's a lot of fun!"

"We're having plenty of fun over here," I said. In truth we'd been playing Ultimate Hopscotch, which combines hopscotch, hide-and-seek and Marco Polo. The rules of Ultimate Hopscotch change constantly and a referee is needed to keep track of all the infractions, but even the variations grow boring after awhile.

"This is better," Matthew said.

"No it's not," I said.

Sheila sprinted down to the edge of the creek. "I want a ride."

Lisa came out from behind a pile of old broken concrete. "Me, too."

The twins gave me a beseeching look as Wendy asked, "Can we go, too, Pauline?"

Peggy tugged on my hand. "Pretty please?"

"I'm not going to stop you," I said crossly. "But you know what happens if you go too far."

Matthew waited until the water took him close to the bank, then stepped over the side and tried to pull the boat ashore. He wasn't quite strong enough, though, and the tide threatened to suck it away. Sheila grabbed the sides of the dinghy.

"Come on, Pauline," she said. "Help us."

"I can do it," Matthew said stubbornly.

I folded my arms. "It's his idea. Let him do it."

Matthew grabbed the bow, gritted his jaw and yanked with all his strength. The dinghy came up onto the ground. Like a true gentleman (a true gentleman in a blue dress) Matthew helped everyone climb aboard and asked, "Are you sure you don't want to come, Pauline?"

"I'm positive."

"We don't need her," Lisa said to the other girls.

"You do if you want a push off." I left them stranded there and went inside the mill to look for the Silent Girl. No one had seen her for a few days and we were worried she had strayed again. It might be weeks or months before she reappeared. Rachel, combing her hair by the window, was less concerned with the Silent Girl than she was with picking a fight.

"You're just jealous because they like Michelle more than they like you," she said.

One of the ghost kittens was curled up in a patch of sunlight, and I dangled a piece of string in front of it until one tiny eye opened.

"You're afraid because you can't intimidate her."

I dragged the string on the floor, letting the kitten pounce and catch it.

"And you don't like her because she's prettier than you are," Rachel said. Her smile vanished when I reached over and pulled her precious hair.

"Ouch!" she cried. "Why are you so mean all the time?"

"Because all of you are so stupid! She's a he and his name is Matthew, not Michelle. He's just some crazy kid who wants to be something he's not."

"Maybe we're all crazy! Didn't you ever think of that?" Rachel's voice cracked. "Maybe we're all stuck here because we want something we can never have."

With that she ran off and disappeared in the shadows. I could hear her sniffling as if I'd really hurt her. Stupid girl, but she's probably right. Lisa wants sweets, Sheila wants to be with a boy and Peggy wants to stop itching. Wendy cries because she misses her mother. Sean craves cigarettes and Little David wants to go home. We all want something and maybe that wanting keeps us here, but trust me — making yourself not want something is very hard to do, especially when you're just a kid.

The sound of laughter brought me to the window. Working together, Matthew and the girls had managed to get the boat back into the water. They floated away without a thought or care about me. Sick of them, sick of the mill and completely sick of being dead, I made my way across the marsh to the overgrown lot where the old drive-in once stood. For a long time I sat amid rusty speaker poles, trying to imagine a movie on the tattered screen. No one bothered me until Matthew showed up.

"What do you want?" I asked.

"I'm just exploring." He kicked at some broken pieces of concrete. "I've never been to a drive-in."

"It closed a long time ago."

"You know a lot of history and stuff, don't you?" he asked.

"More than everyone else."

Matthew gave me one of his squinty-eyed looks. "So you must have heard of Christine Jorgensen."

I folded my arms and bluffed. "What about her?"

"Never mind," he said, as if it weren't really important. He lifted his head and turned toward the lights of Rumney, which had started to twinkle in the dusk. Time is like that when you're dead — sometimes hours pass like minutes, or minutes pass like hours, or you think only a day's gone by but it's been a month.

"I want to live with all of you in the mill," he said.

"It's only for girls."

"You told Mike he was the one who was prejudiced, but you were really talking about yourself."

The accusation stung. "It's not prejudice when it's just common sense."

"Your common sense, not mine. I know what I am. I died for — " Matthew stopped himself from finishing that sentence. No one had said anything about how he'd died. He threw his hands up in the air and started to walk toward town.

"You can't go there," I said. "It's too far. Don't you know that yet?"

He gave me a challenging look. "Scared? Go back and watch the kids."

We circled around the makeshift flower memorial that marked someone's fatal accident and crossed the highway into Rumney proper. The nearest neighborhood was full of crab apple trees poking through the sidewalks and small houses with broken cars in their yards. Although it was summertime, no one was out playing or walking dogs. We could see the lights of televisions through open windows and heard some mother yelling at her kids.

"You miss this, don't you?" Matthew asked.

I shrugged. "Maybe."

We passed the Rumney library, a marble building with tall windows, iron gates and a golden dome. The millionaire Andrew Carnegie had donated the money to build it. When I was alive I would visit almost every day to see my grandmother, the head librarian. We kept going past the post office and the elementary school and up a hill to houses that overlooked the marsh. I felt myself getting tighter and tighter, an elastic band stretched too far, but I didn't say anything and neither did Matthew.

Finally he stopped and pointed. "That's home."

The brown house had a sagging porch and worn roof. Weeds had overrun the flowerbeds. The small, crowded kitchen overlooking the garden smelled like old garbage. Someone had covered the counters with newspapers, magazines, bills, tissue boxes, jumbo size cereal boxes, junk food and just plain junk.

"Ma?" Matthew called out. "You home?"

He went into the next room but I stayed to look at the pictures on the refrigerator. Matthew had been cute in kindergarten, but as he grew older he looked sadder and sadder. I didn't see any brothers or sisters or even a father, but some of the photos had been jaggedly cropped with scissors. The divorce must have been nasty. The newspaper clippings were about Matthew in school plays, Matthew in Little League and Matthew's funeral mass at the Lady of Fatima church. No cause of death was given.

Adjacent to the kitchen was a small dining room and just beyond that a living room where the TV was playing for Matthew's mother.

She sat half-curled up in a faded blue recliner, looking small and old. Baby portraits and old black-and-white pictures hung in dusty frames all over the walls. None of the men looked like they could have been Matthew's father, although some might have been grandparents or great-grandparents.

Matthew bent down and kissed his mother's forehead. "Just came to say hi, Ma."

She didn't stir. Matthew stroked her cheek, his eyes bright, and I thought maybe he had forgotten about me standing there. (The tightness had grown so bad I didn't think either of us would be able to stay much longer.) Just a few blocks from the library was my own house and family, our bright kitchen without any clutter in it, our living room decorated with Mom's oil paintings and Dad's high-school trophies. Visiting my parents would hurt too much and emphasize everything I've lost, but maybe for Matthew the pain of visiting hurt less than the pain of staying away.

"You've got to take care of yourself, Ma," Matthew said.

Stepping away to give him some privacy, I bumped against a desk piled high with more mail. The return addresses were from lawyers, bill collectors and the state prison in Rowe. Four letters from the prison had not been opened. A different idea about Matthew's father emerged, but before it could fully form Matthew straightened and said, "I'll show you my stuff."

"We should get back — " I tried to tell him, but he had already gone upstairs to a small room under the eaves. In the light from the hallway I saw posters of baseball players and banners from different teams. The lamp was shaped like a baseball bat. White baseballs had been sewn onto the blue bedspread. I saw nothing girlish or feminine at all, which meant he'd been tricking us along.

"You lied — " I began, but Matthew shook his head.

"Watch," he said.

The light shifted. The room, like the mill, rolled itself back through weeks and months. Matthew's father, a skinny man so tall he had to bend over or hit his head on the ceiling, appeared with a blue dress clutched in hand. Foam flecked his lips.

"I told you, no more goddamned dresses!"

On the bed, an image of Matthew scrambled to his feet. "But Dad — "

"You're not a girl!" Matthew's father punched him in the face so hard that his head whipped around and a crack came from his neck. "Boys are boys and girls are girls!"

More punches followed, blows of anger and denial and shame. The Matthew beside me did nothing as the vision of his death played out. For all our petty tricks, ghosts are mostly powerless. We can only watch and witness and grieve for what we've lost.

"Boys are boys and girls are girls," the ghostly Matthew said. "Isn't that what you think, too?"

I turned away from the terrible images to watch a different scene emerge from the past. On a rainy afternoon a young Matthew, maybe only six or seven, twirled beside his bed in a ballerina's costume. He was clumsy and awkward and obviously not a girl, but when he lifted his head he looked happier than I had ever seen him.

"Matthew — " I started, but at that very moment the elastic holding me to the marsh snapped. The force of it yanked me backward through a great gray tunnel that seemed to last forever. This was the little death, the penalty for straying too far from the marsh. Everything I knew or thought faded away. When I could see and hear again, the mill's windows were full of autumn light and the twins were holding my hands. From somewhere far away Rachel was singing a beautiful and sad song.

"We're so glad you're back," Wendy said.

"You were gone for a very long time," Peggy said.

"What about Matthew?" I asked, but no one had seen him.

The wild roses by the creek were dying on the day Rachel, Lisa and I went down to the paint factory. Mike and Sean were kicking a half-crushed can back and forth in the broken parking lot. A living person might have thought it was just the wind. Soon the leaves would turn and the skies would darken, but at least winter days are short and spring always returns.

"The Queen Bee returns," Mike said when he saw me. "Too bad. It was so quiet while you were gone."

"Shut up," I said.

"We came to play with Matthew," Lisa said.

Mike kicked the can so hard it sailed past Sean's shoulder. "Who said the little sissy's back?"

"Don't be stubborn." Rachel spoke with a hint of affection that I would never understand. "Wendy saw him on the marsh yesterday."

Sean retrieved the can. "He's not here. Try the pier."

Behind the factory lay a winding path some local kids use as a shortcut to go drink or make out at a rotting old pier. We followed it to where the setting sun made the creek's oil patches gleam like gold. A lone tugboat was moving downstream, its pilot so close we could see him eating a sandwich and potato chips. Matthew was sitting with his legs dangling over the water. I hadn't told anyone about how he died. We each have our own stories to tell, and years and decades in which to tell them.

Lisa sat beside him. "What are you doing?"

Matthew didn't look up. "Just wondering what would happen if I jump in."

"You wouldn't drown," I said.

"It's not fair that this isn't heaven," he said. Maybe he'd thought stretching himself too far was a way to escape the marsh, but I could have told him otherwise. We are trapped in the mud and tides as surely as the reeds and wildflowers.

"Pauline says you can come live with us if you want," Lisa said.

Matthew met my gaze but then turned his head.

"Not out of pity," he said.

"Not out of pity," I said. "It'll be good to have a new girl around. But you have to learn to play Ultimate Hopscotch, and help Lisa find her doll when she loses it, and listen to all of Rachel's sappy songs."

"They're not sappy," Rachel protested.

Lisa smiled. "Sometimes they're sappy."

"Deal," Matthew said, and became Michelle from that day forward.

The three of them started back. I lingered to watch the tugboat. The sun warmed my face and the breeze smelled like salt and diesel. A sudden impulse made me wave my arms and yell "Can you see me?" but the pilot of the tug only drank his coffee and kept on course for the harbor. If it's true that wanting is what keeps us chained to this world, I'll never be free. I want my life back. I want to sleep in my old bed, smell my mother's perfume, sit in a hard classroom chair, eat pizza and Chinese food, play fetch with Roscoe and even get my period again. I want to grow up and have a boyfriend, a husband and children. I want to travel to Africa, to the Amazon and to Australia, and that's just the beginning. But there are no foreseeable beginnings in my future, only middles that turn and turn upon themselves like grindstones.

Still, a girl can dream. Even if she wasn't born a girl. And with that in mind I followed Michelle and the others back to mill.

Boys

Carol Emshwiller

In this story, the boys' club and girls' club have grown up, which only makes them more dangerous.

We need a new batch of boys. Boys are so foolhardy, impetuous, reckless, rash. They'll lead the way into smoke and fire and battle. I've seen one of my own sons, aged twelve, standing at the top of the cliff shouting, daring the enemy. You'll never win a medal for being too reasonable.

We steal boys from anywhere. We don't care if they come from our side or theirs. They'll forget soon enough which side they used to be on, if they ever knew. After all, what does a seven-year-old know? Tell them this flag of ours is the best and most beautiful, and that we're the best and smartest, and they believe it. They like uniforms. They like fancy hats with feathers. They like to get medals. They like flags and drums and war cries.

Their first big test is getting to their beds. You have to climb straight up to the barracks. At the top you have to cross a hanging bridge. They've heard rumors about it. They know they'll have to go home to mother if they don't do it. They all do it.

You should see the look on their faces when we steal them. It's what they've always wanted. They've seen our fires along the hills. They've seen us marching back and forth across our flat places. When the wind is right, they've heard the horns that signal our getting up and going to bed and they've gotten up and gone to bed with our sounds or those of our enemies across the valley.

In the beginning they're a little bit homesick (you can hear them smothering their crying the first few nights) but most have anticipated their capture and look forward to it. They love to belong to us instead of to the mothers.

If we'd let them go home they'd strut about in their uniforms and the stripes of their rank. I know because I remember when I first had my uniform. I was wishing my mother and my big sister could see me. When I was taken, I fought, but just to show my courage. I was happy to be stolen — happy to belong, at long last, to the men.

Once a year in summer we go down to the mothers and copulate in order to make more warriors. We can't ever be completely sure which of the boys is ours and we always say that's a good thing, for then they're all ours and we care about them equally, as we should. We're not supposed to have family groups. It gets in the way of combat. But every now and then, it's clear who the father is. I know two of my sons. I'm sure they know that I, the colonel, am their father. I think that's why they try so hard. I know them as mine because I'm a small, ugly man. I know many must wonder how someone like me got to be a colonel.

(We not only steal boys from either side but we copulate with either side. When I go down to the villages, I always look for Una.)

TO DIE FOR YOUR TRIBE IS TO LIVE FOREVER. That's written over our headquarters entrance. Under it, NEVER FORGET. We know we mustn't forget but we suspect maybe we have. Some of us feel that the real reasons for the battles have been lost. No doubt but that there's hate, so we and they commit more atrocities in the name of the old ones, but how it all began is lost to us.

We've not only forgotten the reasons for the conflict, but we've also forgotten our own mothers. Inside our barracks, the walls are covered with mother jokes and mother pictures. Mother bodies are soft and tempting. "Pillows," we call them. "Nipples" and "pillows." And we insult each other by calling ourselves the same.

The valley floor is full of women's villages. One every fifteen miles or so. On each side are mountains. The enemy's, at the far side, are called

The Purples. Our mountains are called The Snows. The weather is worse in our mountains than in theirs. We're proud of that. We sometimes call ourselves The Hailstones or The Lightnings. We think the hailstones harden us up. The enemy doesn't have as many caves over on their side. We always tell the boys they were lucky to be stolen by us and not those others.

When I was first taken, our mothers came up to the caves to get us back. That often happens. Some had weapons. Laughable weapons. My own mother was there, in the front of course. She probably organized the whole thing, her face, red and twisted with resolve. She came straight at me. I was afraid of her. We boys fled to the back of the barracks and our squad leader stood in front of us. Other men covered the doorway. It didn't take long for the mothers to retreat. None were hurt. We try never to do them any harm. We need them for the next crop of boys.

Several days later my mother came again by herself – sneaked up by moonlight. Found me by the light of the night lamp. She leaned over my sleeping mat and breathed on my face. At first I didn't know who it was. Then I felt breasts against my chest and I saw the glint of a hummingbird pin I recognized. She kissed me. I was petrified. (Had I been a little older I'd have known how to choke and kick to the throat. I might have killed her before I realized it was my mother.) What if she took me from my squad? Took away my uniform? (By then I had a red and blue jacket with gold buttons. I had already learned to shoot. Something I'd always wanted to do. I was the first of my group to get a sharpshooters medal. They said I was a natural. I was trying hard to make up for my small size.)

The night my mother came she lifted me in her arms. There, against her breasts, I thought of all the pillow jokes. I yelled. My comrades, though no older than I and only a little larger, came to my aid. They picked up whatever weapon was handy, mostly their boots. (Thank goodness we had not received our daggers yet.) My mother wouldn't hit out at the boys. She let them batter at her. I wanted her to hit back, to run, to save herself. After she finally did run, I found I had bitten my lower lip. In times of stress I'm inclined to do that. I have to watch out. When you're a colonel, it's embarrassing to be found with blood on your chin.

So now, off to steal boys. We're a troop of older boys and younger men. The oldest maybe twenty-two, half my age. I think of them all as boys, though I would never call them boys to their faces. I'm in charge. My son, Hob, he's seventeen now, is with us.

But we no sooner creep down to the valley than we see things have changed since last year. The mothers have put up a wall. They've built themselves a fort.

I immediately change our plans. I decide this will be copulation day, not boys day. Good military strategy: Always be ready for a quick change of plan.

The minute I think this, I think Una. This is her town. My men look happy, too. This is not only easier, but lots more fun than herding a new crop of boys.

Last time I came down at copulation time I found her – or she found me, she usually does. She's a little old for copulation day, but I didn't want anybody but her. After copulation, I did things for her, repaired a roof leak, fixed a broken table leg.... Then I took her over again, though it wasn't needed, and caused my squad to have to wait for me. Got me a lot of lewd remarks, but I felt extraordinarily happy anyway.

Sometimes on boys night I wonder, what if I stole Una along with boys? What if I dressed her as a boy and brought her to some secret hiding place on our side of the mountain? There are lots of unused caves. Once our armies occupied them all, but that was long ago. Both us and our enemies seem to be dwindling. Every year there are fewer and fewer suitable boys.

Una always seems glad to see me even though I'm ugly and small. (My size is a disadvantage for a soldier, though less so now that I have rank, but the ugliness...that's how I can tell which are my sons... small, ugly boys, both of them. Too bad for them. But I've managed well even so, all the way up to colonel.)

Una was my first. I was her first, too. I felt sorry for her, having to have me for her beginning to be a woman. We were little more than children. We hardly knew what we were doing or how to do it. Afterwards she cried. I felt like crying myself but I had learned not to. Not just learned it with the squad, but I had learned it even before they took me from my mother. I wanted to be taken. I roamed far out into the scrub, waiting for them to come and get me.

The pain in my hip started when I was one of those boys. It wasn't from a wound in a skirmish with the enemy, but from a fight among ourselves. Our leaders were happy when we fought each other. We'd have gotten soft and lazy if we didn't. I keep my mouth shut about my injury. I kept my mouth shut even when I got it. I thought if they knew I could be so easily hurt they'd send me back. Later, I thought if they knew about it, I might not be allowed to come on our raids. Later still I thought I might not be able to be a colonel. I don't let myself limp though sometimes that makes me more breathless than I should be. So far it doesn't seem as if anybody's noticed.

We regroup. I say, "Fellow nipples and fellow pillows...." Everybody laughs. "When have they ever stopped men? Look how womanish the walls are. They'll crumble as we climb." I scrape at a part with the tip of my cane. (As a colonel, I'm allowed to have a cane if I wish instead of a swagger stick.)

We're not sure if the women want to stop copulation day or boy gathering day. We hope it's the latter.

Boost up the smallest boy with a rope on hooks. The rest of us follow.

I used to be that smallest boy. I always went first and highest. Times like this I was glad for my size. I got medals for that. I don't wear any of them. I like playing at being one of the boys. Being small and being a colonel is a good example for some. If they knew about my bum leg I'd be an even better example of how far you can get with disabilities.

We scale the walls and drop into the edges of a vegetable garden. We walk carefully around tomatoes and strawberry plants, squash and beans. After that, raspberry bushes tear at our pants and untie our high-tops as we go by. There's a row of barbed wire just beyond the raspberries. Easy to push down.

I feel sad that the women want to keep us out so badly. I wonder, does Una want me not to come? Except they know we're as determined as mothers. At least I am when it comes to Una.

Una has always been nice to me. I often wonder why she likes me. I can understand somebody liking me now that I'm a colonel with silver on my epaulets, and a silver handled cane, but she liked me when I was nothing but a runty boy. She's small, too. I always think Una and I fit together except for one thing, she's beautiful.

We swarm in, turn, each to our favorite place, the younger ones to what's left over, usually other young ones. But then here we are, swarming back again, into their central square, the place with the well, and stone benches, and their one and only tree. Around the tree are the graves of babies. The benches are the mourning benches. We sit on them or on the ground. There's nobody here, not a single woman nor girl nor baby.

Then there's the sound of shooting. We move from the central square – we can't see anything from there. We hide behind the houses at the edges of the gardens. Our enemy stands along the top of the wall. We're ambushed. We flop down. We have no rifles with us and only two pistols, mine and my lieutenant's. This wasn't supposed to be a skirmish. We have our daggers, of course.

Those along the wall don't seem to be very good shots. I raised my pistol. I'm thinking to show them what a good shot really is. But my lieutenant yells, "Stop! Don't shoot. It's mothers!"

Women all along the wall! And with guns. Hiding under wall-colored shields. Whoever heard of such a thing.

They shoot, but a lot are missing, I think on purpose. After all, we may be the enemy, but we're the fathers of many of their girls and many of them. I wonder which one is Una.

The women are angrier than we thought. Perhaps they're tired of losing their boys to us and to the other side. I wouldn't put it past them not to be on any side whatsoever.

Our boys begin to yell their war cry but in a halfhearted way. But then...one shot...a real shot this time. Good shot, too. One wonders how a woman could have done it. One wonders if it was a man who taught her. The boys are stunned. To think that one of their mothers or one of their sisters would shoot to kill. This is real. We hadn't thought they'd harm us any more than we ever really harm them.

It was my lieutenant they killed. One bloodless shot to the head. For that boy's sake I'm glad at least no pain. He was wearing his ceremonial hat. I wasn't wearing mine. I never liked that fancy heavy hat. I suppose they really wanted to kill me, but had to take second best since they couldn't tell which one I was. Una would know which one was me.

The boys scatter – back to the center square with its mourning tree. The women can't see them back there. I stay to check on the dead lieutenant and to get his dagger and pistol. Then I limp back to where the boys are waiting for me to tell them what to do. Limp. I relax into it. I don't care who sees. I haven't exactly given up, though perhaps I have when it comes to my future. I'll most likely be demoted. To be captured by women....All twenty of us. If I can't get out of this in an efficient and capable way, there goes my career.

I hope they have the sense to come rescue us with a large group. They'll have to make a serious effort. I hope they don't try to fight and at the same time try to save the women for future use.

But then we hear shooting again and we look out from behind the huts near the wall and see the women have turned their guns outwards. At first we think it's us, come to rescue us, but it's not. That's not our battle cry, not our drum beats....We can't see from behind the walls so some of us go up on the roofs. There's no danger, all the rifles are facing outwards, but our boys would have braved the roof without a word, as they always do.

It's not our red and blue banners. It's their ugly green and white.

It's the enemy come to take advantage of our capture. We wish the women would get out of the way and let us go so we could fight for ourselves. Those women are breaking every rule of battle. They're lying flat along their wall. Nobody can get a fair shot at them.

It goes on and on. We get tired of watching and retreat to the square. We reconnoiter food from the kitchens. We eat better than we usually do. The food is so good we wish the women would let up a bit so we can enjoy it without that racket. Where did they get all these weapons? They must have found our ammunition caves and those of our enemy, too.

The women do a pretty good job. By nightfall our enemy has fled back into their mountains and the women are still on top of their wall. It looks as if they're going to spend the night up there. It's a wide wall. Not as badly built as I told the boys it was.

We find beds for ourselves, all of them better than our usual sleeping pads. I go to Una's hut and lie where I had hoped to have a copulation.

Cats prowl and yowl. All sorts of things live with the women. Goats wander the streets and come in any house they want to. All the animals expect food everywhere. Like the women, our boys are soft hearted. They feed every creature that comes by. I don't let on that I do too.

This whole thing makes me sad. Worried. If I could just have Una in my arms, I might be able to sleep. I have a "day dream" of her creeping in to me in the middle of the night. I wouldn't even care if we had a copulation or not.

In the morning boys climb to the roofs again to see what's up. They describe women lying under shields all along the walls and they can see some of the enemy lying dead away from the walls. I need to climb up and see for myself. Besides it's good for the boys to see me taking the same chances they do.

I send the boys off and I take their place. I look down on the women along the wall. I see several rifles pointed at me. I stand like a hero. I dare them to shoot. I take all the time I want. I see wall sections less crowded with women. I take out my notebook (no leader is ever without one) and draw a diagram. I take my time until I have the whole wall mapped out.

I could take out my pistol and threaten them. I could shoot one but it wouldn't be very manly to take advantage of my high point. Were they men I'd do it. But then they do the unmanly thing. They shoot me. My leg. My good leg. I go down, flat on the roof. At first I feel nothing but the shock...as if I'd been hit with a hammer. All I know is I can't stand up. Then I see blood.

Though they're on the wall, they're lower. They can't see me as long as I keep down. I crawl to the edge where boys help me. They carry me back to Una's bed. I feel I'm about to pass out or throw up and I become aware that I've soiled myself. I don't want the boys to see. I've always been a source of strength and inspiration in spite of or because of my size.

One of those boys is Hob, come to help me, my arm across his shoulders. I lean in pain but keep my groans to myself.

"Sir? Colonel?"

"I'm fine. Will be. Go."

I wish I could ask him if he really is my son. They say sometimes the women know and tell the boys.

"Don't you want us to ..."

"No. Go. Now. And shut the door."

They leave just in time. I throw up over the side of the bed. I lie back — Una's pillow all sweated up not to mention what I've done to her quilt.

Una can make potions for pain. I wish I knew which, of the herbs hanging from her ceiling, might help me. But I'd not be able to reach them anyway.

I lie, half conscious, for I don't know how long. Every time I sit up to examine my leg, I feel nausea again and have to lie back. I wonder if I'll ever be able to lead a charge or a raid for boys or a copulation day. And I always thought, when I became a general (and lately I felt sure I'd be one) maybe I'd find out what we're fighting for — beyond, that is, the usual rhetoric we use to make ourselves feel superior. Now I suppose I'll never know the real reasons.

The boys knock. I rouse myself and say, "Come." Try, that is. At first my voice won't sound out at all and then it sounds more like a groan than a word. The boys tell me the women have called down from the wall. They want to send in a spokesman. The boys want to let him in and then hold him hostage so that we'll all be let out safely.

I tell them the women will probably send in a woman.

That bothers the boys. They must have had torture or killing in mind but now they look worried.

"Tell them yes," I say.

It must smell terrible in here. I even smell terrible to myself, and it's uncomfortable sitting in my own mess. I prop myself up as best I can. I hope I can keep to my senses. I hope I don't throw up in the middle of it. I put my dagger, unsheathed, under the pillow.

At first I think the boys were right, it's a man, of course a man. Where would they have found him, and is he from our side or theirs? That's important. I can't tell by the colors. He's all in tan and gray. He's not wearing any stripes at all so I can't tell his rank. He stands, at ease. More than at ease, utterly relaxed, and in front of a colonel.

But then...I can't believe it, it's Una. I should have known. Dressed as a man down to the boots. I have such a sense of relief and after that joy. Everything will be all right now.

I tell the boys to get out and shut the door.

I reach for her, but the look on her face stops me.

"You shot me in the leg on purpose, didn't you! My good leg!"

"I meant to shoot the bad one."

She opens all the windows, and the door again, too, and shoos the boys away.

"Let me see."

She's gentle. As I knew she'd be.

"I'll get the bullet out, but first I'll clean you up." She hands me leaves to chew for pain.

As she leans, so close above me, her hair falls out of her cap and brushes my face, gets in my mouth as it does when we have copulation day. I reach to touch her breast but she pushes me away.

I should kill her for the glory of it...the leader of the women. I'd not be thought a failure then. I'd be made a general in no time.

But, as she pulls away the soiled quilts, she finds my dagger first thing. She puts it in the drawer with her kitchen knives.

I think again how...(and we all know, only too well) how love is a dangerous thing and can spoil the best of plans. Even as I think it, I want to spoil the very plans I think of. I mean if she's the leader then I could deal with her right now, as she leans over me – even without my dagger. They may be good shots, but can they wrestle a man? Even a wounded one?

"I chose you because I thought, of all of them, you might listen."

"You know I won't ever be let come down to copulation day again."

"Don't go back then. Stay here and copulate."

"I have often thought to bring you up to the mountain dressed as a man. I have a place all picked out."

"Stay here. Let everybody stay here and be as women."

I can't answer such a thing. I can't even think about it.

"But then what else do you know except how to be a colonel?"

She washes me, changes the bed, and throws the bed clothes and my clothes out the door. Then she gets the bullet out. I'm half out of my head from the leaves she had me chew so the pain is dulled. She bandages me, covers me with a clean blanket, puts her lips against my cheek for a moment.

Then stands up, legs apart. She looks like one of our boys getting ready to prove himself. "We'll not stand for this anymore," she says. "It has to end and we'll end it, if not one way, then another."

"But this is how it's always been."

"You could be our spokesman."

How can she even suggest such a thing. "Pillows," I say. "Spokesman for the nipples."

Goodness knows what the mothers are capable of. They never stick to any rules.

"If the answer is no, we'll not have anymore boy babies. You can come down and copulate all you want but there'll be no boys. We'll kill them."

"You wouldn't. You couldn't. Not you, Una."

"Have you noticed how there are fewer and fewer boys? Many have already done it."

But I'm in too much pain and dizzy from the leaves she gave me, to think clearly. She sees that. She sits beside me, takes my hand. "Just rest," she says. How can I rest with such ideas in my head? "But the rules."

"Hush. Women don't care about rules. You know that."

"Come back with me." I pull her down against me. This time she lets me. How good it feels to have us chest to chest, my arms around her. "I have a secret place. It's not a hard climb to get there."

She pulls back. "Colonel, sir!"

"Please don't call me that."

Then I say...what we're not allowed to say or even think. It's a mother/child thing, not to be said between a man and a woman. I say, "I love you."

She leans back and looks at me. Then wipes at my chin. "Try not to bite your lip like that."

"It doesn't matter anymore."

"It does to me."

"I liked.... I like...." I already used the other word, why not yet again. "I love copulation day only when with you."

I wonder if she feels the same about me. I wish I dared ask her. I wonder if my son.... Is Hob hers and mine together? I've always hoped he was. She's made no gesture towards him. She hasn't even looked at him any more than any other boy. This would have been his first copulation day had the women not built their wall.

"Rest," she says. "We'll discuss later."

"Is it just us? Or are you saying the same thing to the enemy? They could win the war like that. It would be your fault."

"Stop thinking."

"What if no more boys on either side, ever?"

"What if?"

She gives me more of those leaves to chew. They're bitter. I was in too much pain to notice that the first time. I feel even sleepier right away.

I dream I'm the last of all the boys. Ever. I have to get somewhere in a hurry, but there's a wall so high I'll never get over it. Beside, my legs are not there at all. I'm nothing but a torso. Women watch me. Women, off across the valley floor as far as I can see and none will help. There's nothing to do but lie there and give the war cry.

I wake shouting and with Una holding me down. Hob is there, helping her. Other boys are in the doorway looking worried.

I've thrown the blanket and the pillow to the floor and now I seem to be trying to throw myself out of bed. Una has a long scratch across her cheek. I must have done that.

"Sorry. Sorry."

I'm still as if in a dream. I pull Una down against me. Hold her hard and then I reach out for Hob, too. My poor ugly boy. I ask the unaskable. "Tell me, is Hob mine and yours together?"

Hob looks shocked that I would ask such a thing, as well he should. Una pulls away and gets up. She answers as if she was one of the boys. "Colonel, sir, how can you, of all people, ask a thing like that." Then she throws my own words back at me. "This is how it's always been."

"Sorry. Sorry."

"Oh, for heaven's sake stop being so sorry!"

She shoos the boys from the doorway but she lets Hob stay. Together they rearrange the bed. Together she and Hob make broth for me and food for themselves. Hob seems at home here. It's true, I'm sure. This is our son.

But I suppose all this yearning, all this wondering, is due to the leaves Una had me chew. It's not the real me. I'll not pay any attention to myself.

But there's something else. I didn't get a good look at my leg yet, but it feels like a serious wound. If I can't climb up to our stronghold, I'll not ever be able to go home. I shouldn't, even so, and though my career is in a shambles....I shouldn't let myself be lured into staying here as a copulator for the rest of my life. I can't think of anything more dishonorable. I should send Hob back to the citadel to report on what's happened and to get help. If he was found trying to escape, would Una let the women kill him?

I try to get Hob alone so I can whisper his orders to him. Only when Una goes out to the privy do I get the chance. "Get back to the citadel. Cross the wall tonight. There's no moon." I show him my map and where I think there are fewer women. I want to tell him to take care, but we don't ever say such things.

In the morning I tell Una to tell my leaders to come in to me. I'm in pain, in a sweat, my beard is itchy. I ask Una to clean me up. She treats me as a mother would. Back when my mother did it, I pulled away. I wouldn't let her get close to me. I especially wouldn't let her hug or kiss me. I wanted to be a soldier. I wanted nothing to do with mother things.

All the boys are looking scruffy. We take pride in our cleanliness, in shaving everyday, in our brush cuts, and our enemy is as spic and span as we are. I hope they don't launch an offensive today and see us so untidy.

I'm glad to see Hob isn't with them.

I find it hard to rouse myself to my usual humor. I say, "Pillows, nipples," but I'm too uncomfortable to play at being one of the boys.

I'd prefer to recuperate some, but the boys are restless already. I can't be thinking of myself. We'll storm the wall. I show them the map. I point out the less guarded spots. I grab Una. Both her wrists. "Men, we'll need a battering ram."

Wood isn't easy to get out here on the valley floor. This is a desert except along the streams, but every village has one tree in the center square that they've nurtured along. As here, baby's graves are always around it. In other villages, most are cottonwood, but this one is oak. It's so old I wouldn't be surprised if it hadn't been here since before the village. I think the village was built up around it later.

"Chop the tree. Ram the wall." I tell them. "Go back to the citadel. Don't wait around for me. Tell the generals never to come here again, neither for boys nor for copulation. Tell them I'm of no use to us anymore."

The women won't be able to shoot at the boys chopping it down. It's hidden from all parts of the wall.

When they hear the chopping, the women begin to ululate. Our boys stop chopping, but only for a moment. I hear them begin again with even more vigor.

Here beside me Una ululates, too. She struggles against me but I hang on.

"How could you? That's the tree of dead boys."

I let go.

"All the babies buried there are boys. Some are yours."

I can't let this new knowledge color my thinking. I have to think of the safety of my boys. "Let us go, then."

"Tell them to stop."

"Would you let us go for the sake of a tree?"

"We would."

I give the order.

The women move away from a whole section of the wall, they even provide their ladders. I tell the boys to go. There's no way they could carry me back and no way I could ever climb to the citadel again.

No sooner are the boys gone, even to the last tootle of the fifes, the last triumphant drum beat.... (We always march home as though victorious whether victorious or not.) Hearing them go, I can't help but groan, though not from pain this time. No sooner have the mothers come down from the wall, but that I hear, ululating again. Una stamps in to me.

"What now?"

"It's Hob. Your enemy.... Your enemy has dropped him off at the edge of your foothills."

I can see it on her face.

"He's dead."

"Of course he's dead. You are all as good as dead."

She blames me for Hob. "I blame myself."

"I hate you. I hate you all."

I don't believe we'll be seeing many boys anymore. I would warn us if I was able, I would be the spokesman, though I don't suppose I'll ever have the chance.

"What will the women do with me?"

"You were always kind. I'll not be any less to you."

What am I good for? What use am I but to stay here as the father of females? All those small, ugly, black-haired girls.... I suppose all of them biting their lower lips until they bleed.

Genre: A Word Only a Frenchman Could Love

(A Talk Given at the Public Library Association Preconference on Genre, in Seattle, February 2004)

Ursula K. Le Guin

Here's an essay for folks who picked up this book not realizing that some might categorize it as science fiction. It's also an essay for folks who decided as soon as they saw the names on the cover that this was science fiction – and so snatched it up immediately. And it's even an essay for those who wonder why so many people seem to find it necessary to categorize what they read into one genre or another.

The concept of genre is a valid one. We need a method for sorting out and defining varieties of narrative fiction, and genre gives us a tool to begin the job. But there are two big problems in using the tool. The first is that it's been misused so often that it's hard to use it rightly – like a good screwdriver that's all bent out of shape because some dork tried to pry paving stones apart with it.

"Genre" is a generic word – naturally! – for "a kind or style, especially of art or literature," says the OED, and more specifically a term for paintings of a certain type and subject matter – "scenes and subjects of common life."

Now, "scenes and subjects of common life" nicely covers the subject matter of the realistic novel, which is often the literary equivalent of genre painting. But when the term came over into literature, for some reason it came to mean anything but the realistic novel, and was applied to fictions whose subject matter is some degrees removed from common life – westerns, murder mysteries, spy thrillers, romances, horror stories, fantasies, science fiction, and so on. An odd reversal, but no harm in it.

The subject matter of realism is broader than that of any genre except fantasy; and realism was the preferred mode of modernism. By relegating fantasy to kiddylit, modernist critics left the realistic novel with the widest field and could see it as the biggest kind of fiction. So the word "genre" began to imply inferiority, and came to be commonly misused, not as a description, but as a negative value judgment. Most people now understand "genre" to be an inferior form of fiction, defined by a label, while realistic fictions are simply called novels or literature.

So we have an accepted hierarchy of fictional types, with "literary fiction," not defined, but consisting almost exclusively of realism, at the top. All other kinds of fiction, the "genres," are either spaced out in rapidly descending order of inferiority or simply tossed into a general garbage-heap at the bottom. This judgmental system, like all arbitrary hierarchies, promotes ignorance and arrogance. It has seriously deranged the teaching and criticism of fiction for decades, by short-circuiting useful critical description, comparison, and assessment. It condones imbecilities on the order of, "If it's science fiction it can't be good, if it's good it can't be science fiction."

And judgment by genre is particularly silly and pernicious now that the whole idea of genre itself is breaking down.

For that's the other problem with our good tool; the screwdriver is the wrong shape for the slots, the screws are all screwy. Much of the best fiction being written doesn't fit into the genres any more, but combines, crosses, miscegenates, transgresses, and reinvents them. Seventy years ago Virginia Woolf was questioning the possibility of writing realistic fiction honestly. Many honest writers have given up the attempt.

Terms such as "magical realism" are hastily conceived labels slapped across great, widening cracks in the conventional structure of narrative. They often disguise more than they reveal. Major novelists, great writers appear outside any recognized category — tell me what kind of fiction it is that José Saramago writes? It is not realism; no, it certainly isn't; but it is, it very certainly is literature.

The breakdown is occurring even across a major boundary, the definition of fiction and nonfiction. Jorge Luis Borges said that he considered all prose literature to be fiction. Fiction, for Borges, thus includes history, journalism, biography, memoir, Cervantes' *Don Quixote*, Pierre Menard's *Don Quixote*, the works of Borges, *Peter Rabbit*, and the Bible. It seems a large category, but it may prove more intellectually practicable than any attempt to salvage useless distinctions.

And yet the categories established by genre are not only perpetuated, cemented in, by the stereotyped thinking of reviewers, by the ingrained habits and superstitions of publishers, and by the shelving and descriptive practices of booksellers and libraries; they also are — have been and still are — useful, perhaps necessary, to the appreciation of fiction. If you don't know what kind of book you're reading, and it's not a kind you're used to, you probably need to learn how to read it. You need to learn the genre.

Useless and harmful as a value category, genre is a valid descriptive category. It may be most useful historically; it may cause more confusion than clarity in defining a postmodern work. But where definition by genre applies and is applied fairly, it is invaluable both to readers and to writers.

For example: A writer sets out to write science fiction but isn't familiar with the genre, hasn't read what's been written. This is a fairly common situation, because science fiction is known to sell well but, as a subliterary genre, is supposed to be not worth study — what's to learn? It doesn't occur to the novice that a genre is a genre because it has a field and focus of its own, its appropriate and particular tools and rules and techniques for handling the material, its traditions, and its experienced, appreciative readers: that it is, in fact, a literature. Ignoring all this, our novice is just about to reinvent the wheel, the spaceship, the space alien, and the mad scientist, with cries of innocent wonder. The cries will not be echoed by the readers. Readers familiar with that genre have met the spaceship, the alien, and the mad scientist before. They know more about them than the writer does.

In the same way, critics who set out to talk about a fantasy novel without having read any fantasy since they were eight, and in ignorance of the history and extensive theory of fantasy literature, will make fools of themselves, because they don't know how to read the book. They have no contextual information to tell them what its tradition is, where it's coming from, what it's trying to do, what it does. This was liberally proved when the first Harry Potter book came out and a lot of literary reviewers ran around shrieking about the incredible originality of the book. This originality was an artefact of the reviewers' blank ignorance of its genres (children's fantasy and the British boarding-school story), plus the fact that they hadn't read a fantasy since they were eight. It was pitiful. It was like watching some TV gourmet chef eat a piece of buttered toast and squeal, "But this is delicious! Unheard of! Where has it been all my life?"

Ignorance as a critical qualification is celebrated every time a literary pundit exhibits his sophistication by performing the time-hallowed ceremony of the Ritual Sneers at Tolkien.

We do urgently need to try to rethink genre, in order to reform the practices of critics and reviewers and the assumptions of readers, and to bring the description of fiction into some kind of relation to reality. I admit that the temptation to pull a Borges is very strong — to just say, Genre is dead! All fiction is Literature! Long live Fiction!

But what's the use saying it when you are going to run your head right against the solid obstruction of category labeling and shelving practice, from the conception of the book, the contract, the cover, to the bookstores and libraries? How can you tell reviewers to stop shoving books into outmoded categories where they don't fit, when the publishers themselves absolutely insist on the category labels — and when many, perhaps most of the authors, would scream bloody murder if they didn't get the genre label and cover and category that keeps their book from getting lost among all the other books in all the other genres?

Marketing rules, OK? I have no illusions that intelligence could possibly replace marketing in this or any other matter. Commercial genrification has its reasons. They are not intelligent reasons, but they are intelligible.

Consumerism also rules. If the books aren't labeled, if they aren't shelved by genre, if they don't have a little bitty label saying SF or M or YA, a whole lot of customers and library users will come storming the counter or the desk, shouting Where is my Fiction Fix? I want a Fantasy, I can't read all that realistic stuff! I want a Mystery, I can't read all that plotless stuff! I want a Masterpiece of Grim Realism, I can't read all that imaginary stuff! I want Mindless Fluff, I can't read all that literary stuff! Etc., etc.

To give each reader an annotated author-title list of whatever their fiction addiction is, so they can go find the books on the shelves, is a perfectly fair solution, offered by many libraries. But addicts don't like it. They want books to be easy the way fast food is easy. They want to go to the shelf and stick out their hand and get a fix.

Have you ever noticed initials on the fly leaf of a series mystery at the library – sometimes a whole row of them down the leaf? They're so people will know they've read that one already, because looking at the story itself wouldn't tell them anything, since it's exactly like all the other books in that series by that author. This is addiction. But the only harm I can see in it is that it keeps people from reading good stuff. And they might not read the good stuff anyway, because they've been scared into thinking that literature can't possibly include anything about horses, spaceships, dragons, dreams, spies, monsters, animals, aliens, or dark, handsome, taciturn men who own large houses in remote bits of England. Oh, Darcy, they need you! But they've been scared away from Darcy, or never allowed a glimpse of him. And the commercial fiction machine feeds their hunger for story with junk food – commercial, mechanical, formula fiction.

Any genre, including realism, can be formulized and made commercial. Genre and formula are two different things. But the assumption that they are the same thing allows the lazy-minded critic and professor to ignore all genre literature, dismissing it, unread, as unreadable.

To put a genre label on a book is to ensure it a safe audience, but a limited audience. Publishers go for safe, and so they like genre labels. But not always. With low-risk, big-name authors, safety lies in assuming that the author's literary reputation would be damaged by the admission that one or more of their books belongs to a genre other than literary realism. So when *Oryx and Crake* came out, Margaret Atwood and her publisher denied that she'd ever had anything to do with science fiction — despite the fact that the novel is science fiction in every sense of the term, though unfortunately rather unoriginal science fiction — and despite the fact that *The Handmaid's Tale* also is science fiction, of an equally familiar type though of far higher quality, in fact of superlative quality.

Atwood knows perfectly well what she's writing; I heard her describe *The Handmaid's Tale* as science fiction, reading from it at Harbourfront, the year it came out. But by the time it appeared the publishers had hushed her up and forcibly established her literary virginity, which has remained unspotted ever since. This time, to my grief, she felt it necessary to misdescribe and even sneer at "space" fiction and to describe her book by one of those feeble euphemisms — "speculative fiction" or something. Her marketing department evidently lives in terror that she'll lose the Nobel Prize if her science fiction is recognized as such. So the poor book was doomed to lukewarm civility from the literary reviewers and exasperated silence from the people who could in fact review it usefully, the critics who know and like the genre.

If Atwood had taken the risk of saying straight out, even of *boasting* that her book is science fiction, she would have done literature considerable good, and I believe not damaged her own standing except in the eyes of the most reactionary and mandarin litterateurs, with whom she has notoriously little patience. But Atwood has taken so many risks, I have no heart to blame her for not taking this one. (Note, March 2004: I hear that she has in fact broken out of the marketing department's closet and said that of course the *Handmaid* and *Oryx* are science fiction. Brava Margaret!)

I do admire the courage of Doris Lessing, a real literary lion, a woman who can roar, for making her publisher publish her three science fiction novels as science fiction, and talking about them as science fiction, and even attending the Worldcon. She saw no call to badmouth anybody else to protect her precious reputation. I do not see that her reputation has in fact suffered from her excursion into genre; but of course Lessing has always been a transgressor, always crossing sacred boundaries. No cage for that lion.

I too have crossed some genre barriers, in fact about as many as I could. It's not a matter for me of stooping to an occasional amusing bit of slumming in the kiddylit ghetto or the Sci Fi gutter. I live there, in the ghettos and gutters. I am a street person of the city of fiction. And every now and then I come lumbering up like some sort of Sewer Monster out of the depths of Genre onto the spotless lawns of Literary Realism – since realism, to my mind, is simply another genre, another domain of fiction, and all mine if I want it.

Thinking about the maneuvers performed by self-defined "literary" novelists to preserve their purity from genre pollution, I realized that I am in the unusual position of being able to perform the same poses and contortions – only backwards.

How am I to protect my unspotted name as a science fiction writer from the scorn of those who might think I have been shamelessly performing acts of realism in public?

Thus: How dare you call me a realist? My book *Searoad* has nothing to do with the commercial realism found in all the chain bookstores. I call the book "Social Reality Enhancement." Realistic novels are for lazy-minded, semi-educated people whose atrophied imagination allows them to appreciate only the most limited and conventional subject-matter. Realistic fiction, or Re-Fi as its fans call it, is an outworn genre, written by unimaginative hacks who rely on mere mimesis. If they had any self-respect they'd be writing memoir, but they're too lazy to fact-check. Of course I never read Re-Fi, but my children keep bringing home these garish realistic novels and talking about them, so I know that it's an incredibly narrow genre, completely centered on one species, incredibly culture-bound, full of wornout clichés and predictable situations – the quest for the father, mother-bashing, obsessive lust, suburban guilt, etc, etc. All it's good for is being made into mass-market movies. Given its old-fashioned means and limited subject-matter, realism is quite incapable of describing the complexity of contemporary experience.

Now, would you believe that tripe? There's some truth in it — but it's tripe. *All judgment of literature by genre is tripe. All judgment of a category of literature as inherently superior or inferior is tripe.*

A book can't be judged by its cover — or by its label. A book can be judged only by reading it.

There are many bad books. There are no bad genres.

Of course there are genres that are unappealing to individual readers. A reader who liked or valued all kinds of narrative equally would be undiscriminating to the point of imbecility. Some people honestly can't read fantasy with any pleasure. I honestly can't read porn or most political thrillers with pleasure. I have friends who cannot read *any* fiction with pleasure; they need what they can consider or pretend to be facts. These differences point, again, to the underlying validity of the concept of literary genre.

But they do not justify any judgment of literature by genre.

There are commercial subcategories, such as some series mysteries, subteen grossout books, strict formula romances, which are so narrowly prescribed, so rigidly diminished in emotional and intellectual scope, that a genius would go mad trying to write one of serious merit. But if you incline to sneer at romance as an intrinsically inferior fictional category may I invite you to read — since evidently you have not read them — the works of Charlotte and Emily Bronte?

All judgment of literature by category or genre is tripe.

So what are we going to do, now? What use is the whole concept of genre, if you can't damn whole categories of fiction with it so that you never have to bother learning how to read them, and if the fiction writers are going to keep crossing over, ignoring boundaries, slipstreaming, interbreeding like a barnful of cats — but at the same time publishers and booksellers and librarians cling immovably to the old, false, rigid divisions, because they're commercially unrisky, and because they make it easy for people to find certain types of books without being exposed to any alien forms of literature that might possibly take over their minds and put new ideas into them?

I mean, God forbid that we should mix genres on the shelves. What if I went to Powell's or my branch library for Philip K. Dick and found him next to Charles Dickens – how terrible! Or if I went looking for the new Steven Saylor mystery and had to go *right past* the Patrick O'Brien sea stories! Or, of course, vice versa. Let alone being exposed to some sort of western by Molly Gloss or something indescribable by Karen Fowler or Carol Emshwiller or Virginia Woolf or Jane Austen that isn't like any of the other books at all. If fiction, all fiction, were shelved alphabetically by author, what misery and confusion would result! People would have to know the alphabet! It is unthinkable.

Could I suggest that we think about it?

[excerpts from]

Set This House in Order: A Romance of Souls

Matt Ruff

The borders between sf and "literary fiction" have never been as strong as some people would like them to be, and they've been blurring even more lately. Ursula Le Guin's essay discusses these borders; for those interested in more on this topic, www.artistswithoutborders.org is a valuable site to explore, and Michael Chabon's introduction to his anthology, *McSweeney's Mammoth Treasury of Thrilling Tales*, is required reading. Arguments about definitions of these genres go back to the beginnings of sf criticism – leading to editor and critic Damon Knight's famous solution, "Science fiction is what I point to when I say 'This is science fiction.'"

Anthony Boucher, a founding editor of *The Magazine of Fantasy & Science Fiction*, used to say he published stories *of interest* to readers of fantasy and science fiction...which meant that he would occasionally publish stories without any actual fantasy content. The magazine's continues this tradition today, and so do we. Over the years, Tiptree juries have recommended a number of stories whose sf content has been (at best) minimal.

This year's winner is an exceptional novel by Matt Ruff, *Set This House in Order: A Romance of Souls*. Ruff's first two novels were firmly within the field: *Fool on the Hill* is a fantasy and *Sewer, Gas & Electric: The Public Works Trilogy* is near-future science fiction.

Set This House in Order, though, is a contemporary novel about multiple personality disorder (now renamed dissociative identity disorder by the American Psychiatric Association), and on publication it was virtually ignored by the SF press. One of the jurors read it and suggested it for award consideration.

The novel is about two people with mpd. With the help of a therapist, one has devised an elaborate scheme to deal with his disorder: a virtual house inside his head where each of his personalities has a room to inhabit and a role to play. At the beginning of the novel, the other knows there is something wrong with her, but not what it is.

Ruff based this concept on an acquaintance who had created an internal structure to deal with his own problems, and from this was able to craft a remarkable work of imagination, of speculative psychology.

If you don't immediately see the "Tiptree" aspect of the story in the excerpts from the beginning of the novel here, you *will* see — as you are introduced to both Andrew Gage and Penny Driver — that each contains a multitude of souls of varying gender, maturity and socialization. And you'll want to know more.

ANDREW:

My father called me out.

I was twenty-six years old when I first came out of the lake, which puzzles some people, who wonder how I could have an age without having a past. But I get puzzled, too: most people I know can't remember being born, and what's more, it doesn't bother them that they can't remember. My good friend Julie Sivik once told me that her earliest memory was a scene from her second-birthday party, when she stood on a chair to blow out the candles on her cake. It's all a blank before that, she said, but she didn't seem upset by it, as if it were the most natural thing in the world to be missing two years of her life.

I remember everything, from the first moment: the sound of my name in the dark; the shock of the water; the tangle of the weeds at the bottom of the lake where I opened my eyes. The water is black down there, but I could see sunlight on the surface far above me, and I floated towards it, drawn up by my father's voice.

My father waited for me on the lakebank with Adam and Jake and Aunt Sam. Behind them stood the house, with Seferis up in the pulpit keeping an eye on the body; and from the windows overlooking the lake, and from the edges of the forest, I could feel the others watching me, too shy to show themselves. Gideon must have been watching too, from Coventry, but I didn't know about him then.

I suppose I should explain about the house. Aunt Sam says that a good storyteller only reveals important information a little at a time, to keep the audience interested, but I'm afraid if I don't explain it all now you'll get confused, which is worse than not being interested. So just bear with me, and I promise to try not to bore you later.

The house, along with the lake, the forest, and Coventry, are all in Andy Gage's head, or what would have been Andy Gage's head if he had lived. Andy Gage was born in 1965 and murdered not long after by his stepfather, a very evil man named Horace Rollins. It was no ordinary murder: though the torture and abuse that killed him were real, Andy Gage's death wasn't. Only his soul actually died, and when it died, it broke in pieces. Then the pieces became souls in their own right, coinheritors of Andy Gage's life.

There was no house back then, just a dark room in Andy Gage's head where the souls all lived. In the center of the room was a column of bright light, and any soul that entered or was pulled into the light found itself outside, in Andy Gage's body, with no memory of how it had gotten there or what had happened since the last time it was out. As you can imagine, this was a frightening and terrible existence, made more terrible by the continuing depredations of the stepfather. Of the seven original souls who descended from Andy Gage, five were later murdered themselves, broken into still more pieces, and even the two survivors were forced to splinter in order to cope. By the time they got free of Horace Rollins, there were over a hundred souls in Andy Gage's head.

That was when the real struggle began. Over many years, the two surviving original souls — Aaron, who is my father, and Gideon, my father's brother — pieced together enough of a sense of continuity to figure out what had happened to them. With the help of a good doctor named Danielle Grey, my father worked to establish order. In place of the dark room, he constructed a geography in Andy Gage's head, a sunlit countryside where the souls could see and talk to one another. He created the house, so they'd have a place to live; the forest, so they'd have somewhere to be alone; and the pumpkin field, so the dead could be decently buried. Gideon, who was selfish, wanted no part of any of this, and did everything he could to wreck the geography, until my father was forced to exile him to Coventry.

The effort required to complete the house exhausted my father, and left him with little enthusiasm for dealing with the outside world.

But somebody had to run the body; and so, on the day the last shingle was nailed in place, my father went down to the lake and called my name.

Something else that puzzles me about other people is that a lot of them don't know their purpose in life. This usually does bother them – more than not being able to remember being born, anyway – but I can't even imagine it. Part of knowing who I am is knowing why I am, and I've always known who I am, from the first moment.

My name is Andrew Gage. I was twenty-six years old when I first came out of the lake. I was born with my father's strength, but not his weariness; his persistence, but not his pain. I was called to finish the job that my father had begun: a job that he had chosen, but that I was made for.

I met Penny Driver two months after my twenty-eighth birthday – or two months after my second birthday, depending on how you want to count it.

Jake was up first that morning, as he is most mornings, barreling out of his room around sunrise, thundering down the stairs to the common room, the clamor of his progress setting off a chain reaction of wakings among the other souls in the house. Jake is five years old, and has been since 1973, when he was born from the wreckage of a dead soul named Jacob; he is a mature five, but still basically a little kid, and not very good about respecting other people's need for quiet.

Jake's stomping roused Aunt Sam, who started up cursing; and Aunt Sam's cursing woke Adam, who has the room next to hers; and Adam, who is old enough to respect other people's need for quiet, but often chooses not to, let out a series of war whoops until my father banged on the wall and told him to knock it off. By then, everyone was awake.

I might have tried to ignore it. Unlike the others, I don't sleep in the house, I sleep in the body, and when you're in the body, even the loudest house-noises are just echoes in Andy Gage's head that can be tuned out at will – unless they come from the pulpit. But Adam knows this, of course, and whenever I do try to oversleep, he's out on the pulpit in no time, crowing like a rooster until I take the hint. Some days I make him crow himself hoarse, just to remind him who's boss; but on this particular morning, my eyes were open as soon as Jake hit the stairs.

The room where I slept — where the body slept — was in a renovated Victorian in Autumn Creek, Washington, twenty-five miles east of Seattle. The Victorian belonged to Mrs. Alice Winslow, who had first taken my father on as a boarder back in 1992, before I even existed.

We rented part of the first floor. The space was large but cluttered, clutter being an inevitable side effect of multiplicity, even if you make an effort to keep real-world possessions to a minimum. Just lying there in bed, and without even turning my head, I could see: Aunt Sam's easel, brushes, and paints, and two blank canvases; Adam's skateboard; Jake's stuffed panda; Seferis's kendo sword; my books; my father's books; Jake's little shelf of books; Adam's *Playboy* collection; Aunt Sam's stack of art prints; a color television with remote that used to be my father's but now belonged to me; a VCR that was three-fifths mine, three-tenths Adam's, and one-tenth Jake's (long story); a CD player that was one-half mine, one-quarter my father's, one-eighth Aunt Sam's, and one-sixteenth apiece Adam's and Jake's (longer story); a rack of CDs and videotapes of various ownerships; and a wheeled hamper of dirty clothes that no one wanted to lay claim to, but was mostly mine.

That's what I could see without even looking around; and besides the bedroom, there was a sitting room, a big walk-in closet, a full bathroom that was full in more ways than one, and the kitchen that we shared with Mrs. Winslow. The kitchen wasn't so cluttered, though; Mrs. Winslow cooked most of our meals for us, and strictly limited our personal food storage to one shelf in the refrigerator and two shelves in the pantry.

I got us out of bed and into the bathroom to start the morning ritual. Teeth came first. Jake really enjoys brushing for some reason, so I let him do it, stepping back into the pulpit and giving him the body. I stayed alert. Jake, as I've mentioned, is a child; but Andy Gage's body is adult and five-foot-seven, and hangs on Jake's soul like a suit of clothes many sizes too big. He moves clumsily in it, and often misjudges the distance between his extremities and the rest of the world; and as we've only got the one skull between us, if he bends over to get a dropped toothpaste cap and bashes his head on the corner of the sink, it is a group tragedy. So I kept a close eye on him.

This morning there were no accidents. He did his usual thorough job of brushing: side to side, up and down, getting every tooth, even the tricky ones in back. I wish he could handle the flossing as well, but that's a little too dexterous for him.

I took the body back and had a quick squat on the toilet. This is my job most mornings, though my father occasionally asks to do it – the pleasure of a good shit, he says, being one of the few things he misses from outside. Adam also volunteers sometimes, usually just after the latest *Playboy* has arrived; but I generally don't indulge him more than once or twice a month, as it upsets the others.

After the toilet came exercise. I stretched out on the bath mat beside the tub and let Seferis run through his routine: two hundred sit-ups followed by two hundred push-ups, the last hundred evenly divided between the right and left arms. I came back from the pulpit to muscle burn and a lather of sweat, but I didn't complain. The body's stomach is as flat as a washboard, and I can lift heavy things.

Next I gave Adam and Aunt Sam two minutes each under the shower, starting with Aunt Sam. They used to alternate who went first, but Aunt Sam likes the water a lot warmer than Adam does, and Adam was always "forgetting" to adjust the temperature control before handing off the body, so now every day it's Aunt Sam, then Adam, then me – and Adam knows if he gives me ice water or an eyeful of soap suds, he'll lose his shower privileges for a week.

When my turn came I washed up quickly (the others rarely bother to do any real scrubbing), rinsed and toweled off, and went back into the bedroom to get dressed. My father came out on the pulpit to help me pick clothes. Away from home I have control of the body full-time, so daytime wardrobe really ought to be my responsibility alone, but Aunt Sam says I was born with no fashion sense, and I think my father feels guilty about that.

"Not that shirt," he suggested, after I'd laid my initial selection on the bed.

"Does it clash with the pants?" I asked him, trying to remember the rule. "I thought blue jeans went with everything."

"They do go with everything," my father said. "But some clothes clash with everything, even blue jeans."

"You think it's ugly?" I held up the shirt and examined it more critically. It was a bright yellow plaid, with red and green checks. I'd gotten it along with a bunch of other bargains at a spring clearance sale, and I thought it looked cheerful.

"I know it's ugly," my father said. "If you really like it, you can wear it around here, but I wouldn't recommend it for public viewing."

I hesitated. I did like the shirt, and I hate having to give things up just because of what other people might think. But I also really want other people to think well of me.

"It's your choice," my father said patiently.

"All right," I said, still reluctant. "I'll wear something else."

We finished dressing. I put my watch on last, and checked it against the clock on the nightstand beside my bed. 7:07 A.M., the clock said, MON APR 21. My watch agreed about the day and date, but not about the time.

"Two minutes off," my father observed.

I gave a little shrug. "The watch runs slow," I reminded him.

"You should get it repaired, then."

"I don't need to get it repaired. It's fine the way it is."

"You should fix the VCR clock, too."

This was a longstanding bone of contention between us. My father used to own dozens of clocks, as protection against missing time; but I was less concerned with that, never having lost so much as a second as far as I knew, and had cut back to one clock per room. We'd fought about that decision, and about my failure to keep the remaining clocks perfectly synchronized. My casual attitude towards the VCR clock in particular drove my father crazy: after a power outage or an accidental unplugging, it might flash 12:00:00 for days before I bothered to reset it.

"It's really not that important," I said, more harshly than I intended to. I was still disappointed about the shirt. "I'll get around to it."

My father didn't answer, but I could tell he was frustrated: when I wouldn't look directly at the VCR, I could feel him trying to use the body's peripheral vision.

"I will get around to it," I insisted, and left the bedroom. I passed through the sitting room — whose own clock was a scandalous minute ahead of the one on the nightstand — and went down the side hallway to the kitchen, where Mrs. Winslow had breakfast waiting.

"Good morning, Andrew," Mrs. Winslow said, before I'd spoken a word. She always knew. Most mornings it was me at first, but even if I'd given the body to someone else, Mrs. Winslow would have known, without being told. She was like Adam in that sense, an almost magical reader of persons. "Did you sleep well?"

"I did, thank you." Ordinarily it's polite to repeat the question back, but Mrs. Winslow was a chronic insomniac. She slept less well than anyone I knew, except for Seferis, who doesn't sleep at all.

She'd been up since five at least, and had started cooking when she'd heard the shower. It was a measure of both her kindness and her affection for us that she was willing to do this; like everything else in the morning, breakfast is a shared activity, and no small effort to prepare. I sat down not to one meal but to a hybrid of several, each serving carefully proportioned, starting with half a plate of scrambled eggs and a mug of coffee for me. I ate my fill, then let the others take the body, each soul greeting Mrs. Winslow in turn.

"Good morning, my dear," Aunt Sam said grandly. Aunt Sam's breakfast portion consisted of a cup of herbal tea and a slice of wheat toast with mint jelly; she used to smoke half a cigarette, too, but my father made her give it up in exchange for a little extra time outside. She sipped at the tea and nibbled daintily at her toast until Adam got impatient and started clearing his throat from the pulpit.

"Good morning, gorgeous," said Adam with mock flirtatiousness.

Adam likes to pretend he is a great ladies' man. In reality, women between the ages of twelve and sixty make him nervous, and if Mrs. Winslow's hair hadn't been gray, I doubt he'd have had the courage to be so fresh with her. As he devoured his breakfast – half an English muffin and a bacon strip – he gave her his idea of a seductive wink; but when Mrs. Winslow winked back, Adam startled, sucked bacon down the wrong pipe, and ended in a fit of coughing.

"Good morning, Mrs. Winslow," Jake said, his high voice raspy from Adam's choking fit. He dug awkwardly into the little bowl of Cheerios she set out for him. She poured him a tiny glass of orange juice, too, and he reached too quickly for it. The glass (which was really made of plastic; this had happened before) went flying.

Jake froze. If he'd been with anyone but Mrs. Winslow, he would have fled the body altogether. As it was, he hunched up, fists clenched and muscles tense, bracing for a smash across the knuckles or a punch in the face. Mrs. Winslow was careful not to react too suddenly; she pretended not to even notice at first, then said, very casually: "Oh dear, I must have put that too close to the edge of the table." She got up slowly, crossed to the sink, and wet a rag to mop up the spill.

"I'm sorry, Mrs. Winslow!" Jake blurted. "I –"

"Jake dear," Mrs. Winslow said, wiping the tabletop, "you do know that Florida is a huge state, don't you? They have lots of orange juice there; plenty more where this came from." She refilled his glass, handing it directly to him this time; he took it gingerly in both hands. "There," Mrs. Winslow said. "No harm done. It only *looks* like gold." Jake giggled, but he didn't really relax until he was back inside the house.

Seferis only nodded good morning. His breakfast was the simplest of all: a small plate of salted radishes, which he popped into his mouth one at a time and crunched like candy. Mrs. Winslow had started in on her own breakfast by then, warmed-over biscuits with marmalade. When the lid stuck on the marmalade jar, she offered it to Seferis.

Seferis's size ratio to the body is the inverse of Jake's: his soul is nine feet tall, and crammed into Andy Gage's modest frame he radiates energy and strength. He got the jar lid off with a simple twist of thumb and forefinger, a trick I couldn't have managed even using the same muscles.

"*Efcharisto*," Mrs. Winslow said, as Seferis handed the jar back to her with a flourish.

"*Parakalo*," Seferis replied, and crunched another radish.

When the last of the food had been consumed, Mrs. Winslow switched on the little black-and-white TV on the kitchen counter, and poured a fresh mug of coffee for my father, who came out to visit with her for a while. They liked to watch the news together. Mrs. Winslow used to watch with her husband, and I guess my father's company brought that back for her in some way; likewise, sitting with Mrs. Winslow gave my father a sense of the normal family life he'd always wished for. But this morning was less pleasant than most. The lead news item at the bottom of the hour was an update on the Lodge camping tragedy; it upset my father even more than the VCR clock, and blackened Mrs. Winslow's mood as well.

Maybe you remember the Lodge story; it never received as much national coverage as it might have, because of another similar case in the news at the same time, but people did hear about it. Warren Lodge was a groundskeeper from Tacoma who'd gone camping in Olympic National Park with his two daughters. Two days after the start of the camping trip, the state police spotted Mr. Lodge's jeep weaving between the lanes on Route 101 and pulled him over. Mr. Lodge, who appeared delirious and had a deep scratch across his scalp, claimed that a cougar had invaded the campsite and attacked him, knocking him unconscious. When he came to, he found his daughters' tent slashed to ribbons, their sleeping bags torn and bloody; the girls themselves — Amy, twelve, and Elizabeth, ten — were nowhere to be found, although he'd searched for many hours.

It could have been true. Cougar attacks are not uncommon in the Pacific Northwest, and Mr. Lodge looked strong enough to survive a wrestling match with a big cat, if he got lucky. But watching him on TV — the day after the police pulled him over, he called a press conference to plead for volunteers to help search for his girls — I felt a growing sense of unease. Mr. Lodge's story *could* have been true, but something about the way he told it was wrong. It was Adam, looking out from the pulpit into Mr. Lodge's tear-stained face, who first put my intuition into words: "*He's* the cougar."

Ever since then — almost a full week, now — we'd been waiting for the police to reach the same conclusion. So far there hadn't been a whisper of a suspicion in public, although Adam said the cops had to be thinking about it, unless they were totally incompetent. My father, meanwhile, had pledged that if Mr. Lodge weren't arrested soon, he was going to call the Mason County DA's office himself, or have me do it.

"Do you really think he killed them?" Mrs. Winslow asked now, as the newscast replayed Mr. Lodge's plea for volunteers; the update was just a rehash of previous reports, with an added note that the searchers had all but abandoned hope of finding the girls alive.

My father nodded. "He killed them, all right. And that's not all he did to them."

Mrs. Winslow was quiet for a moment. Then she said: "Do you think he's insane? To kill his own children?"

"Crazy people don't try to hide their crimes," my father said. "He knows what he did was wrong, but he doesn't want to face the consequences. That's not insane. That's selfish."

Selfish: my father's worst epithet. Mrs. Winslow didn't ask the obvious next question, the one I always wondered about, which was Why? Even granting a total disregard for the welfare of others, what would make someone *want* to do to another human being what Mr. Lodge had done to his own daughters? Mrs. Winslow didn't ask that question, because she knew my father didn't have an answer, though he'd spent most of his life searching for one. She didn't ask any other questions, either, only sat there in angry silence as my father finished his coffee and the newscast turned to other matters. Soon it was time for us to leave for work; my father kissed Mrs. Winslow on the cheek and gave me back the body.

There was a family portrait that hung in the Victorian's entrance foyer: a younger, darker-haired Mrs. Winslow with her late husband

and her two sons, all of them standing on the front lawn of the Victorian back before it was renovated. I always slowed down a little going past that photo, ever since my father had told me the story of what happened; today I actually stopped, until Mrs. Winslow came up behind me and steered me forward out the front door.

Outside, the sky was unseasonably clear, the only visible clouds huddled in a group around Mount Winter to the east. Mrs. Winslow handed me a bag lunch (one complete meal; lunch isn't shared). She wished me a good day, then took a seat in the swing chair on the porch to wait for the morning mail. The postman wasn't due for another few hours yet, but she'd wait just the same, just as she always waited, bundling up in an old quilt if it got too cold.

"Will you be all right, Mrs. Winslow?" I asked before leaving. "Do you need anything?"

"I'll be fine, Andrew. Just come home safe, that's all I need."

"Don't worry," I told her. "If anyone tries anything, I'll have them outnumbered." This is an old multiple's joke, usually good for a polite smile at least, but today Mrs. Winslow only patted my arm and said: "Go on, then. Don't make yourselves late."

I started down the front walk. At the sidewalk I turned back to look; Mrs. Winslow had picked up a magazine and was reading, or pretending to read. She looked very small against the side of the Victorian, very small and very alone — *really* alone, in a way I could only imagine. I wondered what that must be like, and whether it was easier or harder than always having other souls for company.

"Don't worry about her," Adam said from the pulpit. "She'll be fine."

"I think the newscast really bothered her."

"It didn't *bother* her," Adam mocked me. "It pissed her off. And it should. You want to worry, worry about people who don't get mad, hearing about a thing like that."

I waved to Mrs. Winslow one last time and made myself start walking. When we were down the block and the Victorian was out of sight behind us, I said: "Do you think they'll catch him? Warren Lodge, I mean."

"I hope so," said Adam. "I hope he gets punished, whether they catch him or not."

"What do you mean?"

"It's just a thing that happens sometimes. Sometimes people think they've gotten away with something, think they've fooled everybody, only it turns out they haven't. They get punished after all."

"How?" I asked. "By who?"

But Adam didn't want to talk about it anymore. "We'll just hope a policeman gets him," he said. Then he went back in the house, and didn't come out again until we were almost at the Factory.

MOUSE:

Mouse is lying in a strange bed, in a strange house, with her hand pressed between the thighs of a man she has never seen before. She doesn't know what day it is, or what city; she has no idea how she got here.

A moment ago it was Sunday evening, April 20th, and she was sitting in the kitchen of her apartment, checking the movie listings in the *Seattle Times*. She was drinking a glass of red wine – never a good idea, but she had an overwhelming craving for it, and someone had left an open bottle in the cupboard above her sink. So she poured herself a glass, took a sip, and traced her finger down the column of showtimes, trying to decide between *The English Patient* and the new Jim Carrey movie.

– and now she is *not* there. There's no sense of having lost consciousness; all she did was blink, and suddenly everything is different. Where she was clothed and seated, she is now naked and lying on her side. The fresh taste of wine has become the stale aftertaste of vodka and cigarettes – she doesn't drink hard liquor or smoke, but she recognizes that aftertaste as if she does both, a lot. The cool roughness of the newsprint under her finger has become the warm clasp of flesh around her hand. And the face of a stranger has materialized, just inches from her own, snoring gin fumes.

She doesn't scream. She wants to, but a lifetime of losing time –

and covering up the fact — has left her skilled at controlling her reactions. She screams inside; outside she only squeaks, a short sharp note like a hiccup. Even this is muted, as her lips clamp together to bottle the sound before it can grow.

It's a bad one. Losing time is never good — it is a symptom of insanity, which in turn is evidence of what a worthless and terrible person she is — but there are degrees of badness, and finding herself in bed with a stranger ranks near the bottom of the scale. Not that this is as bad as it could be: this stranger is asleep, at least, and only her hand is touching him. Mouse has come back from missing time into tight embraces, into the middle of intimate conversations; once she found a man on top of her, pushing her legs apart, and that time she did scream out loud.

This isn't that bad, but it is bad enough. And yet even as she thinks that, thinks what a horrible insane person she must be to find herself in these situations, another part of her mind she thinks of as the Navigator detaches itself, rises above her fright and self-loathing and becomes coolly analytical, seeking to reorient her in place and time. It feels like morning; dim gray light seeps through the window of this tiny bedroom, suggesting dawn. Just which morning is harder to figure. Monday morning, she hopes; that would mean she's only lost a night. But subjectively, there's no difference between losing a single night and losing a whole week — and she has lost whole weeks before, even whole months. Once, when she was younger, she lost an entire year. No matter the duration, all missing time feels exactly the same: like no time at all.

There are ways to tell, though. With her free hand she touches her scalp to see if her hair has grown. Mouse likes to keep her hair short and as plain as possible, but during her blackout periods she forgets this; the sudden development of a hairstyle is often her first clue that she has lost significant time. This time her hair length doesn't seem to have changed — a good sign. Then she remembers that she bit the inside of her cheek during lunch on Sunday. Her tongue probes the spot and finds the wound still there, still fresh.

Monday morning, then. Most likely. And if it has only been one night, and if she spent most of that night...*being with*...the stranger beside her, she can't have traveled far. She must still be in the Seattle area, close to home. That's both good and bad: good, because finding her way back shouldn't be too difficult; bad, because she might have told him where she lives.

She tugs at her captive hand. It pulls loose easily, but as she withdraws it her forearm brushes the cold rubbery lump of a used condom lying on the bed sheet. A cry of disgust passes her lips before she can stop it.

The stranger's eyes move beneath still-closed lids; his own hand comes up, pawing at his mouth and nose. He snorts. And then, as Mouse holds her breath, he rolls over, turns his back to her. He settles again into sleep; but the sound of his snoring has changed now, becoming shallower, closer to true waking.

The Navigator gets her moving before fear can paralyze her. She's light; the bedsprings hardly notice as she slips off the edge of the mattress. She ends up in a crouch on the floor beside the bed and freezes there, listening, but this time the stranger doesn't react.

Her clothes are over by the bedroom door. Her shoes and jeans are, anyway; she doesn't actually recognize the black lace panties or the pink tank top, but as they are part of the same pile it seems reasonable to assume they belong to her too. She notes with passing annoyance that there's no bra. Though she's small enough that she doesn't actually need to wear one, she thinks it looks slutty not to. Not that she's in a position to complain about looking slutty.

She dresses as quickly and quietly as possible. As she does so, she scans the room for other possessions. When you don't know what you brought with you, you can't be sure you aren't forgetting something, but she finally concludes that there is nothing else – and if there is, she can only hope that it's not irreplaceable.

Dressed and ready to leave, she checks herself in the mirror that hangs on the back of the bedroom door, and notices for the first time the obscene phrase printed across the front of the tank top. At first she thinks it's a trick – the words must be written on the mirror somehow, as a curse or an admonition to the kind of woman who would find herself sneaking out of this room at dawn. But no – she looks down – the words are on her clothing, on *her*.

She cannot go outside like this. Her anxiety rising in a tight spiral, she turns and scans the room again. A carelessly discarded sweater lies draped over the top of a dresser beside the bed. It's not her sweater – it's too big – but it will serve to cover her until she gets home. She snatches it up, dislodging several small articles from the dresser top; they clatter noisily to the floor. The stranger stirs, and Mouse, clutching the sweater, bolts from the room.

The cramped passageway outside the bedroom reminds her of the side-corridor of a train sleeper car, with windows along one wall and doors along the other. This triggers a fresh wave of alarm as she wonders if she might really be on a train. But no, the Navigator points out, real train corridors aren't this messy; passengers aren't allowed to store their personal effects in the halls. And besides, it's not moving.

What kind of house looks like a train car, but isn't one? A trailer-house, she realizes. She's in a trailer. This simplifies finding a way out: if the bedroom is at one end of the trailer, the exit must be somewhere towards the other end.

She follows the corridor. Halfway down the trailer's length, it opens out into a living-room/dining-area furnished in classic trailer-trash style: there is a sagging couch, a battered TV set, a fake plug-in fireplace, a splintery dining table piled high with beer cans and dirty plates. A counter with a peeling linoleum top separates the living room from a tiny kitchenette, where more beer cans are stored.

Trailer trash. It is ridiculous, but Mouse is shamed by the tawdriness of the place, shamed far more deeply by that than by the simple fact of being here at all. For all the times this sort of thing has happened to her, she has never once woken up in a nice house. It is as if the mad spirit that constantly disrupts her life meant to impress upon her that this is what she deserves, that gutter is the best she can aspire to. Never mind that she strives to keep her own home tasteful, orderly, and neat – she will always come back to this.

She has to get out of here. The trailer's outside door is in the far corner of the living room, by the entrance to the kitchenette; Mouse hurries to it. She puts on the sweater – it fits her more like a poncho, and reeks of beer and cigarettes – and opens the door. A chilly dawn wind blows in past her, rattling the beer cans on the table.

And Mouse thinks: *What about a coat?*

It was cold last night; wouldn't she have worn a coat? On the verge of escaping, she turns back again, and spies two coats on the floor in front of the phony fireplace. One of them, a scuffed leather jacket, looks like it might fit her, although, like the panties and the tank top, she doesn't actually recognize it.

She hesitates. If it is her jacket, she should take it; she wants to leave nothing of hers behind, nothing that might allow *him* to trace her. On the other hand, she is already stealing the sweater; if the jacket is not hers either, and she steals it too, *he* might call the police. What to do?

The sound of movement from the direction of the bedroom ends her indecision. She leaves the leather jacket behind and scoots out the door, even as a man's voice calls sleepily: "Hello?"

Outside, on the trailer's wooden stoop, Mouse finds a copy of the *Seattle Post-Intelligencer*, still wrapped in its plastic delivery bag. She checks the date, and learns that she was right: today is Monday, April 21st, 1997. She has only lost a night. It would be difficult to overstate her relief at this confirmation.

Mouse's car is parked in the street right in front of the trailer. No question that it's hers; it is a Buick Centurion, an unmistakable big black hulk of an automobile. She bought it used for $1,000 down and forty-eight additional monthly payments of $150, which she is still making. It is not the car she wanted. The car she *thought* she was buying was a Honda Civic, much smaller and much more economical, but somehow she ended up signing a sales contract for the Buick instead.

Whoever was driving the car last night has a thing or two to learn about parallel parking. Not only does it have one wheel up on the curb, it is facing the wrong way. But the driver was not totally careless: the Centurion's doors are all locked, and Mouse can see looking through the window that the keys are not in the ignition. She checks the pockets of her jeans and discovers that the keys are not there, either.

"No," Mouse whispers. "No, no, *no* — " She was so close to getting away! She begins to go through her pockets a second time, turning them inside out.

"Hey," a voice calls to her.

Mouse squeaks. A handful of pocket change goes flying; nickels and pennies patter across the roof of the Centurion like flat hailstones.

The stranger is standing at the top of the stoop. Ignoring the chill, he has come outside wearing only a T-shirt and a dingy pair of boxer shorts. The leather jacket is slung over his arm, and with his left hand he is jangling a set of keys. "You won't get far without these," he tells her.

Mouse swallows hard. Is he taunting her? The Navigator doesn't think so; his tone is not malicious, and he seems preoccupied with blinking the sleep out of his eyes. But he does not come down off the stoop or make any move to offer her the keys.

"Listen," the stranger continues, stifling a yawn. He gestures lazily at the trailer behind him. "You want to come back in for some breakfast? Or if you wait a few minutes, we can go out somewhere ..."

Mouse shakes her head, trying not to look scared. But the stranger sees something in her expression; his own expression sharpens with concern.

"Hey," he says. "You're not bugging out on me about last night, are you? I mean, I know we were both pretty fucked up, but...you do remember, right? I asked you, I asked you *twice*, if you were sure you wanted to come back here with me. And you said you did. You said sure."

Yes, his expression is full of concern. But it is not concern *for* her, she realizes; it is concern *about* her. "You remember that, right?"

"I have to go," Mouse tells him.

"You said *sure*," the stranger insists. "I mean, you want to regret it now, light of day and all, that's your fucking prerogative, but what you said last night..."

"I have to go," Mouse repeats, louder this time.

"Sure, in a minute. I just want to be clear we both understand what happened. I want to be clear — "

Maledicta the Foul-Speaker, tiring of this bullshit, shoves Mouse aside and stalks forward, screaming: "Shut up and give her the fucking keys, cocksucker!"

Mouse blinks. She has teleported from the curb to the bottom of the stoop. Her hands are balled into fists, and her throat is tight, as if she'd just been shouting. The stranger is staring at her.

"All right," he tells her, his voice placating. "All right, Jesus, calm down! I'm not trying to keep you here, I just — "

" — fucking bitch!" Mouse is back at the curb, holding the leather jacket and turning a key in the Centurion's driver's door. Over her shoulder she sees the stranger, now at the foot of the stoop, staggering in a circle with one hand cupping his groin and the other pressed to the side of his face, which appears to be bleeding. "You fucking *bitch*, what did you — "

Silence. Mouse is sitting in her car in the parking lot of a bank. The car's engine is off but the keys are in the ignition; the leather jacket lies on the passenger seat beside her. Outside, the sky is brighter than it was.

Mouse just sits with her hands gripping the steering wheel, waiting to see if the scene will shift again. She watches a digital clock-thermometer on the side of the bank-building cycle from time to date to temperature; the time slowly increments, and the temperature rises by a degree, but there are no sudden jumps and the date remains constant.

Mouse begins to relax, and as she does, it occurs to her that she knows where she is now. The bank building is new, but across the street from it are a number of older storefronts that she recognizes.

She is in Seattle's University District, not five blocks from the basement flat where she lived when she was a student at the U. of Washington.

She can get home from here. She is eager to do so, to change out of the obscene tank top and get rid of it, along with the foul-smelling sweater. But first, at the Navigator's insistence, Mouse checks around the inside of the car for a list.

Today's list is stuffed in the Centurion's glove compartment, along with a half-empty pack of Winston cigarettes and a vodka flask that Mouse pretends not to see. Hastily jotted on a crumpled bar napkin, the list enumerates half a dozen chores and appointments, with space to check off each one after it is completed. Item number one, in letters twice as high as the rest, reads: REALITY FACTORY — 8:30 A.M. DRESS NICE! BE ON TIME!!!

In one sense, Mouse does not need to be reminded about her new job. She has thought of little else since Friday evening, when she first found out about it. In fact it was mainly to stop herself worrying — to get it out of her mind for a few hours — that she hit on the idea of going to see a movie last night, and took down the bottle of wine from her cupboard.

But last night feels like it was less than an hour ago, and Mouse still has it in her head to think that her new job starts tomorrow. The list drives home the fact that tomorrow has become today. Mouse looks at the bank clock again and realizes with dismay that she does not have time to go home. If she still lived in her old U. District flat she might make it, she might even manage a quick shower, but her current apartment on Queen Anne Hill is a fifteen-minute drive in the wrong direction. If she wants to get to Autumn Creek by 8:30, she needs to get on the freeway in the next ten minutes.

"Oh God..." Mouse tugs at the hem of the sweater she is wearing, feels how filthy it is. She looks at the bank clock. "Oh God." DRESS NICE, says the list, BE ON TIME, but there is no way now that she can do both. She hasn't even started her new job yet and already she has screwed up.

"You worthless piece of shit," Mouse says, catching sight of herself in the Centurion's rearview mirror. She slams her fist down into her thigh, pounding rhythmically, hard enough to bruise: "Worthless piece of *shit*, worthless piece of *shit*, worthless piece of *shit* —"

The bank clock marks another minute gone by. Mouse stops hitting herself; she switches on the Centurion's engine and guns it, drives screeching out of the lot. Two blocks down, stopped at a traffic light, she feels indecision tearing at her again. Which is worse: to come to work late but well-groomed, or to come to work on time but looking like trash?

A loud bang interrupts her reverie. A big man in a U.W. Huskies sweatshirt, crossing the street in front of her, has just bounced a basketball off the Centurion's hood. It wasn't an accident; the man noticed that Mouse was talking to herself and decided to scare her. Catching the ball on the rebound, he laughs, happy to have made her jump.

It is too much. Mouse disappears. Malefica comes, Malefica the Evil-Doer, who is Maledicta's twin sister. She taps the accelerator pedal; the Centurion lurches forward into the crosswalk, catching the Huskies fan in the shins. It's just a nudge, just enough to make him drop the ball and fall face forward onto the hood. Just enough to scare him.

It *does* scare him, for a moment. Malefica sees the fear in his eyes. But then he makes a bad mistake: he thinks to himself that Malefica is just a little girl, that she does not really know what she is doing here, who she is messing with. His fear turns to anger; he starts pushing himself up off the hood, meaning to come around and rip open the driver's door.

Malefica depresses the accelerator pedal again, holding it down. The Centurion rolls forward at five, then ten miles per hour, pushing the Huskies fan backwards. Fear recaptures him. "Hey!" he shouts, the soles of his shoes skidding over the pavement, his palms slapping at the car's hood. "Hey! Hey! HEY!" Fear becomes terror as he locks gazes with Malefica through the windshield and reads her intention; he throws himself to the side even as she floors the accelerator.

Still gathering speed out the far side of the intersection, Malefica checks the rear view: back at the crosswalk, the Huskies fan is picking himself up off the ground. He is shouting something after her, waving his fist, but it's hard to look threatening when you've just pissed yourself.

Malefica laughs. She is a little girl, yes, but a little girl with a *big fucking car*, and no one had better try to fuck with her. At the next corner she rolls right past a stop sign, scattering another three pedestrians with a blast of the Centurion's horn.

— and Mouse is driving east on Interstate 90 towards Autumn Creek, her decision made, though she does not recall making it. The air in the Buick is dense with cigarette smoke; Mouse takes a hand off the wheel to slap at a dribbling of ash on the front of the stolen sweater and nearly loses control of the car.

"Oh God..." Mouse steadies the Centurion and pulls it over into the slow lane. She rolls her window down; the smoke clears, but the rush of cold air does nothing for the sweater, which still reeks. *She* still reeks.

Maybe she can say she was sick last night. Sick to her stomach: she ate something bad for dinner, and was up half the night with cramps... and too late, she realized that she'd forgotten to do her laundry ...

Yes, Mouse thinks, with a thrill of elation. It is short-lived. Yes, they might believe that — they might even be proud of her, coming in on time for her first day, despite having been sick. But Mouse knows full well that there will be other mistakes, other screw-ups requiring excuses, and there are only so many lies she can hope to get away with. Eventually, they will see through her. Eventually, inevitably, they will know her for what she truly is.

Worthless piece of shit...

Judging the Tiptree

Suzy McKee Charnas

Social boundaries are not fixed — they shift and change as society evolves. So too, the Tiptree Award changes as gender exploration that was once revolutionary becomes accepted. Each year, the judges who choose the winner of the Tiptree Award discuss and, to some extent, reinvent the award. Here is one judge's description of that process.

In March of 1991 Karen Fowler contacted me about the brand-new Tiptree Award and asked me to be one of several judges for its debut year. As one of the old (or at least older) guard, I'd been on a number of panels of judges in science fiction and fantasy by then. I'd always accepted such invitations because the reading forced me to become current with what was going on and who was kicking up interesting dust.

Judging for an award is exhilarating. Judging panels tend to be filled with colleagues who are enthusiastic and dedicated, thoughtful, eager to share observations about the current state of the field, and entertainingly hot in debating for and against various entries and in assessing their strengths and weaknesses.

On the other hand, awards can be divisive, disappointing; and too conservative — or too ahead of the curve — to do the up-and-comers any good. Over the years I'd seen how awards themselves, and all the panoply of procedure and internal politics they tend to involve, can become institutionalized dinosaurs busily chewing up time, energy, and friendships in the genres they were meant to honor and celebrate.

And yet the damned things do proliferate like rabbits. A webpage on the science fiction magazine *Locus* site breaks them down by category (www.locusmag.com/sfawards/), including a list of ten awards that have gone "defunct"; awards appear to have become a big enough genus to have species die-off and yet persist.

Did we really need *another* award?

Well, for me this was only a token challenge, really. I like the beginnings of new things for their free-form energy. In this case, the purpose and the proposed company looked unusually alluring. The clincher was the idea that some really first-rate chocolate would be part of the prize awarded. I could see that this was definitely a project by, for, and about my kind of crowd.

So after about two seconds of deliberation, I said, "Yes! Sure! I'd love to!" Looking back over my file of correspondence for that year, I am gratified to see that I can personally take credit for the "explores and expands gender roles" language that is now used to describe the type of science fiction and fantasy we are looking for. (That gives me a nice, warm, *chocolatey* feeling).

Early in July, my fellow judge Vonda McIntyre got things moving by sending around to the rest of us a letter describing what she'd been reading so far and which titles she recommended to the rest of us. Debbie Notkin, also a judge and our panel's invaluable coordinator, suggested sending letters like this around periodically among ourselves as the main process of our judgeship, with maybe a conference call at the end for final deliberations.

A little bit later, judge Bruce McAllister (yes, from the start we wanted men on the panel, to signal that the award was not just for women authors and readers) wrote asking us all to think about defining just what qualities we were looking for, and to supply titles from the past exemplifying our ideas of what a Tiptree Award winner might look like and why.

We were off. That means — we started asking questions. Some of these questions were the same ones I'd encountered on other judging panels; but the most interesting ones were raised by the particular nature of this award, and its location right in the intersection of speculative fiction and a spectrum of gender politics in wild-eyed flux.

These are the kinds of questions we raised with each other over the following eight or nine months:

What *did* James Tiptree, Jr. stand for, literarily speaking? And, assuming we could figure that out, was that how we want to define the standards of this award, years after her death? Would she approve? Was Tiptree a feminist herself, and if so by whose definition? Did it matter? What do *we* want this award to *do?*

Are we going to call it a "feminist award" outright?

If we don't call it a "feminist award", is that just ducking the question (because, well, it *is*, isn't it?), and won't people rightly find this stance evasive at best? Yet if we do call it a feminist award, might that lead people to conclude (as many did anyway) that a male author can't win it even if his work qualifies and outshines the competition? Wouldn't many readers and writers and critics, both within our ghetto and outside it, dismiss an explicitly feminist award as a prize for Leftist propaganda? (The anti-feminist backlash was in full cry by this time.) We do want to be taken seriously, but how much do we care what critics and carpers think, given that no matter what we do we can't control how others perceive what we're doing anyway?

Does the winning story have to say something new about gender, or can it say something old in a new way, or just really, really brilliantly?

How much science fiction or fantasy does a book have to have in it to be considered for the Tiptree? What if it has only some vivid dream sequences but it's a good book and it has important feminist themes? What if it's really horror, or almost? Wouldn't that make our choice redundant,or at any rate overlap the territory of several other genre-specific awards? Would that matter?

Can we talk without rancor about a book that some judges hate? This raises serious, germane questions in an in-your-face manner that some will find deeply offensive but that makes ideas keep kicking around in your head long after you've finished reading. Does the first Tiptree winner have to be "nice," only offending people we are quite content to see offended? What kind of message will our first choice send, and how important is that? (Keep in mind: we still didn't know for certain that this was going to be something more than a one-shot event.)

Do we include fiction from all over, not just the U.S.; and if we do, how do we keep watch for foreign work so we don't miss great work from England or New Zealand or India?

Do we want to give the first Tiptree to a well-established science fiction author, which might be perceived as the old girls rewarding one of their own for hanging in there (for the most part there's been precious little other official encouragement, god knows, and we do want to encourage veterans not to quit in despair)? Or do we want it to go to someone up-and-coming, to reward an unusually fine fledgling effort in a cooling cultural climate?

Isn't it just supposed to be about The Best Book/Story, *regardless* of individual careers and circumstances? Only realistically speaking, every award also has all kinds of political meaning, so shouldn't we consider that up front? But given that those impacts are pretty vague and speculative at best, how much should such factors weigh in the balance against the sheer writerly quality of the works considered?

Should we choose a good entry from a well-known and well-rewarded mainstream author who already has a strong feminist reputation to remind the literary world that serious science fiction and fantasy writers measure themselves against the best from the mainstream literary world and wish their work to be respected by that world in turn? Should we penalize good work *because* it's from recognized feminist authors in the mainstream (after all, they don't need the supposed spotlight of an award as much as doubly-ghettoized feminist science fiction and fantasy authors do)?

Does literary fiction's devotion to the virtue of realistic detail enhance and ground the speculative elements in mainstream author X's book, or quench them in banality? What the blazes do we do with "magic realism," which is (or is not) just fantasy in fancy dress?

What if we *can't* agree? Would starting out our award with a tie be seen as wishy-washy? What if some of us disagree with a choice so strongly that we wish to issue a minority opinion? Would that weaken the award, or strengthen it?

Is the male sense of alienation (predominant in science fiction of the time, in cyberpunk specifically) different from the female sense of alienation? Has this author caught the differences and similarities in a striking way? Do we care about alienation per se, a staple of all kinds of modern fiction?

What if the ideas are wonderful but the characters are pure pinewood? What if the characters are riveting, but no advance of any discernable kind is made in ideas – although the ideas expressed are solid ones that can, unfortunately, still bear repeating and repeating and repeating, because for most of the culture basic assumptions about gender have not progressed very far? Where *is* the cutting edge, and how do we know?

How do we explain that once upon a time having a story with one major female character, say a space pilot, was groundbreaking, but that's no longer cutting edge nor even particularly feminist? How do we avoid discouraging writers, particularly but not exclusively male writers of some experience who start from so far back that their best efforts seem antiquated? We don't want to squelch the efforts of those who have just caught on and who are truly trying to catch up, or appear to be disrespectful of the writers of both sexes who have brought us, by now outdated stages, to the point at which having a female space pilot is an ordinary element of any science fiction story.

How do we make sure that people find out about not just our winner(s) but about all the other good, interesting, provocative work that we've considered? We want everyone who's pushing ahead with issues that interest us to be rewarded for it, at least by some interest and attention being drawn to their work if not by an actual prize. (The solution here was the annotated list of considered works, a list published that first year on paper and distributed at WisCon and bake sales everywhere; lists are now available at the Tiptree website).

When you say "lightweight," do you really mean "easy to read"? And is that a good reason to handicap a book? What if there seem to be some wonderful gender ideas somewhere at the heart of a story, but the writing is poetically obscure? Do we want to give the award to a really dense, challenging read, knowing most readers, science fiction or otherwise, won't take it on? But shouldn't readers be nudged into attempting work that's more difficult than what they normally pick up, because of the rewards to be gained and the broadened reading tastes that might result?

What do we do about a book in a series, when we love the whole series for its interesting play with gender concepts but — this isn't the best book of the series so far? Don't we want to reward and recognize the author for the series as a whole? But is this the right way and the right time to do it?

There was no one to answer all these questions but us. How happily we wrangled and rumbled and mumbled all this over, energized by the excitement of discovery, of free discussion, and having lots of time to do it in because there weren't all that many submissions to consider. Publishers (and authors) either hadn't heard of us or didn't know what kind of book or story we were looking for (for which they could hardly be blamed, since we were hammering that out ourselves as we went along). We asked for recommendations from the people who came to the bake sales at conventions, and from editors and critics.

But a lot of what we read we had to go out and find for ourselves. That we did not find an overwhelming amount of material to consider is reflected in the fact that our annotated short list ran to only five entries; there was no long list that first year. When we began, we thought of the award as primarily for short fiction, although we all agreed that a terrific novel would do, too. My judges' panel turned up very little short fiction that seemed eligible but a number of novels.

In the end, our winners were Eleanor Arnason's *A Woman of the Iron People* and Gwyneth Jones' *White Queen*, strikingly different works representing disparate science fiction virtues and concerns and widely varied approaches to gender exploration. The decision to share the award this way not only solved the conflict between supporters of two excellent books but also stamped the award itself with the flexibility and inclusiveness that we felt was a crucial element of the Tiptree concept.

We were tired, happy, pleased to be done, and excited about actually presenting the fruit of our labors to both worthy recipients. Part of the fun for us was this demonstration that Pat Murphy's inspired idea, a casual suggestion made at least partly in jest, had become a reality. The Tiptree Award idea had been carried by a broad-based tide of enthusiasm and goodwill to a resounding affirmation that feminism in science fiction and fantasy was not dead or even sleeping, but alive, ALIVE!!

It was a triumph, for everyone, with the promise of more to come. As originally envisioned, the Tiptree Award could have been just a one-off, a commando strike that would not be repeated until a particularly rich year demanded another mission. But soon it became apparent that anyone who tried to halt the Tiptree Award Juggernaut after 1991 would be pelted off the stage with stale truffles. Bake sales were booming, there were plans afoot for a Tiptree cookbook, and a way had clearly been prepared to channel all this bubbling energy – the energy of women and men who had been feeling choked by the misogynist backlash both within and without the science fiction and fantasy field – into (where else?) the future.

That was back in 1992. Flash-forward: my novel *The Conqueror's Child* won the 1999 Tiptree. As had become customary over the intervening period, I was invited to be a Tiptree Award judge. Since I had already served Karen Fowler said I could not be faulted for declining. Declining! Not a chance.

Things, of course, were different. Part of the interest for me was to see just how different. For starters, we had e-mail for our deliberations – almost instant conversation. The acquisition and distribution of nominated material was much more organized. Finding short fiction and foreign fiction had become the job of specific judges on the panel, broadening the field of consideration well beyond novels published in the US. In fact the overall volume of reading was much increased (this probably made us all a bit more ruthless with each entry). The award was better known , as was the salient fact that the winner received a check, as well as a fine piece of art and some chocolate. So we had lots of material to consider (including a great deal of fiction that fell nowhere within our purview — but hey, these wildly inappropriate but optimistic submissions meant that publishers were eager to get our attention for their authors, which was a welcome development).

We judges were asked to introduce ourselves to each other, a step that had been necessary for only one or two people on the first jury. Science fiction as a world of colleagues was larger now — all the judges didn't already know each other.

Over the years since the first time I had judged, some ground rules had evolved, so we didn't need to hash out as many general issues. Everyone knew now that this was an award for interesting and exciting fantasy and science fiction informed by a feminist awareness. We no longer concerned ourselves with what James Tiptree/Alice Sheldon would have thought, considering it sufficient for our purposes that in her working life she had personally blurred the line between male and female writers in her own authorial identity, to great and lasting effect.

Many either/or questions had been firmly settled. In the intervening years, awards had gone to male authors as well as female, to old as well as young, to new as well as established, to mainstream or academic authors venturing successfully onto our turf, to short work and long work, to difficult writing and to writing of limpid clarity. We were more confident, more established, more clear about our mission; we worried less about appearances and impact. The whole award process had, not surprisingly, matured.

Then the questions began to fly:

What, in each of our minds, would make a good contender now? What are we looking for now — and how is it different from what we might have looked for in past years? Literature, with some aspect of gender as a central issue, obviously; but with feminism under increasingly heavy fire from the Reactionary Right maybe our winner *ought* to have some very clear political intent? But we don't want to work from a defensive position, a position of perceived weakness, do we? And we certainly don't want to reward outright propaganda (no matter how much we agreed with it), right?

Was there still, ten years on, a need, a place, for the Tiptree at all?

What if the book is fascinating and thoughtful almost all the way through, but the ending is a letdown? Can the book be a failure, but the gender-bending elements enough of a success to merit the award?

Do warmth, delicacy, and charm trump brilliant writing and invigorating intellectual rigor?

Does it have to be grim and pessimistic to be a winner?

Why are so many novels series-books, and should that make a difference?

What do we do about a book in which the science fiction is a rather undercooked maguffin and the real emphasis is on character and a recognizably modern setting, but the exploration of motherhood is complex, unusual, and bold?

What do we do if there are lovely gender challenges just dropped into a book that's one volume of a huge-scale space opera, with hardly any attention paid beyond that? Isn't it deeply feminist to assume (and depict) a crucial change in gender matters *without* bothering to examine it deeply, as if it were just accepted as a normal part of things? But if the author's central interests clearly lie elsewhere in a given work, should that startling but rather casual gender treatment enable this book to beat out a less accomplished book in which gender-bending is powerfully foregrounded?

Does established science fiction author X's new book have to be not only better than anything else on our list of contenders but at least as good as the best of X's own previous work to take the prize?

Some of the questions that came up will always come up. Matters of the ideal balance between science fiction and fantasy idea-content and character development, say, can only be settled with regard to specific works (if then), not as some sort of general rule. On every panel of judges, there will be a book-of-substance that finds an enthusiastic champion in one judge, a bored or actively offended critic in another. Questions about the interplay between storytelling and politics will always be thrown off by the friction between books and current reality, and the answers must be specific to the time.

In 1999, we settled on Hiromi Goto's *The Kappa Child*, an entry from a Canadian small press. This novel swept the field with its irresistible charm, originality, and beauty. To our delight, Hiromi Goto not only came in person to WisCon to accept her award but brought her mom with her. Validation doesn't get much better than that.

How will the Tiptree Award process look to its panel of judges five years from now, assuming—and I do assume—that there will be such a panel? The same, and different, and in some respects (I hope) still inchoate — if there is a panel, and a Tiptree Award. Conditions in a living field of artistic endeavor never stop changing, and an award will of necessity change too or else wither into deserved obscurity. This is even truer of an award designed to meet a specific need than of a prize that looks only for authorial achievement without any further qualification (although of course there are *always* qualifications, however unstated and unrecognized they may be).

It may be that the Tiptree Award will fold its tent once and for all —not after its first year but after its thirteenth, or its eighteenth, or its twenty-fifth. I think that the question of whether the award should continue must return with each year, given that this award is so vitally connected to an essential and constantly changing complex of ideas, values, and practices: the gender divide in humankind.

From what I can see, the gender gap has narrowed in some places, but is as wide as ever in others. As scientific advances expand our control over all aspects of sex and reproduction and as politics reacts to the scientific advances, gender issues grow ever more complex. Consequently the conversation, the discussion, the wrangle, the screaming battle over what gender is and what it means and what it should or should not mean continues, hot and hotter. I hope that one of the major venues of that conversation (in Western cultures at least, and increasingly in other cultures with a taste for open-ended inquiry) will continue to be science fiction and fantasy. To my mind and in my experience, that's where the most free and imaginative and outrageously inventive discussion of any important issue finds a natural home.

If there is no Tiptree Award in 2021, I wouldn't be all that surprised. But if there is, and if I were to be asked to be a judge again, I'd jump at the chance — assuming I still had any jump left in me.

The first question raised among the judges would be familiar, and rightly so: "What are we looking for, exactly, in our winner? What do we think this award should be doing now?"

Meanwhile, please pass the chocolate.

The Catgirl Manifesto: An Introduction

by Christina X

FOR RICHARD CALDER

With all the writing and reading about gender that's been done in the last thirty years, some aspects of the topic are still close to taboo. In "The Catgirl Manifesto: An Introduction," Richard Calder gets up close and personal with one of those topics: the way certain female attributes seem to render a large number of men incapable of rational reaction. Calder, "writing as Christina X," has disguised his tale as an academic essay, so this "story" has no characters and no plot. Nonetheless, the jury (and your editors) found it quite gripping. The tone, the style, and the London setting all seemed to call for keeping the British spellings on this one piece.

The most important elements of an erotic art linked to our knowledge about sexuality are not to be sought in the ideal, promised to us by medicine, of a healthy sexuality, nor in the humanist dream of a complete and flourishing sexuality, and certainly not in the lyricism of orgasm and the good feelings of bio-energy (these are but aspects of its normalizing utilization), but in this multiplication and intensification of pleasures connected to the production of the truth about sex. The learned volumes, written and read; the consultations and examinations; the anguish of answering questions and the delights of having one's words interpreted; all the stories told oneself and to others, so much curiosity, so many confidences offered in the face of scandal, sustained — but not without trembling a little — by the obligation of truth; the profusion of secret fantasies and the dearly paid right to whisper them to whoever is able to hear them; in short, the formidable "pleasure of analysis" (in the widest sense of the latter term) which the West has been cleverly fostering for several centuries: all this constitutes something

> like the errant fragments of an erotic art that is secretly transmitted by confession and the science of sex. Must we conclude that our *scientia sexualis* is but an extraordinarily subtle form of *ars erotica*, and that it is the Western, sublimated version of that seemingly lost tradition?
>
> — Michel Foucault, *The History of Sexuality, Volume 1, An Introduction*

The following manifesto (indeed, *the* manifesto, as it has come to be known) was initially deconstructed in terms of its most obvious antecedents: the calls-to-arms of the Futurists, Dadaists, and Surrealists, and (in light of the fact that it is signed by a woman and has such a transgressive agenda) other so-called, if less celebrated, manifestos, such as Valerie Solanas's SCUM manifesto and the CLIT statements — texts, that is, that constitute acts of *poetic terrorism*.

The manifesto first came to public attention in June 1997 after an op-ed article appeared in the London *Independent*. With a dismissive humour typical of early reports, parliamentary correspondent Ian Rathschilde wrote: "MPS' offices have been overwhelmed by mass mailings of a quasi-pornographic piece of agitprop. This so-called 'manifesto' has elicited more than snorts of disgust. Indeed, a certain cabal of Tories — perhaps recalling how well their 'Back to Basics' campaign fared — are by all accounts planning to raise the matter during Prime Minister's question time. Not merely to once again remind the public of the size of the average parliamentarian's mailbag, it seems, but to appropriate that high ground only recently relinquished to the heirs of sixties permissiveness. The offending manifesto, it is argued, is the work of a maenad-like contingent of 'Blair's Babes.' Its sole objective? To bury conservatism as thoroughly as many in the party once thought it possible to bury socialism in the days when they could not count on New Labour to do the job…"

A spate of articles in the national dailies followed. And soon afterwards, the manifesto — sealed in plain manila envelopes affixed with occult symbols associated with the rites of Enochian sex-magick — began to show up in public places (places corresponding, roughly, to the psychogeographical "hotspots" listed in section two of the manifesto itself): "...the towpaths of canals, deserted night-time wharves, abandoned warehouses, factories, shopping malls, the moonlit arches of monstrous bridges, the platforms and tunnels of metropolitan railway stations, the fire-escapes of tenement blocks, the shadow-haunted depths of condom-littered alleyways..."

The impact on British youth culture was profound. The summer of 1997 was, in some respects, similar to that of 1977, when punk found a short-lived apotheosis in the conjunction of the Sex Pistols and the Queen's Silver Jubilee. As with punk, the new, wholly radical slew of music and street fashion inspired by the manifesto's lurid aesthetic (an aesthetic which, in turn, was surely adumbrated by the dark excesses of twentieth-century nihilism) was first championed by art-school students. St Martin's in London's Charing Cross Road represented the vanguard. There, rants, fads, and crazes were quickly coalescing into a cult. Indeed, a vox pop carried out in St Martin's lobby and published in *Dazed and Confused* revealed that more than one student considered the manifesto's catalogue of conspiracy to be not only intoxicating, but also true.

Commentators have often wondered at the gullibility of these young men and women. How, they wonder, could students (most of whom might be expected to possess a more-than-average degree of analytical intelligence) take on board the grotesque suspensions of disbelief necessary for accepting the manifesto's cod-scientific premise? The manifesto is, after all, fantastical in the extreme, and resembles nothing so much as pulp science fiction. The following passage, for example (from the "Phylogenesis" section) details the mutagenic effects of a 1972 supernova flare-up in Leo Minor:

> The physical traits, in themselves, were stark. In a survey of five-hundred Reinhardt and non-Reinhardt females (which tabulated sexual attractiveness according to an ascending scale of universal indices such as classic 0.7 hip-to-waist ratio and regularity of feature), those 5% who had mutant DNA not only topped every category, but did so by substantial margins. Yet

this attractiveness was not, strictly speaking, beauty. Beauty is human. Instead, Reinhardt females were said to possess an exceptional, unwholesomely sweet, prettiness. A prettiness informed by a feverish, hysterical, ever-present passion, which gave them the appearance of being forever sickening for forbidden fruit. Their physiognomy was classified as "neotenic" — a biological term that refers to the retention of larval, immature, or juvenile characteristics in the adult of the species. Renoir had celebrated the glamour of the neotenic. (Albert Aurier, the critic and Symbolist poet, had described Renoir's female subjects as possessing the "beautiful, deep, azure, enameled eyes of dolls, of adorable dolls, with flesh molded of roseate porcelain." Why, asked Aurier, should Renoir depict woman as beautiful "since it suffices to show that she is pretty. Why show her as intelligent, or even as stupid, why as false, as disagreeable? She is pretty! Why should she have a heart, a brain, a soul? She is pretty! Be reasonable, like me, and don't make such a fuss over the pseudovitality of that marvellous and oh so adorably pretty little automaton…") Reinhardt females were certainly Renoiresque, but theirs was a corrupted innocence — the look of an *ingénue* permanently in heat, as if Renoir had collaborated with Delacroix, Rops, and Moreau. It lent them that aspect of *morbidity* that was later to have such devastating consequences.

The behavioural traits, however, were even starker. These included extreme degrees of exhibitionism; an overriding need to be admired and pampered; infantilism; hyperaesthesia; a hatred of maternity and childbirth; and a tendency to spite, deceit and treacherousness in direct proportion to deferred gratification. In test after test, the Reinhardt psyche was revealed to be a seething miasma of sexual obsession. But surely the most bizarre, and disturbing, trait was one that would surely have been classified as a communicable disease, if its effects on others had not been so obviously psychosomatic: a desire — as instinctive as the silky murderousness of a cat's — to drive human males insane with lust. Not figuratively, but literally. In this, Reinhardt

> females proved themselves all too successful. (The sexual aura of the Reinhardt's subject was, it seemed, as real as a "normal" human being's electrical field, if incomparably more powerful.) Men who came into contact with them, or who were seduced, and even men who did as little as fantasize about them, sometimes fell victim to a form of voyeuristic catatonia or "nympholepsy." Characteristically, a nympholept would lose all interest in life and spend his days in bed, or staring mutely out of a window, self-hypnotized by images of the *filles fatales* that infested his overheated imagination. Some such invalids were even prone to seizures. The medical establishment spoke of nympholepsy in terms of "nymphic autism",[1] pointing out that there are accounts in medical literature of people who are not autistic in the sense of suffering from a developmental disorder but are described as "autistic" in reference to the more general, dictionary-definition of autism meaning "absorption in fantasy."

An *absorption in fantasy* – the manifesto almost seems to be describing its readers, or at least those who were to become its acolytes. But why *this* fantasy? Those fleeing "the real" might have chosen something more sophisticated; that they didn't points to some dark, hermetic power lurking at the manifesto's heart, obscured by the clichés and self-repetitive tropes of sado-masochistic erotica. According to Susan Sontag (in her essay *The Pornographic Imagination*): "...'the obscene' is a primal notion of human consciousness, something much more profound than the backwash of a sick society's aversion to the body. Human sexuality is, quite apart from Christian repressions, a highly questionable phenomenon, and belongs, at least potentially, among the extreme rather than the ordinary experiences of humanity. Tamed as it may be, sexuality remains one of the demonic forces in human consciousness – pushing us at intervals close to taboo and dangerous desires, which range from the impulse to commit sudden arbitrary violence upon another person to the voluptuous yearning for the extinction of one's consciousness, for death itself." We must look, then, beyond the manifesto's stage props, its theatrical machinery. The following excerpt, focusing on the British government's creation and sanctioning of WIDOW, seems culled from a science fiction novel that might have been written by Krafft-Ebing; yet as we all know, it continues to warp the fabric of everyday life by a process of reverse-mimesis. Like unbelievers entering a ruined chapel spray-painted with graffiti, we find ourselves in the awkward position of acknowledging that here is *a reality greater than our own.*

> Normal males had little chance of arresting catgirls; they were too easily seduced, too often the victim of nympholepsy. A catgirl's sexual defence/offence mechanisms, though mysterious, were real. And *Felis femella* prowled the world's cities with little fear of being apprehended, or even censured. But the handful of special recruits who formed the top-secret unit called WIDOW (Worldwide Investigation into Death, Orgasm and Womanhood) had proved themselves immune. In fact, not only did they have an unfailing ability to recognize a Reinhardt female on sight, without benefit of corroborative DNA testing, but also had a deep-seated, obsessive need to bring them to justice. And, for these men, justice meant death.
>
> Were they barbarians? Savages? Contemptible butchers? In Sade's *Philosophy in the Boudoir* a distinction is made between two forms of cruelty. The first comes from stupidity; the other is "the fruit of extreme organic sensibility." Sade describes men who have such "organic sensibility" through the mouth of his libertine-philosopher, Dolmancé: "If they are driven to extremes of cruelty, their goals are determined by intelligence and niceness of feeling — in short by their sensitivity. Cruelty liberates their feelings." Such were the men of WIDOW.

Why did reverse-mimesis occur? Perhaps because the manifesto's first acolytes were, if nothing else, celebrants of the postmodern, the post historical — indeed, the *post* everything — adrift in a world of contested meanings brimful with parody and pastiche. The manifesto created believers out of those who found themselves abandoned to an already unstable universe.

By summer's end, copies of the manifesto were mailed directly to television companies, this method of distribution and its outcome fitting the pattern of a classic "media prank" such as utilized by the likes of Malcolm McLaren and his spiritual mentor, Abbie Hoffman.

(According to its practitioners, the art of the media prank lies in telling people *what they want to hear*; to mimic and manipulate mass media by exploiting its sensationalism; and to expose the contradictions of the mass media, and, by extension, the contradictions and essential fraudulence of all modern control systems.)

The watershed came with a Channel 4 documentary screened on 6 September 1997, entitled "Postmodern sadism: sick vogue or new religion?" According to the voiceover that began the programme (over images of inner city housing estates and teenage girls attired in hyperskirts, tutus, Empire-waisted babydolls, thigh boots, and a host of fashion accessories that, over the course of the summer, had come to define the now familiar *prêt à porter* "popcat" style[2]): "Jean Paul Sartre once said that though French literature is known, outside France, for its humanism and rationalism, it had always produced works that were secret and black, such as those by Sade, Lautréamont, and Bataille. If we can accept that agitprop, or Outsider Art, is literature, too, then maybe Britain has appropriated that tradition." In hindsight, the most remarkable aspect of the programme was the appearance of the 90-year-old Dominique Aury, who (as "Pauline Réage") had written the classic *Story of O*. Aury claimed that Dr Evegny Reinhardt, the manifesto's key figure, was a real person, and moreover, that she had known him when he had worked at the Pasteur Institute in Paris. (This represented the first instance of semantic displacement — the colonization of reality by the meta-virus, or meme, buried in the manifesto's heart.) Aury remarked: "In those days, he was friend to many literary figures, though he was particularly close to Robbe-Grillet. But he was like myself. Not only books provoked his fantasies. And talking to him, I learnt that a common experience bound us together. The experience of childhood. I had a very power-

ful subjective life when I was a little girl. And my fantasies continue
all through my adolescence, an adolescence that had been as lonely a
his. He had his own fairy tales, you see, just as did I. For him, it wa
the tales of the succubus. Tales of the daughters of Lilith.[3] There ar
spirits, demonic spirits that are so beautiful, so expert at lovemakin
that after enjoying one a man could not possibly be content with
mere mortal woman. And such was his fate, after he had been visite
by the little succubus he called Omphale…"

On 11 November 1997, the television schedules announced a fol
low-up, entitled "Phylogenesis: Dr Evegny Reinhardt, Painter.
Channel 4's press office denied that any such programme had bee
commissioned, let alone scheduled for broadcast. And yet, despit
these denials, the programme aired at its appointed time. A 30-mi
ute documentary with rudimentary production values, it focuse
on Reinhardt's early years, when he had painted several portraits,
was said, of adolescent succubi, conjured up by demoniacal litanie
gleaned from the work of Dr John Dee and Edward Kelly – Magd
lena, Scarlett, Cliticia, Faye, Vanity, Narcissa, Séverine, Faustina…
and the Omphale that Aury had mentioned in her interview.

The remainder of the programme constituted an evaluation
Reinhardt's artistic output. A few days later, paintings attributed t
him (which Sotheby's was later to describe as belonging to his "med
umistic" period) started to appear on the world art market. Yet eve
attempt to locate the man failed. The Pasteur Institute had no "Rei
hardt" on their records, and the international scientific communit
professed ignorance of his work.

It was at this point that, for reasons still not wholly clear, the ma
ifesto was suppressed. Random House had planned a first-run
100,000 copies, but the stock was destroyed while still at the prin
ers. Dark rumours abounded that a "Part II" was in the offing, i
contents so explosive as to be adjudged liable to precipitate a level
controversy, and indeed panic, that would far exceed that surroun
ing the Marian apparitions at Fatima. It is likely, however, that go
ernment was using these rumours as an excuse to do what many ha
urged from the beginning. That is, to circumvent the Obscene Pub

cations Act by invoking national security, and having Special Branch officers seize both copies and distributors of the manifesto under existing anti-terrorism legislation.

Freud, in questioning why the taboo on the perversions is sustained with such rigidity, said that it was because "they exerted a seductive influence, as if at bottom a secret envy of those who enjoy them had to be strangled." Marcuse, in his re-evaluation of Freud, argued that "the perversions express rebellion against the subjugation of sexuality under the order of procreation, and against the institutions which guarantee this order."

Envy and fear. The British establishment, and those legal and moral systems of control that guaranteed its authority, were under threat, and it reacted as it had done on so many similar occasions: by traducing, demonizing, and illegitimizing the threat, transplanting it from the realm of discourse into the realm of silence. We may conclude by quoting Angela Carter (from *The Sadeian Woman*): "It is fair to say that, when pornography serves — as with very rare exceptions it always does — to reinforce the prevailing system of values and ideas in a given society, it is tolerated; and when it does not, it is banned..."

The government — criticized, in liberal quarters, for high-handed censorship — soon had an opportunity to gag even its most vociferous opponents. In the wings, mass hysteria was simmering. It would soon come to the boil, providing a growing coalition of reactionary forces with a *casus belli*.

The "Feline Spring" of 1998 would herald an annunciation. In May of that year the choreomania struck. Its parallels with the European dancing crazes of the fourteenth century were immediately evident. Raves that had often involved hundreds, or thousands, of people, now involved hundreds of thousands in open-air venues the length and breadth of the British Isles. They would last for weeks and, as the crisis deepened, months. Previous e-fuelled raves had been largely peaceful; this new phenomenon was characterized by violent, Dionysian frenzy. And those most affected were female members of the neo-pagan cult that had spontaneously emerged out of the exigencies of the manifesto's *Weltanschauung*. Symptoms included screaming, hallucinations, convulsive movements, chest pains, hypervent lation, crude sexual gestures, and other pathologies consistent wit episodes of epidemic hysteria. Dehydrated, exhausted, a dance might be hospitalized and, after routine examination, be found t display the same mental (and some said even physical[4]) characte istics as those catalogued by Reinhardt when his *pro bono* work wit deviant, mentally disturbed, young women, had led him to speculat that he had discovered a new species, or subspecies, of human being

It seemed logical, then, for those females afflicted with the dancin craze to be categorized as suffering from "Reinhardt's syndrome."

The dance mania continued to spread. In a wild fusion c flamenco, pole-dancing, can-can, tango, and, most importantly, bel dance ("Dance is the oldest art, the heart of all ritual," Reinhardt ha said. "And belly dance is the oldest of dances"[5]), each dancer strov to interpret the entire repertoire of "dances of death" cited by th unnamed WIDOW agent in the manifesto's "Private Dancer" sectio and in Reinhardt's analysis of "Death and the Maiden" in the sectio entitled "Sex-death and its Significance for the Evolution of th Human Orgasmic Response":

> The vision of "The Dance of Death" took a new form at the end of the 15th century when it was transformed into the subject of "Death and the Maiden." Many paintings of dances of death had already represented a figure of Death meeting a beautiful young virgin, but they seldom contained any trace of eroticism. But with "Death and the Maiden" a bond between sexuality and death became evident. In this iconography, the nubile young woman was no longer involved in a dance, but in a voluptuous act of communion that became more erotic as time went by.

Reinhardt goes on to discuss various renderings of the "Death an the Maiden" theme:

> Two works, both dated 1517, demonstrate the transition between the dance of death and the theme of death and the

maiden. In a painting by Niklaus Manuel Deutsch, Death is a rotting corpse. With one hand he grasps a girl by her neck, while with the other, he grasps her vulva. Hans Baldung Grien's study has Death seizing a girl by the hair and forcing her to go down into a tomb. The naked girl – her mouth plaintive, her face scalded with tears – does not resist.

In 1894 Edvard Munch completed his own version. Here, Death is a skeleton. But in this engraving, Munch suggests a victory of Love over Death. The girl is not frightened of, or threatened by, Death; instead, she embraces him passionately. The embrace becomes an affirmation of Life. As such, it is a painting that prefigures the psychopathology of *Felis femella*, and the dawn of a strange new world.

Those young women who had adopted the manifesto as a fashion and life-style bible danced so furiously and unremittingly that many died from their exertions in the manner of Stravinsky's heroine in *Le Sacre du Printemps*. The themes of "The Dance of Death" and "Death and the Maiden" thus became one.

These dancers were rarely students. They had no truck with, or indeed knowledge of, the intellectual currents that constituted post-modern theory. Yet they occupied a similar landscape of extreme doubt and vertigo. The eve of the new millennium was notable for the universal scepticism many people displayed towards a media-confabulated "reality." (For example, the curious debate between NASA and those conspiracy theorists that claimed the moon landings had been an elaborate hoax was but one example of a slowly emerging belief that all aspects of life amounted to little more than a huge con trick.) The medieval dancing crazes had been attributed to periods of social stress: crop failures, famine, social upheaval, and, of course, the Black Death. Contemporary social scientists pointed to qualitatively similar levels of stress as providing the probable cause of the dancing craze's late twentieth-century counterpart. More specifically, they cited the stress of the *hyperreal*.

The choreomania of 1998 represented some kind of self-psychotherapeutic attempt to cope with a world where fact was becoming fiction, and fiction, fact, by a desperate rejection of uncertainty, and a leap into faith.

The faith, or new reality, that the dancers embraced, was the reality of the manifesto. And in turn, the manifesto embraced them, as they were subsumed into its terrible world.

In early 1999 an editorial in the London *Times* opined: "Late nineteenth-century fantasies of feminine degeneracy, such as codified by Lombroso and Ferrero, seem to be enjoying something of a renaissance. Alas, the current public mood has made us all susceptible to such quackery. It is cool, rigorous scientific enquiry that we need now, answers to the questions posed by this 'manifesto's' wretched influence. What we certainly do not need is biological folklore. Let the public be reminded: there was no supernova flare-up. *And the human race is not manifesting signs of having mutated into a new species.*"

Pressure groups had emerged – many inspired, and championed, by the more popular elements of the press – that had used Lombroso and Ferrero's *The Female Offender* (described by one cultural historian as a "nasty exercise in phrenological fanaticism") as source material for their political tracts. The group that called itself *The Society of Concerned Humans* was particularly vocal in employing Lombroso and Ferrero's brand of forensic rhetoric to campaign for the registration of all females diagnosed as suffering from Reinhardt's syndrome.

Lombroso and Ferrero had argued that degeneration was built into "the very nature of woman" and that it induced them "to seek relief in evil deeds." When maternal sentiment was found wanting and was replaced by "strong passions and intensely erotic tendencies" then "the innocuous semi-criminal present in the normal woman must be transformed into a born criminal more terrible than any man." Reinhardt females, they concluded, were "big children" whose "evil tendencies" were "more numerous and more varied than men's...awakened and excited they produce results proportionately greater."

Though the opinions of *The Society of Concerned Humans* were as outrageous as they were vulgar, the biological-medical model of crime that had gained ascendancy by the end of the twentieth century lent their opinions and recommendations a veneer of respectability — enough, at least, to satisfy middle England. According to the biological-medical model, disease — the sole cause of criminal delinquency — is seen as the motivator for crime, not as a mitigator. Much of this argument rests on evidence of damage, caused by birth or accident, to the frontal lobe of the brain. *The Society of Concerned Humans* pointed to similar evidence provided by brain scans on Reinhardt's subjects. This was thought to corroborate the biological-medical model and confirm the existence of the Lombroso-Ferrero "criminally erotic woman" who possesses not only "blind and innate perversity" but also *innate criminality*.

Like the mutants portrayed in the manifesto, those with Reinhardt's syndrome were rapidly being perceived as belonging to a subset of humankind. More radical pressure groups — on the very fringes of political respectability — even dared to use the term *Untermädchen*.

But those who wished to carry the argument opted for a term that, if prurient and disparaging, was far less inflammatory: *Sphinx*.

The sphinx has a woman's head and bosom and a lion's claws and rump. She is half-human, half-cat. Her name means "The Throttler." She represents an unnameable mystery. And she kills the male.

This nomenclature, of course, like so much else, paralleled fictional events in the manifesto:

> The tabloid press took notice. In highly charged, sensationalistic accounts of those whom — citing the constellation in which the supernova had occurred and the dangerous, feline beauty of those born under its aegis — the public had started to call *sphinxes*, newspapers such as the *Sun* and *Star* dutifully sought a more demotic appellation. Before long, sub-editors began to blue pencil "sphinx" and substitute "catgirl."
>
> The new appellation stuck (along with the less commonly used synonym "sexcat") and came into widespread usage. And though some Reinhardt females — particularly those who thought, or cared, about the future of their "breed" — often re-

verted to using "sphinx" among themselves, most, from this time onward, referred to themselves as *catgirls*.

As did their living analogues.

Reports of "Reinhardt's syndrome" came in from all over Europe and the Americas, and, at last, the Far East and Africa, offering proof that it was a worldwide phenomenon. Liberal democracies were left in a quandary about what, in anything, to do about the problem, if indeed "problem" it was.

The terms "folk devil" and "moral panic" are widely attributed to Stanley Cohen, who in the early 1970s produced a detailed sociological investigation of the Mods and Rockers. Cohen argues: "Societies appear to be subject...to periods of moral panic. A condition, episode, person or group of persons emerges to become defined as a threat to societal values and interests... The moral barricades are manned by editors, bishops, politicians and other right-thinking people; socially accredited experts pronounce their diagnoses and solutions; ways of coping are evolved or resorted to; the condition then disappears, submerges or deteriorates."

The late twentieth century was an age of moral panic. There had been other concessions to the irrational: periodic riots over immigration, the "war on drugs" and the hue and cry over child abuse (and paradoxical fears about the supposed criminality of children). However, one of the key necessary indicators of a true moral panic — that is, volatility — was missing from the "catgirl" equation. The manifesto's influence showed no signs of dissipating.

At certain points in history collective hysteria had evolved into a new worldview. The witch-craze[6] of the sixteenth and seventeenth centuries was, perhaps, the most notable example — a "panic" that, over the course of decades, became an all-encompassing conceptual framework from which it became almost impossible for people to extricate themselves without drawing down suspicion and retribution. The hysteria surrounding the "catgirl problem" was to evolve in a similar manner, but with far greater speed.

Perhaps a collective fear of the "other"[7] had been too long frustrated. Perhaps "Reinhardt's syndrome" represented one "moral panic" too many. Whatever the reasons, it seemed that, after so many years of waiting for another apocalypse, the world at last cried out. And the darkness answered.

The London *Times* performed a U-turn and in a leader of late 1999 revealed that the intelligentsia was questioning the Cohen model as fervently as the mass of the British public: "Are we really in such a 'panic'? Perhaps not. The Cohen model creates the possibility of normalizing and legitimizing the governing classes in society and de-legitimizing those who hold alternative positions or experiences by branding them as 'deviant' and associating them with 'panic' behaviour. But groups such as *The Society of Concerned Humans* have valid cause for concern, even if this newspaper has often disagreed, and disagreed strongly, with their rhetoric. It is time we stopped marginalizing those who dare to put into words what we are all secretly thinking. New Labour must be challenged if we are not to look forward to a new millennium filled with madness and chaos ..."

Both the public and those in power began to think the unthinkable, allowing for the birth of a new "episteme."

Foucault's "episteme" is a system of possible discourses that comes to dominate each historical era. Foucault showed how power and knowledge fundamentally depend on each other, so that the extension of one is simultaneously the extension of the other. In so doing, rationalism requires — even creates — social categories of the mad, criminal, and deviant against which to define itself.

Reinhardt females were judged to be insane, and what is more, criminally insane — not just a variation of *Homo sapiens*, but its own subspecies — and thus open to being sectioned under the Mental Health Act and the new eugenics laws.

In March 2001, in an attempt to stem rising public concern (as concupiscence and moral reproach jostled for editorial space in a slew of red-letterhead dailies) the European Union and the United States instituted a compulsory program of psychosexual testing for all females over 12 years of age (the age when the traits associated with the syndrome began to emerge). The programme revealed that, within the EU's borders alone, over a half million girls and young women were "Reinhardt's." In the same year, EU and American health authorities began to treat an increasing number of male patients with early symptoms of nympholepsy. When the first nympholeptic deaths were reported, public concern — fuelled by the screams and howls of the tabloid press — segued into anger.

Within months, those testing positive were put on national, and later, international registers, and closely monitored by social services and law enforcement agencies. Civil liberties groups were quickly silenced. Soon, Asia, Africa and South America followed suit, though in many developing countries so-called "prophylactic measures" were more stringent, up to and including forcible internment for those who did not comply with the new legislation.

As many had predicted, the programme of testing and registration forced many with "Reinhardt's" underground. They disappeared into the anonymity of the big cities, with few apologies, and fewer regrets. In the manifesto, these runaways were popularly known as "strays" or "feral cats", as opposed to the "domestic" variety that lived under licence.

In the mirror of the real world, it was, of course, the same. And for some years now, of course, it has remained the same, even until the present day.

It is now 2003. And at the time of writing this introduction, it is impossible to know exactly what will follow. It seems likely, however, that despite a period of remission, events in the real world will quite likely soon begin to once more reflect and mimic those detailed in the manifesto:

> Within a few years, the eldest among the runaways had taken the younger females under their wing. They organized themselves into sorority-like "litters." These young women had been made outcasts. And in revenge, they would drive the world insane with lust.

> As more and more females were born with "Reinhardt's," so the percentage of "strays" increased, until the WHO estimated the global tally to be in the millions. Their clandestine influence on everyday life was felt at every level of society. Within five years of the publication of Reinhardt's original paper, many believed "strays" had seduced so many key men in entertainment, industry, politics and finance, that the mental health of much of the world's population would be seriously undermined — a state of affairs that, if unchecked, would lead to the collapse of economies, cultures and, eventually, civilization.

Is the manifesto an analogue of our world, or our world, an analogue of the manifesto? It no longer matters. The dancer has become indiscernible from the dance. What is undeniable is that the manifesto has a social-political, and moreover, a psychological agenda, which we are all currently struggling to either resist or assimilate. The manifesto's purpose is, quite simply, to change people, and in changing them, to change the world. But we are in no position to know where change, whether voluntary or involuntary, will lead us.

Will it be into madness, such as that which awaited the mythical, or semi-mythical, Dr Reinhardt?

> After his return from the Middle East, where he had gone under the name of Lambshead[8] (said by some to be his original name), he might be seen walking along Oxford Street handing out his cheaply-printed pamphlets, seeking to convince any who would stop to listen that a new world order was about to come into existence, a new way of thinking and feeling. "Reality is at bottom a social and linguistic construct," he would say. "Scientific knowledge, far from being objective, reflects and encodes the dominant ideologies and power relations of the culture that produced it. But a new reality is at hand! A new knowledge! And it is one that will be our salvation..."
>
> The eroticization of death, he argued, was the best, and indeed only consolation human beings might expect of life in an

impersonal and savage universe. Men and women were by nature cruel; but the erotic — especially when elevated to a transcendent level — alchemized cruelty into lust, and lust into beauty. The flare-up of 1972 was no supernova, he went on to aver, but something artificially created, whereby the collective morphogenetic field of a dying interstellar civilization might ride the gamma-ray light cones that would allow it to parasitize our minds and bodies, and thus live again. We were all becoming, Dr Reinhardt said, something gloriously "other"...

On August 12, 2005, shortly after launching his "counter-hegemonic" Website advocating terrorist acts of "postmodern sado-masochism," Dr Reinhardt was committed to Her Majesty's secure mental institution in Broadmoor, England — another, but not, of course, the last, victim of nympholepsy.

Is, or was, the manifesto's enigmatic author really a woman? If so, perhaps she might have agreed with French academic Julia Kristeva's statement, that *woman as such does not exist. She is in the process of becoming*, just as the world of the early twenty-first century is in a state of becoming, its reality subsumed by the manifesto's own. A libertine feminist, she might also have found herself haunted by a certain exchange between Lady Clairwil and Juliette in Sade's *Juliette*: "What I should like," says Clairwil, "is to find a crime, the effects of which would be perpetual, even when I myself do not act, so that there would not be a single moment of my life, even when I was asleep, when I was not the cause of some chaos, a chaos of such proportions that it would provoke a general corruption or a disturbance and that even after my death its effects will still be felt." Juliette's reply is succinct: "Try your hand at moral crime, the kind one commits in writing."

It is impossible, at this present juncture, to estimate the precise nature of this moral crime, that is, the *writerly* crime of the manifesto itself, just as it is impossible to calculate the manifesto's long-term effects — whether they will be perpetual, producing a wave of chaos that will engulf generation after generation, or whether they will subside. In 2003 the undermining of paramount reality by a subversive, chthonic force affects the whole globe; in consequence, it is logical to assume that it also affects the integrity of this introduction.

If it does, we may at least confidently assert that change has been coming for a long time. The manifesto is, in many respects, only a crystallization of a deep current of perversity that had previously manifested itself in film clips, a paragraph from a book, an advertisement hoarding, or any other number of pop-cultural fragments. With hindsight, it is possible to see that these moments of epiphany suggested that another world, a parallel world, both more and less real than our own, was pressing against the thin membrane that divided our mutual realities. It was only a matter of time before that membrane ruptured and abandoned us to the dark, fiery plane of existence that the Priestesses of Lilith call New Babylon.

We have surely not seen the worst. Soon, we may look back upon the last seven years merely as a rehearsal for the manifesto's apocalyptic *dénouement*.

In a meeting that came to be known to later historians as the "Star Chamber Conference of May 24, 2004," WIDOW drew up its plans for dealing with strays and ferals, that is, young women classified as *Untermädchen* or *beautiful vermin*.

The surviving minutes of that meeting, and the accompanying extermination order, with all its attendant protocols, are quite specific, and, according to whether one subscribes to a humanistic or suprahumanistic perspective, either damning, or inspiring.

In the summer of 2004, the world's media had begun to report an unusual number of sex-murders, all of which seemed, according to the forensic evidence, to have been committed by a serial killer, or group of killers employing similar methods. It was then that WIDOW learned the necessity of using a large backup team of "normal" men to dispose of bodies before they could be reported to the police. But gossip and speculation continued to spread.

At the beginning of October 2005 a team of investigative

journalists working for BBC television eventually blew the conspiracy wide open. The details of the "extermination order" had been leaked. Public outrage, and the scandal surrounding many top-ranking public servants and politicians, however, quickly subsided. There was no attempt at a cover-up. And, after some minimum posturing, most governments and their electorates acquiesced to what seemed a necessary horror.

For only WIDOW was capable of dealing with what was now known as "the catgirl menace." Far from being disbanded, the organization acquired new powers, and a huge budget.

In a startling bureaucratic *coup d'état*, WIDOW, which still only numbered a few dozen men, assumed full control of the security apparatus of which, until then, it had constituted a mere part. Almost overnight the unit was transformed into an organization that no longer hid behind closed doors, but proudly announced its policies and *modus operandi* to the world.

The name WIDOW disappeared. The gynocides claimed that they were taking upon themselves a sacerdotal task. Their mission, they said, was a crusade. They were "Inquisitors," and they served what would now be universally referred to as the "Inquisition."

Proud, haughty, and convinced of the rectitude of their cause, they walked the streets in their new, all-black uniforms — a wardrobe consisting of riding boots, skintight leather trousers (complete with studded codpiece), thick belts (from which usually hung a handgun, rapier, and stiletto knife), leather doublets, and long, flowing cloaks equipped with monk-like cowls.

Now that it had been acknowledged that, far from reviled perverts, they were gentlemen-killers set upon a sacred mission who held the world's fate in their hands, people showed them respect. Even awe. And the Inquisitors used their power accordingly.

A great, neo-Gothic structure was erected in central London, memorably described in one tour guide as looking like "a collaboration between Brunel and Buñuel, Borromini and

> Bosch." It was the Inquisition's HQ, and also served as a gigantic prison. The fascia above its gates diplayed a quotation from Nietzsche: "Almost everything we call higher culture is based on the spiritualization of *cruelty*."

We all tremble at the prospect of the final rending of the veil, when our own reality becomes indistinguishable from the manifesto's. As such, our decision to publish this *samizdat* edition of *The Catgirl Manifesto* has been problematic. The editors are not acolytes and have a purely academic interest in the text *per se*. However, despite the obvious dangers to themselves of arrest and imprisonment, they believe that open debate – free of government influence and censorship – can only be for the good. Too much superstitious hyperbole has surrounded the manifesto. And this deplorable state of exegesis has existed largely, we feel, because governments around the world are at pains to keep the manifesto on the *index expurgatorius*, assiduously doing all in their power to make sure that it never again enters the public domain.

Of course, there is a complicating factor: the rumour that "Part II" of the manifesto is more than a rumour. It is said that the late Monica Lewinsky[9] (whom so many female acolytes have adopted as an icon and celebrated as a martyr) was instrumental – after long court battles – in acquiring a classified portion of the text hitherto unseen by the editors. Though we acknowledge that something like a "Part II" may actually exist, any speculation about its nature, or its likely effects, must necessarily fall outside our remit.[10]

The complete text of the manifesto, as currently available, follows. Is it a confrontation, a challenge to a spiritless world, or the invocation of a vicious, fascistic tyranny? Now that we are all certain that we live in an age where there is slippage along the fault lines of parallel universes, there are some who will choose to embrace the earthquake, and some who will choose to flee.

But surely no one may ignore.

NOTES:

1. Despite being obvious psychobabble, the term "nymphic autism" was subsequently used by health care workers who attended to the aftermath of the "Feline Spring" of 1998, shortly before "Reinhardt's syndrome" itself entered the medical vocabulary.

2. A different, wholly human, kind of catgirl had existed in Japanese pop culture for some years prior to the manifesto entering the public domain. *Nekomimi* (that is, "catgirl") fashion had played a significant role in kogaru street culture. Its emphasis on *kawaii* ("cuteness") and *cosplay* ("costume play") provided the elements of what was to become a female acolyte's requisite personal style. That summer the "Elegant Gothic Lolita" look that had had Japanese girls dressing up in outfits that would traditionally be worn by Victorian dolls, was imported and transformed into the "Industrial Gothic Lolita" look. (School uniforms in a variety of styles, Eton jackets, extra baggy jumpers, and floppy white loose socks vied with or complemented plastic skirts, stockings, perilous high heels, chains, and exotic corsetry.) For Reinhardt females, life was a neurotic masquerade, in which they continuously fretted about how to maintain the delicate balance between *cuteness* and *whorishness*.

3. Interestingly, the conclusion to *Story of O* presents the reader with an image of Lilith. O is brought to a party naked but for an owl mask — a mask inspired, it is said, by one worn by the artist Leonor Fini, who was to go on to illustrate a luxury edition of *Story of O* in the 1960s. Lilith, according to Hebrew legend, was not only Adam's first wife, but also the Queen of Hell and Mother of the Succubi. In Greek mythology, the Little Owl was the bird sacred to Pallas Athene, the goddess of wisdom and death. But the owl symbolism goes deeper, pointing to O as a Lilim, or daughter of Lilith, for whom the owl was also holy. The figure of Lilith — the dark side of the Great Goddess — is secondary only to the figure of Reinhardt in the manifesto's iconography. Indeed, if Reinhardt is a prophet — which, these days, so many consider him to be — then Lilith is his revelation.

4. While it is true that many subjects had undergone lipoplasty, augmentation mammaplasty, abdominoplasty, and, of course, *umbilicoplasty*, cosmetic surgery could not alone explain the depth and intensity of metamorphosis, leading some researchers to propose a new biological paradigm involving a physical equivalence between memes and genes.

5. The idea that all belly dancers wear rubies in their navels dates, it is often said, from fifties Hollywood, and is a legacy of the Hayes code: a series of rules and guidelines for the movie industry created after the Fatty Arbuckle scandal and the backlash it engendered. Bejewelling the navel was Hollywood's way of getting around the censors' demands that the navel should not be shown.

However, the question of the "ruby in the navel" is, in reality, far more complex, and the practice (both in fifties movies, such as King Vidor's *Solomon and Sheba*, in which Gina Lollobrigida sports a rubricate umbilicus, and, more recently, as adopted by pop icons such as Britney Spears and Shakira) may well be a response to atavism.

In the ancient world, the "Town of the Sacred Courtesans" was Uruk, a place sacred to Ishtar, the goddess of love, beauty, fertility, and war. Ishtar was the Sumerian goddess Inanna given a Semitic name. She was the courtesan of the gods. In Babylonian times, when the Goddess cultures flourished, Lilith was called the "hand of Innana." It was her duty to gather men from the street and bring them into the temple, to be served by the cult's sacred prostitutes. Lilith, Innana, and Ishtar are often portrayed in statuary and relief as possessing a *burning navel*.

Ishtar, the goddess of fertility, was also the goddess of death. She performed a "dance of seven veils" when she descended into the underworld to reclaim her paramour, Tammuz. The ruby is emblematic of her wounded belly, the bleeding fulcrum of female sexuality and life. When Salome danced the dance of the seven veils, she danced a dance of death, not only for the Prophet whose new religion so opposed the old, but for herself. As such, her dance was both seductive and autoerotic, like all belly dance and, indeed, all dances of death.

The contemporary fashion of navel piercing is then perhaps a subconscious attempt to represent and embody the *burning navel* and all that it stands for. This atavism has been foregrounded, of course, by the manifesto, whose female acolytes worship images of the Queen of Sheba and Salome — both celebrated as avatars of Lilith — as well as less well-known incarnations of the Goddess, such as Helen of Troy, Lucrezia Borgia, and Mata Hari. Male acolytes, too, of course, have responded to the question of "the ruby in the navel" by not only arguing that it is symbolic of WIDOW's decision to exterminate *Felis femella* by ritual, umbilical wounding, but that it demonstrates that the manifesto reveals to humankind more general, symbolic truths pertaining to sex, death and the "self-enthrallment" of the Reinhardt female.

6. The witch-craze was a pogrom against women. It embodied *sex crime*. Until the mid-1500s, the much-quoted scripture Exodus 22:18 had used the gender-neutral *maleficos* for the word "witch." By the mid-sixteenth century, new translations were feeding the fires of gynocide. In Luther's Bible Exodus 22:18 reads "*Die Zauberinnen soltu nicht leben lassen*." ("Thou shalt not suffer a witch to live.") But in this translation the word for witch refers solely to females. In *La Saincte Bible*, published in 1566, the word chosen for witch is also feminine. 'Thou shalt not suffer a witch to live' had come to mean 'Thou shalt not suffer a woman to live.' By the 1600s witchcraft was considered a sex offence and prosecutors were predisposed to conceive of witches as beautiful, predatory young women. Fellatio was considered a particularly heinous criminal act. It was a form of vampirism whereby the demonic female — with her insatiable lust for seminal fluid — would suck out a man's essence and thus weaken and contaminate him.

7. According to Lacan, a child's sense of self arrives externally, from a reflection, or from the imaginary. The child enters the social world through the "symbolic order" represented most crucially by *language*. Language belongs to the Father and the patriarchal order of the phallus. Power in language is the phallus. Women "are excluded — forever outcast as 'the other' — as creatures *without* language. This is due to the fact that they cannot escape from the imaginary into the symbolic order, as males can." The manifesto states that after moving to London in 2005 to take up a position at University College, Dr Reinhardt published a paper in the *British Journal of Psychiatry*. He argued that the mental aberrations of human females with mutant DNA were best understood with reference to files made available to him by WIDOW. In the course of their work WIDOW had written up reports of their kills that included photographs, video footage and transcripts of recordings of young women *in extremis*. It was when *in extremis*, argued Dr Reinhardt, that the mutant female revealed the essence of her psyche. By so doing, he concluded, she revealed an evolutionary "quantum leap" in orgasmic response that, if it spread to the general population, would herald a fearful new age.

Dr Reinhardt's central thesis was that the death, or sex-death, of the mutant female, was in many ways pre-scripted, an erotic performance improvised about certain unchanging motives and themes. It was, in other words, like so many other elements of her behaviour, seemingly hardwired into the brain. The seven major *leitmotifs* of the sex-death were found to follow no specific order, and would often repeat themselves, or add a hitherto unique variation, in a single "performance"; but the most common order, following a progression involving apprehension, threat, initial wounding, torture, to the final death scene, was as follows: 1) cycles of perverse disbelief; 2) lewd infantilism; 3) pleas to be made into a "pet"; 4) frotteurism; 5) display rituals; 6) begging for mercy; 7) begging for the *coup de grâce*.

The second *leitmotif* — affecting speech, in terms of vocabulary, syntax, and pronunciation — is the characteristic most emblematic of the Reinhardt subject's "otherness" and her status as outcast child.

8. Some biographical information about Thackery T. Lambshead currently resides on the Web and in the apocryphal *The Thackery T. Lambshead Guide to Eccentric and Discredited Diseases*. It is the opinion of the editors of this edition of *The Catgirl Manifesto* that Reinhardt and Lambshead were brothers, perhaps even twins.

9. Monica Lewinsky graduated with a degree in psychology from Lewis and Clark College in the spring of 1995. Shortly thereafter, she accepted an unpaid internship at the White House, where she became the most internationally celebrated fellatrix of modern times. Some feminists have argued that Lewinsky was the victim of sexual opportunism at the hands of her boss, President William Jefferson Clinton. The Starr report, however, suggests that she was engaged, not only in seduction, but also in a process of self-enthrallment typical of *Felis femella* and the exploitative and, ultimately, self-destructive relationships they enter into with

demonic males. Kenneth Starr is, obviously, as much a prototype "Inquisitor" as Lewinsky herself is an early example of a "catgirl." In Section II of the Starr narrative, '1995: Initial Sexual Encounters,' she admits to having read an early version of the manifesto that had, it seems, been in circulation in the US long before the full version appeared in the UK.

The second volume of her autobiography is notable for her illuminating, post-feminist critique of Reinhardt's paper in the *British Journal of Psychiatry*. In this famous quote she focuses on his categorization of the sixth *leitmotif* of sex-death:

"When Dr Reinhardt talks of 'begging for mercy' he mistakenly assumes that it is the victim's desire to *placate* her prospective killer that is uppermost in her mind. With Bill and me this was only half the story. Though fellatio is no longer taboo, it remains the case that most women condition themselves to believe that the only pleasure they themselves may expect from the act is gained from the degree of pleasure they afford their men. (It is not so long ago that human females were thought incapable of receiving real pleasure or satisfaction from *penetrative* sex — a time when the clitoris was either unknown, or held to be pernicious.) It is true: I was the President's slave, his plaything, his little kittenish *pet*. But for a catgirl, fellatio — though desperate — is also vampiric. I *was* concerned to placate; I feared rape, of course, just as, later, *post-coitum*, I feared the slow, painful death that Kenneth Starr seemed to promise me. (Revealed, for all to see, in the sub-text of my deposition, and promised, these days, to so many of my kind by "the catgirl manifesto's" male acolytes!) I feared Presidential power, its delicious authority. But I was always in control, the consumer, not the consumed. And I took far, far more than I ever gave. The only relationship the slave fears is that of friendship. I am a Reinhardt female, and if I adore fellatio, I also adore treachery and deceit. Like all incompletely domesticated female animals, catgirls make *dangerous* pets. Bill should have known that before he played with me..."

10. N.B. Following Monica Lewinsky's recent execution, some few days before this *samizdat* manifesto was due to go to press, her estate has proclaimed that "Part II" will be published within months and that it will be like a trump that calls an end to this age and brings about the reign of Lilith.

Looking through Lace

Ruth Nestvold

One of the first winners of the Tiptree Award, *A Woman of the Iron People*, by Eleanor Arnason, features an anthropological team studying the native peoples of another planet. Ruth Nestvold's story, firmly in that tradition, depicts an all-male team having trouble deciphering a world where the indigenous people have very distinct men's and women's cultures. Bringing in a woman linguist might help more if the anthropologists didn't have their own gender preconceptions. The team can't understand why some things seem so obvious and others so mysterious; as with some other stories in this book, if you know what you're looking at you may not see it.

Toni came out of the jump groggy and with a slight headache, wishing the Allied Interstellar Research Association could afford passage on Alcubierre drive ships – even if they did collapse an unconscionable amount of space in their wake. For a moment, she couldn't remember what the job was this time. She sat up and rubbed her eyes while the voice on the intercom announced that they would be arriving at the Sagittarius Transit Station in approximately one standard hour.

Sagittarius. Now she remembered. The women's language. Suddenly she felt much more awake. For the first time, she was on her way to join a first contact team and she had work to do. She got up, washed her face in cold water at the basin in her compartment (at least AIRA could afford private compartments), and turned on the console again, calling up the files she had been sent when given her assignment to Christmas.

"List vids," she said. It was time she checked her theoretical knowledge against the real thing again. Just over three weeks she'd had to learn the Mejan language, one week on Admetos after getting her new assignment and two weeks in transit. From the transit station it would be another week before she finally set foot on the planet. Even with the latest memory enhancements, it was a daunting challenge. A month to learn a new language and its intricacies. A month to try to get a feel for a culture where women had their own language, which they never spoke with men.

That had been her lucky break. Toni was the only female xenolinguist in this part of the galaxy with more than a year's experience. And suddenly she found herself promoted from grunt, compiling grammars and dictionaries, to first contact team.

She scrolled through the list of vids. This time, she noticed a title which hadn't caught her attention before.

"Play 'Unknown Mejan water ritual.'"

To judge by the AIC date, it had to be a video from one of the early, pre-contact-team probes. Not to mention the quality. The visuals were mostly of the bay of Edaru, and the audio was dominated by the sound of water lapping the shore.

But what she could see and hear was fascinating. A fearful young hominid male, tall and gracile, his head shaved and bowed, was being led out by two guards to the end of a pier. A small crowd followed solemnly. When they arrived at the end, another man stepped forward and, in the only words Toni could make out clearly, announced that Sentalai's shame would be purged. (Assuming, of course, that what had been deciphered of the men's language to this point was correct.) The older man then motioned for the younger man to remove his clothes, fine leather garments such as those worn by the richer of the Edaru clans, and when he was naked, the two guards pushed him into the water.

Three women behind them conferred briefly. Then one of the three stepped forward and flung a length of lace after the young man.

Toni stared as the crowd on the pier walked back to shore. She could see no trace of the man who had been thrown in the water. According to her materials, the Mejan were excellent swimmers, growing up nearly as much in the water as out, and it should have been easy for him to swim back to the pier. But for some reason he hadn't.

It reminded her of nothing so much as an execution.

The entry bay of the small space station orbiting Christmas was empty and sterile, with none of the personal details that a place accumulated with time, the details that made it lived-in rather than just in use. Toni was glad she would soon be moving to the planet's surface. Blank walls were more daunting than an archaic culture and an unknown language anytime.

Two men were there to meet her, and neither one was the team xenolinguist.

The elder of the two stepped forward, his hand outstretched. "Welcome to the *Penthesilea*, Dr. Donato."

"Thank you, Captain Ainsworth. It's a pleasure to meet you. And please, call me Toni."

Ainsworth smiled but didn't offer his own first name in exchange. Hierarchies were being established quickly.

"Toni, this is Dr. Samuel Wu, the new xenoteam sociologist."

From their vid communications, Toni had expected to like Sam Wu, and now she was sure of it. His smile was slow and sincere and his handshake firm. Besides, he was in a similar position on the team, having been brought into the project late after the original sociologist, Landra Saleh, had developed a serious intolerance to something in the atmosphere of Christmas, despite the battery of tests they all had to go through before being assigned to a new planet.

"Nice to meet you in person, Toni," Sam said.

"Nice to meet you too." Toni looked from one to the other. "And Dr. Repnik? Was he unable to leave the planet?"

There was a short silence. "Uh, he thought Dr. Wu could brief you on anything that has come up since the last communication you received. Continued study of the language has precedence at this point."

Toni nodded. "Of course." But that didn't change the fact that another xenolinguist could brief her better than a sociologist — especially one who had only been on the planet a week himself.

As Ainsworth led her to her quarters aboard ship, she drew Sam aside. "Okay, what's all this about?"

"I was afraid you'd notice," he said, grimacing.

"And?"

"I guess it's only fair you know what you'll be up against. Repnik didn't think a female linguist needed to be added to the team, but Ainsworth insisted on it."

Toni sighed. She had been looking forward to working with Repnik. Of the dozen inhabited worlds discovered in the last century, he had been on the xenoteams of half of them and had been the initial xenolinguist on three. He had more experience in making sense of unknown languages than anyone alive. And the languages of Christmas were a fascinating puzzle, a puzzle she had thought she would get a chance to work on with one of the greatest xenolinguists in the galaxy. Instead, she would be a grunt again, an unwanted grunt.

"Here we are," Ainsworth said, as the door to one of the cabins opened at his touch. "We'll have the entrance reprogrammed as soon as you settle in."

"Thank you."

"We'll be going planetside tomorrow. I hope that's enough time for you to recover from your journey."

It never was, but it was all she was going to get. "I'm sure it will be."

"Good, then I will leave you with Dr. Wu so that he can brief you on anything you still need to know."

She set her bag down on the narrow bed and gazed out the viewport at the planet, a striking sight. The discovery team that had done the first fly-by of the Sgr 132 solar system had given it the name Christmas. The vegetation was largely shades of red and the ocean had a greenish cast, while the narrow band of rings alternated shades of green and gold. There was only one major continent, looking from the viewport now like an inverted pine tree, like Christmas wrapping paper with the colors reversed. One more day, and she'd finally be there.

Sam stepped up behind her. "Beautiful, isn't it?"

"And how." She gazed at the planet in silence for a moment and then turned to Sam. "So how did Repnik think he would be able to gather data on the women's language without a female xenolinguist?"

"He wanted to plant more probes and use the technicians and crew of the *Penthesilea*."

She shook her head. "But they're not trained in working with an alien language."

"That's what Ainsworth said." He raised one eyebrow and smiled. "Except he added that they were needed on the ship for the jobs they had been hired to do."

Toni chuckled despite the ache in her gut. "I think I'm going to be very grateful you're on this team, Sam."

Sam grinned. "Ditto."

From: The Allied Interstellar Community General Catalogue. Entry for Sgr 132-3, also known as Christmas, or Kailazh (land) in the native tongue.

The third planet in the system of Sgr 132 is 1.2 AU from its sun, has a diameter of 15,840 kilometers, a density of 3.9, and 0.92G. The day is 16.7 standard hours and the year 743 days (1.42 Earth years). It is iron poor but rich in light metals. Satellites: three shepherd moons within a thin ring of debris. Land mass consists largely of one supercontinent covering most of one pole and extending south past the equator. It is now known to be a seeded planet of hominid inhabitants with a number of plants and animals also related to Terran species. Date of original colonization of the planet as yet unknown. Technological status: pre-automation, primitive machines, rudimentary scientific knowledge. There is no written language.

The first thing Toni noticed when she stepped off the shuttle was the scent of the air, tantalizing and slightly spicy, as if someone were baking cookies with cardamom and cinnamon.

The second thing she noticed was the gravity. Christmas had slightly lower gravity than Earth, but Toni had grown up on Mars, and it certainly felt more like home than Admetos had. Her joints still ached from the large planet's crushing gravity. Thank god she had been transferred.

The rings were only the third thing she noticed. They arched across the southern sky like some kind of odd cloud formation, pale but still visible in the daylight.

Sam saw the direction of her gaze. "Wait until you see them at sunset."

Toni nodded, smiling. "I wanted to say I can imagine, but I'm not sure I can."

Irving Moshofski, the xenoteam geologist, stepped forward to introduce himself and shook Toni's hand. "Nice to meet you, Dr. Donato. Gates and Repnik are waiting for us in town."

They followed Moshofski to their ground transportation, an open carriage drawn by descendants of Terran horses, but taller and with lighter bone structure. This pair was a reddish-brown much deeper than the bays of Earth.

Toni took another deep breath of the air. "I swear, if they hadn't already named it Christmas for the colors, they would have changed the name to Christmas when they smelled the place."

"Everyone familiar with Terran Western culture says that," Moshofski said.

She climbed up into the open carriage behind Ainsworth and noted that it was well sprung, the workmanship of the wood smooth, and the leather seats soft. Their driver was a young Mejan man, tall and willowy, his skin a lovely copper color. As they settled into their seats, Toni greeted him in Alnar ag Ledar, "the language of the sea" — the universal language used by men and women on Christmas to communicate with each other.

Their driver lifted the back of his hand to his forehead in the Mejan gesture of greeting. "Sha bo sham, tajan."

She returned the gesture and turned to Ainsworth, suppressing a chuckle. "Why did he call me 'mother'?"

"That seems to be a term of respect for women here."

"At least that's something. But it looks like I still have a lot to learn."

Ainsworth nodded. "We all do. We strongly suspect the Mejan are withholding information from us. They're very reluctant to begin any kind of treaty negotiations with the Allied Interstellar Community."

"They don't trust us," Moshofski said.

Toni shrugged. "Is there any reason why they should?" She leaned forward to address the driver, speaking rapidly in the men's language. "Moden varga esh zhamkaned med sherned?" *Do you trust the men from the sky?*

The driver looked over his shoulder at her and chuckled. "Roga desh varga an zhamnozhed, tajan." *Like I trust the stars.* Toni noticed that the laughing eyes in his copper-brown face were an extraordinary smoky green color.

She raised one eyebrow. "Moshulan sham beli?" *Not to fall on you?*

He laughed out loud and Toni leaned back in her seat, grinning.

The landing base was about ten kilometers outside of the biggest town, Edaru, and she studied the landscape avidly during the trip. She loved the sights and scents and sounds of strange worlds, the rhythms of a new language, the shape and color of plants she had never seen before. For someone from Earth, the red hues of the landscape on Christmas might have conjured associations of barrenness, although the rich shades from magenta to burnt umber were from the native vegetation itself, the wide, strangely-shaped leaves of the low-growing plants and the fronds of the trees. But it never would have occurred to Toni to associate reds and umbers with barrenness. For someone from Neubrandenburg on Mars, red was the color of homesickness.

Toni didn't notice Edaru until they were practically upon it. They came over a rise and suddenly the city, crowded around a large bay, was spread out before them. The buildings were low and close to the water; despite occasional flooding, the Mejan were happiest as close to the sea as possible.

At the sight of their vehicle, people came out of their houses, standing in doorways or leaning on windowsills to watch them pass. A number lifted the backs of their hands to their foreheads in the Mejan gesture of greeting.

Christmas was one of the half-dozen seeded planets in the known universe, and as on other such planets, the human population had made some physical adjustments for life in the given environment, most obviously in their height and the prominent flaps of skin between their fingers. But to Toni, who had spent two years now on Admetos among what the human members of AIRA referred to as the giant ants, they didn't appear very alien, or at least only pleasantly so. The people she saw were tall, light-boned, dark-skinned and wide-chested, with long hair in various hues which they wore interlaced with thin braids enhanced by colorful yarn. She was surprised at how little difference there was in the styles worn by the men and the women — not what she would have expected from a world where the women spoke a separate, "secret" language.

Ships and boats of various sizes were docked at the wharves, and one large ship was sailing into port as they arrived. The materials sent to her had described them as primitive craft, but she found them graceful and beautiful. The long, low stone houses had rows of windows facing the sea and were ornamented with patterns of circles and waves in shades of red and purple and green and blue on a background of yellow. Some larger houses were built in a u-shape around a central courtyard. Toni stared and smiled and waved. It looked clean and peaceful, the children content and the women walking alone with their heads held high.

The common house — the main government building of Edaru — was located in the center of town near the wharves. Councillor Lanrhel himself was waiting for them, the back of his hand touching his forehead in greeting. She couldn't help thinking it looked like he was shading his eyes to see them better.

Lanrhel was a handsome man, even taller than the average Mejan, with streaks of gray in his reddish-brown hair, looking almost like an extra shade in the colors of his braids. The pale, tooled leather of his short cape, which was worn in the long warm half of the year, was the same length as his tunic, reaching just past the tops of his thighs. He stood in the doorway, his open palm in front of his forehead, and Toni returned the gesture as she approached the building. When Lanrhel didn't relax, she glanced at Sam and Ainsworth, unsure what to do. Perhaps she had not made the gesture correctly. She repeated it and said in the best local dialect she could manage, "Negi eden an elamed elu mazhu velazh Edaru. An rushen eden sham." Which meant as much as I'm-honored-to-be-a-guest-in-Edaru-thank-you. Except that the language of the Mejan had no verb for "to be" and tenses were expressed in auxiliary verbs which could go either before or after the main verb, depending on the emphasis.

The councillor smiled widely and lowered his arm, and Toni winced, realizing she had used the male first person pronoun. Her first official sentence on Christmas and it was wrong. She was glad Repnik wasn't there. Sam and Ainsworth didn't seem to notice that she'd made a mistake, but when she glanced back at the driver with the smoky green eyes, she saw that he too had a grin on his wide lips.

"We are happy to have you visit our city," Lanrhel said and led them into the common house. They crossed a central hallway and entered a large room where about a dozen people were seated in comfortable chairs and sofas in a circle. Low tables were scattered in the center, and on them stood strange-looking fruits in glossy bowls made of the shells of large, native beetles. Decorative lace hangings graced the walls.

Lanrhel announced them and the others rose. Toni was surprised to see almost as many women as men, all garbed in soft, finely tooled leather of different colors. Leather was the material of choice of the Mejan, and their tanning methods were highly advanced. Sam had speculated it was because they lived so much with water, and leather was more water-resistant than woven materials.

She recognized Repnik immediately. She knew his face from photos and vids and holos; thin and wiry, with deep wrinkles next to his mouth and lining his forehead. Despite age treatments, the famous linguist looked old, used-up even, more so than the images had led her to believe. He was also shorter than she expected, barely topping her eyebrows.

He came forward slowly to shake her hand. "Ms. Donato?" he said, omitting her title.

Two could play that game. "Mr. Repnik. I'm honored to be able to work with you."

His eyes narrowed briefly. "It really is unfortunate that you were called to Christmas unnecessarily. I'm sure you will soon see that there is little contribution for you to make here. Despite the sex barrier, I've managed to collect enough material on my own to make some conclusions about the women's dialect."

Sam had warned her on ship, but Repnik's unwelcoming attitude still stung. She did her best not to let it show, keeping her voice level. "A dialect? But it was my understanding Alnar ag Eshmaled couldn't be understood by the men."

"Ms. Donato, surely you are aware that speakers of different dialects often cannot understand each other."

She bit her lip. If she was going to have a hand in deciphering the women's language, she had to get along with him. Instead of arguing, she shrugged and gave Repnik a forced smile. "Well, as they say, a language is a dialect with an army and a navy. And that's not what we have here, is it?"

Repnik nodded. "Precisely."

Jackson Gates, the team exobiologist, moved between them and introduced himself, earning Toni's gratitude. He was a soft-spoken, dark-skinned man with graying hair and beard, obviously the type who cared little about cosmetic age treatments. She judged his age at barely over fifty.

Lanrhel then introduced her to the other members of the Edaru council. The oldest woman, Anash, came forward and presented Toni with a strip of decorative lace, similar to the beautiful hangings on the walls. Toni lifted the back of her hand to her forehead again and thanked her.

The multitude of introductions completed, they sat down on the leather-covered chairs and couches, and Ainsworth asked in barely passable Mejan if anything had been decided regarding treaty negotiations with AIC. Lanrhel looked at Toni, and she repeated the request, adding the correct inclinations and stripping it of the captain's Anglicized word order. Why hadn't the councillor referred to Repnik? She'd been studying like a fiend for the last month, but surely his command of the language was better than hers.

Lanrhel leaned across the arm of his chair and murmured something to Anash. Toni caught mention of the treaty again, and the words for language, house, and her own name. Anash looked across the circle at her and smiled. She returned the smile, despite the headache she could feel coming on. The first day on a new planet was always difficult, and this time she'd had conflict brewing with her boss even before she got off the shuttle. But next to Anash, another woman had pulled out her crocheting (a far cry from the stiff formality of the official functions she'd had to endure on Admetos), a man with eyes the color of the sea on Christmas had joked with her, and she still had a sunset to look forward to.

And no one was going to toss her into the ocean just yet. She hoped.

From: Preliminary Report on Alnar ag Ledar, primary language of Christmas. Compiled 29.09.157 (local AIC *date) by Prof. Dr. Dr. Hartmut Repnik, h.c. Thaumos, Hino, Marat, and Polong, Allied Interstellar Research Association first contact team xenolinguist, Commander, Allied Interstellar Community Forces:*

> The language of the Mejan people of Christmas is purely oral with both inflecting and agglutinating characteristics. Tense information seems to be given exclusively in an inflected auxiliary which takes the place of helping verbs and modals while also providing information on the addressee of the sentence. Nouns are gendered, masculine and feminine, but with some interesting anomalies compared to known languages. Adjectives are non-existent. The descriptive function is fulfilled by verbs (e.g. jeraz, "the state of being green").

The arc of the rings lit up like lacework in the last rays of the setting sun, while the sky behind it showed through purple and orange and pink. Toni took a deep breath and blinked away the tears that had started in her eyes at the shock of beauty. Beside her, Sam was silent, too wise to disturb her enjoyment of the moment.

They were sitting on the veranda of the house AIRA had rented for her and any other women from the ship who had occasion to come planetside. Together they watched as the colors faded and the sky grew dark. The small moons accompanying the rings appeared, while the brilliant lace became a dark band, starting in the east and spreading up and over.

"Maybe that's why they seem to set such a high store by lace," Toni finally said when the spectacle was over.

Sam nodded. "I've thought of that too."

She took a sip of the tea, sweet and hot with a flavor that reminded her subtly of ginger, and leaned back in her chair, pulling her sweater tighter around her. The night grew cold quickly, even though it was early fall and Edaru was in the temperate zone.

"What have you learned about the role of women since you've been here?" Toni asked.

"Well, since they will only talk to the men of Edaru, it's a bit difficult finding out anything. But they don't live in harems, that's for sure."

"Harems" was Repnik's term for the houses of women, although they could come and go as they pleased and the houses were off-limits for men completely, as far as the first contact team could determine.

She laughed, briefly and without humor. "I wonder what bit him."

Sam was quiet so long, she turned to look at him. In the flickering light of the oil lamp, his face was shadowed, his expression thoughtful. They had a generator and solar batteries for electricity in Contact House One and Two, but they tried to keep use of their own technology to a minimum.

"I don't think he ever had a life," Sam finally said. "Most people are retired by the time they reach 100. But look at Repnik – what would he retire to? His reputation spans the known universe, but it's all he's got. There's no prestige in hanging out on a vacation planet, and I doubt if he knows how to have fun."

His generous interpretation of Repnik's behavior made her feel vaguely guilty. "True. But I still get the feeling he's got something against women."

"Could be. I heard he went through a messy divorce a few years back – his ex-wife was spreading nasty rumors about him. I'm glad I'm not the woman working under him."

"Bad choice of words, Sam."

He smiled. "Guilty as charged."

Mejan "music" from a house down the hill drifted up to them, an odd swooshing sound without melody which reminded Toni of nothing so much as the water lapping the shore. Some native insects punctuated the rhythm with a "zish-zish, zish-zish" percussion, but there were no evening bird sounds. According to Jackson Gates, the only native life forms of the planet were aquatic, amphibian, reptilian or arthropod. There were no flying creatures on Christmas at all – and thus no word for "fly" in the Mejan language. Since the arrival of the xenoteam, the term "elugay velazh naished" ("move in the air") had come into use.

It was impossible for contact to leave a culture the way it was before. Leaving native culture untouched was an article of belief with AIRA, but it was also a myth.

Toni finished her tea and put down her mug. "It's occurred to me that Repnik's being led astray by the fact that Christmas is a seeded planet. Most of the other languages he worked on were of non-human species."

"Led astray how?"

"Well, when they look so much like us, you expect them to *be* like us too. Language, social structures, the whole bit."

"It's a possibility. Just don't tell him that."

"I'll try. But I have a problem with authority, especially when it's wrong."

Sam chuckled. "I don't think Repnik is serious about the harems, though. It's just his idea of a joke."

"Yeah, but there are also some odd things about the language which don't seem to go along with his analysis. Grammatical gender for example. Repnik refers to them as masculine and feminine, but they don't match up with biological sex at all. If he's right, then 'pirate' and even 'warrior' are both feminine nouns."

"I don't have any problem with that."

Toni pursed her lips, pretending to be offended. "But *I* do."

"I probably get them wrong all the time anyway."

"Don't you use your AI?" Like herself, Sam had a wrist unit. AI implants had been restricted decades ago because they led to such a high percentage of personality disorders.

He shrugged. "I don't always remember to consult it. Usually only when I don't know a word."

"And there's no guarantee the word will be in the dictionary yet or even that the AI will give you the right word for the context if it is."

"Exactly."

Toni gazed out at the night sky. Stars flickered above the horizon, but where the rings had been, the sky was black except for the shepherd moons. Below, the bay of Edaru was calm, the houses nestled close to the water, windows now lit by candlelight or oil lamps. She wondered where the green-eyed driver was, wondered what the Mejan executed people for, wondered if she would get a chance to work on the women's language.

She repressed the temptation to sigh and got up. "Come on, I'll walk you back to the contact house. I need to talk to Ainsworth before he returns to the ship."

The legend of the little lace-maker
Recorded 30.09.157 (local AIC date) by Landra Saleh, sociologist, first contact team, SGR 132-3 (Christmas / Kailazh).

As long as she could remember, Zhaykair had only one dream – to become the greatest maker of lace the Mejan had ever known. All young girls are taught the basics of crocheting, but Zhaykair would not stop at that. She begged the women of her village to show her their techniques with knots, the patterns they created, and she quickly found the most talented lace-maker among them. Saymel did not belong to Zhaykair's house, but the families reached an agreement, and the little girl was allowed to learn from Saymel, although the job of Zhaykair's house was raising cattle.

But before she had seen nine summers (*note: approximately thirteen standard years — L.S.*), Zhaykair had learned all Saymel had to teach her. She begged her clan to allow her to go to the city of Edaru, where the greatest lace-makers of the Mejan lived. Her mothers and fathers did not want to send her away, but Saymel, who could best judge the talent of the young girl, persuaded them to inquire if the house of Mihkal would be willing to train her.

The elders sent a messenger to the Mihkal with samples of Zhaykair's work. They had feared being ridiculed for their presumption, but the messenger returned with an elder of the house of Mihkal to personally escort Zhaykair to the great city of Edaru.

Zhaykair soon learned all the Mihkal clan could teach her. Her lace was in such great demand, and there were so many who wanted to learn from her that she could soon found her own house. Her works now grace the walls of all the greatest families of the Mejan.

"If Repnik refuses to allow you to work on the women's language, I'm not sure what I can do to help," Ainsworth said.

"Then why did you send for me?" She hardly felt the cool night air against her skin as their open carriage headed for the AIC landing base. If she hadn't returned to the contact house with Sam, she would have missed Ainsworth completely. A deliberate move, she suspected now.

"I thought I could bring him around."

"Can't you order him?"

"I don't think that would be wise. With a little diplomacy, you can still persuade him. In the long run he will have to see that he needs you to collect more data."

Toni rubbed her temples. The headache she'd first felt coming on during the introductions in the common house had returned with a vengeance. "He'll probably try to use remote probes."

"He already has. But since none of us are allowed in the women's houses, they can't be placed properly. We've tried three close to entrances and have lost them all."

"What happened to them?"

"One was painted over, one was stepped on and one was swept from a windowsill and ended in the trash."

They pulled up next to the temporary landing base, and the light from the stars and the moons was replaced by aggressive artificial light. Ainsworth patted her knee in a grandfatherly way. "Chin up, Donato. Do your work and do it well, and Repnik will recognize that you can be of use to him. We'll get the women's language deciphered and you will be a part of it. That's what you want, isn't it?"

"Yes." Maybe everyone was right and she was just overreacting to Repnik's reluctance to let her work on the women's language. It was certainly nothing new for AIRA researchers to feel threatened by others working in the same field and be jealously defensive of their own area of expertise. Toni had seen it before, but that didn't mean she had to like it. Her first day on Christmas was not ending well. At least she'd had the sunset.

The captain got out of the carriage and waved at her as the driver turned it around and headed back into town.

When they were nearing the city again, Toni leaned forward, propping her arms on the leather-covered seat in front of her. The driver was the same one they'd had this morning. Strange that she'd been so fixated on Ainsworth and her own problems that she hadn't even noticed.

He glanced over his shoulder at her and smiled but said nothing.

Toni took the initiative. "Sha bo sham."

"Sha bo sham, tajan." The planes of his face were a mosaic of shadow and moonlight, beautiful and unfamiliar.

"Ona esh eden bonshani Toni rezh tajan, al?" *Me you call Toni not mother, yes?*

He laughed and shook his head in the gesture of affirmative, like a nod in Toni's native culture. "Bonlami desh an. Tay esh am eladesh bonshani Kislan." *Honored am I. And you me will call Kislan.*

She smiled and offered her hand as she would have in her own culture. He transferred the reins to one hand, then took her own hand gently and pressed it to his forehead. His skin was warm and dry. She couldn't see his smoky green eyes in the starlight, but she could imagine them. When he released her hand, she could have sworn it was with reluctance.

Perhaps the day was not ending so badly after all.

The women of Anash's family, the house of Ishel, were gentle but determined — they would not allow Toni to learn Alnar ag Eshmaled, "the language of the house," from them until she promised not to teach it to any men. Which of course was impossible. The point of research funded by AIRA was for it to be published and made accessible to everyone in the known galaxy. You couldn't restrict access to data on the basis of sex. On the basis of security clearance perhaps, but not on the basis of sex.

"Bodesh fadani eshukan alnar ag eshmaled," Anash said, her expression sympathetic. *No man may speak the language of the house.* Permission-particle-tense-marker-present-female addressee verb negative-marker-subject object: with the mind of a linguist, Toni broke down the parts of the sentence, trying to see if the women favored different sentence structures than the men.

So they weren't going to speak their language with her. She had spent her first two days setting up house and getting her bearings, and now that she finally had an appointment with some of the women of the planet, she learned that Repnik was right — she wouldn't be able to do the job she had come here to do. But at least they had welcomed her into the women's house and were less careful with her than with the men of the contact team. With the camera in her AI, she had recorded Anash and Thuyene speaking in their own language several times. She felt a little bad about the duplicity – she'd never had to learn a language by stealth before – but if she was going to do the job she came here to do, she didn't have a choice. And when it came right down to it, AIRA never asked anyone's permission to send out the probes used in the first stages of deciphering a new language. Stealth always played a role.

But what a dilemma. AIRA was required to make their knowledge of new worlds public. Not to mention Toni would only be able to make her reputation as a xenolinguist if she could publish the results of her research. Perhaps they could work something out with AIRA that would make it possible for her to study the women's language.

"May I still visit this house?" Toni asked in the men's language.

Anash smiled. "We are happy to welcome the woman from the sky. And perhaps you can teach us the language you speak as the men of the sky teach the men of the people."

"Why is it that you will speak with the men of Edaru and not with the men of the first contact team?"

The smile vanished from Anash's face. "They are offensive." In the Mejan language it was more like "exhibit a state of offensiveness," a verb used for descriptive purposes, but it was nonetheless different from the verb "to offend," which connoted an individual action.

"What have they done?" Toni asked.

The older woman's face seemed to close up. "They speak before they are spoken to."

Was that all it was? The men of the contact team had offended the Mejan sense of propriety? "So men of a strange house may not speak to a woman without permission?"

"They may not. That intimacy is only granted within families."

How simple it was after all: someone had merely made the mistake of not asking the right questions. She had read stories of contact teams which had suffered misunderstandings from just such a mistake. But how were you supposed to know which questions to ask when dealing with an alien culture? It was no wonder the mistake had been made over and over again.

And their team had the excuse of having lost their sociologist after less than a week.

Toni rose and lifted the back of her hand to her forehead. "I will come again tomorrow at the same time if that is convenient."

"I will send word."

Toni started to nod and then caught herself and shook her head. Visiting a new world was exhausting business.

DG: *sci.lang.xeno.talk*
Subject: We aren't redundant yet (was Why I do what I do)
From: A.Donato@aira.org
Local AIC *date: 21.10.157*

<insultingly uninformed garbage snipped>

Okay, I'll explain it again, even though I've been through this so many times on the DGs it makes my head spin.

No, we can't just analyze a couple of vids made by a drone and come up with a language. Even with all the sophisticated equipment for recording and analysis which we now possess, at some stage in deciphering an alien tongue we're still dependent on the old point and repeat method. The human element of interaction, of trial and error, remains a necessary part of xenolinguistics. IMNSHO, the main reason for this is that analyzing an alien language, figuring out the parts of speech and the rules at work (which is the really tough part, and not simple vocabulary), is more than just "deciphering" — a very unfortunate word choice, when it comes right down to it. "Deciphering" implies that language is like a code, that there is a one-to-one correspondence between words, a myth which supports the illusion that all you have to do is substitute one word for another to come up with meaning. Language imperialists are the worst sinners in this respect, folks with a native tongue with pretensions towards being a diplomatic language, like English, French or Xtoylegh.

People who have never learned a foreign language, who have always relied on the translation modules in their AIs to do a less-than-perfect job for them, often can't conceive how difficult this "deciphering" can be, with no dictionaries and no grammar books. An element you think at first is an indefinite article could very well be a case or time marking. You have no idea where the declensions go, no idea if the subject of the verb comes first or last or perhaps in the middle of the verb itself.

No linguistics AI ever built has been idiosyncratic enough to deal satisfactorily with the illogical aspects of language. Data analysis can tell you how often an element repeats itself and in which context, it can make educated guesses about what a particular linguistic element *might* mean, but the breakthroughs come from intuition and hunches.

AIs have been able to pass the Turing test for two centuries now, but they still can't pass the test of an unknown language.

As she left the women's house, Kislan was coming down the street in the direction of the docks.

"Sha bo sham, Kislan."

"Sha bo sham, Toni." He pronounced her name with a big grin and a curious emphasis on the second syllable. After three days planetside, she was beginning to see him with different eyes. She recognized now that the colors braided into his hair signified that by birth he was a member of the same family as Councillor Lanrhel himself and he had "married" into the house of Ishel, one of the most important merchant clans in the city of Edaru. It seemed the council of Edaru had sent a very distinguished young man as transportation for their guests.

And he was part of some kind of big communal marriage.

"Where are you off to?" she asked.

"The offices of Ishel near the wharves. A ship has returned after an attack by pirates and we must assess the damage."

"Are pirates a problem around here?"

Kislan shook his head in the affirmative. "It is especially bad in the east."

They stood in the street awkwardly for a moment, and then Kislan asked, "Where do you go now? May I walk with you?"

"Don't you have to get to work?"

He shrugged. That at least was the same gesture she was used to. "There is always time for conversation and company."

Toni grinned. "I'm on my way back to the contact house."

Kislan turned around and fell into step next to her. She asked him about his work and he asked her about hers, and it occurred to her how odd it was that this particular social interaction was so much like what she had grown up with and seen on four planets now.

Talking and laughing, they arrived at the contact house in much less subjective time than it had taken Toni to get to the house of Anash – and it was uphill. She watched Kislan stride back down to the wharves, starting to worry about her own peace of mind.

But when she entered the main office of the contact house, she had other things to worry about.

"I hope you will remember to remain professional, Donato," Repnik said.

Toni resisted the urge to retort sharply and sat down on the edge of a table. There were no AIRA regulations forbidding personnel from taking a walk with one of the natives – or even sleeping with one, as long as the laws of the planet were not broken. "Kislan was telling me about how they lost a ship to pirates. What do we know about these pirates?"

"Not much," Sam said. "Ainsworth wants to do some additional surveillance of the eastern coast."

"How did your meeting with Anash go?" Repnik asked.

She took a deep breath. "They won't speak their language with me until I promise no men will ever learn it."

Repnik shrugged. "I told you your presence here was unnecessary."

Didn't he even have any intellectual curiosity left, any desire to figure out the puzzle? Whether he resented her presence or not, if he still had a scientific bone left in his body he would be taking advantage of having her here.

She stood and began to pace. "Wouldn't it be possible to work out a deal with AIRA? Something that would allow us to reach an agreement with the women on their language? If Alnar ag Eshmaled had a special status, then only certain researchers would have access to the information."

"You mean, *women* researchers."

Toni stopped pacing. "Well, yes."

"Which would mean I, the head of this contact team, would be barred from working on the women's language."

She barely registered the minor victory of Repnik now referring to Alnar ag Eshmaled as a language. She had painted herself into a very hazardous corner. "I was only thinking of how we could keep from offending the women."

"And how you could get all the credit for our findings."

"I didn't—"

Repnik stepped in front of her, his arms crossed in front of his chest. "I would suggest that you try to remember that you're an assistant here."

Toni didn't answer for a moment. Unfortunately, that *wasn't* the way she remembered the description of her assignment to Christmas. But it had named her "second" team xenolinguist. Which meant if Repnik saw her as an assistant, she was an assistant. "Yes, sir. Anything else?"

"Tomorrow morning I would like you to work on compiling a more extensive dictionary with the material we have collected in the last several weeks."

"Certainly, sir."

She picked her bag up off the floor and left Contact House One for the peace and safety of Contact House Two before she could say anything else she would regret. How could she have been so stupid? In terms of her career, it would have been smarter to suggest using her visits to install surveillance devices, even if that would have been questionable within the framework of AIRA regulations. But of course Repnik would never agree to a strategy that would leave her to work on one of the languages of Kailazh exclusively.

When would she learn?

Toni pushed open the door of her house, slipped off her jacket and hung it over the back of a chair. Well, she was not about to break the laws of her host planet, Repnik or no Repnik, so before she hooked her mobile AI into her desk console, she set up a firewall to keep the men on the team from learning the women's language by accessing her notes.

Once her privacy was established, she told the unit to replay the women's conversation, and the sounds of their voices echoed through the small house while she got herself something to eat.

"Index mark one," she said after the first short conversation was over, and her system skipped ahead to the next conversation. The first thing she noticed was that the women's language had some rounded vowel sounds which were absent in the men's, something like the German umlaut or the Scandinavian "ø." There were a couple of words which sounded familiar, however.

She finished the bread and cheese and tea and wiped her mouth on a napkin. "System, print a transcript of the replayed conversations using the spelling system developed by Repnik, and run a comparison with the material already collected on the men's language."

"Any desired emphasis?"

"Possible cognates, parallel grammatical structures, inflections."

While the computer worked, she laid out the printed sheet of paper in front of her on the desk. Sometimes she found it easier to work in hard copy than with a projection or on a screen. Doodling with a pencil or pen on paper between the lines could help her to see new connections, possibilities too far-fetched for the computer to take into consideration – but exactly what was needed for dealing with an arbitrary, illogical human system like language.

The transcript was little more than a jumble of letters. Before the initial analysis, the computer only added spaces at very obvious pauses between phonemes. Pencil in hand, Toni gazed at the first two lines, the hodgepodge of consonants and vowels.

Tün shudithunföslodi larasethal segumshuyethunrhünem kasemalandaryk.

Athneshalathun rhün semehfarkari zhamdentakh.

The last recognized unit of meaning looked like a plural. Plural was formed in the men's language by adding the prefix "zham-" to the noun, and there was no telling if those particular sounds were the same in the women's language, or even if the plural was built the same, but it at least gave her a place to start.

There was a faint warning beep and the computer announced in its business-like male voice, "Initial analysis complete."

Toni looked up. "Give me the possible cognates. Output, screen." A series of pairs of words replaced an image of the landscape of Neubrandenburg.

Dentakh – tendag.

But why would the women be discussing pirates in the middle of a conversation about languages?

When she had gotten home, Toni had felt another stress headache coming on, but now it had disappeared completely and without drugs. She had a puzzle to solve.

"Print out the results of the analysis," she said, pulling her chair closer to the table holding the console.

She went to work with a smile.

From: Preliminary Report on Alnar ag Eshmaled, secondary language of Kailazh (Christmas). Compiled 28.11.157 (local AIC *date) by Dr. Antonia Donato, second xenolinguist, Allied Interstellar Research Association first contact team. (Draft)*

> The men's and women's languages of Kailazh (Christmas) are obviously related. While this does not completely rule out an artificially constructed secret language, as has been observed in various cultures among classes wanting to maintain independence from a ruling class, the consistency in the pho-

netic differences between the cognates thus discovered seems to indicate a natural linguistic development. A further argument against a constructed language could be seen in sounds used in the women's language which are nonexistent in the men's language.

Interestingly enough, the women's language appears to have the more formal grammar of the two, with at least two additional cases for articles (dative and genitive?), as well as a third form for the second person singular, all of which are unknown in Alnar ag Ledar. To confirm this, however, much more material will need to be collected.

She'd had approximately three hours of sleep when her mobile unit buzzed the next morning. She burrowed out from under the pile of blankets and switched on audio. She didn't want anyone seeing her just yet.

"Yes?" she said and snuggled back into her warm nest of covers.

Repnik's voice drifted over to her and she grimaced. "Donato, do you realize what time it is?"

"No. I still don't have the display set up," she replied, trying to keep the sleep out of her voice. "And I must have forgotten to set my unit to wake me last night. Sorry."

An impatient "hmpf" came from her system. "Jump lag or no jump lag, I'd like you over here now."

The connection ended abruptly and Toni pushed the covers back and got up, rubbing her eyes. Nights were simply too short on Christmas, especially when you didn't go to bed until the sun started to come up.

Leather togs on and coffee down, she was soon back at Contact House One, keying in and correcting terms in the preliminary version of the dictionary. After giving her his instructions, Repnik had left with Sam for a tour of the tannery outside of town, where they would ask questions and collect data and make discoveries. Like usual, Gates and Moshofski were already out looking at boulders and bushes and beasts.

While she was left with drudgery.

It was funny how something she had done regularly for the last five years now seemed much more tedious than it ever had before. Toni loved words enough that even constructing the necessary databases had always held a certain fascination. Besides, it was a means to an end, a preliminary step on the ladder to becoming a first contact xenolinguist working on her own language.

Now it was a step down.

She spent the morning checking and correcting new dictionary entries automatic analysis had made, consulting the central AI on her decisions, and creating links to grammatical variations and audio and visual files, where available. And all that on only three hours of sleep.

"Fashar," the computer announced. "Lace, the lace. Feminine. Irregular noun. Indefinite form fasharu."

Toni did a search for "rodela," another word for lace in the Mejan language, and then added links between the words. Under the entry "fashar," she keyed in, "See also 'rodela' (lace) and 'rodeli' (to create lace or crochet)." She would have to ask Anash if there was a difference between "rodela" and "fashar" – as yet, nothing was noted in their materials.

Outside the door of the lab, she heard the sound of voices, Sam and Repnik returning from field work. Having fun.

"Fashela," the computer announced. "Celebrate. Verb, regular."

"That's the attitude," Toni muttered.

The door opened, and Repnik entered, followed by Sam, who looked a little sheepish. Getting chummy with the top of the totem pole.

Repnik sauntered over to her desk. "How is our dictionary coming along?" he asked in that perky voice bosses had when they were happy in the knowledge that they were surrounded by slaves.

"I'm up to the 'f's now in checking entries and adding cross references. Our material is a little thin on specific definitions, though."

The faint smile on his face thinned out and disappeared. He looked offended, but Toni had only been pointing out a minor weakness, common in early linguistic analysis of new languages. Man, was he touchy. She would have to tread carefully. "I've been tagging synonyms where we don't have any information on the kinds of situations where one word or the other would be more appropriate. Would you like to ask the Mejan about them or should I?"

"Make a note of it," Repnik said shortly.

"Certainly, sir."

"I have another meeting with Councillor Lanrhel. I'll see you both again tomorrow."

"But —"

"Tomorrow, Donato."

When he was gone, Toni joined Sam next to the small holo well they had set up in the lab, where he was viewing a scene of what looked like a festival.

"I learned something the other day in the women's house that you might find interesting."

"Bookmark and quit," Sam said to the holo projector before facing her. "That's right, I wanted to ask you about that, but you left pretty abruptly yesterday."

Toni pulled over a chair and straddled it, leaning her forearms on the back. "I know. I should have stuck around. Maybe I'm overreacting, but I'm starting to get the feeling Repnik wants to make me quit."

Sam shook his head. "You *are* overreacting. Your suggestion yesterday, logical as it was, was practically calculated to make him feel threatened. Just give him some time to get used to you."

"I'll try."

"So, what did you find out?"

Toni chuckled. "Right. Anash told me yesterday that there's no specific taboo on women speaking with strange men. The reason they won't speak with the men of our team is because they offend them by speaking before they are spoken to."

Sam's eyes lit up. "Really?"

She nodded. "Do you know if you're guilty of offensive behavior yet?"

"I don't think so. When I got here, Repnik told me there was a taboo against strangers speaking with Mejan women *at all*, so I didn't even try. Wow. This changes everything."

"Yup. I wanted to get together with Anash and Thuyene again this afternoon. I could ask then if we could meet outside of the women's house sometime and you could join us."

"Maybe you should find out first how I *am* supposed to conduct myself."

"The young one with the hair of night and eyes like a *likish?*" Anash asked. A likish was one of the native amphibian creatures of Kailazh, with both legs and fins and a nostril/gill arrangement on its back which reminded Toni vaguely of whales. She had yet to see a likish, but she had seen pictures, and she could appreciate the simile. Not having adjectives, Alnar ag Ledar could be quite colorful if the speaker chose some other way to describe something than using the attribute verbs.

"*Al*," Toni said. Yes.

Anash gazed at her with a speculative expression — or at least what looked like one to Toni. Her eyes were slightly narrowed, her head tilted to one side, and her lips one step away from being pursed. "That one has not himself offended any of the women of Edaru," the older woman finally said. "You say he is a specialist in understanding the ways of a people?"

"Yes. He has replaced Landra Saleh, who I believe you met before she became ill."

"Then we will meet with him two days from now in the common house."

That would mean she'd have to give up her surreptitious recordings in the women's house for the day, but helping Sam would be worth it. She felt as if she had given him a present, he was so happy when she told him.

The day of their appointment, they walked together down the hill to the center of town, Toni sporting a new leather cape she had purchased for a couple of ingots of iron from the string she wore around her neck. Iron was much more precious on Kailazh than gold. She examined the stands they passed. Most of the vendors they saw were men, but occasionally a lone woman sat next to the bins of fruits and vegetables or the shelves of polished plates and bowls made from the shells of oversized bugs. Such a female vendor would have to deal with male customers alone, some of whom would necessarily be strangers. Perhaps now that they had started asking the right questions, they could learn something more of the rules governing intersexual relations.

"From what you've learned since you arrived, do you know when one of those ceremonial gifts of lace is appropriate?" she asked, trying to act naturally, but still feeling like a circus animal. People peered out of their windows at them as they passed, and children ran up to them, giggling and staring, or hid behind their mothers' or fathers' legs. It hadn't been any different on Admetos, but the beings there had looked like ants. These were people.

"No. But it seems to be something only given by women. We aren't on sure enough ground yet to start messing with symbolic gestures."

Toni gave a playful snort of disgust. "You've already been here two weeks. What have you been doing in all that time?"

Sam chuckled. "I may not trust myself with symbols, but we could certainly bring Anash a bottle of that lovely dessert wine that Edaru is famous for. Have you tried it yet?"

"I'm still trying to stick mostly to foods I'm familiar with. I don't want to end up offworld like your predecessor."

"Well, once you get daring, take my word for it, it's an experience you don't want to miss. And according to Jackson, the fruit *kithiu* which they use to make *denzhar* is descended from plain old Terran grapes."

"Okay, you've convinced me. Where's the nearest wine dealer?"

The merchant was a man, so Toni didn't have a chance to see what the interaction would be between Sam and a female merchant. They paid with a small bead each from the strings of precious metals they wore around their necks, and arrived at the common house just as Kislan was helping Anash and Thuyene out of an open carriage. To her surprise, Toni felt a pang resembling jealousy. These two women both belonged to Kislan's family, and while Anash was probably old enough to be his mother, Thuyene wasn't much more than Toni's age; probably less biologically on this world without age treatments. Her glossy reddish-brown hair hung in a single thick braid to her waist, laced with the colors of her birth clan and her chosen clan. Her amber eyes were full of life and intelligence. And Kislan was in some kind of group marriage arrangement with her. Did he hold her hand a little longer than Anash's? Or was her feverish, human-male-deprived imagination just taking her for a ride?

Anash waved. Toni gave herself an inner shake and returned the gesture.

"I'm glad you didn't have to wait," Anash said. "I was afraid business went long." She looked at Sam curiously, but he said nothing, just lifting the back of his hand to his forehead in the gesture of greeting. Kislan said something rapidly to the women of his family in a low voice that Toni couldn't understand. She looked away, hoping her face wasn't as flushed as she felt.

The room Anash led them to in the common house was smaller than the one where they had met on Toni's arrival, a comfortable, sunny room with large windows facing a central courtyard and lace hangings decorating the walls.

"Samuel Wu has brought you a gift in hopes that relations between you may begin in a spirit of harmony and trust," Toni said as they took seats on upholstered brocade sofas. This was the first time she had seen furniture covered in anything besides leather, and she wondered if this room was usually reserved for special occasions.

Kislan sat down beside her, and Toni felt her pulse pick up and her cheeks grow hot.

Anash addressed Sam directly. "Sha bo sham, Samuel. We thank you, both for the thought and the respect that goes with it. We will be happy to tell you of Mejan ways and are curious to hear about the ways of the stars."

Sam got the bottle of denzhar out of his bag while Toni checked the AI at her wrist to make sure she had set it for record mode. Across from her, Thuyene pulled a crocheting project out of her own bag, and Toni suppressed a smile.

"Sha bo sham, tajan," Sam said, leaning across and presenting the wine to Anash. "I am honored to be able to speak with you and hope that the gift is welcome."

They had chosen well. A pleased smile touched Anash's lips as she accepted the bottle, and Toni almost sighed in relief.

Sam began by asking about the specific rules governing interaction between men and women and learned that other than the disrespect shown if a man not of a woman's family spoke before being spoken to, there was a whole battery of taboos concerning what was appropriate when and with whom and at what age. It reminded Toni vaguely of what she had read of Victorian England – except for the group marriages, of course. They never got to the topic of sex proper, however; Sam was obviously doing his best to tread carefully, and open discussion of sexual practices was taboo in the majority of cultures in the galaxy.

"Boys move into the house of men when they are weaned, correct?" Sam asked.

Anash shook her head. Toni felt the heat from Kislan's body next to her.

"Is there any kind of ritual associated with the move?"

"To leave the mother is to leave the sea, so there is a celebration on the beach called *mairheltan*."

Kislan spoke up. "It is the first memory I have, the *mairheltan*."

"And the ritual?" Sam asked.

"The boy who is to leave the house of women goes into the water with the mother and comes back out by himself," Thuyene said. "Then there is a feast with fish and dashik, and the child receives a leather cape and a length of lace."

She used the term "roda ag *fashar*" not "rodel" when she spoke of lace. Toni remembered the dictionary entries she'd been working on and couldn't help asking an off-topic question. "What exactly is the difference between 'fashar' and 'rodel'?"

Thuyene lifted up the crocheting she was working on. "This is 'rodela.'" She pointed to a wall hanging just past Kislan's shoulder. "This is 'fashar.'"

It was all lace to Toni, but she was beginning to see the difference. "So 'fashar' is the piece when it is finished?"

"Not always. The 'fashar' given to a boy when he joins the house of men only begins. The women of his house can add to the 'fashar' he is given as a boy."

Toni would have liked to ask more, but Sam was already asking another question himself. "If a boy has already begun to talk before he leaves the house of women, how is it he doesn't learn to speak the women's language?"

Anash chuckled. "His mother corrects him if he speaks the language that is wrong."

Sam laughed and looked at Kislan, who smiled and shrugged. Toni could see how that would be a very effective method.

The meeting continued until the light through the windows began to grow dim, and ended with a promise to show Sam around town the next day to see some of the places where women worked in Edaru. Anash couldn't accompany him herself, but she would see to it that one of the women of her house met him tomorrow morning at the Mejan equivalent of a café in the main square. Of course, he still was not allowed to visit any of the houses of women, but his enthusiasm at the sudden progress in his research was obvious in his voice and posture.

Toni had learned quite a bit herself that afternoon. It was surprising what you could discover if you only knew which questions to ask. Anash and Thuyene had been astonished at some of the things they told them about their native cultures as well, in particular the institution of marriage, which they only seemed to be able to understand in terms of property, of one partner "belonging" to the other.

She had done her best to suppress her awareness of Kislan beside her, but the discussion of different forms of partnership had unfortunately had quite the opposite effect. As a human male of Kailazh, he was both familiar and exotic at the same time. All the senses in her body were screaming "potential partner" for some illogical and primordial reason, and she had the uncomfortable sensation that Kislan was aware of her in a similar way. He hadn't spoken much, and neither had she. Instead, they had sat there, the lovely view of the red fern and coral-like vegetation visible through the window across from them.

On one level, Toni was relieved when Anash called an end to the meeting. On another, she wished she could continue to sit there and talk for hours, learn more about social arrangements on Christmas, find out how the Mejan viewed their own history. And on the primal level, she was humming. Feeling that kind of physical attraction again after so long, almost knee to knee and elbow to elbow, was mind- and body-racking.

She barely looked at Kislan as they took their leave, mentally kicking herself for the way she was responding to his physical presence.

"Their reaction to marriage forms in Terran culture was interesting, don't you think?" Sam said when they were out of earshot of the common house.

"You mean in terms of property?" Toni asked.

"Exactly. I wish we could find out more about their history. It makes me wonder if slavery might not be too far removed in the Mejan consciousness. Oh, and thank you."

"What for?"

Sam smiled that slow smile she had learned to like so much from the vids they had sent each other. "For giving me a crack at half a society."

The Legend of the Three Moons

Once, in the early days of the Mejan, after the Great War, there was a very attractive young man, more handsome than any other in all of the thirteen cities. When he came of age, Zhaykair, mother of the house of Sheli, asked if he would join their family, and he came willingly. The house had a good reputation for the fine lace it produced, and the women of the house were beautiful, their necks long, their shoulders wide, and their skin glossy.

A sister of the house looked on the man with desire and wished to have him for herself alone. The husband saw her beauty, her hair the color of night and her eyes like a dashik flower, and he swore to do anything for her; she made his blood run hotter than any woman he had ever seen. The sister went mad at the thought of him lying with other women, and she made him promise he would resist all others for her sake.

Zhaykair saw what her sister was doing and how it poisoned the atmosphere in the house. She went to the councillor to ask what he thought should be done with the young man.

"We will bring them before us and ask them what is more important, the peace of the house or their love."

So the sister and the husband were brought before the council. The mother gazed at the sister with sadness and said, "I cannot believe that you would disturb the peace of the house this way."

The sister began to cry. The husband jumped up, his hand raised against Zhaykair. When the sister saw what he intended to do, she threw herself upon him, but not before he had struck the mother.

By law, the husband had to be given back to the sea for striking a mother. The sister refused to let him go alone, and they returned to the sea together.

Zhaykair could not bear the thought of what had happened in her house and the sister's betrayal, and she followed them soon after. The sea in her wisdom wanted to make a lesson of them and gave the three lovers to the sky.

And now the sister, who never wanted to share the young man with another, must share him with Zhaykair every night. Sometimes it is the sister who is closer and sometimes the mother, but only for a short time does the sister ever have him to herself.

The next day, Toni met with the women on their own turf again. She was shown into the cental courtyard by a beautiful young woman wearing the colors of Ishel and Railiu in the thin dark braids scattered through her heavy hair. The air was crisp and the sun bright, and they wandered among the houses, Anash and Thuyene pointing out more of the complex. The first contact team referred to the residences of the families of Edaru as "houses" for the sake of simplicity – in actuality, they consisted of several buildings, with the young girls living in one, the mothers of the youngest children with their babies and toddlers in another, and the grown women with no children below the age of about three standard years in a third. There was also a smaller version of the Edaru common house, with a family refectory and rooms where all could gather and talk, play games, tell stories. Perhaps superficially the setup did resemble a harem, but it obviously wasn't one.

"I hope you did not lose much in the pirate attack," Toni said during a lull in the conversation.

Anash looked grim. "Too much."

"This is the second ship attacked this summer," Thuyene added.

Suddenly, Toni realized how she might be able to get the Mejan to agree to the AIC treaty. Anash was obviously one of Lanrhel's main advisors, and he would listen to what she had to say. "So you also have a problem with pirates," she said casually.

"Why do you say 'also'?" Anash asked.

"There are many pirates among the stars too. That is the purpose of the Allied Interstellar Community – to form a common defense against the pirates of the sky."

Of course, that wasn't the only purpose: interstellar trade and research were at least equally important, with the emphasis on the trade. But Toni doubted she could interest anyone on Kailazh in trade with distant points of light that figured prominently in stories told in the evening to pass the time.

"But why should we fear them?" Thuyene asked. "We do not travel the stars, so they cannot attack the ships of the people."

"It's not that easy," Toni said, suppressing thoughts of how the other woman might be spending her nights in the Ishel main house with Kislan. "They might come here."

Anash started. "Attack Edaru? From the sky?"

"Certainly from the sky."

In their surprise, they didn't think to lower their voices when they turned to each other, and Toni was able to capture a rapid but lengthy conversation on her wrist unit.

Finally they turned back to her. "How can that be?"

"As soon as this world was discovered, the news of another culture was known to all the worlds with access to the network of the community of the stars." But, of course, the word she used in the Mejan language wasn't actually "network": the term the first contact team used to approximate the interstellar exchange of information referred to the trade of professional couriers who traveled between the thirteen cities, dispensing messages and news.

"I see," Anash said. "And in this way, we become a part of this community before we even give permission." She used some kind of qualifier for "permission" which Toni was unfamiliar with, but she didn't deem it the right time to ask what it meant. Anash lifted the back of her hand to her forehead, and Toni's heart sank — she was being dismissed.

"Thuyene will see you out of the house," Anash said and turned on her heel.

Together they watched her stride back to the central building. "You should have told us sooner," Thuyene said quietly.

"I didn't know it was so important."

"I believe you. There is much we still do not know about each other."

That was certainly true.

When she returned to Contact House One, she found Sam sitting tensely in his desk chair and Repnik standing next to him, his arms folded in front of his chest.

Repnik turned, not relaxing his defensive posture. The stress lines between his eyes were even more pronounced than usual and his face was pale. "I'm glad you've finally arrived, Donato. I hear you took Sam to meet with the women yesterday without my authorization."

Toni blinked. Sam didn't *need* Repnik's authorization. Certainly, Repnik had seniority, but the experts of a first contact team were free to pursue their research however they saw fit. *She*, by contrast, was only second linguist, so it was a bit more logical for Repnik to boss her around.

"Uh, yes."

"I won't have it. I've already told Sam that he is not to meet with the women again unless I arrange it."

Which meant never. The women refused to negotiate with Repnik, that much was clear.

She looked at Sam, his lips pressed together and misery in his eyes.

Toni at least didn't have much to lose. She could put her neck out where Sam obviously wasn't willing to. "But he's chief sociologist."

"And I'm head of the first contact team."

She couldn't believe it. Either he was so fixated on maintaining complete control of the mission that he had lost it – or there was something he didn't want them to find out. She looked him in the eye, her hands on her hips. "Maybe we should see what Ainsworth has to say about that. Computer, open a channel to the *Penthesilea*."

"Access denied."

"What?!"

"Access denied," the computer repeated, logical as always.

"Why?"

"Prof. Dr. Hartmut Repnik has restricted access to communications channels. I am no longer authorized to initiate off-site communications without his permission."

The completely mundane thought darted through Toni's mind that she would no longer be able to participate in the AIC discussion groups. As if that mattered right now.

"I don't want you visiting any of the houses of women without my approval, either," Repnik continued, addressing Toni.

"But we're here to learn about these people."

"And the two of you have been conducting unauthorized research. Now if you'll excuse me, I have AIRA business to attend to."

When Repnik was out of the door, Toni turned to Sam. "Unauthorized research?"

Sam shrugged, looking wretched.

Toni dropped into the chair next to him. "So, you still think I'm overreacting?"

Sam didn't respond to her attempt at a joke. "We're stuck, you know. He's going to tell Ainsworth some story about us now."

She propped her chin in her hand. "You must have done something to set him off. Can you think what it might be?"

He shook his head. "I just told him about the meeting with Anash and Thuyene yesterday."

"So he doesn't want either of us speaking directly with the women. But why?"

Sam shook his head, and Toni got up and began to pace. "Look, Sam, he can't get away with this. If Repnik really does contact Ainsworth about us with some fairy tale, then we'll also have our say, and it should be obvious that he's giving orders that hinder the mission."

"And what if he lies?"

"We have to tell Gates and Moshofski what's up."

"They won't be in until tonight."

They stared at each other in silence for a moment. "I think I need to take a walk."

Sam gave her a weak smile and waved her out the door. "Go. I'll hold down the fort."

Toni walked, long strides that ate up the stone-lined streets. She had devoted most of her adult life to AIRA, and she didn't know what she would do if they threw her out. Given the number of interstellar languages she could speak, there would always be jobs for her, but if she went into translating or interpreting, she would no longer be involved in the aspect of language she enjoyed most, the puzzle of an unknown quantity.

At least she wouldn't have to work with any more ants.

The weather was turning, appropriate to her mood, the gray-green sky heavy with the threat of rain. Toni made her way through narrow side streets to the sea wall at the south end of town. The green ocean below crashed against the wall, sending shots of spray up to the railing where she stood, and the wind tangled her hair around her face. She pulled her leather cape tighter around her body and gazed out to sea. The lacy rings of sunset probably would not be visible tonight, blocked out by the coming storm.

She heard a footstep behind her and turned. Kislan. He gazed at her with eyes that matched the sea, and she realized she had come out here close to the docks hoping they would run into each other.

He raised the back of his hand to his forehead and she returned the gesture. "Sha bo sham, Kislan."

"Sha bo sham, Toni."

Her name in his language sounded slower, more formal, less messy, the "o" rounded and full, the syllables distinct and clear. She wondered what "Antonia" would sound like on his lips. She'd never liked the name, but she thought she might if he said it.

"How do you greet a friend, someone you are close to?" Toni asked.

"Sha bo foda," he said. "Dum gozhung 'sha.'" *Or simply "sha."*

"Can we use 'fo' and 'foda' with each other?" she asked, offering her hand in the gesture of her homeworld.

He nodded, ignoring her hand. He didn't want to use the informal "you" form with her. He wouldn't take her hand anymore either, although he took Thuyene's when he was only leaving for an afternoon. But then, Thuyene was one of his wives, and she most certainly was not. She leaned her hip on the railing, gazing at the gray-green sea below the dark gray sky. There was no reason to feel hurt and every reason to feel relief. He was a part of the Ishel family, and she still didn't understand the way loyalty was regarded in these complex relationship webs. Not something to get messed up with.

Tears began to collect at the corners of her eyes and she wiped them away angrily. To her surprise, Kislan turned her to him and took her chin in one hand.

"Tell me," he said. The Mejan very rarely used the command form and there was something shocking about it. It startled Toni into more honesty than she had intended.

"This is all so difficult."

He shook his head slowly and she gave a humorless laugh. Then her intellectual knowledge managed to seep through her emotional reaction. He wasn't disagreeing with her.

She twisted her face out of his hand and turned around to grip the railing at the top of the sea wall. A pair of arms encased in soft leather came around her and a pair of hands with their strange, wonderful webbing settled on hers. "You don't understand. It is not allowed for us to speak so with each other."

His chest was wide and hard against her back, welcome and strong. She had the unrelated, illogical thought that he probably had the high lung capacity of most of the Mejan, and wondered how long he could stay underwater comfortably.

"Al," Toni said, *yes*, unsure what exactly she was saying "yes" to.

Then there were a pair of lips, soft and warm, against the back of her neck, and it was too late to consider anything. She was in way over her head, infatuated with a man who had about a dozen official lovers.

His arm moved around her shoulders and he steered her away from the railing along the sea wall, away from the city. "It hurts me to see you weep. I would keep you from being alone."

To their left, the stone walls were painted in bright colors, colors to make the heart glad, shades of yellow and red and sea green.

She pulled herself together and dried her cheeks with the back of her hand. "It's no good. We barely understand each other."

"You speak our language very well."

"It's more than that. Our ways differ so much, when you say one thing, I understand another. We can't help but see each other through the patterns we know from the cultures we grew up with. Like looking through lace — the view isn't clear, the patterns get in the way."

Kislan shook his head — affirmation, she reminded herself. "Yes, I see. But I would never hurt you, Toni."

"Ah, but you do. I know it's not deliberate, but just by being a man who lives by the rules of the Mejan, you hurt me."

He shook his head again. "It has to do with the relationship between men and women in the culture where you come from?"

"Yes." Toni didn't trust herself with gestures.

They had nearly reached the end of the sea wall, and there were no buildings here anymore. Kislan took her hand in his own webbed one.

"You would want to have me for yourself?" Kislan asked. "Like the sister in the legend of how the moons got into the sky?"

"It is the way things are done in the world I come from," Toni said defensively.

He smiled at her. "That is a story that lives in my heart."

She stopped, surprised. "I thought it was meant to show the People how not to behave, a lesson."

Kislan laughed out loud. "Have you no stories in your culture that are meant to teach but tempt instead?"

Of course they did. Human nature was stubborn and contrary, and no matter what the culture, there would always be those who would rebel, who would see something different in the stories than what was intended. Even in a relatively peaceful, conformist society like that of the Mejan.

"Yes, there are some similarities."

They leaned against the railing and looked out at the harbor of Edaru, at the graceful, "primitive" ships swaying with the waves. The sea was unquiet, the sky still heavy.

Kislan let his shoulder rest against hers. "Although I know nothing about the worlds on the stars, I can understand a little how you cannot always make sense of our way of doing things. The People live all along the coast here, and the rule of the house is the same for all. But the pirates on the other side of the land and on the islands to the east live by rules hard for us to understand."

"What rules do they live by?"

"They have no houses and no loyalty. They buy and sell not only goods but also *zhamgodenta*."

That was a term Toni had not yet heard. "What does *godenta* mean?"

"That is a word for a person who is bought and sold."

Slavery. Sam had been right.

From: Mejan creation myth
Recorded 01.10.157 (local AIC *date) by Landra Saleh, sociologist, first contact team,* SGR *132-3 (Christmas/Kailazh).*

> The war between the Kishudiu and the Tusalis lasted so many years and cost so many lives, there were no longer any women left who had not known a life without war. Soon there were no longer any men left at all.
>
> The women of the Kishudiu and Tusalis looked around them at the destruction of their homes, saw that there was nothing left to save and no enemies left to fight. Together, they took the last ships and fled by sea.
>
> After sailing for almost as many days as the war had years, they came to a beautiful bay on the other side of the world, a haven of peace, a jewel. Edaru.

Jackson Gates and Irving Moshofski were already there when Toni returned to Contact House One. Two pairs of dark eyes and one pair of gray turned to her in unison when she entered the lab.

"This is unprecedented," Jackson said.

"I hope so," Toni said. "But since this is the only first contact team I've ever been on, my experience is a bit limited."

The men smiled, and the atmosphere became a shade less heavy.

"One of us will have to be here in the lab at all times in case the *Penthesilea* makes contact," Moshofski said. "I checked the systems, and there doesn't seem to be a way for any of us to override Repnik's commands."

"So we have to wait until Ainsworth can do it," Toni said.

The other three nodded.

"I was beginning to wonder what Repnik was up to," Jackson said quietly. "He made a point of telling me you were having an affair with the young man who acted as your chauffeur from the landing base."

Toni swallowed. "I—no—I'm attracted to him, but, I—no." Then through her embarrassment she realized what he had said. "You mean Kislan wasn't your chauffeur when you first arrived?"

"No. We had a much older man driving us."

"Hm. Was he also a member of the ruling clans?"

"I don't remember offhand the colors he wore in his hair, but I don't think so."

"Interesting." So why had they sent her Kislan?

There was little else they could arrange without contact to the *Penthesilea*, so they said goodnight to each other and sought their separate quarters. With all of the day's upheavals, Toni had almost forgotten the recording she had made in the morning.

It was a gold mine—or an iron mine, from the Mejan point of view. And it wasn't just the long conversation between Thuyene and Anash or the snippets from the other women in the Ishel family: the discoveries started from the unknown qualifier Anash had used when speaking to her. After analyzing the recordings of the women's language for similar occurrences of "kasem," she was almost certain it was a possessive pronoun.

Both the possessive and the genitive were unknown in the men's language—the linguistic forms for ownership.

Toni leaned back in her chair and regarded the notes she had made in hard copy, the circles and question marks and lines and arrows. So what did she have? She had phonetic differences which seemed to indicate that the men's language had evolved out of the women's language and not the other way around. She had a gendered language in which the genders of the nouns didn't match up with gendered forms of address. She had warriors being named in one breath with pirates and pirates being named in one breath with language. She had a language spoken by men and named after the sea—and the sea was associated with the mother. She had grammatical cases that didn't exist in the men's language, a pairing which normally would lead her to conclude that the "secondary language" was the formalized, written language. If you looked at Vulgar Latin and Italian or any other of the common spoken languages in the European Middle Ages on Earth, it was the written language which had maintained the wealth of cases, while the romance languages which evolved out of it dispensed with much of that.

But the Mejan had no written language.

She had a boss who was doing his utmost to keep them from learning too much about the culture of the women.

And she had a man with eyes the color of a stormy green sea. A man who was married to about a dozen women at once.

All she had were questions. Where were the answers?

The next morning, Toni found Kislan on the docks, speaking with a captain of one of the ships belonging to his family. It probably would have been more logical to seek out Anash, but Toni didn't feel very logical.

When he saw her striding their way, Kislan's eyes lit up, and her gut tightened in response. She touched her forehead with the back of her hand. "Sha bo dam," she said, using the plural second person. "I hope I'm not interrupting anything?"

Kislan nodded denial. "We are expecting a shipment of leather goods, and I merely wanted to see if it had arrived." He introduced Toni to the captain, Zhoran. She noted the threads braided into his hair, saw that he too wore the colors of both Lanrhel's family and the Ishel, and she looked at him more closely. His coloring was lighter than Kislan's and he was obviously older, his golden-brown hair showing the first signs of gray at the temples. The bone structure was very similar, though. She wondered if they were brothers.

Toni touched Kislan's elbow briefly. "May I speak with you alone?"

"Let's go to the office."

Toni followed him a short way down a street leading away from the docks, away from the busy, noisy atmosphere like that of any center for trade and travel. Despite the presence of horses and carriages, despite the color of the vegetation on the hills and the scent of the air, it reminded her a little of the many transit stations between wormhole tunnels that she had passed through on her travels. It looked nothing alike, but there was an energy level, an atmosphere, which was much the same.

Kislan had a small office in the rambling administration building of his family's trading business. On a table in the center of the room stood a counting machine similar to an abacus, and against one wall was a heavy door with a lock, the first lock Toni had even seen on Kailazh. But no desk. With no system of writing, there was apparently no need for a desk.

When the door was closed behind her, Kislan pulled her into his arms and held her tightly. "Time has crawled by since you left me yesterday," he murmured next to her hair.

The words and the arms felt incredibly good, but Toni couldn't allow herself to get involved with him, especially when she still didn't know whether fooling around outside the house was a sin or not. To judge by the legends she was familiar with, trying to monopolize a sexual partner was definitely a sin. Which was enough of a problem by itself.

She slowly disentangled herself from Kislan's embrace. "I didn't seek you out for this. I wanted to ask you about something I don't understand, something that might help me understand more."

"Yes?"

"In your creation myth, all the men are killed in the war between the Kishudiu and the Tusalis. But how can the women start a new society without men? Is there any explanation in the myth for that?"

Kislan shrugged. "What explanation is needed? All of the men died; the warriors, *zhamhainyanar*."

"Hainyan? I don't know that word yet. What does it mean?"

"Hainyan is the word for the man when a man and a woman are together as a family."

"But I thought that was 'maishal'?"

"No, no. Hainyan is an old word. For the way it used to be. Much as you told us in the land you come from." He seemed to be both repelled and fascinated by the thought, and Toni remembered how he and Anash and Thuyene could only understand the marriages of

Terran and Martian culture in terms of possession.

If Toni was right, and "yanaru" was the word for woman in Alnar ag Eshmaled, then the root of "hain-yan" could be "over-woman."

A husband – like on the world she came from.

"But that still doesn't explain how the Mejan came to be," she said.

"They made their slaves their husbands." This time he used the word "maishal."

Toni stared at him. The women had owned the men when they first came here. Their language had possessive cases, the men's language – the language evolving from the dialect of the slaves? – did not. And the pirates to the east, the men who kept slaves – was the word for pirate perhaps the original word for men in the women's language? That would explain why they had been discussing "pirates" when Toni asked if she could learn their language.

Suddenly things started coming together for her like a landslide. And she was almost certain Repnik had figured it out – which was why he was doing his best to hinder their research.

Because he couldn't be chief linguist on a planet where the chief language was a women's language.

She wondered what had really happened to Landra Saleh.

"I must speak with Repnik."

"Why?"

"I think I know now why he was trying to forbid me to talk to the women."

"He did that?"

"Yes."

"But how can he have the authority? Authority belongs to the mother." *Tandarish derdesh kanezha tajanar.* He used the attitude particle "der-" for "a fact that cannot be denied."

Toni stared at him, her mind racing. Authority belongs to the mother. Tandarish – tajanar. "Tan" and "tajan" could well have the same root, which would mean the authority of the mother was even embedded in the word itself.

She pulled a notebook and pen out of her shoulder bag, sat down in one of the chairs, and jotted down the possible cognates with the women's language, along with the old word for husband. And slave. She was trying to come up with a cognate for the first half of the word "godent" when Kislan interrupted her.

"What are you doing?" he asked, sitting down in the chair next to her and peering over her shoulder.

She didn't have any words for what she was doing in his language and so she tried to describe it. "I have an idea about the language of the People, and I wanted to make the symbols for the words before I forget."

"I have seen the men of the contact team do this before, but I thought it was something like painting." He laughed out loud. "I didn't understand, none of us did. Among us, the men are not responsible for making *dalonesh*."

Toni wasn't familiar with the last word. "What does *dalonesh* mean?"

Kislan shrugged. "Events, history, business – anything that should be passed on."

Records. He was speaking of records. But in order to have records, you had to have a written language.

"Rodela," Toni murmured. They had been even more dense than she had thought. The crocheting the women did was *writing*, making the records of important meetings, and who knew what else.

"Yes," Kislan said, his voice thoughtful. "That means that among the people from the sky both men and women learn *rodela?*"

Both men and women learn crocheting, Toni's brain translated for her stubbornly and she had to laugh. "I'm sorry. Repnik had translated 'rodela' with a word for a hobby among women on the world where he comes from. The answer to your question is yes, on the worlds I know, Earth, Mars, Jyuruk and Admetos, we all learn writing."

"I have often thought it would be good to know, but men are not regarded as masculine if they learn *rodela*."

Men are not regarded as masculine if they learn crocheting. Certainly not. That fit very well into the mind set the first contact team had brought with them to Christmas. But in order to understand Kislan's statement, more than "rodela" would have to be changed. Toni suspected to get at the underlying attitude, you would have to change the gender of the words as well: *Women are not regarded as feminine if they learn writing.*

That was the attitude that was behind what Kislan had said. He had not mentioned "rodela" like something he could easily do without, he had mentioned it with regret, like something being denied to him. Even if you translated the words with their correct meanings, the sense of the sentence could not be communicated.

Toni took a deep breath. Suddenly everything about the Mejan looked completely different. The world had tilted and turned upside-down, and now the Christmas tree was right-side up. She couldn't believe how blind they had been, how blind *she* had been. Except, perhaps, Repnik.

Of course, the first contact team had been plagued by bad luck from the start — or was it? — with no sociologist, no one to talk to the women, and a xenolinguist who was deliberately deceiving everyone. But that did not excuse the extent of the misunderstanding, and it certainly did not excuse her. She had felt something was off, but she had allowed her own inherited attitudes to keep her from figuring out what it was.

"And the wall hangings," she asked, getting up and beginning to pace. "Those are...?"

He shrugged. "Genealogies, histories, famous stories. Fashar."

Documents, books perhaps. Another word which would have to be changed. Translated as "lace" in the present dictionary. The books, the writing, had been there right in front of their faces all the time.

She stopped pacing and faced him. This had implications for their whole analysis of the language. "I have to speak with Repnik."

"Dai eden mashal." Which meant the same as "good" but was expressed in verb form. And if she had said the same thing to another woman, it would have been "dai desh mashal."

But she would probably never trust her knowledge of another language again.

The story of the young poet
Recorded 30.09.157 by Landra Saleh, retranslated 06.12.157 (local AIC *date) by Antonia Donato.*

As long as she could remember, Zhaykair had only one dream — to become the greatest poet the Mejan had ever known. All young girls are taught the basics of writing, but Zhaykair would not stop at that. She begged the women of her village to teach her their way with words, the patterns they created, and she quickly found the most talented writer among them. Saymel did not belong to Zhaykair's house, but the families reached an agreement, and the little girl was allowed to learn from Saymel, although the job of Zhaykair's house was raising cattle.

But before she had seen nine summers, Zhaykair had learned all Saymel had to teach her. She begged her clan to allow her to go to the city of Edaru, where the greatest poets of the Mejan lived. Her mothers and fathers did not want to send her away, but Saymel, who could best judge the talent of the young girl, persuaded them to inquire if the house of Mihkal would be willing to take her on.

The elders sent a messenger to the Mihkal with some of Zhaykair's poems. They had feared being ridiculed for their presumption, but the messenger returned with an elder of the house of Mihkal to personally escort Zhaykair to the great city of Edaru.

Zhaykair soon learned all the Mihkal clan could teach her. Her poetry was in such great demand, and there were so many who wanted to learn from her, that she could soon found her own house. Her works now grace the walls of all the greatest families of the Mejan.

Toni found Repnik in the main square of Edaru, leaving the school of the house of Railiu, where boys memorized a wealth of Mejan legends and songs and were taught basic mathematics and biology and navigational skills.

But no crocheting.

"Sir!" Toni called out, rushing over to him. "I need to speak with you. Can we perhaps return to the contact house?"

"*You* can return to the contact house, Donato. I am going out to lunch with Sebair, the rector of the Railiu school."

Sebair strolled next to Repnik with his hand to his forehead, and Toni returned the gesture, greeting him less graciously than she should have.

"Sha bo sham, tajan," Sebair said, smiling anyway.

"Mr. Repnik," Toni persisted. "I really need to speak with you. It's very important."

"I'm sure it is. But you have a job to do, and what you have to tell me can wait until I get back to the lab."

Toni took a deep breath. "I know. What you've been trying to hide."

Repnik's stride faltered, but his confidence didn't, at least not as far she could tell. "I have no idea what you're talking about."

"I know that as far as the Mejan are concerned, I am the head of this team. And I know that they *do* have a system of writing."

Repnik stopped in his tracks. "You know *what?*"

So he hadn't gotten that far. He wasn't a good enough actor to fake that stare of surprise. Toni felt a surge of satisfaction.

"And I also know that you've been trying to hinder the research of the first contact team."

An angry flush covered the chief linguist's face. "Ms. Donato, you are hallucinating."

"I don't think so. Don't you want to know what the system of writing is?"

Repnik snorted. "There is none. I knew before you came that a woman dealing with a woman's language would lead to problems."

Finally, Toni could no longer control her temper. "Obviously not as many problems as a man dealing with a men's language," she spat out.

She saw his hand come up as if the moment were being replayed in slow motion. She knew it meant he was about to slap her, but she was too surprised to react. From that observing place in her mind, she saw Sebair start forward and try to stop Repnik, but then the flat of his palm met her cheek, and the sting of pain sent tears to her eyes.

She lifted her own palm to cover the spot, while utter silence reigned in the main square, everyone gaping at her and her boss. Then, just as suddenly, chaos broke out. The men who had been going about their business only minutes before converged upon Repnik and wrestled him to the ground. Toni stood frozen, staring at the scene in front of her.

Repnik had struck a mother.

The old man struggled beneath the three young men who held him down. "What is the meaning of this?" he asked in Alnar ag Ledar.

Suddenly Lanrhel was there next to them. Toni wondered when he had joined the fray. "Let him rise."

The voluntary guards pulled Repnik to his feet, and Lanrhel faced him. "You know enough of our laws to know that to strike a mother means you must be returned to the sea."

"She is no mother."

Lanrhel didn't even bother to answer, turning instead to Toni. "Tajan, do you need assistance?"

Toni was too confused for a second to come up with the right gesture and she shook her head. "No, it's nothing. Let him go, please."

A firm hand took her elbow. Anash. "Come."

"But Repnik..."

"Come. He must go with Lanrhel now."

Toni allowed herself to be led away to the common house and a small, private room. A basin of water was brought, and Anash pushed her into a chair and bathed her stinging cheek gently.

"You won't really throw him out to sea, will you?" Toni finally asked.

"I don't know yet what we will do. We have a dilemma."

They certainly did. Toni didn't even know if Repnik could swim. And if he could, he wouldn't be allowed to swim to shore. She didn't like him, but — a death sentence for a slap? "You can't give him back to the sea. He's not from this world. Where he's from, it's not a crime to slap a woman."

"Then it should be," Anash said grimly.

Anash was defending her, but it didn't feel like it. "Don't do this to him."

"How can you defend him after all the disrespect he has shown you?"

If Toni hadn't felt so horrible, she almost would have been tempted to laugh. That was the kind of reasoning shown by aristocracies and intolerant ruling powers throughout the ages. Repnik hadn't been right to try to keep the truth from the first contact team, but he hardly deserved to walk the plank.

Until this morning, she'd thought these women needed to be defended from the likes of Repnik. Now everything was on its head, everything.

As if to prove her point, Kislan entered the room, shutting the door gently behind him. He stared at her expectantly, and she finally remembered to greet him.

"Sha bo sham, Kislan."

"Sha bo sham, Toni." He approached and gave her a kiss, right in front of Anash.

His clan knew. They'd given him to her. Like a present. She was the visiting dignitary, and he was her whore. Had he thrown himself in her way willingly, or had he been sent?

Toni pushed herself out of the chair and wandered over to the window. The central square of Edaru was unusually quiet for this time of day, just before the midday meal. People stood in small groups of two or three, speaking with earnest faces, spreading the news. By evening, the whole city would know that a man of the people from the sky had committed a grave crime against the sole woman of the contact team. If nothing was done, not only would Anash's authority be undermined, the first contact team would be seen as lawless and immoral.

She lifted her gaze above the rooftops of the buildings on the other side of the square, to the lacy pattern formed by the rings of Christmas in the sky.

The sky. The old man wouldn't thank her, but she might have a way to save him, keep him from being thrown into the ocean, send him home safely.

"I have an idea," she breathed. "Criminals are returned to the sea, because that is where they are from, yes?"

Anash shook her head, watching Toni carefully.

"And the people of the first contact team do not come from the sea, they come from the sky."

"You are right," the older woman said. "This might be a solution."

She was the visiting dignitary, she had to remember that. "It is the only solution we can consider," she said in what she hoped was a voice of command.

Anash gazed at her as an equal. "Then we will give him back to the sky."

The ceremony took place on a sunny but cool afternoon three days later. Before arrangements could be made with the *Penthesilea*, they had to wait until the ship made contact itself. The taciturn Moshofski handled that end once Ainsworth overrode Repnik's commands, while Toni spent her time at the house of Ishel and in consultations with Lanrhel – aside from the one-sided shouting matches with Repnik, who was being kept under guard in the common house. Repnik had made it very clear that he intended to take Toni to interstellar court on charges of mutiny and conspiracy.

And if AIRA believed him, she was saving him to dig her own grave.

A construction resembling a pier was hastily built on a plain outside of town, between Edaru and the landing base. Although it wasn't conveniently located for the town residents, several thousand people had made the trip to see Repnik returned to the sky. With his head shaved, the old man looked even older, gaunt and bare and bitter.

Toni wished she didn't have to watch, let alone participate. The rest of the first contact team had elected to stay at home.

With a guard on either side, Repnik was accompanied down the waterless pier, Anash, Toni and Thuyene a few paces behind. A shuttle from the *Penthesilea* waited at the end, Lanrhel and Ainsworth beside the door. Finally Repnik and his guards reached the councillor, and Lanrhel announced in his booming voice, "Mukhaired ag Repnik bonaashali derladesh." *Repnik's shame will now certainly be purged.* He then ordered the older man to strip. When Repnik refused, his guards stripped him forcibly.

Toni looked away. His humiliation was painful to see, his skinny, white flesh hanging loosely on his bones. He would hate her for the rest of his life, and she could hardly blame him.

Then Anash's hand on her elbow was urging her forward, pressing a bit of lace into her hand. A written record of his time on Christmas. Toni looked up and flung the *fashar* through the open doors of the shuttle.

Ainsworth nodded a curt goodbye, turned, and followed Repnik. The doors whisked shut and the shuttle lifted off the ground.

After the ceremony, Anash led her to a small carriage to take her back to town. She was no longer surprised that the driver was Kislan again, and only a little surprised that Anash didn't join them.

Kislan was her present, after all.

If only she knew what to say, what to feel. He was still just as handsome, but he didn't draw her in the same way. She didn't like what it said about herself that she suddenly saw him so differently. Now he was a supplicant, whereas before he was exotic and distant, a man of good standing in a powerful clan.

She couldn't have the same feelings for someone who had been given to her.

"What's wrong, Toni?" Kislan asked gently after she hadn't spoken for minutes. His pronunciation of her name was a little like that of her Italian grandmother, and she had the odd impulse to cry.

"I don't know. I can't figure anything out."

"I thought you did not like Repnik?"

"No."

"Then why are you upset?"

"Things are so much stranger here than I thought. I'm confused. I need to think things out."

"And thinking things out includes me, yes?"

For a moment, Toni couldn't answer. "Yes."

She arrived at Contact House One just as the lacy show of evening was beginning again, her heart and mind a mess. The world was on its head and there were holes in the sky.

At the sound of hooves and wheels on the cobblestones, Sam, Jackson and Moshofski came out to the door of the courtyard, their expressions solemn.

Sam helped her down. "Ainsworth contacted us from the shuttle. They had to sedate Repnik."

Toni closed her eyes briefly. "I'm so sorry."

"No need, Donato," Jackson said. "Repnik was deliberately hindering AIRA work."

"We've started wondering what really happened to Landra," Moshofski added.

"I've been wondering about that too."

"We mentioned our suspicions to Ainsworth, and there will be an investigation," Jackson said. "And given the social structures on Christmas, you're to head the first contact team in future when dealing with the Mejan."

A smile touched Moshofski's serious features. "But in the lab, I'm the boss. Seniority, you know."

She could hardly believe it. "Certainly."

"Sam baked a cake to celebrate the two promotions," Jackson said. "Shall we test his talents?"

"I'll follow you in a minute."

The three men filed into the contact house, and she came around the carriage to Kislan's side. "I never wanted to hurt you."

He gazed back at her, not answering.

Toni looked away, at the sky above, the fabulous sunset over Edaru. "I'm sorry. I will come see you again soon and we can talk. Perhaps I can teach you our way of writing."

His eyes lit up. "Yes." He placed his free hand on her shoulder and nodded at the sky. "It's beautiful, isn't it?" *It is-in-a-state-of-beauty, yes?*

Toni shook her head. "Yes."

"Tiptree" and History

Joanna Russ

Alice Sheldon was a very complex person. Noted feminist author Joanna Russ formed a very close friendship with Sheldon through correspondence. This essay presents her insightful view of Alice Sheldon and the enemies she struggled against.

The visionaries come first. Scattered, and unsupported except by each other, they're the first to say right out loud and in public that Something Hurts and It Is Not Good. When they club together you have radical actions like WITCH hexing Wall Street or the first women to camp out in Greenham Common. These are the people who are laughed at if they're noticed at all, although the laugher often has an ugly edge, evidence that the radicals have hit an important social nerve. When the assertion that It Hurts and It Is Not Good has spread, the unity of the grassroots may become impressive and frightening. Then those who have a stake in the status quo will use repression and lies that go beyond laughter. There will be factions as the radicals find that their interests and temperaments aren't identical. Lots of those who crowd through the door opened by the radicals will try to disassociate themselves from the radicals. And so on and so on.

Academic critics who notice James Tiptree Jr.'s work (they're not many) seem to me to find the genesis of "Tiptree's" pessimism in Alice Sheldon's unusual and difficult childhood as the only surviving child of her explorer and writer parents. Childhood experience matters, of course — it does to everyone — but there is an important social context these critics are neglecting.

Tiptree was born at the wrong time. That is, the social movements relevant to her personal condition came too late in her life to help her. If she'd been born (as I was) in the late 1930s she would have gone through adolescence in the Horrible 1950s but she well might have been young enough in the late 1960s to benefit from the theoretical and practical support of both feminism and gay liberation. And although being born in a particular place can be changed in later life, being "stuck" in time never ends. From Alli's teens through her sixties she fought lifelong battles on at least two fronts. She fought not only without allies but without the clarity of what Judith Herman has called a conceptual life raft, i.e. the analysis that makes something not only personal but also political.

Alice Sheldon not only led the kind of vocational life women of her generation were not supposed to lead (the first enemy); she was a lesbian. She was (like some others I have met) a lesbian who never dared to have a real love affair, although (as she once wrote to me) "it was always girls and women who lit me up."

Nothing in Sheldon's life or Tiptree's fictional worlds went beyond that "lighting up" of erotic attraction. Indeed many of her stories insist that what lies beyond the attraction is simply (and awfully) death. "A Momentary Taste of Being" is one of these stories and there are many others like it in her work. Consider, for example, the almost transparent story "The Only Neat Thing To Do," in which two "children" as Tiptree calls them – the human girl is fifteen and the alien is feminine if not female — are sent "hand in hand" to commit suicide by diving into a star. Their suicide, we're told, is the only alternative to being sexual together, which would be literally far more disastrous.

Sheldon's one-sided, unexpressed attractions are not unusual among lesbians even now. I have met women in their seventies and eighties who are still terrified of what may happen to their families or their Social Security payments if their lesbianism becomes public knowledge. I met one woman in her eighties who had a lover for the very first time in her eighties. Another, in her sixties, retreated in fear from a lesbian support group when someone pointed out to her that her life need not remain isolated, loveless, and dishonest.

There was a third enemy Alice Sheldon faced and this one, I think, finally did kill her. It also made her unlikely, I believe, to challenge compulsory heterosexuality openly or to take real feminist risks.

Alli was chronically depressed. She once wrote me that it was only during vacations, which she and her husband spent in the Yucatan, that she felt really happy. A return to McLean, Virginia, where they lived, always meant a return of depression. At another time she wrote me that a trip to British Columbia plunged her into the worst depression of her life. Neither she nor her doctor could make sense of this pattern. Neither could I...then. Now I can. It was precisely at the time she shot her husband (who had lost his eyesight) and then herself that the mental dysfunction called Seasonal Affective Disorder, SAD, was first coming into public notice. SAD is a type of chronic depression caused (in those susceptible to it) by a lack of intense sunlight. In Northern countries, where sunlight is pale and weak and the winter days are short, people susceptible to SAD may become clinically depressed in the autumn and winter or even be constantly depressed during the whole year.

In the Yucatan, near the equator, Alli was happy; in Virginia, farther north, she was depressed. In British Columbia with its pale, pale daylight, she was utterly miserable. If only she had lived a little longer she might have heard about SAD and so might her doctor. I think the knowledge might have saved her life.

Stories are created by living, enjoying, suffering real people. That's why I've emphasized the personal in Tiptree's life in this essay. I write it also because I loved Alli dearly although we never met. I'll always remember the blue-ink octopi she drew on her post cards. In her letters she worried about me and I addressed her as everything from Traptingle to Trumpetbump to Trippletroop. She was my dear and lovely friend. I'm a New York Jew from a liberal-radical family and everyone knows how loud *we* are (yelling is necessary in New York City because if you don't yell, nobody can hear you in the subway). Alli was from a WASP family with considerable social pretensions—at one point, they insisted she come out as a debutante. My response to unhappiness and disappointment has always been combative; Alli could not, I think, take that route. Alli once wrote that lab rats squeak if they are squeezed and that when life squeezed her, writing was her way of "squeaking." How superbly she "squeaked" and how lucky we are that she did! "A Momentary Taste of Being" ends with the narrator's telling us that he doesn't dream any more. Traptroop kept on dreaming, immeasurably enriching her readers' lives and other writers' stories. Here are some of those stories.

NOTE:

Sheldon's metaphor about squeaking/writing comes from her essay "A Woman Writing Science Fiction and Fantasy" in *Women of Vision*, edited by Denise Du Pont.

What I Didn't See

Karen Joy Fowler

Writing may be a solitary profession, but writers don't work in a vacuum. Many stories are written in response to others, and ongoing dialogues can be the inspiration for fiction. To cite one example, Joanna Russ's apocalyptic *We Who Are About To...* was a conscious response to Marion Zimmer Bradley's *Darkover Landfall*.

"What I Didn't See" grew from multiple sources:

Feminist theorist Donna Haraway wrote a book called *Primate Visions*, including a chapter which discusses a 1921 African expedition led by Carl Akeley. One member of that expedition, Mary Hastings Bradley, wrote a book about her experiences exploring Africa with her five-year-old daughter. That young daughter grew up to write stories of her own, including "The Women Men Don't See" by James Tiptree, Jr.

Fowler also cites the influences of primate studies, King Kong, Belgian Congo politics, Tarzan, harems, spiders, and perilous card games.

In the Tiptree story, the male narrator is on a small chartered plane transporting two women to a destination he could never imagine. (It is included in her collection *Her Smoke Rose Up Forever*, a new edition of which is being published by Tachyon at about the same time as this anthology.) In this story, much the same thing happens...maybe.

This story was shortlisted for the Tiptree Award in 2002 (stories by Founding Mothers, board members, and other people close to the award are ineligible to win). Perhaps because it was originally published on the online sf site SCIFICTION (www.scifi.com/scifiction), Fowler's tale created some controversy for its lack of science fiction content. Nonetheless, it was awarded the Nebula Award for Best Short Story of 2003 by the Science Fiction and Fantasy Writers of America. We include it here because of the relationship of its content to the Tiptree Award, because it's made trouble in just the ways we like to support, and because we're so very proud that one of our own Founding Mothers (and one of your editors) won the Nebula.

I saw Archibald Murray's obituary in the *Tribune* a couple of days ago. It was a long notice, because of all those furbelows he had after his name, and dredged up that old business of ours, which can't have pleased his children. I, myself, have never spoken up before, as I've always felt that nothing I saw sheds any light, but now I'm the last of us. Even Wilmet is gone, though I always picture him such a boy. And there is something to be said for having the last word, which I am surely having.

I still go to the jungle sometimes when I sleep. The sound of the clock turns to a million insects all chewing at once, water dripping onto leaves, the hum inside your head when you run a fever. Sooner or later Eddie comes, in his silly hat and boots up to his knees. He puts his arms around me in the way he did when he meant business and I wake up too hot, too old, and all alone.

You're never alone in the jungle. You can't see through the twist of roots and leaves and vines, the streakish, tricky light, but you've always got a sense of being seen. You make too much noise when you walk.

At the same time, you understand that you don't matter. You're small and stuck on the ground. The ghosts of paths weren't made for you. If you get bitten by a snake, it's your own damn fault, not the snake's, and if someone doesn't drag you out you'll turn to mulch just like anything else would and show up next as mold or moss, ferns, leeches, ants, millipedes, butterflies, beetles. The jungle is a jammed-alive place, which means that something is always dying there.

Eddie had this idea once that defects of character could be treated with doses of landscape: the ocean for the histrionic, mountains for the domineering, and so forth. I forget the desert, but the jungle was the place to send the self-centered.

We seven went into the jungle with guns in our hands and love in our hearts. I say so now when there is no one left to contradict me.

Archer organized us. He was working at the time for the Louisville Museum of Natural History and he had a stipend from Collections for skins and bones. The rest of us were amateur enthusiasts and paid our own way just for the adventure. Archer asked Eddie (arachnids) to go along and Russell MacNamara (chimps), and Trenton Cox (butterflies), who couldn't or wouldn't, and Wilmet Siebert (big game), and Merion Cowper (tropical medicine), and also Merion's wife, only he turned out to be between wives by the time we left, so he was the one who brought Beverly Kriss.

I came with Eddie to help with his nets, pooters, and kill jars. I was never the sort to scream over bugs, but if I had been, twenty-eight years of marriage to Eddie would have cured me. The more legs a creature had, the better Eddie thought of it. Up to point. Up to eight.

In fact Archer was anxious there be some women and had specially invited me, though Eddie didn't tell me so. This was smart; I would have suspected I was along to do the dishes (though of course there were the natives for this) and for nursing the sick, which we did end up at a bit, Beverly and I, when the matter was too small or too nasty for Merion. I might not have come at all if I'd known I was wanted. As it was, I learned to bake a passable bread on campfire coals with a native beer for yeast, but it was my own choice to do so and I ate as much of the bread myself as I wished.

I pass over the various boats on which we sailed, though these trips were not without incident. Wilmet turned out to have a nervous stomach; it started to trouble him on the ocean and then stuck around when we hit dry land again. Russell was a drinker, and not the good sort, unlucky and suspicious, a man who thought he loved a game of cards, but should have never been allowed to play. Beverly was a modern girl in 1928 and could chew gum, smoke, and wipe the lipstick off her mouth and onto yours all at the same time. She and Merion were frisky for Archer's taste and he tried to shift this off onto me, saying I was being made uncomfortable, when I didn't care one way or the other. I worried that it would be a pattern and every time one of the men was tired on the trail they'd say we had to stop on my account. I told Eddie right away I wouldn't like it if this was to happen. So by the time we were geared up and walking in, we already thought we knew each other pretty well and we didn't entirely like what we knew. Still, I guessed we'd get along fine when there was more to occupy us. Even during those long days it took to reach the mountains — the endless trains, motor cars, donkeys, mules, and finally our very own feet — things went smoothly enough.

By the time we reached the Lulenga Mission, we'd seen a fair bit of Africa – low and high, hot and cold, black and white. I've learned some things in the years since, so there's a strong temptation now to pretend that I felt the things I should have felt, knew the things I might have known. The truth is otherwise. My attitudes toward the natives, in particular, were not what they might have been. The men who helped us interested me little and impressed me not at all. Many of them had their teeth filed and were only ten years or so from cannibalism, or so we were informed. No one, ourselves included, was clean, but Beverly and I would have tried, only we couldn't bathe without the nuisance of being spied on. Whether this was to see if we looked good or only good to eat, I did not wish to know.

The fathers at the mission told us that slaves used to be led through the villages in ropes so that people could draw on their bodies the cuts of meat they were buying before the slaves were butchered, and with that my mind was set. I never did acknowledge any beauty or kindness in the people we met, though Eddie saw much of both.

We spent three nights in Lulenga, which gave us each a bed, good food, and a chance to wash our hair and clothes in some privacy. Beverly and I shared a room, there not being sufficient number for her to have her own. She was quarreling with Merion at the time though I forget about what. They were a tempest, those two, always shouting, sulking, and then turning on the heat again. A tiresome sport for spectators, but surely invigorating for the players. So Eddie was bunked up with Russell, which put me out, because I liked to wake up with him.

We were joined at dinner the first night by a Belgian administrator who treated us to real wine and whose name I no longer remember though I can picture him yet – a bald, hefty man in his sixties with a white beard. I recall how he joked that his hair had migrated from his head to his chin and then settled in where the food was plentiful.

Eddie was in high spirits and talking more than usual. The spiders in Africa are exhilaratingly aggressive. Many of them have fangs and nocturnal habits. We'd already shipped home dozens of button spiders with red hourglasses on their backs, and some beautiful golden violin spiders with long delicate legs and dark chevrons underneath. But that evening Eddie was most excited about a small jumping spider, which seemed not to spin her own web, but to lurk instead in the web of another. She had no beautiful markings; when he'd first seen one, he'd thought she was a bit of dirt blown into the silken strands. Then she grew legs and, as we watched, stalked and killed the web's owner and all with a startling cunning.

"Working together, a thousand spiders can tie up a lion," the Belgian told us. Apparently it was a local saying. "But then they don't work together, do they? The blacks haven't noticed. Science is observation and Africa produces no scientists."

In those days all gorilla hunts began at Lulenga, so it took no great discernment to guess that the rest of our party was not after spiders. The Belgian told us that only six weeks past, a troupe of gorilla males had attacked a tribal village. The food stores had been broken into and a woman carried off. Her bracelets were found the next day, but she'd not yet returned and the Belgian feared she never would. It was such a sustained siege that the whole village had to be abandoned.

"The seizure of the woman I dismiss as superstition and exaggeration," Archer said. He had a formal way of speaking; you'd never guess he was from Kentucky. Not so grand to look at – inch-thick glasses that made his eyes pop, unkempt hair, filthy shirt cuffs. He poured more of the Belgian's wine around, and I recall his being especially generous to his own glass. Isn't it funny, the things you remember? "But the rest of your story interests me. If any gorilla was taken I'd pay for the skin, assuming it wasn't spoiled in the peeling."

The Belgian said he would inquire. And then he persisted with his main point, very serious and deliberate. "As to the woman, I've heard these tales too often to discard them so quickly as you. I've heard of native women subjected to degradations far worse than death. May I ask you as a favor then, in deference to my greater experience and longer time here, to leave your women at the mission when you go gorilla hunting?"

It was courteously done and obviously cost Archer to refuse. Yet he did, saying to my astonishment that it would defeat his whole purpose to leave me and Beverly behind. He then gave the Belgian his own thinking, which we seven had already heard over several repetitions – that gorillas were harmless and gentle, if oversized and overmuscled. Sweet-natured vegetarians. He based this entirely on the wear on their teeth; he'd read a paper on it from some university in London.

Archer then characterized the famous Du Chaillu description – glaring eyes, yellow incisors, hellish dream creatures – as a slick and dangerous form of self aggrandizement. It was an account tailored to bring big game hunters on the run and so had to be quickly countered for the gorillas' own protection. Archer was out to prove Du Chaillu wrong and he needed me and Beverly to help. "If one of the girls should bring down a large male," he said, "it will seem as exciting as shooting a cow. No man will cross a continent merely to do something a pair of girls has already done."

He never did ask us, because that wasn't his way. He just raised it as our Christian duty and then left us to worry it over in our minds.

Of course we were all carrying rifles. Eddie and I had practiced on bottles and such in preparation for the trip. On the way over I'd gotten pretty good at clay pigeons off the deck of our ship. But I wasn't eager to kill a gentle vegetarian – a nightmare from hell would have suited me a good deal better (if scared me a great deal more.) Beverly too, I'm guessing.

Not that she said anything about it that night. Wilmet, our youngest at twenty-five years and also shortest by a whole head – blond hair, pink cheeks, and little rat's eyes – had been lugging a tin of British biscuits about the whole trip and finishing every dinner by eating one while we watched. He was always explaining why they couldn't be shared when no one was asking. They kept his stomach settled; he couldn't afford to run out and so on; his very life might depend on them if he were sick and nothing else would stay down and so forth. We wouldn't have noticed if he hadn't persisted in bringing it up.

But suddenly he and Beverly had their heads close together, whispering, and he was giving her one of his precious biscuits. She took it without so much as a glance at Merion, even when he leaned in to say he'd like one, too. Wilmet answered that there were too few to share with everyone so Merion upset a water glass into the tin and spoiled all the biscuits that remained. Wilmet left the table and didn't return and the subject of the all-girl gorilla hunt passed by in the unpleasantness.

That night I woke under the gauze of the mosquito net in such a heat I thought I had malaria. Merion had given us all quinine and I meant to take it regularly, but I didn't always remember. There are worse fevers in the jungle, especially if you've been collecting spiders, so it was cheerful of me to fix on malaria. My skin was burning from the inside out, especially my hands and feet, and I was sweating like butter on a hot day. I thought to wake Beverly, but by the time I stood up the fit had already passed and anyway her bed was empty.

In the morning she was back. I planned to talk to her then, get her thoughts on gorilla hunting, but I woke early and she slept late.

I breakfasted alone and went for a stroll around the Mission grounds. It was cool with little noise beyond the wind and birds. To the west, a dark trio of mountains, two of which smoked. Furrowed fields below me, banana plantations, and trellises of roses, curving into archways that led to the church. How often we grow a garden around our houses of worship. We march ourselves through Eden to get to God.

Merion joined me in the graveyard where I'd just counted three deaths by lion, British names all. I was thinking how outlandish it was, how sadly unlikely that all the prams and nannies and public schools should come to this, and even the bodies pinned under stones so hyenas wouldn't come for them. I was hoping for a more modern sort of death myself, a death at home, a death from American causes, when Merion cleared his throat behind me.

He didn't look like my idea of a doctor, but I believe he was a good one. Well-paid, that's for sure and certain. As to appearances, he reminded me of the villain in some Lillian Gish film, meaty and needing a shave, but handsome enough when cleaned up. He swung his arms when he walked so he took up more space than he needed. There was something to this confidence I admired, though it irritated me on principle. I often liked him least of all and I'm betting he was sharp enough to know it. "I trust you slept well," he said. He looked at me slant-wise, looked away again. *I trust you slept well.* I trust you were in no way disturbed by Beverly sneaking out to meet me in the middle of the night.

Or maybe — I trust Beverly didn't sneak out last night.

Or maybe just I trust you slept well. It wasn't a question, which saved me the nuisance of figuring the answer.

"So," he said next, "what do you think of this gorilla scheme of Archer's?" and then gave me no time to respond. "The fathers tell me a party from Manchester went up just last month and brought back seventeen. Four of them youngsters — lovely little family group for the British Museum. I only hope they left us a few." And then, lowering his voice, "I'm glad for the chance to discuss things with you privately."

There turned out to be a detail to the Belgian's story judged too delicate for the dinnertable, but Merion, being a doctor and maybe more of a man's man than Archer, a man who could be appealed to on behalf of women, had heard it. The woman carried away from the village had been menstruating. This at least the Belgian hoped, that we'd not to go up the mountain with our female affliction in full flower.

And because he was a doctor I told Merion straight out that I'd been light and occasional; I credited this to the upset of travel. I thought to set his mind at ease, but I should have guessed I wasn't his first concern.

"Beverly's too headstrong to listen to me," he said. "Too young and reckless. She'll take her cue from you. A solid, sensible, mature woman like you could rein her in a bit. For her own good."

A woman unlikely to inflame the passions of jungle apes was what I heard. Even in my prime I'd never been the sort of woman poems are written about, but this seemed to place me low indeed. An hour later I saw the humor in it, and Eddie surely laughed at me quickly enough when I confessed it, but at the time I was sincerely insulted. How sensible, how mature was that?

I was further provoked by the way he expected me to give in. Archer was certain I'd agree to save the gorillas and Merion was certain I'd agree to save Beverly. I had a moment's outrage over these men who planned to run me by appealing to what they imagined was my weakness.

Merion more than Archer. How smug he was, and how I detested his calm acceptance of every advantage that came to him, as if it were no more than his due. No white woman in all the world had seen the wild gorillas yet — we were to be the first — but I was to step aside from it just because he asked me.

"I haven't walked all this way to miss out on the gorillas," I told him, as politely as I could. "The only question is whether I'm looking or shooting at them." And then I left him, because my own feelings were no credit to me and I didn't mean to have them anymore. I went to look for Eddie and spend the rest of the day emptying kill jars, pinning and labeling the occupants.

The next morning Beverly announced, in deference to Merion's wishes, that she'd be staying behind at the mission when we went on. Quick as could be, Wilmet said his stomach was in such an uproar that he would stay behind as well. This took us all by surprise as he was the only real hunter among us. And it put Merion in an awful bind — we'd more likely need a doctor on the mountain than at the mission, but I guessed he'd sooner see Beverly taken by gorillas than by Wilmet. He fussed and sweated over a bunch of details that didn't matter to anyone and all the while the day passed in secret conferences — Merion with Archer, Archer with Beverly, Russell with Wilmet, Eddie with Beverly. By dinnertime Beverly said she'd changed her mind and Wilmet had undergone a wonderful recovery. When we left next morning we were at full complement, but pretty tightly strung.

It took almost two hundred porters to get our little band of seven up Mount Mikeno. It was a hard track with no path, hoisting ourselves over roots, cutting and crawling our way through tightly woven bamboo. There were long slides of mud on which it was impossible to get a grip. And always sharp uphill. My heart and my lungs worked as hard or harder than my legs and though it wasn't hot I had to wipe my face and neck continually. As the altitude rose I gasped for breath like a fish in a net.

We women were placed in the middle of the pack with gun-bearers both ahead and behind. I slid back many times and had to be caught and set upright again. Eddie was in a torment over the webs we walked through with no pause as to architect and Russell over the bearers who, he guaranteed, would bolt with our guns at the first sign of danger. But we wouldn't make camp if we stopped for spiders and couldn't stay the course without our hands free. Soon Beverly sang out for a gorilla to come and carry her the rest of the way.

Then we were all too winded and climbed for hours without speaking, breaking whenever we came suddenly into the sun, sustaining ourselves with chocolate and crackers.

Still our mood was excellent. We saw elephant tracks, large, sunken bowls in the mud, half-filled with water. We saw glades of wild carrots and an extravagance of pink and purple orchids. Grasses in greens so delicate they seemed to be melting. I revised my notions of Eden, leaving the roses behind and choosing instead these remote forests where the gorillas lived – foggy rains, the crooked hagenia trees strung with vines, golden mosses, silver lichen; the rattle and buzz of flies and beetles; the smell of catnip as we stepped into it.

At last we stopped. Our porters set up which gave us a chance to rest. My feet were swollen and my knees stiffening, but I had a great appetite for dinner and a great weariness for bed; I was asleep before sundown. And then I was awake again. The temperature, which had been pleasant all day, plunged. Eddie and I wrapped ourselves in coats and sweaters and each other. He worried about our porters, who didn't have the blankets we had, although they were free to keep a fire up as high as they liked. At daybreak, they came complaining to Archer. He raised their pay a dime apiece since they had surely suffered during the night, but almost fifty of them left us anyway.

We spent that morning sitting around the camp, nursing our blisters and scrapes, some of us looking for spiders, some of us practicing our marksmanship. There was a stream about five minutes walk away with a pool where Beverly and I dropped our feet. No mosquitoes, no sweat bees, no flies, and that alone made it paradise. But no sooner did I have this thought and a wave of malarial heat came on me, drenching the back of my shirt.

When I came to myself again, Beverly was in the middle of something and I hadn't heard the beginning. She might have told me Merion's former wife had been unfaithful to him. Later this seemed like something I'd once been told, but maybe only because it made sense. "Now he seems to think the apes will leave me alone if only I don't go tempting them," she said. "Lord!"

"He says they're drawn to menstrual blood."

"Then I've got no problem. Anyway Russell says that Burunga says we'll never see them, dressed as we're dressed. Our clothes make too much noise when we walk. He told Russell we must hunt them naked. I haven't passed that on to Merion yet. I'm saving it for a special occasion."

I had no idea who Burunga was. Not the cook and not our chief guide, which were the only names I'd bothered with. I was, at least (and I do see now, how very least it is) embarrassed to learn that Beverly had done otherwise. "Are you planning to shoot an ape?" I asked. It came over me all of sudden that I wanted a particular answer, but I couldn't unearth what answer that was.

"I'm not really a killer," she said. "More a sweet-natured vegetarian. Of the meat-eating variety. But Archer says he'll put my picture up in the museum. You know the sort of thing – rifle on shoulder, foot on body, eyes to the horizon. Wouldn't that be something to take the kiddies to?"

Eddie and I had no kiddies; Beverly might have realized it was a sore spot. And Archer had made no such representations to me. She sat in a spill of sunlight. Her hair was short and heavy and fell in a neat cap over her ears. Brown until the sun made it golden. She wasn't a pretty woman so much as she just drew your eye and kept it. "Merion keeps on about how he paid my way here. Like he hasn't gotten his money's worth." She kicked her feet and water beaded up on her bare legs. "You're so lucky. Eddie's the best."

Which he was, and any woman could see it. I never met a better man than my Eddie and in our whole forty-three years together there were only three times I wished I hadn't married him. I say this now, because we're coming up on one of those times. I wouldn't want someone thinking less of Eddie because of anything I said.

"You're still in love with him, aren't you?" Beverly asked. "After so many years of marriage."

I admitted as much.

Beverly shook her golden head. "Then you'd best keep with him," she told me.

Or did she? What did she say to me? I've been over the conversation so many times I no longer remember it at all.

In contrast, this next bit is perfectly clear. Beverly said she was tired and went to her tent to lie down. I found the men playing bridge, taking turns at watching. I was bullied into playing, because Russell didn't like his cards and thought to change his luck by putting some empty space between hands. So it was me and Wilmet opposite Eddie and Russell, with Merion and Archer in the vicinity, smoking and looking on. On the other side of the tents the laughter of our porters.

I would have liked to team with Eddie, but Russell said bridge was too dangerous a game when husbands and wives partnered up and there was a ready access to guns. He was joking, of course, but you couldn't have told by his face.

While we played Russell talked about chimpanzees and how they ran their lives. Back in those days no one had looked at chimps yet so it was all only guesswork. Topped by guessing that gorillas would be pretty much the same. There was a natural order to things, Russell said, and you could reason it out; it was simple Darwinism.

I didn't think you could reason out spiders; I didn't buy that you could reason out chimps. So I didn't listen. I played my cards and every so often a word would fall in. Male this, male that. Blah, blah, dominance. Survival of the fittest, blah, blah. Natural selection, nature red in tooth and claw. Blah and blah. There was an argument then as to whether by simple Darwinism we could expect a social arrangement of monogamous married couples or whether the males would all have harems. There were points to be made either way and I didn't care for any of those points.

Wilmet opened with one heart and soon we were up to three. I mentioned how Beverly had said she'd get her picture in the Louisville Museum if she killed an ape. "It's not entirely my decision," Archer said. "But, yes, part of my plan is that there will be pictures. And interviews. Possibly in magazines, certainly in the museum. The whole object is that people be told." And this began a discussion over whether, for the purposes of saving gorilla lives, it would work best if Beverly was to kill one or if it should be me. There was some general concern that the sight of Beverly in a pith helmet might be, somehow, stirring, whereas if I were the one, it wouldn't be cute in the least. If Archer really wished to put people off gorilla-hunting, then, the men agreed, I was his girl. Of course it was not as bald as that, but that was the gist.

Wilmet lost a trick he'd hoped to finesse. We were going down and I suddenly saw that he'd opened with only four hearts, which, though they were pretty enough, an ace and a king included, was a witless thing to do. I still think so.

"I expected more support," he said to me, "when you took us to two," as if it were my fault.

"Length is strength," I said right back and then I burst into tears, because he was so short it was an awful thing to say. It took me more by surprise than anyone and most surprising of all, I didn't seem to care about the crying. I got up from the table and walked off. I could hear Eddie apologizing behind me as if I was the one who'd opened with four hearts. "Change of life," I heard him saying. It was so like Eddie to know what was happening to me even before I did.

It was so unlike him to apologize for me. At that moment I hated him with all the rest. I went to our tent and fetched some water and my rifle. We weren't any of us to go into the jungle alone so no one imagined this was what I was doing.

The sky had begun to cloud up and soon the weather was colder. There was no clear track to follow, only antelope trails. Of course I got lost. I had thought to take every possible turn to the right and then reverse this coming back, but the plan didn't suit the landscape nor achieve the end desired. I had a whistle, but was angry enough not to use it. I counted on Eddie to find me eventually as he always did.

I believe I walked for more than four hours. Twice it rained, intensifying all the green smells of the jungle. Occasionally the sun was out and the mosses and leaves overlaid with silvered water. I saw a cat print that made me move my rifle off of safe to ready and then often had to set it aside as the track took me over roots and under hollow trees. The path was unstable and sometimes slid out from under me.

Once I put my hand on a spider's web. It was a domed web over an orb, intricate and a beautiful pale yellow in color. I never touched a silk so strong. The spider was big and black with yellow spots at the undersides of her legs and, judging by the corpses, she carried all her victims to the web's center before wrapping them. I would have brought her back, but I had nothing to keep her in. It seemed a betrayal of Eddie to let her be, but that sort of evened our score.

Next thing I put my hand on was a soft looking leaf. I pulled it away full of nettles.

Although the way back to camp was clearly downhill, I began to go up. I thought to find a vista, see the mountains, orient myself. I was less angry by now and suffered more from the climbing as a result. The rain began again and I picked out a sheltered spot to sit and tend my stinging hand. I should have been cold and frightened, but I wasn't either. The pain in my hand was subsiding. The jungle was beautiful and the sound of rain a lullaby. I remember wishing that this was where I belonged, that I lived here. Then the heat came on me so hard I couldn't wish at all.

A noise brought me out of it — a crashing in the bamboo. Turning, I saw the movement of leaves and the backside of something rather like a large black bear. A gorilla has a strange way of walking — on the hind feet and the knuckles, but with arms so long their backs are hardly bent. I had one clear look and then the creature was gone. But I could still hear it and I was determined to see it again.

I knew I'd never have another chance; even if we did see one later the men would take it over. I was still too hot. My shirt was drenched from sweat and rain; my pants, too, and making a noise whenever I bent my knees. So I removed everything and put back only my socks and boots. I left the rest of my clothes folded on the spot where I'd been sitting, picked up my rifle, and went into the bamboo.

Around a rock, under a log, over a root, behind a tree was the prettiest open meadow you'd ever hope to see. Three gorillas were in it, one male, two female. It might have been a harem. It might have been a family — a father, mother and daughter. The sun came out. One female combed the other with her hands, the two of them blinking in the sun. The male was seated in a patch of wild carrots, pulling and eating them with no particular ardor. I could see his profile and the gray in his fur. He twitched his fingers a bit, like a man listening to music. There were flowers — pink and white — in concentric circles where some pond had been and now wasn't. One lone tree. I stood and looked for a good long time.

Then I raised the barrel of my gun. The movement brought the eyes of the male to me. He stood. He was bigger than I could ever have imagined. In the leather of his face I saw surprise, curiosity, caution. Something else, too. Something so human it made me feel like an old woman with no clothes on. I might have shot him just for that, but I knew it wasn't right — to kill him merely because he was more human than I anticipated. He thumped his chest, a rhythmic beat that made the women look to him. He showed me his teeth. Then he turned and took the women away.

I watched it all through the sight of my gun. I might have hit him several times — spared the women, freed the women. But I couldn't see that they wanted freeing and Eddie had told me never to shoot a gun angry. The gorillas faded from the meadow. I was cold then and I went for my clothes.

Russell had beaten me to them. He stood with two of our guides, staring down at my neatly folded pants. Nothing for it but to walk up beside him and pick them up, shake them for ants, put them on. He turned his back as I dressed and he couldn't manage a word. I was even more embarrassed. "Eddie must be frantic," I said to break the awkwardness.

"All of us, completely beside ourselves. Did you find any sign of her?"

Which was how I learned that Beverly had disappeared.

We were closer to camp than I'd feared if farther than I'd hoped. While we walked I did my best to recount my final conversation with Beverly to Russell. I was, apparently, the last to have seen her. The card game had broken up soon after I left and the men gone their separate ways. A couple of hours later, Merion began looking for Beverly who was no longer in her tent. No one was alarmed, at first, but by now they were.

I was made to repeat everything she'd said again and again and questioned over it, too, though there was nothing useful in it and soon I began to feel I'd made up every word. Archer asked our guides to look over the ground about the pool and around her tent. He had some cowboy scene in his mind, I suppose, the primitive who can read a broken branch, a footprint, a bit of fur and piece it all together. Our guides looked with great seriousness, but found nothing. We searched and called and sent up signaling shots until night came over us.

"She was taken by the gorillas," Merion told us. "Just as I said she'd be." I tried to read his face in the red of the firelight, but couldn't. Nor catch his tone of voice.

"No prints," our chief guide repeated. "No sign."

That night our cook refused to make us dinner. The natives were talking a great deal amongst themselves, very quiet. To us they said as little as possible. Archer demanded an explanation, but got nothing but dodge and evasion.

"They're scared," Eddie said, but I didn't see this.

A night even more bitter than the last and Beverly not dressed for it. In the morning the porters came to Archer to say they were going back. No measure of arguing or threatening or bribing changed their minds. We could come or stay as we chose; it was clearly of no moment to them. I, of course, was given no choice, but was sent back to the mission with the rest of the gear excepting what the men kept behind.

At Lulenga one of the porters tried to speak with me. He had no English and I followed none of it except Beverly's name. I told him to wait while I fetched one of the fathers to translate, but he misunderstood or else he refused. When we returned he was gone and I never did see him again.

The men stayed eight more days on Mount Mikeno and never found so much as a bracelet.

Because I'm a woman I wasn't there for the parts you want most to hear. The waiting and the not-knowing were, in my view of things, as hard or harder than the searching, but you don't make stories out of that. Something happened to Beverly, but I can't tell you what. Something happened on the mountain after I left, something that brought Eddie back to me so altered in spirit I felt I hardly knew him, but I wasn't there to see what it was. Eddie and I departed Africa immediately and not in the company of the other men in our party. We didn't even pack up all our spiders.

For months after, I wished to talk about Beverly, to put together this possibility and that possibility and settle on something I could live with. I felt the need most strongly at night. But Eddie couldn't hear her name. He'd sunk so deep into himself, he rarely looked out. He stopped sleeping and wept from time to time and these were things he did his best to hide from me. I tried to talk to him about it, I tried to be patient and loving, I tried to be kind. I failed in all these things.

A year, two more passed, and he began to resemble himself again, but never in full. My full, true Eddie never did come back from the jungle.

Then one day, at breakfast, with nothing particular to prompt it
he told me there'd been a massacre. That after I left for Lulenga th
men had spent the days hunting and killing gorillas. He didn't de
scribe it to me at all, yet it sprang bright and terrible into my mind
my own little family group lying in their blood in the meadow.

Forty or more, Eddie said. Probably more. Over several days. Ba
bies, too. They couldn't even bring the bodies back; it looked so ba
to be collecting when Beverly was gone. They'd slaughtered the goril
las as if they were cows.

Eddie was dressed in his old plaid robe, his gray hair in uncombe
bunches, crying into his fried eggs. I wasn't talking, but he put hi
hands over his ears in case I did. He was shaking all over from weep
ing, his head trembling on his neck. "It felt like murder," he said.
"Just exactly like murder."

I took his hands down from his head and held on hard. "I expect it
was mostly Merion."

"No," he said. "It was mostly me."

At first, Eddie told me, Merion was certain the gorillas had taken
Beverly. But later, he began to comment on the strange behavior of
the porters. How they wouldn't talk to us, but whispered to each
other. How they left so quickly. "I was afraid," Eddie told me. "So upset about Beverly and then terribly afraid. Russell and Merion, they
were so angry I could smell it. I thought at any moment one of them
would say something that couldn't be unsaid, something that would
get to the Belgians. And then I wouldn't be able to stop it anymore.
So I kept us stuck on the gorillas. I kept us going after them. I kept us
angry until we had killed so very many and were all so ashamed, there
would be no way to turn and accuse someone new."

I still didn't quite understand. "Do you think one of the porters
killed Beverly?" It was a possibility that had occurred to me, too; I admit it.

"No," said Eddie. "That's my point. But you saw how the blacks
were treated back at Lulenga. You saw the chains and the beatings.
I couldn't let them be suspected." His voice was so clogged I could

hardly make out the words. "I need you to tell me I did the right thing."

So I told him. I told him he was the best man I ever knew. "Thank you," he said. And with that he shook off my hands, dried his eyes, and left the table.

That night I tried to talk to him again. I tried to say that there was nothing he could do that I wouldn't forgive. "You've always been too easy on me," he answered. And the next time I brought it up, "If you love me, we'll never talk about this again."

Eddie died three years later without another word on the subject passing between us. In the end, to be honest, I suppose I found that silence rather unforgivable. His death even more so. I have never liked being alone.

As every day I more surely am; it's the blessing of a long life. Just me left now, the first white woman to see the wild gorillas and the one who saw nothing else – not the chains, not the beatings, not the massacre. I can't help worrying over it all again, now I know Archer's dead and only me to tell it, though no way of telling puts it to rest.

Since my eyes went, a girl comes to read to me twice a week. For the longest time I wanted nothing to do with gorillas, but now I have her scouting out articles as we're finally starting to really see how they live. The thinking still seems to be harems, but with the females slipping off from time to time to be with whomever they wish.

And what I notice most in the articles is not the apes. My attention is caught instead by these young women who'd sooner live in the jungle with the chimpanzees or the orangutans or the great mountain gorillas. These women who freely choose it – the Goodalls and the Galdikas and the Fosseys. And I think to myself how there is nothing new under the sun, and maybe all those women carried off by gorillas in those old stories, maybe they all freely chose it.

When I am tired and have thought too much about it all, Beverly's last words come back to me. Mostly I put them straight out of my head, think about anything else. Who remembers what she said? Who knows what she meant?

But there are other times when I let them in. Turn them over. Then they become, not a threat as I originally heard them, but an invitation. On those days I can pretend that she's still there in the jungle, dipping her feet, eating wild carrots, and waiting for me. I can pretend that I'll be joining her whenever I wish and just as soon as I please.

The Snow Queen: A Tale in Seven Stories

Hans Christian Andersen

TRANSLATED BY DIANA CRONE FRANK AND JEFFREY FRANK

Much has been written about how folk stories and fairy tales have been diminished in the past century to mere fiction for children. In recent decades, writers – especially fantasy writers – have been reclaiming these stories for adults. Some of these are retellings of the stories in their original periods (Lisa Goldstein's "Ever After," or Patricia C. Wrede's *Snow White and Rose Red*); others have recast them in contemporary times (Donald Barthelme's *Snow White*, or Jane Yolen's *Briar Rose* as set during the Nazi Holocaust). Editor Terri Windling has pioneered in this area with a series of fairy tale novels for Ace and Tor (starting with *The Sun, the Moon and the Stars* by Steven Brust) and a series of anthologies on this theme with Ellen Datlow (starting with *Snow White, Blood Red*).

A writer who retells a fairy or folk tale often wants to point out some relevance of the old story to the contemporary world. Thus it is not surprising that many of these retellings have some new political or social perspective, and thus it is not surprising that gender roles and gender expectations are frequently re-examined in these fictions.

In 1998, "Travels with the Snow Queen," Kelly Link's modern take on a Hans Christian Andersen story, won a Tiptree Award. Her story uses the events of Andersen's tale to take her character on a very different journey.

This wasn't the first contemporary retelling of the story. Perhaps most famously, Joan D. Vinge used it as the basis for her Hugo Award-winning science fiction novel of the same name in 1980. Patricia McKillip's 1993 version can be found in the *Snow White, Blood Red* anthology.

This year, Kara Dalkey's original look at the same story caught the attention of the jury. "The Lady of the Ice Garden" is set in Japan's militaristic Kamakura period, but more than the setting is different here. Girida and Keiken are not simple analogues of Andersen's Gerda and Kai; they have their own motivations and end up in their own places.

These modern versions of the Snow Queen story present fresh insights not only about gender assumptions but about storytelling itself. Running the two together was irresistible. And in case many of you have not had the opportunity to read the original recently, we decided to include that as well, in the acclaimed new Frank translation.

All right, let's get started! When we're at the end of the story, we'll know more than we do now, because there was an evil troll, one of the worst – it was the devil. One day, he was in a really good mood; he had made a mirror that had special qualities: It would shrink everything that was good and beautiful to almost nothing, and it would magnify whatever was worthless and ugly and make it seem even worse. The most beautiful landscapes looked like boiled spinach, and the nicest people appeared loathsome; or they appeared to stand on their heads with their stomachs missing and their faces so twisted that you couldn't tell who they were. If someone had a freckle, you can be sure that it would spread over his nose and mouth. It was great fun, the devil said. If someone had a good, pious thought, the mirror would show a grin – the troll-devil just couldn't stop laughing at his clever invention.

Everyone who was enrolled in troll school (for the devil ran a troll school) spread the word that a miracle had happened. For the first time, they believed, you could see what people and the world were really like. The troll students ran all over the place with the mirror. In the end there wasn't a country or a person that it hadn't distorted; and now they wanted to fly up to heaven and make fun of the angels and God himself. The higher they took the mirror, the harder they laughed; they could barely hold on to it. They flew higher and higher, closer to God and the angels. Suddenly, the mirror, which was still grinning, shook so violently that it slipped from their hands and fell to earth, where it broke into a hundred million, billion, and even more pieces. From that moment the mirror spread more unhappiness than ever.

Some splinters were hardly as big as a grain of sand, and they flew around the whole wide world. If a splinter got into somebody's eyes, it stayed there and made everything look bad. People would see only what was wrong, because every little speck was as powerful as the whole mirror. In fact, some people even got a small piece in their hearts. That was really awful – their hearts then became as hard as chunks of ice. Some pieces of the mirror were so big that you could use them as window-panes, but you wouldn't want to look at your friends through a window like that. Other pieces were used for eyeglasses, and when people put them on to see or to decide a question fairly, that's when things really went wrong. The devil laughed until his sides split – that tickled pleasantly – while tiny pieces of glass kept flying through the air. Now let's see what happens.

SECOND STORY | *A Little Boy and a Little Girl*

In the big city, where there are so many houses and people and not enough room for everyone to have his own little garden, most people must settle for a flowerpot. Two poor children, who nevertheless had a garden a little bigger than a flowerpot, lived there too. They were not brother and sister, but they were as fond of one another as if they were. Their parents lived right next to each other; each family had a room right under the roof, where one house almost bumped into the other. A rain gutter ran between the houses, under the eaves, and each had a window that faced the other. You could go across the rain gutter from window to window in a single stride.

Outside the window each family put a large wooden box for growing herbs and a little rosebush too. One rosebush grew in each box, and they thrived. The parents had set the boxes across the rain gutter so that they almost reached from window to window. The boxes looked like flowering walls; sweet-pea vines hung over the sides, and the long branches of the rosebushes wound around the windows and grew into one another. It was almost like an archway of greenery and flowers. Because the boxes were so high up, the children knew that they shouldn't climb out of them, but they were often allowed to sit on their little stools under the roses. They played so beautifully there.

In winter, of course, that sort of fun was over. The windows were often frosted over. But the children heated copper coins on the stove, pressed them against the frozen windowpanes, and the coins made perfect round peepholes. Through the opening in each window was an affectionate eye belonging to the little boy and the little girl. His

name was Kai, and she was Gerda. In the summer they could g
together in one leap, but in the winter they had to climb lots of ste
down and lots of steps up. Outside, the snow drifted.

“The white bees are swarming,” Grandmother said.

“Do they also have a queen?” the little boy asked, because he kne
that real bees had one.

“Yes, they do,” Grandmother said. “She flies where the swar
is thickest. She's the biggest one of all, and she never stays on th
ground. She flies up again into the black clouds. On lots of wint
nights she flies through the streets and looks through the window
and then they freeze over very strangely — as if they were covered wit
flowers.”

“Yes, I've seen that,” both children said, for they knew that it wa
true.

“Can the Snow Queen come inside?” the little girl asked.

“Let her just come,” the boy said. “I'll put her on the hot stove, an
she'll melt.”

Grandmother smoothed his hair and told more stories.

In the evening, when Kai was half undressed, he climbed up on th
chairs by the window and looked through his little peephole. A coupl
of snowflakes fell outside, and one of them — the largest — stayed o
the edge of a flower box. The snowflake grew bigger and bigger unti
at last, it turned into a woman; she wore the finest white gauze mad
of millions of starlike flakes. She was delicate and beautiful made o
blinding, glimmering ice. Yet she was alive. Her eyes stared out lik
two bright stars, but there was no calm or peace in them. She nod
ded toward the window and waved her hand. The little boy was fright
ened and jumped down from the chair; just then a large bird flew pas
the window.

The next day it was freezing. Then the thaw came and then sprin
— the sun shined, green sprouts peeked out of the ground, swallow
made their nests, windows were opened, and the two children sa
once more in their little garden over the rain gutter, way up above th
top floor.

The roses bloomed unusually well that summer. The little girl ha earned a hymn that mentioned roses, which made her think about er own. She sang it for the little boy, who joined in:

In the valley, the roses grow wild,
There we can speak to the Christ child!

The children held hands, kissed the roses, and looked into God's lear sunshine; they talked to it as if the baby Jesus were there. The ummer days were so lovely, and it was heavenly to be out among the resh rosebushes, which never seemed to stop blooming.

Kai and Gerda were looking at their picture book filled with animals and birds, and then – precisely as the clock on the big church steeple struck five – Kai said, "Ouch! Something stung my heart, and I've got something in my eye!"

The little girl pulled him close; he blinked, but no, there was nothing to see.

"I think it's gone," he said, but it wasn't gone. It was, in fact, one of those glass splinters from the mirror – the troll's mirror. Of course, we all remember that ghastly mirror, which could shrink everything big and beautiful down to something tiny and hideous and could magnify whatever was evil and bad, making every flaw stand out. Poor Kai, he had gotten a tiny piece of it right in his heart. Soon it would be like a lump of ice. It didn't hurt anymore, but the splinter was still there.

"Why are you crying?" Kai asked. "You look so ugly! There's nothing wrong with me. Ugh!" he suddenly shouted. "That rose has been chewed by a worm. And look, it's quite crooked. When you think about it, those roses are disgusting. They look like the boxes they grow in." He kicked the box hard and tore two roses from the bush.

"Kai, what are you doing?" the little girl shouted. When he saw how alarmed she was, he ripped off another rose and ran inside through the window, away from Gerda.

From then on, whenever she showed up with the picture book, he said it was for babies. When Grandmother told them stories, he always had to say "but" – and if he had the chance, he would follow her, put on her glasses, and imitate the way she spoke. It was exactl like her, and it made people laugh. Kai soon learned how to walk an talk like everybody on their street and how to imitate everything tha was different and unattractive about them. People said, "That bo certainly has a good head on his shoulders." But because of the glas splinter in his eye and in his heart, he even teased little Gerda, wh loved him with all her heart.

The little boy's games became quite different from what they ha been. They were so clever now: One winter day, as the snow flake came flying down, Kai went outside with a big magnifying glass spread out the corner of his blue coat, and let the snow fall on it.

"Look through the glass, Gerda!" he said. Every snowflake be came much bigger and looked like a dazzling flower or a star with te points; it was beautiful.

"Look how well designed they are," Kai said. "They're much more interesting than real flowers. There's not a single flaw; they're absolutely perfect as long as they don't melt."

A little later Kai showed up with big gloves; he was carrying a sled on his back. "They're letting me go to the big square, where the other children play!" he shouted right in Gerda's ear. And off he went.

The most daring boys on the square often tied their sleds to the farmers' wagons and rode along for a while. It was great fun. Right in the middle of their games, a large sleigh showed up. It was white all over, and in it sat someone wrapped in thick white fur and a fleecy white hat; the sleigh went twice around the square, and Kai quickly managed to tie his little sled to it and ride along. It went faster and faster, right into the next street; then the person steering the sleigh turned around and gave Kai a friendly nod — as if they knew one another. Each time Kai wanted to unhook his little sled, the person in the sleigh would nod again, and Kai stayed put. They drove right through the gates of the town.

By now the snow was coming down so thickly that the little boy could barely see a thing as he sped along. Quickly, he let go of the rope to get loose from the sleigh, but it didn't do any good. His tiny sled was stuck, and it went as fast as the wind. He shouted very loudly, but no one heard him, and the snow drifted and the sleigh flew along. Occasionally, the sled jumped while rushing across ditches and fences. He was scared; he wanted to say the Lord's Prayer, but all he could remember was his multiplication tables.

The snowflakes got bigger and bigger, and in the end they looked like big white chickens. Suddenly, they jumped out of the way, the big sleigh stopped, and the person in it got up. It was a woman. Her fur coat and the hat were made of pure snow; she stood very tall and straight, brilliantly white. It was the Snow queen.

"We've arrived safely," she said. "But if you think that this is cold, crawl into my bear fur." She invited him into her sleigh and wrapped him in the fur, which felt as if he were sinking into a snowdrift.

"Are you still cold?" she asked and kissed him on his forehead. Oh! Her kiss was colder than ice; it went through him, right to his heart, which, as you know, was almost a lump of ice already. It was as if he was going to die — but only for a moment, and then it felt good. He no longer sensed the cold.

"My sled! Don't forget my sled!" That was the first thing that he remembered. It was tied to one of the white chickens, which flew behind them with the sled on its back. The Snow Queen kissed Kai again, and at that moment he forgot all about Gerda, Grandmother, and everyone at home.

"Now you won't get any more kisses," she said. "Because then my kisses would kill you."

Kai looked at her — she was so beautiful. He could not imagine a wiser, lovelier face. She didn't appear to be made of ice, as she had when she was outside his window, waving to him. In his eyes she was perfect, and he was no longer afraid. He told her that he was good at arithmetic — even fractions — and knew how many square miles there were in the country and "how many inhabitants." She always just smiled, and he realized that he didn't know enough. He looked at great big sky, and she flew off with him — way up to the dark cloud. The wind whistled and roared — as if it were singing old songs. They flew over forests and lakes, over oceans and land. Below, the cold wind shrieked, wolves howled, the snow glistened, and black screech-

ing crows flew past. But above them the moon shined big and brig
and Kai could tell that it would be a very long winter night. Duri
the day he slept at the feet of the Snow Queen.

THIRD STORY | *The Flower Garden and the Woman Who Knew Sorcery*

How was Gerda doing now that Kai was gone? Where was he? No o
knew, and no one could tell her. The other boys could say only th
they had seen him tie his little sled to a magnificent big one that we
down the street and out through the gate of the city. Nobody kn
where he was, lots of tears were shed, and Gerda wept despairin
for a long time. People said that Kai was dead, that he had drowned
the river close to town. Oh, those were long, dark winter days.

Then spring came, with a warmer sun.

"Kai is dead and gone," Gerda said.

"I don't think so!" the sunshine said.

"He's dead and gone," she said to the swallows.

"I don't think so!" they replied, and in the end Gerda didn't thi
so either.

"I'll put on my new red shoes — the ones Kai hasn't seen," she sa
one morning. "Then I'll go down to the river and ask what it know

It was very early. She kissed old Grandmother, who was still slee
ing, put on her red shoes, and walked alone through the gate to th
river.

"Is it true that you've taken my friend? I'll give you my red shoes
you'll give him back to me."

She thought that the waves nodded strangely, so she took off h
red shoes, the most precious thing she owned, and tossed them in
the river. But the shoes landed close to the bank, and right away sma
waves carried them back to her. It was as if the river would not take h
most precious possession because it had not taken Kai. She began t
worry that she hadn't thrown the shoes far enough, and she crawle
into a boat that lay among the reeds. From the far end of the boat sh
tossed her shoes overboard, and because the boat wasn't tied up, th

movement was enough to make it push off from the riverbank. When she felt the boat move, she hurried to get off. But before she could, the boat was already two feet from shore and sailing rapidly away.

Gerda became quite frightened and began to cry, but no one heard her except the sparrows, and they couldn't carry her ashore. Still, they flew along the riverbank and sang as if to comfort her. "Here are we! Here are we!" The boat was carried along by the current; Gerda, in her stocking feet, sat very still. Her little red shoes floated behind, but they could not reach the boat, which was going faster now.

Both sides of the river were beautiful, with lovely flowers, old trees, sheep, and cows on the steep slopes — but not a single person in sight.

"Maybe the river will take me to Kai," Gerda thought, and that made her feel better. She stood up and looked for hours at the beautiful green riverbank. She came to a big cherry orchard with a little house that was all thatched roof and a few strange red and blue windows. Outside stood two wooden soldiers who presented arms for everyone who sailed by.

Gerda called out to them — she thought they were alive — but of course they didn't answer. She got quite close to them; the river pushed the boat right up to the shore.

Gerda shouted even louder, and an old, old woman came out of the house. She was leaning on the crook of her cane and wore a big sun hat with beautiful flowers painted on it.

"You poor little child!" the old woman said. "How did you get out there on that big strong river and drift so far into the wide world?" The old woman waded into the water, grabbed the boat with the crook of her cane, pulled it to shore, and lifted little Gerda out.

Gerda was happy to be on dry land but still a bit afraid of this strange old woman.

"Come here and tell me who you are and how you got here," the woman said.

Gerda told her everything, and the old woman shook her head and said, "Hmm. Hmm." When Gerda had told her all there was to tell and asked if she had seen Kai, the old woman said that he hadn't come by. But, she continued, he probably would, and Gerda shouldn't be so sad; she ought to taste her cherries and look at the flowers. They were far prettier than in any picture book, and each of them had a story to tell. Then she took Gerda by the hand; they went into the little house, and the old woman locked the door.

The windows were set curiously high, and the light shined very strangely through their red, blue, and yellow panes. The most delicious-looking cherries sat on the table, and Gerda wasn't afraid to eat as many as she wanted. While Gerda was eating, the old woman untangled her hair with a golden comb. Her shiny yellow hair curled beautifully, and her friendly round face looked like a rose.

"I've always longed for such a sweet little girl," the old woman said. "You'll see – the two of us are really going to get along." As the old woman combed Gerda's hair, Gerda thought less and less about Kai, who was like a brother to her. The old woman knew witchcraft, but she wasn't an evil witch; she just did a little sorcery for her own amusement – and now she wanted to keep Gerda. So she went into the garden, pointed her cane at the rosebushes, and, although they were in beautiful bloom, they sank into the black earth so that nobody could see where they'd been. The old woman was afraid that if Gerda saw them, she would think about her own roses, remember Kai, and run away.

She led Gerda into the flower garden. It was very beautiful and fragrant. Every flower imaginable from every season was at its peak at the same time. No picture book could be more colorful and beautiful. Gerda jumped with happiness and played until the sun sank behind the tall cherry trees. Then she got into a lovely bed with red silk covers that were filled with blue violets. She slept, and her dreams were as pleasant as a queen's on her wedding day.

The next day in the warm sunshine Gerda played with the flowers. Many days passed. She recognized every flower, but no matter how many there were, she thought that one was missing. Yet she didn't know which one. Then one day she was looking at the old lady's big sun hat – the one with flowers painted on it. The most beautiful flower was a rose; the old woman had forgotten to remove it from her hat when she made the others disappear into the ground. That's what happens when you're not paying attention.

"Of course!" Gerda said. "There aren't any roses!" She jumped around the flowerbeds and looked and looked, but there were none to be found. Then she sat down and cried, but her hot tears fell just where the rosebush had vanished. When her warm tears soaked into the earth, a rosebush suddenly shot up. It was in full bloom, just as it had been when it disappeared. Gerda hugged it, kissed the roses, and thought about the beautiful roses at home, which made her think of Kai.

"I've been here too long," the little girl said. "I've got to find Kai." She asked the roses, "Do you know where he is? Do you think he's dead and gone?"

"He's not dead," the roses replied. "We've been under the ground, where all the dead people are, but Kai wasn't there."

"Thank you," Gerda said. She went to the other flowers and looked into their blossoms and asked them, "Don't you know where Kai is?"

All the flowers stood in the sunlight and dreamed their own fables or fairy tales. Gerda had to listen to many of their stories, but none of the flowers knew anything about Kai.

What did the orange lily say?

"Do you hear the drum — *boom boom?* It only has two notes — *boom boom!* Listen to the sad song of the women — listen to the shouts of the priests. The Hindu wife, in her long red robes, stands on the funeral pyre. Flames leap around her and her dead husband. But the Hindu wife thinks about who is living inside the circle — he whose eyes burn hotter than the flames, whose fiery eyes touch her heart more than the flames that will turn her body into ash. Can the fire in the heart die in the flame of the pyre?"

"I don't understand that at all," Gerda said.

"It's my fairy tale," the tiger lily replied.

What does the morning glory say?

"An old castle hangs over a narrow mountain road. Bindweed grows along its old red walls, leaf by leaf, all the way to the balcony, and a beautiful girl stands there, bending over the railing, looking down the road. No rose looks fresher – no apple blossom floating in the wind is lighter than she is. Her gorgeous silk robe rustles, 'When is he coming?'"

"Is it Kai you mean?" Gerda asked.

"I'm just talking about my own fairy tale, my dream," the morning glory replied.

What does the little daisy say?

"A wide board hangs on ropes between the trees – it's a swing. Two sweet little girls are swinging; their dresses are white like snow, and long green silk ribbons flutter from their hats. Their brother, who's older, stands on the swing, holding on with his arm twisted around the rope. In one hand he holds a little bowl, and in the other a clay pipe; he's blowing soap bubbles. The swing goes back and forth, and the bubbles, with beautiful changing colors, fly off. The last bubble clings to the pipe, shaking in the wind. The swing moves back and forth. Their little black dog, as light as the bubbles, stands on its hind legs and wants to climb onto the flying swing. The dog falls down and yelps angrily, the children laugh, the bubble pops. A swing, a reflection in a bursting soap bubble – that's my song!"

"What you're telling me may be beautiful, but you're saying it so sadly, and you haven't mentioned Kai at all. What do the hyacinths say?"

"There were three beautiful sisters, so transparent and delicate. One had a red dress, the other a blue, and the third sister's was all white. They danced hand in hand by the smooth lake in the clear moonlit night. They weren't elves; they were human children. The air smelled very sweet, and the girls disappeared into the wood. The smell got stronger. Three coffins (and inside them lay the beautiful girls) glided out of the woods and across the lake. Glowworms moved around like small, floating lights. Were the dancing girls asleep or were they dead? The fragrance of the flowers tells us they're dead, and the evening bell tolls for the dead."

"You're making me quite sad," Gerda said. "You have such a strong smell that I can't stop thinking about the dead girls. Is Kai really dead?

The roses had been under the ground, and they said no."

"Ding-dong," the hyacinth bells rang. "We're not ringing for Kai – we don't know him. We sing our own song – it's the only one we know."

Gerda went over to the buttercup, which shined among the glistening green leaves.

"You shine like a little sun," Gerda said. "Tell me: Do you know where I can find my friend?"

The buttercup shone brightly and looked at Gerda again. What song did the buttercup know? Its song was not about Kai, either:

"On the first day of spring, God's warm sun shone on the little courtyard. Its rays shimmered against the white wall of the house next door, and the first yellow flowers, like gold in the warm sunshine, grew nearby. Old Grandmother was outside in her chair; her granddaughter, a poor and pretty servant girl, had come home for a short visit. She kissed her grandmother. There was gold in that blessed kiss – gold from the heart. There was gold in her eyes, gold in the ground where it lies, and gold in the sky at sunrise. There you go – that's my little story," the buttercup said.

"My poor old grandmother!" Gerda sighed. "I'm sure she misses me and weeps for me just as she did for Kai. But I'll be going home again soon and then I'll have Kai with me. Asking the flowers isn't helping me – they only sing their own songs and don't tell me anything." She gathered up her skirt so that she could run faster, but the narcissus smacked her on the leg as she jumped over it. She stopped and looked at the tall flower, asking, "Maybe you know something?" She bent all the way down to it, and what did it say?

"I can see myself! I can see myself!" the narcissus said. "Oh, how good I smell!" In a small attic room a ballerina, half dressed, stands on one foot, then two, and kicks at the whole world. But she's an illusion. She pours water from the teapot onto some cloth that she's holding – it's the bodice of her dress. Cleanliness is next to Godliness. Her white ballet skirt hangs from a peg; it was also washed in the teapot and dried on the roof. She puts on the skirt and ties a saffron-yellow scarf around her neck to make the skirt appear even

whiter. Lift your leg high! See how she shows off her stem! I can se
myself! I can see myself!"

"I don't like that at all," Gerda said. "You don't need to tell m
that." Then she ran to the edge of the garden.

The garden gate was locked, but she jiggled the rusty handle until
shook loose and the gate sprang open. Then Gerda ran barefoot int
the wide world. She looked back three times, but no one followed he
At last, when she couldn't run anymore, she sat down on a big roc
When she looked around, summer was gone — it was late fall. But yo
couldn't tell what season it was in the beautiful garden where the su
always shone and all the flowers bloomed the year around.

"Oh, my — all the time I've wasted!" Gerda said. "It's already fall.
don't dare rest any longer" — and she got up to leave.

Oh, how sore and tired her little feet were. All around her it ha
become raw and cold. The long willow leaves had turned complete
yellow; fog dripped off them, and one leaf fell after another. Only th
blackthorn bush still had berries, which were sour enough to mak
your mouth pucker. How gray and hard the wide world was!

FOURTH STORY | *The Prince and the Princess*

Gerda needed to rest again. Just across from where she sat, a b
crow hopped on the snow. It had been watching her for some tin
when it wiggled its head and said, "Caw, caw — hellaw!" He couldn
pronounce it any better than that, but he was feeling kindly towa
the little girl and asked where in the world she was going all alon
Alone: Gerda certainly understood that word and knew all too we
what it meant to her. She told the crow her whole life story and ask
whether it had seen Kai.

The crow nodded thoughtfully and said, "Could be, could be!"

"What? Really?!" she shouted, and she nearly squeezed the crow
death — that's how hard she kissed him.

"Take it easy! Take it easy!" the crow said. "I think I've seen Ka
but because of the princess he's probably forgotten you."

"He's staying with a princess?" Gerda asked.

"Yes, but listen," the crow said. "It's hard for me to speak your language. If you spoke Crowish, it would be easier to explain."

"I haven't learned it," Gerda said. "But grandma knew it. She also spoke Snobbish. If only I had learned it."

"Never mind," the crow said. "I'll tell you everything as well as I can, but it's sure to be bad anyway." Then he told her what he knew:

"In this kingdom there's a princess who's so incredibly intelligent that she's read every newspaper in the world and forgotten all of them — that's how intelligent she is. The other day, when she was sitting on her throne — and that's not a whole lot of fun, they say — she started to hum a song. To be precise, it went like this: 'Why shouldn't I get married?' And she said, 'Why not?' Then she decided to get married, but she wanted to find a husband who knew what to say when someone spoke to him — not someone who just stood there looking dignified, because that's so boring. She called all her ladies-in-waiting together, and when they heard what she wanted, they thought it would be great fun. 'Oh, I like that idea!' they all said. 'I had almost the same idea the other day.'"

"Believe me, everything I tell you is true," the crow went on. "My sweetheart is a tame bird who's allowed to go anywhere in the castle, and she's told me everything."

Naturally, his fiancée was a crow, because birds of a feather flock together.

"The next day's newspapers had a border of hearts, along with the princess's initials, and they announced that every attractive young man was invited to come to the castle to talk to the princess. She would choose the one who sounded most at home and spoke the best. Yes indeed!" the crow said. "This is as true as the fact that I'm sitting here. People streamed to the castle — it was a mob scene — but nobody was chosen, not on the first day or on the second. In the street, people were all well-spoken, but the moment that they came through the castle gate and saw guards in the courtyard wearing silver, and footmen on the stairs wearing gold, they were stunned. They stood in front of the throne where the princess sat, and they didn't know what to say, so they repeated the last thing she had said — and she didn't want to hear that again. It was as if the suitors inside had fallen asleep with snuff spilling down their fronts. It wasn't until they got out into the street again that they could talk. There was a line of people from the city's gate all the way to the castle. I saw it with my own eyes," the crow continued. "They were hungry and thirsty, but at the castle they didn't get even a glass of lukewarm water. Of course, some of the cleverest had brought sandwiches, but they didn't share with their neighbor, because this is what they thought: If he looks hungry, the princess won't choose him."

"But Kai, little Kai?" Gerda asked. "When did he come? Was he in the crowd?"

"Be patient, be patient – we're almost there. On the third day a short person without a horse or carriage marched boldly right up to the castle. His eyes shined like yours, and he had nice long hair, but his clothes were shoddy."

"It was Kai," Gerda said excitedly. "Oh, I've found him!" She clapped her hands.

"Did he have a little rucksack on his back?" the crow asked.

"No, it was probably his sled," Gerda said, "because he was on a sled when he went away."

"You may be right," the crow said. "I didn't look very carefully. But my tame sweetheart told me all about it. When he came through the castle door and saw the guards dressed in silver and the footmen on the stairs dressed in gold, he wasn't the least bit daunted. He just nodded and said, 'It must be really boring to stand there on the stairs – I'd rather go inside.' Inside, the royal rooms were all lit up; the king's councilors and various excellencies went around barefoot and carried golden plates. It was enough to make anyone solemn. His boots creaked very loudly, but he still wasn't afraid."

"I'm sure it's Kai!" Gerda said. "I know he got new boots – I heard them creak at Grandmother's."

"Oh, yes, they certainly creaked," the crow said. "But he was bold, and went straight to the princess, who sat on a pearl as big as a spinning wheel. All the ladies-in-waiting with their servant girls, and the servant girls with *their* servant girls, and all the lords-in-waiting with *their* servants and their servants' servant boys — all stood at attention around the castle. The closer they stood to the door, the prouder they looked. And the servants' servants' servant boy, who always wears slippers, was so proud that you could hardly bear to look at him."

"That must have been awful," Gerda said. "But Kai got the princess anyway?"

"If I hadn't been a crow, I would have won her — although I'm engaged. People say that he spoke as well as I speak when I'm speaking Crowish — or that's what my tame sweetheart says. He was bold and charming. He wasn't there to propose, only to listen to the wisdom of the princess. He liked what he heard, and she liked him too."

"Yes, that was certainly Kai," Gerda said. "He was so smart he could do numbers in his head — with fractions! Oh, please, won't you take me to the castle?"

"That's easy for you to say," the crow said. "But how do we do it? I'll talk to my tame fiancée; she can probably give us advice. But I've got to tell you, a little girl like you will never get permission to get all the way in."

"Yes, I will!" Gerda said. "When Kai finds out that I'm here, he'll come out and fetch me right away."

"Wait for me by the fence there," the crow said, wiggled his head, and flew off.

As soon as it got dark, the crow came back. "Caw, caw!" he said. "My fiancée sends you many greetings, and here's a little piece of bread for you. She got it in the kitchen — there's enough bread there — and you must be hungry. Anyway, you can't get inside the castle; after all, you're barefoot, and the guards dressed in silver and the footmen in gold won't allow it. But don't cry; we'll get you there. My fiancée knows a small back staircase that leads to the bedroom, and she knows where to get the key."

They went into the garden, past the trees along the wide path, where one leaf fell after another. At the castle, when the lights were put out, one after another, the crow led Gerda to the back door, which stood ajar.

Gerda's heart beat with dread and yearning. It was as if she were about to do something bad, but all she wanted to know was where Kai was. It had to be him. In her mind she could see his wise eyes, his long hair; she could vividly remember the way he had smiled when they had sat under the roses at home. She thought he would be happy to see her — to hear how far she had come for his sake and to know how sad everyone at home had been when he did not return. She felt dread and longing.

Then they were on the staircase; a small lamp burned on a cupboard. The tame crow stood in the middle of the floor. She turned her head every which way and looked at Gerda, who curtsied as Grandmother had taught her.

"My fiancé has said so many nice things about you, Miss Gerda," the tame crow said. "Your vita, as we say, is very touching. If you'll take the lamp, I'll lead the way. We'll go straight there. That way we won't run into anyone."

"I think someone is following right behind us," Gerda said, and something rushed by her like shadows on a wall: horses with flying manes and thin legs, gamekeepers, and ladies and gentlemen on horseback.

"Those are just dreams," the tame crow said. "Dreams take the royals' thoughts out to the hunt, and that's good, because they can see it all better from bed. I want to be sure that if you reach a position of honor and respect, you'll show heartfelt gratitude."

"Don't mention it," the crow from the woods said.

They went into the first room. It was all rosy satin with artificial flowers on the walls. Here the dreams rushed by but so quickly that Gerda was not able to catch sight of the royals. Each room was more magnificent than the one before — it was amazing — and then they were in the bedroom. The ceiling there looked like a great palm tree made of glass — precious glass. In the middle of the floor two beds that resembled lilies hung on stems of gold. One was white, which is where the princess slept; the other was red, and that was where Gerda looked for Kai. She pushed one of the red petals aside and saw a brown neck. "Oh that's Kai!" She shouted out his name, held the lamp close, and dreams galloped into the room again. He woke up, turned his head, and – it was not Kai.

It was only the prince's neck that looked like Kai's, but nevertheless the prince was young and handsome. The princess peeked out from her white lily bed and asked what was going on. Gerda began to cry. She told her entire story and all that the crows had done for her.

"You poor thing!" the prince and the princess said. They praised the crows and said that they weren't the least bit angry at them but that they shouldn't do it again. Meanwhile, the crows would get a reward.

"Do you want freedom?" the princess asked. "Or would you rather have steady jobs as court crows, with benefits – whatever is left over in the kitchen?"

Both crows curtsied and asked for jobs at the court, for they were thinking about their old age and said, "It's so nice to have something for our golden years," as they called it.

The prince got out of his bed and let Gerda sleep in it, but that was all he could do for her. She folded her hands and thought, "How good the people and the animals were." Then she closed her eyes and slept very soundly. All the dreams came flying in, and they looked like God's angels, pulling a little sled. Kai sat on the sled and nodded to her, but it was only a dream, and it was gone again as soon as she woke up.

The next day Gerda was dressed from top to toe in silk and velvet. They invited her to stay at the castle and live in comfort, but all she asked for was a horse, a little carriage, and a pair of small boots. Then she would head out into the wide world again and look for Kai.

She got boots and a fur muff. She was dressed very nicely, and when she wanted to leave, a new coach of pure gold was waiting at the door. The prince and princess's coat of arms shined like a star from the carriage. The coachman, servants, and postilions – for there were postilions too – wore gold crowns. The prince and princess helped Gerda into the coach themselves and wished her good luck. The wild crow, who by now had gotten married, accompanied her inside the coach for the first three miles; he sat next to her, because it

made him sick to ride backward. The tame crow stood on the castl
gate and flapped her wings. She did not come along because she'd ha
a headache ever since she'd gotten a steady job and too much to ea
The coach was lined with sugar pretzels, and the seats were filled wit
fruit and cookies.

"Goodbye, goodbye!" the prince and princess called. Gerda crie
the crow cried — that is how the first few miles passed. Then the cro
said goodbye too, and it was the saddest parting. He flew up into
tree and flapped his black wings for as long as he could see the coacl
which shone like the bright sunshine.

FIFTH STORY | *The Little Bandit Girl*

They drove through a dark forest, but the coach was bright like
flame. It hurt the bandits' eyes — they couldn't stand it.

"It's gold, it's gold!" the bandits shouted as they rushed forwar
and took hold of the horses. They killed the postilions, the coacl
man, and the servants, and yanked Gerda out of the coach.

"She's plump, she's lovely, she's fattened up with nuts," said the o
bandit hag, who had a long bristly beard and eyebrows that covere
her eyes. "She's as good as a little fat lamb — oh, she'll taste so good
She pulled out her shiny knife — the way it glinted was terrifying.

"Ouch!" the hag said suddenly. She had been bitten on the ear b
her own daughter, who clung to her back and looked so unruly an
wild that it was sheer pleasure for a bandit. "You nasty brat!" th
mother said and didn't have the time to chop up Gerda.

"I want her to play with me," the bandit girl insisted. "I want h
to give me her muff, her beautiful dress, and I want her to sleep ne
to me." She bit her mother again, which made the bandit hag jum
up and spin around. All the bandits laughed and said, "Look how sl
dances with her kid!"

"I want to get into the coach," the bandit girl said. She had to ha
her way because she was so spoiled and stubborn. She and Gerda s
in the coach, and they drove over brambles and thorns, deep into tl

woods. The bandit girl was no bigger than Gerda, but she was stronger — her shoulders were broader and her skin was darker. Her eyes were quite black — they looked almost sad. She hugged Gerda and said, "They won't chop you to pieces as long as I don't get mad at you. I guess you're a princess?"

"No," Gerda said and told her all that had happened to her and how fond she was of Kai.

The bandit girl looked solemn, nodded slightly, and said, "I won't let them chop you up, and even if I do get mad at you, I'll do it myself." She dried Gerda's eyes and warmed her hands in the beautiful muff, which was very soft and warm.

The coach stopped. They were in the middle of the courtyard of the bandits' castle, which had a crack that ran from top to bottom. Ravens and crows flew out of holes in the wall, and big bulldogs — each of them looked as if it could swallow an entire person — jumped high in the air. But the dogs didn't bark, because it was forbidden.

A big fire burned on the stone floor in the middle of an enormous old sooty room. Smoke drifted toward the ceiling and had to find its own way out. Soup cooked in a large vat, and hares and rabbits turned on spits.

"You'll sleep here with me and all my little animals," the bandit girl said. They ate and drank and went to a corner that was covered with blankets and straw. Above them, perched on pegs and rafters, were nearly a hundred tame pigeons. They seemed to be asleep, but they stirred slightly when the little girls approached.

"They're all mine," the bandit girl said and quickly grabbed one of the pigeons. She held it by the feet and shook it until it flapped its wings. "Kiss it!" she shouted, and it flapped in Gerda's face. "The wild wood pigeons are up there," she continued and pointed high up the wall to bars that covered a hole. "Those two are wood pigeons — they'll fly off in a second if you don't lock them up properly. And here's my dear old Bae!" she said, yanking the antlers of a reindeer who was tied by a shiny copper ring around his neck. "We have to watch him carefully too or he'll run off with the pigeons. Every single evening

I tickle his neck with my sharp knife — he's afraid of that." The littl
bandit girl pulled a long knife from a crack in the wall and let it slid
across the reindeer's neck. The poor animal kicked; the bandit gi
laughed and dragged Gerda to bed.

"Do you keep the knife with you when you sleep?" Gerda aske
and looked at it a little fearfully.

"I always sleep with the knife," the bandit girl replied. "You neve
know what might happen. But tell me again what you told me befor
about Kai and why you went out in the wide world."

Gerda started from the beginning, while the wild pigeons cooe
in their cage, and the tame pigeons slept. The little bandit girl put he
arm around Gerda's neck and held the knife in her other hand. Sh
made a lot of noise when she slept. Gerda could not close her eyes, fo
she didn't know if she was going to live or die. The bandits sat arounc
the fire singing and drinking, and the bandit hag did somersaults —
oh, it was a terrible sight for a little girl to see.

Then the wood pigeons said, "Grrgh, grrgh! We've seen Kai. A
white hen pulled his sled — he sat in the carriage of the Snow Queen.
When we were still in our nest, her carriage flew by above the forest. Her ice-cold breath killed all the baby birds except the two of us.
Grrgh, grrgh!"

"What are you two saying up there?" Gerda shouted. "Where did
the Snow Queen go? Do you have any idea?"

"She probably went to Lapland, because there's always snow and
ice there. Just ask the reindeer who's tied up over there with a rope."

"Yes," the reindeer said. "There's ice and snow, and it's wonderful
and good. You can jump all around the big shiny valleys. The Snow
Queen has her summer tent there, but her permanent castle is up by
the North Pole on the island called Spitsbergen."

"Oh, Kai, little Kai," Gerda sighed.

"Now lie still," the bandit girl said. "Or else I'll poke you in the
stomach with my knife."

In the morning Gerda told her everything that the wood pigeons
had reported, and the bandit girl looked quite serious. She nodded

her head and said, "It doesn't matter, it doesn't matter. Do you know where Lapland is?" she asked the reindeer.

"Who would know better than me?" the reindeer replied, and his eyes sparkled. "I was born and raised there, and I played there in the snowy fields."

"Listen," the bandit girl said to Gerda. "You can see that all the men are gone. But Ma is still here, and she'll stick around. Late in the morning she'll start to drink from the big bottle. After that, she'll take a little nap, and that's when I can help you." She jumped out of bed, rushed to give her mother a hug, pulled her mother's beard, and said, "Good morning, my own sweet goat!" Her mother pinched her nose so that it turned both red and blue, but she did it all out of love.

When her mother had drunk from her bottle and was taking her nap, the bandit girl went to the reindeer and said, "I really wish I could keep tickling you with my sharp knife, because it's so funny. But never mind. I'll untie your rope and help you get outside, so you can run away to Lapland. But you have to hurry and take this little girl to the Snow Queen's castle, where her friend lives. You know her story, because she talked loud enough and you listened in."

The reindeer jumped for joy. The bandit girl lifted Gerda onto its back, took care to tie her down, and even gave her a little pillow to sit on. "While we're at it," she said, "here are your fur boots, because it will get cold. I'll keep the muff because it's much too pretty, but you won't freeze. Here are my mother's big mittens – they'll reach all the way to your elbow. Put them on. Now your hands look like my horrid mother's."

Gerda was so happy that she cried.

"I don't like it when you whine," the bandit girl said. "Just look happy now! And here are two loaves of bread and a ham so you won't starve." The bread and the ham were tied behind Gerda. The bandit girl opened the door, coaxed all the big dogs inside, and cut the rope with her knife, telling the reindeer, "Now run! But take care of the little girl."

Gerda stretched her big mittens toward the bandit girl and said goodbye. Then the reindeer rushed off through bushes and stubble through a big forest, across swamps and steppes, as fast as it could go. Wolves howled, ravens shrieked, and the sky made a noise like "achoo, achoo" — as if it had sneezed itself red.

"Those are my old Northern Lights," the reindeer said. "Look how they shine!" It ran farther, through night and day. The bread was eaten, the ham too, and then they were in Lapland.

SIXTH STORY | *The Lapp and the Finn*

They stopped at a small house. It looked wretched; the roof almost touched the ground, and the doorway was so low that the people who lived there had to crawl on their stomachs to get in or out. No one was home except for an old Lapp woman who was frying fish next to a whale-oil lamp. The reindeer told her Gerda's whole story, but first he told his own because it seemed much more important; besides, Gerda was so worn out by cold that she could not speak.

"Oh, you poor things," the Lapp woman said. "You still have a long way to go. You have to travel more than a hundred miles into Finnmark because the Snow Queen has her country place there; she fires off blue light every single night. I'll write a few words on a dried codfish, because I don't have any paper. You can give it to the Finn woman up there — she knows more about it than I do."

When Gerda had warmed up and gotten something to eat and drink, the Lapp woman wrote a few words on the dried codfish and told Gerda to keep it safe. She tied Gerda to the reindeer again, and he bounded off. There was a sound of "Phst, phst!" in the air, and all night the most beautiful blue Northern Lights burned in the sky. Then they arrived in Finnmark, where they knocked on the Finn woman's chimney, because she did not even have a door.

It was so hot inside that the Finn woman walked around almost naked. She was tiny and sort of grimy. She helped Gerda out of her clothes and took off her mittens and boots — otherwise Gerda would be far too hot — and put a piece of ice on the reindeer's head. Then she read what was written on the dried fish. She read it three times. By hen she knew it by heart and put the dried codfish into the pot. You could still eat it; she never wasted anything.

The reindeer told his own story first and then Gerda's. The Finn woman blinked her wise eyes but said nothing.

"You're so wise," the reindeer said. "I know that you can tie up all the winds of the world with a thread. When a sailor unties one knot, he'll get a good breeze. If he unties a second, it will blow hard, and when he unties a third and fourth, it'll be so stormy that the trees in the forest will blow down. Won't you give the little girl a drink so she'll get the strength of twelve men and overpower the Snow Queen?"

"The strength of twelve men?" the Finn woman said. "A lot of good that will do!" She went over to a shelf, took down a big rolled-up hide, and unfolded it. The hide was covered with strange letters. The Finn woman read until sweat poured from her forehead.

Once again the reindeer begged the Finn woman to help Gerda. Gerda looked at her pleadingly, her eyes filled with tears. The Finn woman's eyes fluttered again and she pulled the reindeer into a corner. As she put another piece of ice on his head, she whispered, "It's all true. Kai's with the Snow Queen — where he can have everything he wants or imagines. He believes it's the best place in the world, but that's because he has a splinter from the mirror in his heart and a little speck of glass in his eye. Unless they come out, he'll never be human again, and the Snow Queen will keep her power over him."

"But can't you give Gerda some kind of potion to give her power over everything?"

"I can't give her any more power than she already has. Can't you see how much that is? Don't you see how people and animals feel they must help her — how far she's come on just her bare feet? But we mustn't tell her about this power. It's in her heart because she's a sweet innocent child. If she can't get to the Snow Queen herself and get rid of Kai's glass splinters, there's nothing we can do. The Snow Queen's garden starts two miles from here. You have to carry Gerda over there and set her down in the snow by the big bush with red berries. Don't dawdle — and hurry back." The Finn woman lifted Gerda onto the back of the reindeer and he ran as fast as he could.

"I forgot my boots! I forgot my mittens!" Gerda shouted. The
stung her, but the reindeer did not dare stop. He ran until he cam
the big bush with red berries, where he set her down. He kissed
on the mouth and big shiny tears ran over the animal's cheeks. T
he ran back as fast as he could. There she was, poor Gerda, with
shoes, without gloves, in the middle of the fearsome, ice-cold Fi
mark.

She ran on as quickly as she could, but a whole regiment of sn
flakes came toward her. These snowflakes did not fall from the
— it was quite clear and glowed with the Northern Lights. T
rushed along the ground, and the closer they came, the bigger t
got. Gerda remembered how big and strange snowflakes had loo
when she'd seen them through a magnifying glass, but here they w
altogether different — big and scary. They were alive — they w
the Snow Queen's guard — and had the most peculiar shapes. So
looked like big ugly hedgehogs, and others were like snakes knot
together, jabbing with their heads. Some looked like small chu
bears whose hair stood up. They were all shining white; they were
living snowflakes.

Gerda said her prayers, and it was so cold that she could see
own breath — it came out of her mouth like smoke from a chimn
Her breath got denser and denser until it turned into small transp
ent angels who grew larger and larger when they touched the grou
They all wore helmets, they all carried spears and shields, and th
kept coming. By the time Gerda had finished her prayers, a legi
of angels surrounded her. They stabbed the terrible snowflakes w
their spears, and they splintered into hundreds of pieces. So Ger
could move on, cheerful and safe. The angels rubbed her feet a
hands so that she didn't feel so cold, and she walked quickly towa
the Snow Queen's castle.

But before we go on with Gerda's story, we need to see how Ka
doing. He certainly wasn't thinking about Gerda, and he never ima
ined that she was just outside the castle.

SEVENTH STORY | *What Happened in the Snow Queen's Castle and What Happened Later*

The walls of the castle were made of drifting snow, the windows and doors of cutting winds; depending on how the snow drifted, the castle had more than a hundred rooms. They were very bright, lit by the strong Northern Lights. The biggest room stretched for miles, and all the rooms were so large, so empty, so shiny, and so icily cold. No one ever had any fun there — there wasn't even a dance for the polar bears, where the wind made the music and small bears got up on their hind legs to show how refined they were. There were no card games with paw-smacking and backslapping or even a ladies' coffee klatch for the white foxes. The Snow Queen's rooms were empty, enormous, and cold. The Northern Lights flared so regularly that you could calculate the exact moment when they would be at their brightest and at their dimmest. In the middle of this empty, endless, icy room was a frozen lake; it had cracked into a thousand pieces. Amazingly, each piece looked exactly like every other piece. When the Snow Queen was home, she sat in the middle of this lake. It was the Mirror of the Mind, she said — unique and the best thing in the world.

Kai had become quite blue with cold — almost black, in fact — but he did not feel it, because the Snow Queen had kissed away his shivers, and his heart had nearly become a lump of ice. Kai was dragging sharp flat pieces of ice, which he put together in all sorts of ways — the way we use pieces of wood in Chinese puzzles. He was trying to work something out, making most ingenious patterns: an ice puzzle of the mind. To Kai his design seemed wonderful and very important — but that was only because of the glass splinter in his eye. He had been struggling to shape the pieces of ice into a word — *eternity* — but could not figure out how to do it. The Snow Queen had said, "If you can make that design for me, you'll be your own master, and I'll give you the entire world and a pair of new skates." But he could not do it.

"I must rush off to the warm countries," the Snow Queen told him. "I want to take a look at the big black pots" — she was referring

to the volcanoes Etna and Vesuvius. "I want to give them a coat c
whitewash. They need it, and it will look good after the lemons an
grapes have been harvested." Then the snow queen flew away, an
Kai was left all alone in the big, empty, icy room that was miles long
He looked at the pieces of ice and thought and thought until his hea
ached. He was so stiff and still that you would think that he had fro
zen to death.

That was when Gerda came into the castle, through the big gat
made of stinging winds. But she read an evening prayer, and th
winds calmed down as if they were going to sleep. She stepped int
the big, empty, cold room and saw Kai. She recognized him, rushe
to him, hugged him, held him tight, and cried, "Kai, dear Kai! No
I've found you!"

But he sat very still, stiff and cold. Gerda started to cry hot tear
Her tears fell on his chest and reached his heart — thawing out th
lump of ice and melting the piece of mirror lodged in it. He looked a
her as she sang the hymn:

In the valley, the roses grow wild,
There we can talk to Christ child!

Kai burst into tears. He cried so hard that the splinter washed rig
out his eye. He recognized her and let out a shout: "Gerda, swe
Gerda! Where on earth have you been? And where have I been?" H
looked around. "It's really cold in here! And how big and empty it is
He held on to her, and she laughed and cried with joy. It was so wo
derful that even the pieces of ice danced happily around. When th
got tired, they lay down, forming just the word that the Snow Quee
had asked Kai to guess. Now he was his own master, and the Sno
Queen would give him the whole world and a new pair of skates.

Gerda kissed his cheeks, and they turned red; she kissed his eye
and they shined like hers; she kissed his hands and feet, and he b
came healthy and fit. It was all right for the Snow Queen to come ba
now. His freedom was written on the floor in shining pieces of ice.

Kai and Gerda held hands and wandered out of the big castle. They talked about Grandmother and about the roses on the roof, and wherever they went, the winds were quiet and the sun broke through. When they reached the bush with the red berries, the reindeer was waiting. Another young reindeer had come with him; her udder was full, and she gave the children warm milk and kissed them on the mouth. The reindeer carried Kai and Gerda to the Finn woman, where they warmed up in her hot room and got directions to get home. Then they went to the Lapp woman, who had sewn them new clothes and had gotten her sled ready.

The reindeer – with its young companion jumping alongside – followed the children all the way to the border, where they saw green sprouts for the first time. There they said goodbye to the reindeer and Lapp woman. "So long!" they shouted. The first little birds began to chirp, and green buds covered the forest. Then a young girl wearing a shiny red hat and holding two pistols came out of the woods on a magnificent horse. Gerda recognized the horse; it was one of those that had pulled her golden carriage. The rider was the bandit girl. She was bored at home and wanted to go north, and if that did not amuse her, she would go someplace else. She immediately recognized Gerda, and Gerda recognized her – a happy moment.

"You're really something, the way you tramped around," Gerda said to Kai. "We've gone to the end of the world for your sake. I wonder if you deserve it."

Gerda patted the bandit girl on the cheek and asked after the prince and princess.

"They've travelled to foreign countries," the bandit girl told her.

"What about the crow?" Gerda asked.

"Well, the crow is dead," she replied. "His tame sweetheart is a widow. She walks around with a piece of black wool tied to her leg. The way that she complains is pathetic, but it's all nonsense. Tell me what happened with you – how you managed to find him."

Gerda and Kai told her.

"So that's it," the bandit girl said. She grabbed their hands and promised that if she ever came through their town, she would come

to see them. Then she rode away into the wide world as Kai and Gerd
walked off hand in hand. As they walked, it turned into a beautif
spring day, all green and filled with flowers. Church bells rang, an
they recognized the tall towers, the great city. That was where the
lived. They went straight to Grandmother's door — up the stairs t
the living room where everything was just as it had been. The cloc
said tick-tock, the hands turned, and as they walked through the do
they realized that they were grownups now. The roses on the ro
bloomed in the open windows. There were their small chairs. Kai an
Gerda sat down and held each other's hands. They had forgotten,
if it were a bad dream, the cold empty splendor of the Snow Queen
castle. Grandmother sat in God's clear sunshine and read aloud fro
the Bible: "Unless you become like children, you cannot enter th
Kingdom of God."

Kai and Gerda looked at each other and suddenly understood th
old hymn:

In the valley, the roses grow wild,
There we can talk to Christ child!

There they sat, the two of them. They were grownups, and yet th
were children — children in their hearts. And it was summer — warm
wonderful summer.

The Lady of the Ice Garden

Kara Dalkey

Long, long ago, before and before, there once stood two houses side by side in Heian Kyo. They were no more than shacks, in one of the poorer quarters of the city. In each house lived a mother and her only child. Both women were of once noble families that had fallen into political disfavor, and thereby into poverty. Such was the way of those times, after the conflict called Heiji, in the era of Jisho.

One woman had a daughter, whom we will call Girida. The other woman had a son, whom we will call Keiken. Both children grew up together as if they were brother and sister, though they were not.

The two houses shared between them a garden, small but lovingly tended, in which both children played. In the spring, there were plum blossoms and fukujuso, peach blossoms and azalea. In the summer, the little pond in the center of the garden would hold two sacred white lotus blossoms over which the boy and girl would recite the Lotus Sutra. In the autumn, there would be bluebells and cattails and crickets to catch.

But the glory of the little garden was in winter, when snow mercifully covered the patched roofs of the houses and bare boughs of the trees and made every little hillock glitter as if bedecked with silver. Girida and Keiken would chase each other, throwing snowballs and building snow dragons, laughing as if such days would never end.

But end they must. In the winter of the year when Girida turned twelve and Keiken turned thirteen, it happened. It was on a day after an ice storm, and glorious icicles, bright as sword blades, hung from the eaves of the houses and branches of the trees. The boy and girl were chasing one another through the garden when Keiken tripped on a patch of ice and slid into the wall of his house. With a great crack, icicles fell from the eaves. Keiken felt a sharp pain in his left hand, and something got into his eye. "Ei!" he cried out as he stood up.

Girida ran over. "Keiken! Are you hurt?"

Keiken blinked and rubbed his eye. The pain swiftly vanished, though his eye still felt cold.

Girida peered closely at his face. "Did you get something in your eye? I see nothing there."

"It was merely a shard of ice, I think. It has melted now."

"Keiken! Your hand!"

Keiken held up his left hand and saw that a shard of icicle had lodged in the web of flesh between his thumb and forefinger. He plucked out the ice chip and a drop of blood pooled there and then fell, a dark red stain against the pure white snow.

"Keiken, we must take you inside and let mother bandage it."

Keiken looked up at her. And he saw Girida in a way he had never seen her before. He noticed the smudge of mud on her cheek. He noticed the many-times-mended kimono she wore. He noticed the blemishes on her sun-browned face and the slight crookedness of her teeth, the bushiness of her eyebrows. He suddenly despised her. "I will see to it myself," he grumbled. "Go away!"

"But Keiken —"

"Go!"

Girida ran into her house, weeping, and Keiken did not care.

What the two did not know is that this ice storm had been created by oni demons. They had been having a winter battle in the sky, with spears and swords made from ice, polished and sharp as steel. Such oni blades might cut the flesh of demons, but they cut the hearts and souls of mortals. A mortal hurt with such a blade will reject all that he has loved and desire what is worst for him or her. Who knows how it occurred, a stray wind or a mischievous kami, but some of the oni blades had fallen to earth as icicles in the snow.

In the days that followed, Keiken no longer played in the garden with Girida. Instead, he took up a wooden sword and went out into the street where the older boys practiced fighting. At first he had to fight fiercely, no matter what blows fell upon him, in order to gain their respect. When he had proven himself, they began to teach him things he had not known, as he had had no father to raise him.

Keiken learned that the way of the warrior is to never fear death, to believe one is already dead and be prepared to embrace death happily when it comes. He learned that an honorable death is the sweetest thing a man might achieve. He learned that rank was what mattered in society and that a man had best marry well if he had little noble status himself. The boys would laugh about how they would someday use their bodies like swords when bedding fine ladies. Keiken learned much in a short time.

Girida would watch Keiken as he practiced and play-dueled with the other boys. She admired him all the more and tried to put aside the pain of knowing that he no longer wished her company. When Keiken finished each day, she would wave to him as he walked from the street into his house, but he would not acknowledge her. She would call upon his mother in the evening, but Keiken would not come out of his room to speak with her.

Girida's mother noticed her weeping one night and tried to console her. "It is an odd change that comes over young men of that age," her mother said. "Suddenly all they can think of is fighting and boasting and getting the better of their peers. We always assumed that the two of you were surely close in some former life and that you would someday marry. But perhaps that is not to be. A woman's life is harder than a man's and she must bear terrible burdens. Be brave and await what happens."

Weeks passed and winter deepened. One evening, when the air had turned very chill, Keiken remained in the street practicing even after the other boys had gone home. He did not mind the cold at all. It meant he could not feel the blisters on his hands, the aching in his wrists and arms as he swung his sword through the patterns. It seemed a healing cold, and he wished his soul could become as cold as well, to feel no pain, no loneliness, no loss. He watched the cloud of his warm exhalation, like dragon breath, turn to ice crystals in the air.

When at last he stopped to rest, as the twilight was fading, he noticed an ox carriage stopped at the side of the street. It was a fine, covered carriage, clearly of some noble house, and the oxen tethered to it had hides of the purest white.

The curtains of the side windows had a crest of snowflakes, or were they butterflies? Keiken could not tell.

It was not unknown for young noble ladies to stop their carriages and watch the boys practice. Some of the older boys bragged they'd gotten many a night's entertainment in such a fashion. Keiken had the feeling someone from the carriage was watching him.

A slender, white arm emerged from the carriage window. The hand curled and beckoned to him.

Keiken's breath caught in his throat. It is a lady! What if she is a Taira? If I am desired by a lady of the most powerful warrior clan in Heian Kyo, my fortune may be made! Keiken walked to the side of the carriage, his leg muscles aching from the exertion and the cold. "You wish to speak with me?"

"What an admirable young man you are." The woman's voice within was low and melodious, like winter wind through bare tree branches. "Such a fearsome aspect for one so young. Tell me your name and your parentage."

"I am called Keiken," he replied, and then swallowed hard. He wished he could lie about his parentage, but there were severe penalties if caught in such falsehood, particularly in a society where everyone of importance knew everyone else of importance. "As for my heritage, my father is of noble birth but was sent into exile the year after I was born and I am forbidden to speak his name. My mother's as well, though she once served at Court."

"Ah, a boy of well-born, if unfortunate family. Excellent." The back door of the carriage swung open by an unseen hand. "Please, come in and speak with me."

Keiken's heart raced. He was being offered the sort of opportunity the older boys only dreamed of. With no thought of Girida, he went to the back of the carriage and went in.

The woman who sat on the cushioned side-bench within the carriage was astonishing to look upon. She wore layers of white brocade silk kimonos, the color of purity, the color of death, as if she were a Shinto priestess. Her long, coal black hair framed a face white as porcelain, and Keiken could tell she wore no white face powder. She needed none. Her skin was as smooth and unblemished as new-fallen snow. Her eyes were black as obsidian chips, yet they held glinting light, stars in a night sky.

She beckoned him toward her. "I so admired your strength as I watched you." She untied the sash at her waist and let her kimonos fall open, revealing pale, small breasts and a smooth abdomen beneath.

Keiken stumbled into her embrace. Her skin was cold, yet he felt a warming within.

"Show me what you know of swordsmanship," she whispered.

And he did.

Girida worried as Keiken did not return that night. Or the next. Seven days went by. And then another seven. No one seemed to know where he had gone, not even his mother. Girida finally found an old woman who owned an herb and medicine shop on the street where the boys practiced. The old woman shook her head and said only, "He has gone with the Lady of the Ice Garden."

Girida told this to both her mother and Keiken's mother. Neither woman seemed to know any one called by such a name. "But people change names so often," said Girida's mother. "Women, particularly, whenever they change residence. This lady might even be someone we once knew at the Imperial Court."

"Well," sighed Keiken's mother. "If Keiken has made a good match for himself, then I can hardly complain." She glanced at Girida guiltily. "But it is not right that he has not sent word to us."

"Perhaps the little coward does not dare," grumbled Girida's mother. To Girida she said, "We have a distant relative whom, I heard, married recently. She is a daughter of a concubine of a former emperor and so she is sometimes called the Wisteria Princess. Perhaps it is she who took Keiken away, or she might know who did. Do you want to go ask her?"

Girida nodded.

Girida's mother brought out a set of fine, if out of fashion, winter kimonos that she had been saving. "Wear these and at least no one will laugh at you."

Girida obediently put them on, and several pairs of tabi socks to wear under her clogs, and then set out through the snowy streets, to the address her mother gave her. The snow fell thicker and thicker and there were very few people out on the streets. Sometimes Girida had to find her way by feeling along the stone walls surrounding the great mansions in the Palace District. At last she came to the intersection of streets where the mansion she sought was supposed to be. She went to the first large gate she saw and pounded on it with her little fist.

The head of a guard appeared over the gate, his helmet comically piled with snow. "Who is there?"

"If you please, sir," said Girida, bowing respectfully, "Is this the residence of a lady called the Wisteria Princess?"

"It is. Who wants to know?"

"I am Girida, no one of importance. But I believe my friend Keiken is the man she just married. I bring him a message from his mother."

"Give it to me, then."

"If you please, I should like to speak with him myself."

The samurai laughed. "If you are no one of importance, then there is no one inside you are worthy to speak to. Go away." His head disappeared behind the gate again.

Girida sighed heavily. Her feet were very cold and she stamped them. Then she turned to begin her walk home again — and gasped as a dark figure appeared, standing beside her.

"Your pardon, sir," said Girida, bowing again. "I did not see you there."

"That is quite all right."

Girida glanced up. It was an elderly monk in black robes with a big nose who spoke to her. "Your pardon, holy one," she said with even more respect.

"It is terrible weather for a young girl like you to be out. Is anything the matter? Can I be of assistance?"

Girida said, "I do not think so. I thought that my life long friend Keiken might be here at this mansion. We have not heard from him in a long time and his mother and I wish to know if he is well. But even if he is here, it is not possible for me to see him. I am not of sufficient importance to get in."

"There is always a way around trouble," said the monk, with a knowing smile. "There is another entrance – the main gate, in fact. Perhaps you can get in that way."

Girida had her doubts but it seemed foolish to return all the way home without trying once more. "If you lead me to it, holy one, I will gratefully follow."

"This way, then." The monk walked away through the snow and Girida had to hurry to keep up with him. She kept her gaze on the dark shapes of his black robes flapping in the snowy wind.

He rounded the corner of the building first, disappearing from sight. When Girida rounded the corner, she nearly bumped into a man wearing the black robes and tall hat of a nobleman of the First Rank. Girida bowed very low. "Forgive me, most noble lord. I thought you were a monk who was just here, or I would have been more polite."

"I am the monk who was just here."

"But –"

"I am a tengu, and I may take any shape I wish."

"A tengu!" Girida had heard of the demons of the mountains who often took the shape of black birds. Now that she looked at the nobleman, his robes and sleeves did seem to billow out behind him as if he had black wings. "Why are you helping me?"

"Fortune is often unkind. Now and then, I like to see that Fortune does not get its way. I hate a predictable world, don't you?"

Girida did not know if she should agree, but she nodded.

"Good." The tengu nobleman strode up to the main gate in the wall and pounded on the doors.

A small panel slid open in the middle of one door and someone peered out. "Who is there?"

"What do you mean, who is there?" cried the tengu in an imperious voice. "What do you mean leaving me out in the snow like this? Here I am a very important visitor and I am treated like a servant. The Wisteria Princess herself will hear of this! Perhaps even the Chancellor!"

"Your pardon, most noble lord!" said the guard on the other side of the gate. The panel slid shut and soon Girida heard the great wooden bolts drawn from behind the doors. The doors were drawn inward with great speed and the tengu strode arrogantly in.

Girida held her sleeves up modestly in front of her face and hurried after the tengu as if she were his servant.

The tengu led her through a side garden where stone lanterns poked out from beneath mounds of snow. It did not look particularly like an ice garden to Girida, but who could say why people gave themselves the names they did?

She followed him up a flight of wooden steps into a building that formed one wing of the Wisteria Princess's mansion. They entered a room, dimly lit with little oil lanterns. The room was filled with painted folding screens, depicting men on horses hunting wild boar with spears and arrows and noblewomen in fine carriages watching the hunters. The tengu nobleman picked up an oil lamp and carried it along with him. By its flickering light, the painted hunters seemed to follow them, their horses galloping from screen to screen.

"O most noble sir," said Girida, frightened, "the screens seem to be coming to life."

"Do not worry," said the tengu. "They are only dreams. The princess hires a court painter to capture them on paper. The dreams can run from panel to panel but they can never escape. Rather sad, when you think about it."

Girida preferred not to think about it and held up her sleeves on either side of her face so that she did not have to gaze on the desperate, rushing dreams. She followed the tengu into the next chamber, which was hung with silk tapestries the color of cherry blossoms. Each banner was embroidered with wisteria blooms, in purple, blue, and white. "It is her favorite flower," said the tengu, as if reading Girida's thoughts. "Wisteria represents the impermanence of beauty. Shows wisdom on the part of the princess, I would say."

Girida merely thought it sad and gladly hurried on to the next room. There she saw a grand dais carved in the shape of an enormous lotus blossom. In the center lay two people sleeping.

One had very long hair, whom she presumed to be the princess. The other had hair tied up in a topknot, and Girida was certain this must be Keiken.

She rushed to his side and gently shook his shoulder. "Keiken! Keiken! It is me, Girida."

The young man rolled over and gazed at her. It was not Keiken. "Who are you?" he asked sleepily. "Are you one of the dreams?"

The princess also rolled over, and regarded her, but the princess did not seem to be disturbed or angry. "Who are you? This is an awkward place to receive visitors."

Girida blushed with deep embarrassment and bowed low. "I beg your pardon, noble ones. I am called Girida, and I am a distant relative of yours. I have come looking for my dear friend Keiken who has disappeared. He has sent no message to his mother to tell her where he has gone. I have heard only that he is with the Lady of the Ice Garden. I came hoping he was here, or that you might know what this means."

"What an ill-mannered wretch," said the prince who was not Keiken, "that he should not tell his mother where he has gone."

"I do not know of such a lady," said the princess, brushing her long hair back from her face, "but if there is such a one, she must live in the mountains to the north. Only there could an ice garden last any length of time. Perhaps the monks of Kuramadera know of her. As you are a cousin who has fallen on bad fortune, it would be heartless of me not to help you. Let me lend to you my palanquin and my guards so that you may make a pilgrimage to Kuramadera."

Girida bowed very low again. "You are most kind. I doubt that I could ever repay you sufficiently." She turned to thank the tengu also, but he seemed to have disappeared.

The princess waved her hand dismissively. "Is it not said that sympathy in the heart brings benevolence in life? Come, let us get you ready, for I am sure you are eager to leave at once."

And so Girida was fed a fine meal of rice and fish and pickled vegetables. She was given the most fashionable winter kimonos to put on —white shading to blue at the hem, with the outermost kimono bearing a pattern of cranes taking flight. She was led to an elegant wicker palanquin—a large basket, really, hung from two poles. She glanced in and saw the palanquin was full of soft cushions. Eight burly samurai in full armor of iron plates laced with purple silk cords stood ready to take up the wooden beams of the palanquin. The princess gave Girida a box full of rice cakes and pickled plums to eat along the way.

Full of gratitude and hope, Girida again thanked the princess and got into the palanquin, closing the little wicker door behind her. She felt the men take up the carrying poles and they set out upon her journey.

Kuramadera was only a few hours travel from Heian Kyo by foot and so Girida expected they would reach the monastery only shortly after dark. She dozed happily on the cushions as the palanquin swung gently to and fro beneath the poles, in rhythm with the marching of the warriors.

Girida was jolted awake suddenly as the palanquin crashed to the ground. She heard the warriors draw their swords, and then heard the humming of arrows. There were screams from the samurai and shouts and the clashing of metal against metal. Girida drew her knees up to her chest, very afraid.

In a way, the noise went on too long. In a way, it was over too soon. The little wicker door in the palanquin opened, and a strange, ugly face peered in. "Well, what have we here?"

Strong arms reached in and dragged Girida out of the palanquin. She screamed and kicked and shouted, "Leave me alone! The Wisteria Princess will hear of this!" But only rough laughter greeted her complaints. Her outer kimonos were torn off her, leaving her standing, shivering, in only her innermost robe.

Men with torches stood around her, their hair unbound, their garments dirty and frayed. Robbers, clearly. These were known to haunt the forests north of Heian Kyo, sometimes even venturing into the capital itself. This was why the princess had sent warriors to carry the palanquin. But now the samurai lay dead at Girida's feet.

One of the robbers, an old woman with her gray hair done up in a warrior's topknot, walked up to Girida and looked her over sourly. "What a useless bit of fluff this is," the woman robber growled. "She brings no horses or oxen to eat. Looks like we'll have to eat her instead." She drew a knife from out of her obi and pointed it at Girida's neck.

But suddenly something like a monkey jumped on the old woman's back, grabbing her arm. "No, no! Let me keep her! I always wanted a sister, a playmate. Don't kill her!" It leaned forward and bit the old woman's ears.

The old woman cried, "Ow! Ow! Oh, very well, you wicked child. Why is it I can refuse you nothing? Go on, then. We'll find something else to eat."

The creature scrambled off the old woman's back and ran up to stand nearly nose-to-nose with Girida. It was a girl, about Girida's height and age, but her skin was sun-browned and when she smiled Girida could see she was missing teeth. "Hello! Hello!" cried the robber girl. "I am Arai, and you are mine now." Arai grabbed Girida's wrist and dragged her back into the palanquin, squeezing in with her.

Girida was so afraid that she went along with the girl without struggle. Inside the palanquin, she huddled in one corner and silently watched.

The robber girl Arai rolled about on the cushions and beat her fists on the sides of the palanquin. "Carry us! Carry us!" she commanded the robbers outside. To Girida's surprise, the palanquin was hoisted into the air and again she was on her way to...somewhere.

Arai caught sight of the lacquered box and exclaimed, "What is this! Some overlooked riches?" She knocked the top off and gasped. "Rice cakes! And some...withered things."

"They're pickled plums," said Girida, morosely. "They are much prized at Court."

"Then we will eat like emperors!" said Arai. She stuffed a rice cake into her mouth and held the box out to Girida.

Girida shook her head. She was too afraid to be hungry.

"All the more for me, then," said Arai, and she finished the entire box of rice cakes and plums herself.

Girida was astonished that the robber girl was so rude as to not share any with her mother or the other robbers. But Girida did not wish to anger her – after all, Arai had saved her life, and so she said nothing.

At last the palanquin was again set down and the girls were ordered out. Arai went first and pulled Girida out after her by the sleeve. As Girida emerged from the wicker basket she had to rub her eyes to believe what she saw.

At first it looked like a giant bush with fires burning within it. Girida blinked and saw it was a very high wall made of sticks and leaves and thorns. During the day, it would surely look like just another part of the forest.

"Come on!" cried Arai, and she pulled Girida by the arm toward the stick wall. They followed the rest of the robbers through a low opening in the wall and emerged into a torchlit clearing surrounded by little domes made of bent tree branches covered with bark. Robbers were sitting around the clearing, haggling over the clothing and weapons they had stolen off the bodies of the samurai who had accompanied Girida.

Arai pulled Girida into a little opening in the twig wall and Girida found herself in what seemed like an animal's den. The floor was lined with fox and bear skins. Bones and tiny skulls hung from overhead on silken threads. By the far wall, to Girida's surprise, stood a small red deer tethered by a leather collar to a stake in the floor. The deer stared at them and whickered but did not move.

"This is my place," said Arai. With a wave of her hand she set the bones overhead to clacking like wind chimes. "I am the Princess of Bandits."

She went over to the little deer and put her arm around its neck. The deer tried to sidle away but was trapped between Arai and the wall. "This is Beni. I caught him in the woods and now he is mine." She drew a knife from her belt and caressed the deer's neck with the blade. The deer's eyes showed white as it stared at her in terror. "I do this every night," Arai said, grinning. "He is so frightened. Isn't it delicious?"

Girida did not find it pleasant at all. She wished she could free the deer but such an action did not seem wise at the moment.

Arai came back over to her, put an arm around her shoulders, and put the knife blade against Girida's neck. "And I found you in the woods and now you are mine. I order you to tell me everything about yourself. Why were you so foolish as to come into our forest?"

Girida swallowed hard. The knife blade was cold against the skin of her neck, like ice. Wondering if she might live or die by her answer, Girida told Arai of Keiken and her search for the Lady of the Ice Garden. Arai listened with intent eyes.

"But this is a wondrous story!" cried Arai when Girida was finished. "I have never been part of a story like this. I have only been part of stories about robbing and killing and chopping people up and eating them. You must let me help you!" Arai took the knife away from Girida's neck and grabbed her sleeve. She pulled Girida roughly out of her hut and back across the open space where the robbers sat beside their cooking fires.

Girida tried not to make eye contact with the rough men who were staring at her hungrily. Given what Arai had said about chopping and eating people, Girida couldn't be sure they weren't sizing her up for their next meal.

Arai led her to a tiny round hut made of pine branches. Dim light flickered just beyond the cloth-covered doorway. Arai stopped and grabbed Girida's shoulders. "Now, remember. You must show my Obaa great respect, even if she is a robber's grandmother. You understand?"

"Of course," said Girida.

Arai pushed aside the cloth curtain and led Girida in. The hut had a floor of flattened earth covered with woven straw mats. On a little wood platform, on tattered silk cushions, knelt an old woman, her eyes half-shut in blindness. Her face was as browned and wrinkled as pickled plums and her hands were so bony they were almost claws. Yet a benevolence seemed to radiate from her, as if her spirit had distanced itself from her horrible offspring and the deterioration of her body.

"This is something new you bring me, Arai-chan," said the old woman. "It smells like a young garden under winter snow."

"Obaa-san," said Arai, "this is Girida, who is from Heian Kyo and is my age. She came into our forest looking for her lost love Keiken, who has gone with the Lady of the Ice Garden. It is such a wonderful story, I have decided we must help her."

"I am most honored to meet you," said Girida to the old woman, bowing even though it would not be seen.

"Bring her closer," said the old woman.

Arai pushed Girida so that she fell to her knees in front of the old woman. The old woman lightly touched Girida's face and hair. At first, Girida dreaded the touch of those hands, but they were so warm and gentle that soon she didn't mind at all.

"You are on a most dangerous journey," said the old woman. "Even if you reach your goal you may very well fail."

"I know that, Obaa-san," said Girida. "But I feel as though I have no other purpose in life."

"Then I suppose you must continue, even though what you feel is not so," said the old woman.

"How can we help her?" asked Arai, eagerly.

"You cannot," said the old woman, a little sharply. "But your pet whom you keep tied up in your hidey-hole can."

"What, Beni? What can my deer do for her?"

"He is not a real deer. If he had been, you never could have caught him. He is a kirin, who was weakened by transforming himself into a deer. Because you placed a leather collar on him, he cannot return to the heavenly realm from which he came. He has been too long now in contact with sin and impurity, living among us. Perhaps if he does a kindness for this girl, he may earn his return to the Higher Paths."

"But…then I must lose my Beni?" asked Arai.

"You are coming to an age," said the old woman with a wry smile, "when I am sure you will soon have many more males to torment. Go and fetch him."

Arai bowed awkwardly. "As you wish, Obaa-san. I was becoming bored with him anyway." She departed and for long, awkward moments, Girida knelt with the old woman in silence.

Finally, the old woman said, "Much as it displeases me to say so, you would do well to think more like Arai, child. To devote your thoughts so much to only one thing can only lead to sorrow."

"Nonetheless," said Girida, "it is so."

The old woman sighed. "It is ever thus. I allowed my heart to be stolen by a robber king and see what has happened to me."

Arai returned, leading Beni in by the collar. "Here he is. The ungrateful wretch tried to bite me."

"Do not punish him, child. Take his collar off."

Reluctantly, Arai slipped the collar off of the red deer's neck. At once, the deer began to change – its head became more like a dog's or a lion's with long fangs and a wispy beard and mane. Tiny horns sprouted from its forehead. Its tail became more like a donkey's and small flames flickered around its leg joints and shoulders.

"Thank you, kind lady," said the kirin in a flutelike voice, bobbing its head to the old woman. "It takes one of remarkable insight to have discerned my true nature. Surely a place awaits you in my Master's kingdom."

"Not I," said the old woman with a brusque laugh. "My offspring have seen to that. I fear I must endure another turn on the Wheel before I may approach the Pure Land. But if you can help this poor stranger girl who has come among us, you might earn yourself a return."

"To be free of this place I would gladly attempt it. What must I do?"

"Carry her to the northernmost tip of Honshu. There is an Ainu wisewoman there whom I met when I was on a pilgrimage long ago. The wisewoman should be able to help this girl find what she needs."

"Then it is done," said the kirin. So they went outside, the kirin and Arai and Girida. Arai helped Girida get on the kirin's back. Arai was pouting as if she might cry. "Take good care of her, Beni. She's as close to a sister as I ever had."

"Mend your ways," said the kirin to Arai. "May your heart find a more pure path—"

"Don't lecture me," cried the Princess of Bandits, brandishing her knife, "or I will summon my cousins to make a meal of you."

"I am gone," said the kirin and he leaped into the air.

Girida clung tightly to his mane as the kirin cantered over the clouds. The night sky was ablaze with stars and the Bridge arched across the heavens. They flew so fast the wind pulled and tore at her hair and under-robe. She should have been cold, but the flames on the kirin's legs warmed her without burning her. Along the way, Girida talked about Keiken, shouting above the wind into the kirin's ear.

Before long, the kirin alighted on a rocky shore that was lightly dusted with snow. Where the shore met the nearby hills was a single stone hut with smoke drifting out of a hole in the center of its thatched roof.

"Here we are," said the kirin. "Kindly dismount."

Girida slid off his back and together they walked toward the hut. Girida had heard little of the barbarians of the north, the Ainu, and she did not know what to expect. She was almost more afraid of meeting this wisewoman than she had been of the Princess of Bandits.

The kirin knocked at the wooden front door with his fore-hoof and presently it was opened by a short, round woman. She wore a very short cotton kimono, and her bare arms and legs were pale and hairy.

"Oh, it is you," she said to the kirin. "I expected you long ago."

"I was held captive for a time," said the kirin. "Now I bring this girl in hopes that I may be redeemed."

The wisewoman shrugged and stepped away from the door. The

kirin entered as if he had been invited, and Girida followed. A great fire filed a stone circle in the center of the hut. Whole fish were roasting on an iron spit slung across the hearth. The hut was very warm and Girida was suddenly glad she was wearing no more than her one layer of kimono.

"This girl," the kirin continued, as if he'd been asked, "needs to find the Lady of the Ice Garden, who has stolen her dear companion."

The wisewoman made a pitying noise as she picked at her teeth with a fish bone. "Poor girl. No man can be stolen by the Lady of the Ice Garden unless he is more than half willing to be taken." She looked at Girida. "If you go there, you will see things that will be saddening, shocking, and painful to you. Will you still make the journey?"

Girida hesitated only a moment. "Yes. I must. My mind has been filled only with Keiken since he left."

"Must be a small mind indeed to be so easily filled," grumbled the wisewoman. "Very well, then." She picked up a dried fish and began to carve a map into it. She held out the fish to the kirin. "The Lady of the Ice Garden has her winter palace here, in the mountains to the west. Now be off with you."

"Wait!" cried the kirin. "If this Lady is so formidable a foe, should Girida not be given more protection? I know you have many potions and amulets and spells. Can't you give her the strength of ten warriors, or a magical dagger, or *something*?"

The wisewoman stared at the kirin a moment, and then laughed and laughed and laughed, her little round belly shaking. "Oh my, oh my, you have not been long in our world, have you? The Lady of The Ice Garden fights battles of the spirit, not of weapons or strength of muscle. This girl already has all the arms and armor she will ever have, within herself. Whether it will be enough, I cannot say. Oh, wait, there *is* one thing I can give her." The wisewoman bustled over to a wooden chest from which she pulled a robe made from a bear skin. She waddled over to Girida and said, "Wear this."

Girida shied away. "It...is an unclean thing." She glanced uncertainly at the kirin.

The wisewoman sighed. "If you wear it, you will have many more years in which to chant prayers to your blessed Amida for forgiveness. If you freeze to death, you will not."

"It is a small sin," said the kirin, gently, to Girida. "You had better do as she suggests."

So Girida put on the bear-fur robe. They all went outside and the wisewoman hefted Girida onto the kirin's back. "Good fortune to you, child," said the wisewoman. "And *you*," she said to the kirin, "come back to me as soon as you have dropped her off and I will help you find your way home."

"Then I am gone," said the kirin, joyfully, and he leaped into the air. Again, Girida had to hold on with all her strength as the kirin dashed through the clouds up into the peaks that formed the spine of Honshu. They flew so terrifyingly close to the rocky outcroppings that Girida shut her eyes tight so as not to be frightened by what she saw.

Sooner than she expected, the kirin alighted again on solid ground and stopped. "Here we are. Dismount, please."

Girida opened her eyes and slid off his back. It was very, very cold. Her breath seemed to turn to ice before her face. She pulled the bear-skin robe tightly around herself, glad now that she had accepted the wisewoman's gift.

They were standing at a wall of high, thorned bushes, on which grew red berries like drops of blood. The torii gateway before them was carved from cherry wood. Battling oni demons were carved into the uprights and the crossbeam.

"I must leave you now," said the kirin. "May you come to know the Amida's blessing." He rubbed his furry cheek against hers a moment and then he sprung into the air, vanishing swiftly into the surrounding mist.

Girida felt very alone. Nonetheless, she had come too far to let fear paralyze her now. She stepped across the floor-beam of the gate and entered the Ice Garden.

It was beautiful, in a strange way. There were lanterns and bridges carved of ice, grazing deer of ice, flowers of ice crystals, pine trees whose needles were ice shards. Enchanted, Girida crossed one of the ice bridges, walking deeper into the garden.

And then she saw the men. Warriors with fierce expressions standing frozen guard. But their armor was formed of slabs of ice and their swords were sharpened icicles. They stared straight ahead, eyes glazed over, facing some unseen foe. Girida tiptoed past them, but it hardly mattered. They took no notice of her. They could not.

Girida walked up ice-carved steps into the palace itself. She entered a grand hall whose pillars were ice, whose floor was ice, whose low tables were ice. In the center of the room stood a young man whose skin was a pale blue.

"Keiken!" cried Girida and she rushed to him. This time it really was Keiken and she opened her arms to embrace him.

"Stay back!" cried Keiken through jaws frozen shut. "Do not touch me!"

Girida staggered back, hurt as if a needle had been driven into her heart. "But Keiken, it is me, Girida. Your dear friend. Aren't you happy to see me?"

"Why did you come here?" Keiken demanded. "Did I send for you? Did I give you any reason to believe I wanted you to follow me?"

Girida felt hot tears forming in her eyes. "We...we were so worried for you. Your mother does not know where you are. I have thought of nothing but you since you left. Don't these things matter to you?"

"Why should they matter?" growled Keiken. "Are such things a *man's* concern? I contemplate the Vast Emptiness, I celebrate Death, the banishment of fear. I have put pity from my heart and I now look forward to crushing enemies beneath my sandals until only I live to laugh at them. And you dare to come to me sniveling about my mother and your thoughts of me? Hah! I left because I saw what a weak, unworthy creature you are."

The tears began to run down Girida's cheeks, but they were now more tears of anger than of sorrow. She noted that all through his speech, Keiken had not moved. He was frozen in place, becoming like the guardsmen standing out in the garden. For all his brave talk, he was helpless.

Girida rushed up to him and threw her arms around him. She ignored his cries of "What are you doing? Let go of me at once!"

She wept openly on his chest, letting her hot tears flow over his shoulder and down his arm, warming his skin. She felt him begin to move beneath her.

Suddenly, he grabbed her and flung her down to the floor. "What have you done!" he cried, looking down at himself. "I was becoming strong! I was forgetting everything. I had lost my pain. I was feeling nothing. And now you want me to be weak like you. You want me to hurt and cry and need and feel shame and loneliness. I refuse! Do you hear? Don't you see? I was better off frozen. How can you say you care for me when you have *ruined* me?"

Keiken ran from the room. Girida stood up and watched from the veranda as he dashed into the garden and flung himself onto a frozen pond. But ice only covered the surface, and Keiken was soaked as he fell through. He managed to stagger out again, but the coldness of the air froze him swiftly, until he became as stiff and unmoving as the other guards who stood sentinel against a foe that lay only within.

Girida did not know what to do, then. She began to murmur the Lotus Sutra for him, but was stopped when a hand fell upon her shoulder.

Girida spun around. She saw a woman pale as snow, with long hair as black as night, eyes black as obsidian, dressed in kimonos of the palest blue. "Forgive me for being a poor hostess," said the woman, "but I had been occupied elsewhere. You are Girida, are you not? Keiken spoke your name sometimes, while sleeping."

"Please," begged Girida, "release him. Save him. I will give you anything."

"That is not possible, child. He has always been free to go. It is his choice to remain. But I must thank you, for you have done me a service."

"I have?"

"I search for a companion of the greatest strength and wisdom. Yet you have shown me that Keiken was weak. He rejected knowledge of himself. He was unworthy of me. Or of you." She took a stone from her sleeve and threw it at Keiken. He collapsed into a pile of ice shards on the snow.

Girida gasped, putting her hand to her mouth. "No!"

"They are so easily shattered," sighed the Lady of the Ice Garden. "The willow may look down upon the grass that grows at its roots, yet when the mighty storms blow it is the willow that breaks, not the grass. Go home, Girida. There is nothing for you here. There never was."

"Why do you do this?" Girida demanded.

"I am what I am. Men seek me out. For some reason, in this time and this place, many wish to come to me, believing that to know my embrace is the worthiest achievement. I should be flattered but, as you see, the strongest and wisest do not seek me thus and never will. Therefore I am doomed to be eternally disappointed. But you are not. Go home."

Mist gathered around Girida until her sight was obscured. When it lifted, she was standing outside her mother's hovel. The poor, shoddy place never looked so wonderful.

Years passed and Girida married a humble sandal maker. She learned how to carve the wood and handle the accounting. They had children and she laughed and cried and felt great pain and great joy with her family. When her husband and mother died, Girida put on the robes of a Buddhist nun. She became a scholar and a pilgrim, traveling the length of Honshu and writing down the wondrous things she learned and saw. And when at last she came to the Pure Land and met the kirin once more, she was able to say to him, "I have led a full life, and that has been the greatest blessing of all."

Travels with the Snow Queen

Kelly Link

Part of you is always traveling faster, always traveling ahead. Even when you are moving, it is never fast enough to satisfy that part of you. You enter the walls of the city early in the evening, when the cobblestones are a mottled pink with reflected light, and cold beneath the slap of your bare, bloody feet. You ask the man who is guarding the gate to recommend a place to stay the night, and even as you are falling into the bed at the inn, the bed, which is piled high with quilts and scented with lavender, perhaps alone, perhaps with another traveler, perhaps with the guardsman who had such brown eyes, and a mustache that curled up on either side of his nose like two waxed black laces, even as this guardsman, whose name you didn't ask calls out a name in his sleep that is not your name, you are dreaming about the road again. When you sleep, you dream about the long white distances that still lie before you. When you wake up, the guardsman is back at his post, and the place between your legs aches pleasantly, your legs sore as if you had continued walking all night in your sleep. While you were sleeping, your feet have healed again. You were careful not to kiss the guardsman on the lips, so it doesn't really count, does it.

Your destination is North. The map that you are using is a mirror. You are always pulling the bits out of your bare feet, the pieces of the map that broke off and fell on the ground as the Snow Queen flew overhead in her sleigh. Where you are, where you are coming from, it is impossible to read a map made of paper. If it were that easy then everyone would be a traveler. You have heard of other travelers whose maps are breadcrumbs, whose maps are stones, whose maps are the four winds, whose maps are yellow bricks laid one after the other. You read your map with your foot, and behind you somewhere there must be another traveler whose map is the bloody footprints that you are leaving behind you.

There is a map of fine white scars on the soles of your feet that tells you where you have been. When you are pulling the shards of the Snow Queen's looking glass out of your feet, you remind yourself, you tell yourself to imagine how it felt when Kay's eyes, Kay's heart were pierced by shards of the same mirror. Sometimes it is safer to read maps with your feet.

Ladies. Has it ever occurred to you that fairy tales aren't easy on the feet?

So this is the story so far. You grew up, you fell in love with the boy next door, Kay, the one with blue eyes who brought you bird feathers and roses, the one who was so good at puzzles. You thought he loved you – maybe he thought he did, too. His mouth tasted so sweet, it tasted like love, and his fingers were so kind, they pricked like love on your skin, but three years and exactly two days after you moved in with him, you were having drinks out on the patio. You weren't exactly fighting, and you can't remember what he had done that had made you so angry, but you threw your glass at him. There was a noise like the sky shattering.

The cuff of his trousers got splashed. There were little fragments of glass everywhere. "Don't move," you said. You weren't wearing shoes.

He raised his hand up to his face. "I think there's something in my eye," he said.

His eye was fine, of course, there wasn't a thing in it, but later that night when he was undressing for bed, there were little bits of glass like grains of sugar, dusting his clothes. When you brushed your hand against his chest, something pricked your finger and left a smear of blood against his heart.

The next day it was snowing and he went out for a pack of cigarettes and never came back. You sat on the patio drinking something warm and alcoholic, with nutmeg in it, and the snow fell on your shoulders. You were wearing a short-sleeved T-shirt; you were pretending that you weren't cold, and that your lover would be back soon. You put your finger on the ground and then stuck it in your mouth. The snow looked like sugar, but it tasted like nothing at all.

The man at the corner store said that he saw your lover get into a long white sleigh. There was a beautiful woman in it, and it was pulled by thirty white geese. "Oh, her," you said, as if you weren't surprised. You went home and looked in the wardrobe for that cloak that belonged to your great-grandmother. You were thinking about going after him. You remembered that the cloak was woolen and warm, and a beautiful red – a traveler's cloak. But when you pulled it out, it smelled like wet dog and the lining was ragged, as if something had chewed on it. It smelled like bad luck: it made you sneeze, and so you put it back. You waited for a while longer.

Two months went by, and Kay didn't come back, and finally you left and locked the door of your house behind you. You were going to travel for love, without shoes, or cloak, or common sense. This is one of the things a woman can do when her lover leaves her. It's hard on the feet perhaps, but staying at home is hard on the heart, and you weren't quite ready to give him up yet. You told yourself that the woman in the sleigh must have put a spell on him, and he was probably already missing you. Besides, there are some questions you want to ask him, some true things you want to tell him. This is what you told yourself.

The snow was soft and cool on your feet, and then you found the trail of glass, the map.

After three weeks of hard traveling, you came to the city.

No, really, think about it. Think about the little mermaid, who traded in her tail for love, got two legs and two feet, and every step was like walking on knives. And where did it get her? That's a rhetorical question, of course. Then there's the girl who put on the beautiful red dancing shoes. The woodsman had to chop her feet off with an axe.

There are Cinderella's two stepsisters, who cut off their own toes, and Snow White's stepmother, who danced to death in red-hot iron slippers. The Goose Girl's maid got rolled down a hill in a barrel studded with nails. Travel is hard on the single woman. There was this one woman who walked east of the sun and then west of the moon, looking for her lover, who had left her because she spilled tallow on his nightshirt. She wore out at least one pair of perfectly good iron shoes before she found him. Take our word for it, he wasn't worth it. What do you think happened when she forgot to put the fabric softener in the dryer? Laundry is hard, travel is harder. You deserve a vacation, but of course you're a little wary. You've read the fairy tales. We've been there, we know.

That's why we here at Snow Queen Tours have put together a luxurious but affordable package for you, guaranteed to be easy on the feet and on the budget. See the world by goosedrawn sleigh, experience the archetypal forest, the winter wonderland; chat with real live talking animals (please don't feed them). Our accommodations are three-star: sleep on comfortable, guaranteed pea-free boxspring mattresses; eat meals prepared by world-class chefs. Our tour guides are friendly, knowledgeable, well-traveled, trained by the Snow Queen herself. They know first aid, how to live off the land; they speak three languages fluently.

Special discount for older sisters, stepsisters, stepmothers, wicked witches, crones, hags, princesses who have kissed frogs without realizing what they were getting into, etc.

You leave the city and you walk all day beside a stream that is as soft and silky as blue fur. You wish that your map was water, and not broken glass. At midday you stop and bathe your feet in a shallow place and the ribbons of red blood curl into the blue water.

Eventually you come to a wall of briars, so wide and high that you can't see any way around it. You reach out to touch a rose, and prick your finger. You suppose that you could walk around, but your feet tell you that the map leads directly through the briar wall, and you can't stray from the path that has been laid out for you. Remember what happened to the little girl, your great-grandmother, in her red woolen cape. Maps protect their travelers, but only if the travelers obey the dictates of their maps. This is what you have been told.

Perched in the briars above your head is a raven, black and sleek as the curlicued mustache of the guardsman. The raven looks at you and you look back at it. "I'm looking for someone," you say. "A boy named Kay."

The raven opens its big beak and says, "He doesn't love you, you know."

You shrug. You've never liked talking animals. Once your lover gave you a talking cat, but it ran away and secretly you were glad. "I have a few things I want to say to him, that's all." You have, in fact, been keeping a list of all the things you are going to say to him. "Besides, I wanted to see the world, be a tourist for a while."

"That's fine for some," the raven says. Then he relents. "If you'd like to come in, then come in. The princess just married the boy with the boots that squeaked on the marble floor."

"That's fine for some," you say. Kay's boots squeak; you wonder how he met the princess, if he is the one that she just married, how the raven knows that he doesn't love you, what this princess has that you don't have, besides a white sleigh pulled by thirty geese, an impenetrable wall of briars, and maybe a castle. She's probably just some bimbo.

"The Princess Briar Rose is a very wise princess," the raven says, "but she's the laziest girl in the world. Once she went to sleep for a hundred days and no one could wake her up, although they put one hundred peas under her mattress, one each morning."

This, of course, is the proper and respectful way of waking up princesses. Sometimes Kay used to wake you up by dribbling cold water on your feet. Sometimes he woke you up by whistling.

"On the one hundredth day," the raven says, "she woke up all by herself and told her council of twelve fairy godmothers that she supposed it was time she got married. So they stuck up posters, and princes and youngest sons came from all over the kingdom."

When the cat ran away, Kay put up flyers around the neighborhood. You wonder if you should have put up flyers for Kay. "Briar Rose wanted a clever husband, but it tired her dreadfully to sit and listen to the young men give speeches and talk about how rich and sexy and smart they were. She fell asleep and stayed asleep until the young man with the squeaky boots came in. It was his boots that woke her up.

"It was love at first sight. Instead of trying to impress her with everything he knew and everything he had seen, he declared that he had come all this way to hear Briar Rose talk about her dreams. He'd been studying in Vienna with a famous doctor, and was deeply interested in dreams."

Kay used to tell you his dreams every morning. They were long and complicated and if he thought you weren't listening to him, he'd sulk. You never remember your dreams. "Other peoples' dreams are never very interesting," you tell the raven.

The raven cocks its head. It flies down and lands on the grass at your feet. "Wanna bet?" it says. Behind the raven you notice a little green door recessed in the briar wall. You could have sworn that it wasn't there a minute ago.

The raven leads you through the green door, and across a long green lawn towards a two-story castle that is the same pink as the briar roses. You think this is kind of tacky, but exactly what you would expect from someone named after a flower. "I had this dream once," the raven says, "that my teeth were falling out. They just crumbled into pieces in my mouth. And then I woke up, and realized that ravens don't have teeth."

You follow the raven inside the palace, and up a long, twisty staircase. The stairs are stone, worn and smoothed away, like old thick silk. Slivers of glass glister on the pink stone, catching the light of the candles on the wall. As you go up, you see that you are part of a great gray rushing crowd. Fantastic creatures, flat and thin as smoke, race up the stairs, men and women and snakey things with bright eyes. They nod to you as they slip past. "Who are they?" you ask the raven.

"Dreams," the raven says, hopping awkwardly from step to step. "The Princess's dreams, come to pay their respects to her new husband. Of course they're too fine to speak to the likes of us."

But you think that some of them look familiar. They have a familiar smell, like a pillow that your lover's head has rested upon.

At the top of the staircase is a wooden door with a silver keyhole. The dreams pour steadily through the keyhole, and under the bottom of the door, and when you open it, the sweet stink and cloud of dreams are so thick in the Princess's bedroom that you can barely breathe. Some people might mistake the scent of the Princess's dreams for the scent of sex; then again, some people mistake sex for love.

You see a bed big enough for a giant, with four tall oak trees for bedposts. You climb up the ladder that rests against the side of the bed to see the Princess's sleeping husband. As you lean over, a goose feather flies up and tickles your nose. You brush it away, and dislodge several seedy-looking dreams. Briar Rose rolls over and laughs in her sleep, but the man beside her wakes up. "Who is it?" he says. "What do you want?"

He isn't Kay. He doesn't look a thing like Kay. "You're not Kay," you tell the man in the Princess's bed.

"Who the fuck is Kay?" he says, so you explain it all to him, feeling horribly embarrassed. The raven is looking pleased with itself, the way your talking cat used to look, before it ran away. You glare at the raven. You glare at the man who is not Kay.

After you've finished, you say that something is wrong, because your map clearly indicates that Kay has been here, in this bed. Your feet are leaving bloody marks on the sheets, and you pick a sliver of glass off the foot of the bed, so everyone can see that you're not lying. Princess Briar Rose sits up in bed, her long pinkish-brown hair tumbled down over her shoulders. "He's not in love with you," she says, yawning.

"So he was here, in this bed, you're the icy slut in the sleigh at the corner store, you're not even bothering to deny it," you say.

She shrugs her pink-white shoulders. "Four, five months ago, he came through, I woke up," she says. "He was a nice guy, okay in bed. She was a real bitch, though."

"Who was?" you ask.

Briar Rose finally notices that her new husband is glaring at her. "What can I say?" she says, and shrugs. "I have a thing for guys in squeaky boots."

"Who was a bitch?" you ask again.

"The Snow Queen," she says, "the slut in the sleigh."

This is the list you carry in your pocket, of the things you plan to say to Kay, when you find him, if you find him:

1. I'm sorry that I forgot to water your ferns while you were away that time.
2. When you said that I reminded you of your mother, was that a good thing?
3. I never really liked your friends all that much.
4. None of my friends ever really liked you.
5. Do you remember when the cat ran away, and I cried and cried and made you put up posters, and she never came back? I wasn't crying because she didn't come back. I was crying because I'd taken her to the woods, and I was scared she'd come back and tell you what I'd done, but I guess a wolf got her, or something. She never liked me anyway.
6. I never liked your mother.
7. After you left, I didn't water your plants on purpose. They're all dead.
8. Goodbye.
9. Were you ever really in love with me?
10. Was I good in bed, or just average?
11. What exactly did you mean, when you said that it was fine that I had put on a little weight, that you thought I was even more beautiful, that I should go ahead and eat as much as I

wanted, but when I weighed myself on the bathroom scale, I was exactly the same weight as before, I hadn't gained a single pound?

12. So all those times, I'm being honest here, every single time, and anyway I don't care if you don't believe me, I faked every orgasm you ever thought I had. Women can do that, you know. You never made me come, not even once.

13. So maybe I'm an idiot, but I used to be in love with you.

14. I slept with some guy, I didn't mean to, it just kind of happened. Is that how it was with you? Not that I'm making any apologies, or that I'd accept yours, I just want to know.

15. My feet hurt, and it's all your fault.

16. I mean it this time, goodbye.

The Princess Briar Rose isn't a bimbo after all, even if she does have a silly name and a pink castle. You admire her dedication to the art and practice of sleep. By now you are growing sick and tired of traveling, and would like nothing better than to curl up in a big featherbed for one hundred days, or maybe even one hundred years, but she offers to loan you her carriage, and when you explain that you have to walk, she sends you off with a troop of armed guards. They will escort you through the forest, which is full of thieves and wolves and princes on quests, lurking about. The guards politely pretend that they don't notice the trail of blood that you are leaving behind. They probably think it's some sort of female thing.

It is after sunset, and you aren't even half a mile into the forest, which is dark and scary and full of noises, when bandits ambush your escort, and slaughter them all. The bandit queen, who is grizzled and gray, with a nose like an old pickle, yells delightedly at the sight of you. "You're a nice plump one for my supper!" she says, and draws her long knife out of the stomach of one of the dead guards. She is just about to slit your throat, as you stand there, politely pretending not to notice the blood that is pooling around the bodies of the dead guards, that is now obliterating the bloody tracks of your feet, the knife that is at your throat, when a girl about your own age jumps onto the robber queen's back, pulling at the robber queen's braided hair as if it were reins.

There is a certain family resemblance between the robber queen and the girl who right now has her knees locked around the robber queen's throat. "I don't want you to kill her," the girl says, and you realize that she means you, that you were about to die a minute ago, that travel is much more dangerous than you had ever imagined. You add an item of complaint to the list of things that you plan to tell Kay, if you find him.

The girl has half-throttled the robber queen, who has fallen to her knees, gasping for breath. "She can be my sister;" the girl says insistently. "You promised I could have a sister and I want her. Besides, her feet are bleeding."

The robber queen drops her knife, and the girl drops back onto the ground, kissing her mother's hairy gray cheek. "Very well, very well," the robber queen grumbles, and the girl grabs your hand, pulling you farther and faster into the woods, until you are running and stumbling, her hand hot around yours.

You have lost all sense of direction; your feet are no longer set upon your map. You should be afraid, but instead you are strangely exhilarated. Your feet don't hurt anymore, and although you don't know where you are going, for the very first time you are moving fast enough, you are almost flying, your feet are skimming over the night-black forest floor as if it were the smooth, flat surface of a lake, and your feet were two white birds. "Where are we going?" you ask the robber girl.

"We're here," she says, and stops so suddenly that you almost fall over. You are in a clearing, and the full moon is hanging overhead. You can see the robber girl better now, under the light of the moon. She looks like one of the bad girls who loiter under the street lamp by the corner shop, the ones who used to whistle at Kay. She wears black leatherette boots laced up to her thighs, and a black, ribbed T-shirt and grape-colored plastic shorts with matching suspenders. Her nails are painted black, and bitten down to the quick. She leads you to a tumbledown stone keep, which is as black inside as her fingernail polish, and smells strongly of dirty straw and animals.

"Are you a princess?" she asks you. "What are you doing in my mother's forest? Don't be afraid. I won't let my mother eat you."

You explain to her that you are not a princess, what you are doing, about the map, who you are looking for, what he did to you, or maybe it was what he didn't do. When you finish, the robber girl puts her arms around you and squeezes you roughly. "You poor thing! But what a silly way to travel!" she says. She shakes her head and makes you sit down on the stone floor of the keep and show her your feet. You explain that they always heal, that really your feet are quite tough, but she takes off her leatherette boots and gives them to you.

The floor of the keep is dotted with indistinct, motionless forms. One snarls in its sleep, and you realize that they are dogs. The robber girl is sitting between four slender columns, and when the dog snarls, the thing shifts restlessly, lowering its branchy head. It is a hobbled reindeer. "Well go on, see if they fit," the robber girl says, pulling out her knife. She drags it along the stone floor to make sparks. "What are you going to do when you find him?"

"Sometimes I'd like to cut off his head," you say. The robber girl grins, and thumps the hilt of her knife against the reindeer's chest.

The robber girl's feet are just a little bigger, but the boots are still warm from her feet. You explain that you can't wear the boots, or else you won't know where you are going. "Nonsense!" the robber girl says rudely.

You ask if she knows a better way to find Kay, and she says that if you are still determined to go looking for him, even though he obviously doesn't love you, and he isn't worth a bit of trouble, then the thing to do is to find the Snow Queen. "This is Bae. Bae, you mangy old, useless old thing," she says. "Do you know where the Snow Queen lives?"

The reindeer replies in a low, hopeless voice that he doesn't know, but he is sure that his old mother does. The robber girl slaps his flank. "Then you'll take her to your mother," she says. "And mind that you don't dawdle on the way."

She turns to you and gives you a smacking wet kiss on the lips and says, "Keep the shoes, they look much nicer on you than they did on me. And don't let me hear that you've been walking on glass again." She gives the reindeer a speculative look. "You know, Bae, I almost think I'm going to miss you."

You step into the cradle of her hands, and she swings you over the reindeer's bony back. Then she saws through the hobble with her knife, and yells "Ho!" waking up the dogs.

You knot your fingers into Bae's mane, and bounce up as he stumbles into a fast trot. The dogs follow for a distance, snapping at his hooves, but soon you have outdistanced them, moving so fast that the wind peels your lips back in an involuntary grimace. You almost miss the feel of glass beneath your feet. By morning, you are out of the forest again, and Bae's hooves are churning up white clouds of snow.

Sometimes you think there must be an easier way to do this. Sometimes it seems to be getting easier all on its own. Now you have boots and a reindeer, but you still aren't happy. Sometimes you wish that you'd stayed at home. You're sick and tired of traveling towards the happily ever after, whenever the fuck that is — you'd like the happily right now. Thank you very much.

When you breathe out, you can see the fine mist of your breath and the breath of the reindeer floating before you, until the wind tears it away. Bae runs on.

The snow flies up, and the air seems to grow thicker and thicker. As Bae runs, you feel that the white air is being rent by your passage, like heavy cloth. When you turn around and look behind you, you can see the path shaped to your joined form, woman and reindeer, like a hall stretching back to infinity. You see that there is more than one sort of map, that some forms of travel are indeed easier. "Give me a kiss," Bae says. The wind whips his words back to you. You can almost see the shape of them hanging in the heavy air.

"I'm not really a reindeer," he says. "I'm an enchanted prince."

You politely decline, pointing out that you haven't known him that long, and besides, for traveling purposes, a reindeer is better than a prince.

"He doesn't love you," Bae says. "And you could stand to lose a few pounds. My back is killing me."

You are sick and tired of talking animals, as well as travel. They never say anything that you didn't already know. You think of the talking cat that Kay gave you, the one that would always come to you, secretly, and looking very pleased with itself, to inform you when Kay's fingers smelled of some other woman. You couldn't stand to see him pet it, his fingers stroking its white fur, the cat lying on its side and purring wildly, "There, darling, that's perfect, don't stop," his fingers on its belly, its tail wreathing and lashing, its pointy little tongue sticking out at you. "Shut up," you say to Bae.

He subsides into an offended silence. His long brown fur is rimmed with frost, and you can feel the tears that the wind pulls from your eyes turning to ice on your cheeks. The only part of you that is warm are your feet, snug in the robber girl's boots. "It's just a little farther," Bae says, when you have been traveling for what feels like hours. "And then we're home."

You cross another corridor in the white air, and he swerves to follow it, crying out gladly, "We are near the old woman of Lapmark's house, my mother's house."

"How do you know?" you ask.

"I recognize the shape that she leaves behind her," Bae says. "Look!"

You look and see that the corridor of air you are following is formed like a short, stout, petticoated woman. It swings out at the waist like a bell.

"How long does it last?"

"As long as the air is heavy and dense," he says, "we burrow tunnels through the air like worms, but then the wind will come along and erase where we have been.

The woman-tunnel ends at a low red door. Bae lowers his head and knocks his antlers against it, scraping off the paint. The old woman of Lapmark opens the door, and you clamber stiffly off Bae's back. There is much rejoicing as mother recognizes son, although he is much changed from how he had been.

The old woman of Lapmark is stooped and fat as a grub. She fixes you a cup of tea, while Bae explains that you are looking for the Snow Queen's palace.

"You've not far to go now," his mother tells you. "Only a few hundred miles and past the house of the woman of Finmany. She'll tell you how to go — let me write a letter explaining everything to her. And don't forget to mention to her that I'll be coming for tea tomorrow; she'll change you back then, Bae, if you ask her nicely."

The woman of Lapmark has no paper, so she writes the letter on a piece of dried cod, flat as a dinner plate. Then you are off again. Sometimes you sleep as Bae runs on, and sometimes you aren't sure if you are asleep or waking. Great balls of greenish light roll cracking across the sky above you. At times it seems as if Bae is flying alongside the lights, chatting to them like old friends. At last you come to the house of the woman of Finmany, and you knock on her chimney, because she has no door.

Why, you may wonder, are there so many old women living out here? Is this a retirement community? One might not be remarkable, two is certainly more than enough, but as you look around, you can see little heaps of snow, lines of smoke rising from them. You have to be careful where you put your foot, or you might come through someone's roof. Maybe they came here for the quiet, or because they like ice fishing, or maybe they just like snow.

It is steamy and damp in the house, and you have to climb down the chimney, past the roaring fire, to get inside. Bae leaps down the chimney, hooves first, scattering coals everywhere. The Finmany woman is smaller and rounder than the woman of Lapmark. She looks to you like a lump of pudding with black currant eyes. She wears only a greasy old slip, and an apron that has written on it, "If you can't stand the heat, stay out of my kitchen."

She recognizes Bae even faster than his mother had, because, as it turns out, she was the one who turned him into a reindeer for teasing her about her weight. Bae apologizes, insincerely, you think, but the Finmany woman says she will see what she can do about turning him back again. She isn't entirely hopeful. It seems that a kiss is the preferred method of transformation. You don't offer to kiss him, because you know what that kind of thing leads to.

The Finmany woman reads the piece of dried cod by the light of her cooking fire, and then she throws the fish into her cooking pot. Bae tells her about Kay and the Snow Queen, and about your feet, because your lips have frozen together on the last leg of the journey, and you can't speak a word.

"You're so clever and strong," the reindeer says to the Finmany woman. You can almost hear him add *and fat* under his breath. "You can tie up all the winds in the world with a bit of thread. I've seen you hurling the lightning bolts down from the hills as if they were feathers. Can't you give her the strength of ten men, so that she can fight the Snow Queen and win Kay back?"

"The strength of ten men?" the Finmany woman says. "A lot of good that would do! And besides, he doesn't love her."

Bae smirks at you, as if to say, I told you so. If your lips weren't frozen, you'd tell him that she isn't saying anything that you don't already know. "Now!" the Finmany woman says, "take her up on your back one last time, and put her down again by the bush with the red berries. That marks the edge of the Snow Queen's garden; don't stay there gossiping, but come straight back. You were a handsome boy — I'll make you twice as good-looking as you were before. We'll put up flyers, see if we can get someone to come and kiss you.

"As for you, missy," she says. "Tell the Snow Queen now that we have Bae back, that we'll be over at the Palace next Tuesday for bridge. Just as soon as he has hands to hold the cards."

She puts you on Bae's back again, giving you such a warm kiss that your lips unfreeze, and you can speak again. "The woman of Lapmark is coming for tea tomorrow," you tell her.

The Finmany woman lifts Bae, and you upon his back, in her strong, fat arms, giving you a gentle push up the chimney.

Good morning, ladies, it's nice to have you on the premiere Snow Queen Tour. I hope that you all had a good night's sleep, because today we're going to be traveling quite some distance. I hope that everyone brought a comfortable pair of walking shoes. Let's have a head count, make sure that everyone on the list is here, and then we'll have introductions. My name is Gerda, and I'm looking forward to getting to know all of you.

Here you are at last, standing before the Snow Queen's palace, the palace of the woman who enchanted your lover and then stole him away in her long white sleigh. You aren't quite sure what you are going to say to her, or to him. When you check your pocket, you discover that your list has disappeared. You have most of it memorized, but you think maybe you will wait and see, before you say anything. Part of you would like to turn around and leave before the Snow Queen finds you, before Kay sees you. You are afraid that you will burst out crying or even worse, that he will know that you walked barefoot on broken glass across half the continent, just to find out why he left you.

The front door is open, so you don't bother knocking, you just walk right in. It isn't that large a palace, really. It is about the size of your own house and even reminds you of your own house, except that the furniture, Danish modern, is carved out of blue-green ice — as are the walls and everything else. It's a slippery place and you're glad that you are wearing the robber girl's boots. You have to admit that the Snow Queen is a meticulous housekeeper, much tidier than you ever were. You can't find the Snow Queen and you can't find Kay, but in every room there are white geese who, you are in equal parts relieved and surprised to discover, don't utter a single word.

"Gerda!" Kay is sitting at a table, fitting the pieces of a puzzle together. When he stands up, he knocks several pieces of the puzzle off the table, and they fall to the floor and shatter into even smaller fragments. You both kneel down, picking them up. The table is blue, the puzzle pieces are blue, Kay is blue, which is why you didn't see him when you first came into the room. The geese brush up against you, soft and white as cats.

"What took you so long?" Kay says. "Where in the world did you get those ridiculous boots?" You stare at him in disbelief.

"I walked barefoot on broken glass across half a continent to get here," you say. But at least you don't burst into tears. "A robber girl gave them to me."

Kay snorts. His blue nostrils flare. "Sweetie, they're hideous."

"Why are you blue?" you ask.

"I'm under an enchantment," he says. "The Snow Queen kissed me. Besides, I thought blue was your favorite color."

Your favorite color has always been yellow. You wonder if the Snow Queen kissed him all over, if he is blue all over. All the visible portions of his body are blue. "If you kiss me," he says, "you break the spell and I can come home with you. If you break the spell, I'll be in love with you again."

You refrain from asking if he was in love with you when he kissed the Snow Queen. Pardon me, you think, when she kissed him. "What is that puzzle you're working on?" you ask.

"Oh, that," he says. "That's the other way to break the spell. If I can put it together, but the other way is easier. Not to mention more fun. Don't you want to kiss me?"

You look at his blue lips, at his blue face. You try to remember if you liked his kisses. "Do you remember the white cat?" you say. "It didn't exactly run away. I took it to the woods and left it there."

"We can get another one," he says.

"I took it to the woods because it was telling me things."

"We don't have to get a talking cat," Kay says. "Besides, why did you walk barefoot across half a continent of broken glass if you aren't going to kiss me and break the spell?" His blue face is sulky.

"Maybe I just wanted to see the world," you tell him. "Meet interesting people."

The geese are brushing up against your ankles. You stroke their white feathers and the geese snap, but gently, at your fingers. "You had better hurry up and decide if you want to kiss me or not," Kay says. "Because she's home."

When you turn around, there she is, smiling at you like you are exactly the person that she was hoping to see.

The Snow Queen isn't how or what you'd expected. She's not as tall as you – you thought she would be taller. Sure, she's beautiful you can see why Kay kissed her (although you are beginning to wonder why she kissed him), but her eyes are black and kind, which you didn't expect at all. She stands next to you, not looking at Kay at all, but looking at you. "I wouldn't do it if I were you," she says.

"Oh come on," Kay says. "Give me a break, lady. Sure it was nice, but you don't want me hanging around this icebox forever, any more than I want to be here. Let Gerda kiss me, we'll go home and live happily ever after. There's supposed to be a happy ending."

"I like your boots," the Snow Queen says.

"You're beautiful," you tell her.

"I don't believe this," Kay says. He thumps his blue fist on the blue table, sending blue puzzle pieces flying through the air. Pieces lie like nuggets of sky-colored glass on the white backs of the geese. A piece of the table has splintered off, and you wonder if he is going to have to put the table back together as well.

"Do you love him?"

You look at the Snow Queen when she says this and then you look at Kay. "Sorry," you tell him. You hold out your hand in case he's willing to shake it.

"Sorry!" he says. "You're sorry! What good does that do me?"

"So what happens now?" you ask the Snow Queen.

"Up to you," she says. "Maybe you're sick of traveling. Are you?"

"I don't know," you say. "I think I'm finally beginning to get the hang of it."

"In that case," says the Snow Queen, "I may have a business proposal for you."

"Hey!" Kay says. "What about me? Isn't someone going to kiss me?"

You help him collect a few puzzle pieces. "Will you at least do this much for me?" he asks. "For old time's sake. Will you spread the word, tell a few single princesses that I'm stuck up here? I'd like to get out of here sometime in the next century. Thanks. I'd really appreciate it. You know, we had a really nice time, I think I remember that."

The robber girl's boots cover the scars on your feet. When you look at these scars, you can see the outline of the journey you made. Sometimes mirrors are maps, and sometimes maps are mirrors. Sometimes scars tell a story, and maybe someday you will tell this story to a lover. The soles of your feet are stories — hidden in the black boots, they shine like mirrors. If you were to take your boots off, you would see reflected in one foot-mirror the Princess Briar Rose as she sets off on her honeymoon, in her enormous four-poster bed, which now has wheels and is pulled by twenty white horses.

It's nice to see women exploring alternative means of travel.

In the other foot-mirror, almost close enough to touch, you could see the robber girl whose boots you are wearing. She is setting off to find Bae, to give him a kiss and bring him home again. You wouldn't presume to give her any advice, but you do hope that she has found another pair of good sturdy boots.

Someday, someone will probably make their way to the Snow Queen's palace, and kiss Kay's cold blue lips. She might even manage a happily ever after for a while.

You are standing in your black laced boots, and the Snow Queen's white geese mutter and stream and sidle up against you. You are beginning to understand some of what they are saying. They grumble about the weight of the sleigh, the weather, your hesitant jerks at their reins. But they are good-natured grumbles. You tell the geese that your feet are maps *and* your feet are mirrors. But you tell them that you have to keep in mind that they are also useful for walking around on. They are perfectly good feet.

winners and short lists

The Tiptree Award process does not call for a list of nominees from which a winner is chosen, because we feel that creates an artificial set of "losers" instead of a list of books worthy of attention. Instead, each panel releases a winner (or winners) and a "short list" of fiction which the judges consider especially worthy of readers' attention. In some years, the judges publish a "long list" of books they also found interesting in the course of their reading.

Below are the winners and short lists from all years of the award, as well as the long list from 2003. **Entries in boldface** are included in this volume. For more information on all of these works, please visit our website — at www.tiptree.org — for all of the annotated lists.

You are encouraged to join the not-so-secret Secret Feminist Cabal and forward recommendations for novels and short fiction works that explore and expand gender. You'll find a recommendation form on the website. The wider our network of supporters, the more good candidates the judges see every year.

2003 WINNER

Matt Ruff, *Set This House in Order: A Romance of Souls* (Harper-Collins 2003)

2003 SHORT LIST

Kim Antieau, *Coyote Cowgirl* (Forge 2003)

Richard Calder writing as Christina X, "The Catgirl Manifesto: An Introduction" (*Album Zutique* #1, edited by Jeff Vander-Meer, Ministry of Whimsy 2003)

Kara Dalkey, "The Lady of the Ice Garden" (*Firebirds*, edited by Sharyn November, Firebird 2003)
Carol Emshwiller, "Boys" (SCIFICTION 01.28.03)
Nina Kiriki Hoffman, *A Fistful of Sky* (Ace 2002)
Kij Johnson, *Fudoki* (Tor 2003)
Sandra McDonald, "The Ghost Girls of Rumney Mill" (*Realms of Fantasy*, August 2003)
Ruth Nestvold, "Looking through Lace" (*Asimov's Science Fiction*, September 2003)
Geoff Ryman, "Birth Days" (*Interzone*, April 2003)
Tricia Sullivan, *Maul* (Orbit 2003)

2003 LONG LIST
Storm Constantine, *The Wraiths of Will and Pleasure* (Tor 2003)
Jenny Davidson, *Heredity* (Soft Skull Press 2003)
Gregory Frost, *Fitcher's Brides* (Tor 2002)
Sally Miller Gearhart, *The Kanshou* (Spinsters Ink 2002)
Nalo Hopkinson, *The Salt Roads* (Warner 2003)
James Patrick Kelly, "Bernardo's House" (*Asimov's Science Fiction*, June 2003)
Kay Kenyon, *The Braided World* (Spectra 2003)
John Kessel, "Under the Lunchbox Tree" (*Asimov's Science Fiction*, July 2003)
Rosemary Kirstein, *The Lost Steersman* (Del Rey 2003)
Nancy Jane Moore, "Walking Contradiction" (*Imaginings*, edited by Keith R.A. DeCandido, Pocket Books 2003)
Pat Murphy, "The Wild Girls" (*Witpunk*, edited by Claude Lalumière and Marty Halpern, Four Walls Eight Windows 2003)
Ruth L. Ozeki, *All Over Creation* (Viking 2003)
Ed Park, "Well-Moistened With Cheap Wine, The Sailor and the Wayfarer Sing of Their Absent Sweethearts," (*Trampoline*, edited by Kelly Link, Small Beer 2003)
Tim Pratt, "Poor Man's Wife" (*Lady Churchill's Rosebud Wristlet* 13, November 2003)

Tom Purdom, "Path of the Transgressor" (*Asimov's Science Fiction*, June 2003)
Vandana Singh, "The Woman Who Thought She Was a Planet" (*Trampoline*, edited by Kelly Link, Small Beer 2003)
Jo Walton, *Tooth and Claw* (Tor 2003)

2002 WINNERS
M. John Harrison, *Light*
John Kessel, "Stories for Men"

2002 SHORT LIST
Eleanor Arnason, "Knapsack Poems"
Ted Chiang, "Liking What You See: A Documentary"
John Clute, *Appleseed*
Karen Joy Fowler, "What I Didn't See"
Gregory Frost, "Madonna of the Maquiladora"
Shelley Jackson, *The Melancholy of Anatomy*
Larissa Lai, *Salt Fish Girl*
Peter Straub, editor, *Conjunctions 39: The New Wave Fabulists*

2001 WINNER
Hiromi Goto, *The Kappa Child*

2001 SHORT LIST
Joan Givner, *Half Known Lives*
Hugh Nissenson, *The Song of the Earth*
Ken MacLeod, *Dark Light*
Sheri S. Tepper, *The Fresco*

2000 WINNER
Molly Gloss, *Wild Life*

2000 SHORT LIST
Michael Blumlein, "Fidelity: A Primer"
James L. Cambias, "A Diagram of Rapture"

David Ebershoff, *The Danish Girl*
Mary Gentle, *Ash: A Secret History*
Camille Hernandez-Ramdwar, "Soma"
Nalo Hopkinson, "The Glass Bottle Trick"
Nalo Hopkinson, *Midnight Robber*
China Miéville, *Perdido Street Station*
Pamela Mordecai, "Once on the Shores of the Stream Senegambia"
Severna Park, *The Annunciate*
Tess Williams, *Sea as Mirror*

1999 WINNER
Suzy McKee Charnas, *The Conqueror's Child*

1999 SHORT LIST
Judy Budnitz, *If I Told You Once*
Sally Caves, "In the Second Person"
Graham Joyce, "Pinkland"
Yumiko Kurahashi, *The Woman with the Flying Head and other stories*
Penelope Lively, "5001 Nights"
David E. Morse, *The Iron Bridge*
Kim Stanley Robinson, "Sexual Dimorphism"

1998 WINNER
Raphael Carter, "Congenital Agenesis of Gender Ideation"

1998 SHORT LIST
Eleanor Arnason, "The Gauze Banner"
Octavia Butler, *Parable of the Talents*
Ted Chiang, "Story of Your Life"
Stella Duffy, *Singling Out the Couples*
Karen Joy Fowler, *Black Glass*
Maggie Gee, *The Ice People*
Carolyn Ives Gilman, *Halfway Human*
Phyllis Gotlieb, *Flesh and Gold*

Nalo Hopkinson, *Brown Girl in the Ring*
Gwyneth Jones, "La Cenerentola"
James Patrick Kelly, "Lovestory"
Ursula K. Le Guin, "Unchosen Love"
Elizabeth A. Lynn, *Dragon's Winter*
Maureen F. McHugh, *Mission Child*
Karl-Rene Moore, "The Hetairai Turncoat"
Rebecca Ore, "Accelerated Grimace"
Sara Paretsky, *Ghost Country*
Severna Park, *Hand of Prophecy*
Kit Reed, "The Bride of Bigfoot"
Kit Reed, *Weird Women, Wired Women*
Robert Reed, "Whiptail"
Mary Rosenblum, "The Eye of God"
Joan Slonczewski, *The Children Star*
Martha Soukup, "The House of Expectations"
Sean Stewart, *Mockingbird*
Sarah Zettel, *Playing God*

1997 WINNERS
Candas Jane Dorsey, *Black Wine*
Kelly Link, "Travels with the Snow Queen"

1997 SHORT LIST
Storm Constantine, "The Oracle Lips"
Paul Di Filippo, "Alice, Alfie, Ted and the Aliens"
Emma Donoghue, *Kissing the Witch: Old Tales in New Skins*
L. Timmel Duchamp, "The Apprenticeship of Isabetta di Pietro Cavazzi"
Molly Gloss, *The Dazzle of Day*
M. John Harrison, *Signs of Life*
Gwyneth Jones, "Balinese Dancer"
Ian McDonald, *Sacrifice of Fools*
Vonda N. McIntyre, *The Moon and the Sun*

Shani Mootoo, *Cereus Blooms at Night*
Salman Rushdie, "The Firebird's Nest"
Paul Witcover, *Waking Beauty*

1996 WINNERS
Ursula K. Le Guin, "Mountain Ways"
Mary Doria Russell, *The Sparrow*

1996 SHORT LIST
Fred Chappell, "The Silent Woman"
Suzy McKee Charnas, "Beauty and the Opera, or The Phantom Beast"
L. Timmel Duchamp, "Welcome, Kid, to the Real World"
Alasdair Gray, *A History Maker*
Jonathan Lethem, "Five Fucks"
Pat Murphy, *Nadya*
Rachel Pollack, *Godmother Night*
Lisa Tuttle, *The Pillow Friend*
Tess Williams, "And She Was the Word"
Sue Woolfe, *Leaning Towards Infinity*

1995 WINNERS
Elizabeth Hand, *Waking the Moon*
Theodore Roszak, *The Memoirs of Elizabeth Frankenstein*

1995 SHORT LIST
Kelley Eskridge, "And Salome Danced"
Kit Reed, *Little Sisters of the Apocalypse*
Lisa Tuttle, "Food Man"
Terri Windling, editor, *The Armless Maiden and other stories for childhood's survivors*

1994 WINNERS

Ursula K. Le Guin, "The Matter of Seggri"
Nancy Springer, *Larque on the Wing*

1994 SHORT LIST

Eleanor Arnason, "The Lovers"
Suzy McKee Charnas, *The Furies*
L. Warren Douglas, *Cannon's Orb*
Greg Egan, "Cocoon"
Ellen Frye, *Amazon Story Bones*
Gwyneth Jones, *North Wind*
Graham Joyce & Peter F. Hamilton, "Eat Reecebread"
Ursula K. Le Guin, *A Fisherman of the Inland Sea*
Ursula K. Le Guin, "Forgiveness Day"
Rachel Pollack, *Temporary Agency*
Geoff Ryman, *Unconquered Countries*
Melissa Scott, *Trouble and Her Friends*
Delia Sherman, "Young Woman in a Garden"
George Turner, *Genetic Soldier*

1993 WINNER

Nicola Griffith, *Ammonite*

1993 SHORT LIST

Eleanor Arnason, *Ring of Swords*
Margaret Atwood, *The Robber Bride*
Sybil Claiborne, *In the Garden of Dead Cars*
L. Timmel Duchamp, "Motherhood"
R. Garcia y Robertson, "The Other Magpie"
James Patrick Kelly, "Chemistry"
Laurie J. Marks, *Dancing Jack*
Ian McDonald, "Some Strange Desire"
Alice Nunn, *Illicit Passage*
Paul Park, *Coelestis*

1992 WINNER

Maureen McHugh, *China Mountain Zhang*

1992 SHORT LIST

Carol Emshwiller, "Venus Rising"

Ian MacLeod, "Grownups"

Judith Moffett, *Time, Like an Ever Rolling Stream*

Kim Stanley Robinson, *Red Mars*

Sue Thomas, *Correspondence*

Lisa Tuttle, *Lost Futures*

Elisabeth Vonarburg, *In the Mother's Land*

1991 WINNERS

Eleanor Arnason, *A Woman of the Iron People*

Gwyneth Jones, *The White Queen*

1991 SHORT LIST

John Barnes, *Orbital Resonance*

Karen Joy Fowler, *Sarah Canary*

Mary Gentle, *The Architecture of Desire*

Greer Ilene Gilman, *Moonwise*

Marge Piercy, *He, She and It*

RETROSPECTIVE AWARD WINNERS

Suzy McKee Charnas, *Motherlines* (1978)

Suzy McKee Charnas, *Walk to the End of the World* (1974)

Ursula K. Le Guin, *The Left Hand of Darkness* (1969)

Joanna Russ, *The Female Man* (1975)

Joanna Russ, "When It Changed" (1972)

RETROSPECTIVE AWARD SHORT LIST

Margaret Atwood, *The Handmaid's Tale* (1986)

Iain Banks, *The Wasp Factory* (1984)

Katherine Burdekin, *Swastika Night* (1937)

Octavia Butler, *Wild Seed* (1980)
Samuel R. Delany, *Babel-17* (1966)
Samuel R. Delany, *Triton* (1976)
Carol Emshwiller, *Carmen Dog* (1990)
Sonya Dorman Hess, "When I Was Miss Dow" (1966)
Elizabeth A. Lynn, *Watchtower* (1979)
Vonda McIntyre, *Dreamsnake* (1978)
Naomi Mitchison, *Memoirs of a Spacewoman* (1962)
Marge Piercy, *Woman on the Edge of Time* (1976)
Joanna Russ, *The Two of Them* (1978)
Pamela Sargent, editor, *Women of Wonder* (1974), *More Women of Wonder* (1976) and *The New Women of Wonder* (1977)
John Varley, "The Barbie Murders" (1978)
Kate Wilhelm, *The Clewiston Test* (1976)
Monique Wittig, *Les Guerillères* (1969)
Pamela Zoline, "The Heat Death of the Universe" (1967)

acknowledgements

Every year, five thoughtful and careful souls read a mountain of books recommended by readers, publishers, and each other, to determine the winner(s) and shortlisted works for that year's Tiptree Award, rewarded only with stunning collage T-shirts by artist Freddie Baer, cloisonné Space Babe pins, the endless gratitude of the Motherboard, and the reading pleasure of people who use the award lists as reading suggestions. With the advent of this volume, that last reward will increase greatly. Here's who you have to thank for most of the selections in this book.

Michael Marc Levy, science fiction critic and Chair of the Department of English Literature at University of Wisconsin–Stout; Vicki Rosenzweig, a long-time fan, nonfiction writer, and editor; Lori Selke, editor of *Tough Girls: Down and Dirty Dyke Erotica*, and the zine *Problem Child*; Nisi Shawl, whose stories have been published in *Asimov's Science Fiction*, *Strange Horizons*, *Mojo: Conjure Stories* and in both volumes of the groundbreaking *Dark Matter* anthology series; and Maureen Kincaid Speller, critic, reviewer, English literature student and former Arthur C. Clarke Award judge.

Many other people helped both with putting together this book and with doing the work that made the book possible.

Two members of the Tiptree Award Motherboard, Jeanne Gomoll and Ellen Klages, somehow got out of having their names on this anthology, despite all of the superb work they do for the award and the books. If they thought they would get away without being mentioned

at all, they were wrong. Kat Angeli acts as Motherboard treasur
which is how the authors get paid.

The judges can't function without the help of our Tiptree Awa
procurers, who undertake to get recommended books from pu
lishers. This job was established by Susanna Sturgis, carried on e
tremely well by Spike Parsons, and is now ably accomplished by G
W. Thomas.

Jacob Weisman at Tachyon Publications has the faith in this boo
which makes him willing to publish it as the first in a series. Bern
Goodman originally brought the idea to Jacob's notice. Jill Rober
also contributed on Tachyon's behalf. John D. Berry, designer *extrao
dinaire*, has already been through endless iterations of the cover d
sign, and we will no doubt have more reasons to thank him by th
time the interior design is complete. Long before the book nee
proofreading, Ann Smith has been doing time on tedious help wi
manuscript preparation. Sharyn November of Firebird Books ha
been extremely cooperative in supplying copyedited manuscripts i
useful formats.

And finally, we have to thank the legions of members of the Secr
Feminist Cabal: the ones who run bake sales, bake cookies, contrib
ute auction items, recommend books to the jury, and do the legion o
other tasks that make the Tiptree Award both successful and fun. Yo
know who you are.

about the authors

HANS CHRISTIAN ANDERSEN was born in Fyn, Denmark, in 1805. He wrote novels, short stories, travel books, poetry and plays; but he was best known, during his lifetime and after, for his *eventyr* – his fairy tales. He died in 1875.

RICHARD CALDER was born in 1956, in Whitechapel, London. In the mid-seventies he read English Literature at the University of Sussex. After graduating he traveled extensively throughout Southeast Asia and Australia and, upon returning to the UK, subsequently worked in bookselling, independent television, and the American Embassy's press office. He became a full-time author in 1990 after moving from London to Nongkhai, Thailand, a border town overlooking Laos. In 1998 he moved to the Philippines, where he lived for some years in Castillejos, Zambales, and Baguio City. (Both Thailand and the Philippines feature heavily in his work.) After returning to London, and enduring a brief sojourn in the suburbs, he currently resides in another "East" – his native East End.

Richard Calder has been published in *Interzone*, *Science Fiction Eye*, and *Omni*. His novels include the "Dead" trilogy (*Dead Girls*, *Dead Boys*, *Dead Things*), *Cythera*, *Frenzetta*, *The Twist*, *Malignos*, *Impakto*, and *Lord Soho*.

SUZY MCKEE CHARNAS won the Nebula Award for her novella "The Unicorn Tapestry," the Hugo Award for her short story "Boobs," and a Mythopoeic Society Award for her children's book, *The Kingdom of Kevin Malone*. The first two novels of her four-novel Holdfast Chronicles series, *Walk to the End of the World* and *Motherlines*, were awarded the Retrospective Tiptree Award. *The Conquerer's Child*, the conclusion to the Holdfast Chronicles, won the Tiptree Award in 1999. A versatile writer, she has written young adult fantasies, two vampire novels, a mainstream novel about art, ghosts, and land fraud set in New Mexico, short stories, two plays, and the complete revision of the libretto to a musical, *Nosferatu*.

KARA DALKEY was born in 1953 in Los Angeles. She has written/published fifteen novels and a dozen short stories, all fantasy, historical fantasy, or science fiction. Her most recent publications have been *Water*, a trilogy of young adult novels she describes as "the Atlantis and Arthurian myths in a blender." Her most recent short story other than the one in this volume appears in *Tales of the Slayer II*. Kara now lives in the Pacific Northwest, a land of other writers, musicians, and addicts of caffeine. Her current hobbies include spending too much time on computer games and playing electric bass in an oldies rock n' roll band.

CAROL EMSHWILLER says, "I grew up in France and Ann Arbor, Michigan. My dad was a professor there. I was a dreadful student, just squeaking by with Cs and a few Ds. That was because (well, partly) going back and forth from France to here. I was hopelessly confused. So confused I gave up at age eleven. *And* I'm such a slow reader I often wonder why I'm in this job...the teaching of writing and needing to read all the time. But even though I was a bad student, I always did love to read.

"I was a housewife with three children through all the big middle part of my life. I had to struggle for every little moment of writing time I could get.

"My young adult novel, *Mr. Boots*, will come out from either Penguin Putnam or Firebird Books. Also, they'll reissue my Nebula-nominated *The Mount* as a young adult novel. Tachyon Publications will publish my fifth book of short stories sometime next year."

KAREN JOY FOWLER, a Founding Mother of the Tiptree Award, is one of the editors of this volume.

DIANA CRONE FRANK has a Ph.D. in linguistics and produces documentaries for television. JEFFREY FRANK is a senior editor at *The New Yorker* and the author of the novels *The Columnist* and *Bad Publicity*. They live in Manhattan.

URSULA K. LE GUIN has published six books of poetry, twenty novels, over a hundred short stories (collected in eleven volumes), four collections of essays, eleven books for children, and four volumes of translation. Her work includes realistic fiction, science fiction, fantasy, young children's books, books for young adults, screenplays, essays, verbal texts for musicians, and voicetexts for performance or recording. Her awards include a National Book Award, five Hugo Awards, five Nebula Awards, SFWA's Grand Master, the Kafka Award, a Pushcart Prize, the Howard Vursell Award of the American Academy of Arts and Letters, the L.A. Times Robert Kirsch Award, the PEN/Faulkner Award for Short Stories, and the ALA Margaret Edwards Award for Young Adult Fiction. She is also a two-time winner of the James Tiptree, Jr. Award and a winner of the Tiptree Retrospective Award.

KELLY LINK's collection, *Stranger Things Happen*, was a Firecracker nominee, a Village Voice Favorite Book and a Salon Book of the Year – *Salon* called the collection "...an alchemical mixture of Borges, Raymond Chandler, and Buffy the Vampire Slayer." Stories from the collection have won the Nebula, Tiptree and World Fantasy Awards.

Kelly lives in Northampton, MA, and is currently working on a new collection of stories. She received her BA from Columbia University and her MFA from the University of North Carolina at Greensboro. Kelly and her husband, Gavin J. Grant, publish books and a twice-yearly zine, *Lady Churchill's Rosebud Wristlet*, as Small Beer Press.

Sandra McDonald served as a commissioned officer in the US Navy and then went on to unspectacular achievements as a wannabe Hollywood scriptwriter. Having traipsed through the jungles of Guam and braved the wilds of Newfoundland she now resides in a century-old house in Massachusetts overlooking the sea. Her work has appeared in *Realms of Fantasy*, *Strange Horizons*, *Talebones* and more. Visit her website at www.sandramcdonald.com.

In order to feed her writing addiction, Ruth Nestvold works as a contractor in software localization. She has sold short stories to a variety of markets including *Isaac Asimov's Science Fiction Magazine*, *Realms of Fantasy*, *Strange Horizons*, *Andromeda Spaceways*, and NFG. On occasion, she maintains a web site at www.ruthnestvold.com.

Matt Ruff is not a multiple personality, but he is an obsessive personality, a condition for which he self-medicates with marriage to a patient woman. In addition to *Set This House in Order*, he is the author of *Fool on the Hill* and *Sewer, Gas & Electric: The Public Works Trilogy*. He lives in Seattle, Washington.

Joanna Russ, winner of the Nebula and Hugo Awards, is the author of seven novels, including *The Female Man* and *On Strike Against God*. Her critical works include *How to Suppress Women's Writing* and *To Write Like a Woman: Essays in Feminism and Science Fiction*. She was awarded the Retrospective Tiptree Award for her short story "When It Changed" and her novel *The Female Man*.

Geoff Ryman is a Canadian living in London and sometimes in Brazil. His main claim to fame is working on the very first British monarchy and No 10 Downing Street websites back in the mid-90s. His fiction has won the British Science Fiction Association Award twice, the World Fantasy Award, the Arthur C Clarke Award, the John W Campbell Memorial Award, the Eastercon Award and the Philip K Dick Award. It's long been an ambition of his to be listed for the

Tiptree because of the focus on gender issues, and it hasn't happened since 1994, so he's dead chuffed. Next novels: *AIR* and *The King's Last Song*.

ALICE SHELDON/JAMES TIPTREE, JR., needs no introduction here, because she is introduced repeatedly throughout the book.

about the editors

KAREN JOY FOWLER is the author of two story collections and four novels, the third of which, *Sister Noon*, was a finalist for the PEN/Faulkner award. Her first novel, *Sarah Canary*, won the Commonwealth medal for best first novel by a Californian in 1991. Her short story collection *Black Glass* won the World Fantasy Award in 1999; her first two novels were both *New York Times* notable books in their year. Her most recent novel is the bestseller *The Jane Austen Book Club*, published by Putnam in April of 2004. She lives with her husband in Davis, California.

PAT MURPHY has won numerous awards for her science fiction and fantasy writing. In 1987, she won the Nebula, an award presented by the Science Fiction Writers of America, for both her second novel, *The Falling Woman*, and her novelette "Rachel in Love." In 1990, her short story collection, *Points of Departure*, won the Philip K. Dick Award for best paperback original and her novella "Bones" won the World Fantasy Award. Her short fiction has also won the Isaac Asimov Reader's Award and the Theodore Sturgeon Memorial Award and has reached the final ballot for the Hugo Award, presented by the World Science Fiction Convention. Her novel *There and Back Again* won the 2002 Seiun Award for best foreign science fiction novel translated into Japanese. Her most recent novel is *Adventures in Time and Space with Max Merriwell*. When she is not writing science fiction, Pat writes for the Exploratorium, San Francisco's museum of science, art, and human perception. She is a Founding Mother of the James Tiptree Award and a member of the Award's Motherboard.

DEBBIE NOTKIN is an editor and nonfiction writer. She edited *Flying Cups & Saucers*, the first collection of Tiptree-recognized short fiction, published by Edgewood Press in 1998. She edited and wrote the text for photographer Laurie Toby Edison's two books, *Women En Large: Images of Fat Nudes*, and *Familiar Men: A Book of Nudes*. She is the chair of the James Tiptree Award Motherboard and a member of the Motherboard of Broad Universe, an organization with the primary goal of promoting science fiction, fantasy, and horror written by women. She has been an editor and consulting editor for Tor Books and Prima Publishing. Her essays on body image, and on science fiction, have been widely published and she has spoken on these topics all over the United States and in Japan.

JEFFREY D. SMITH was a friend of James Tiptree's and is the literary trustee of her estate. He is a member of the James Tiptree Award Motherboard. He edited "Women in Science Fiction," a groundbreaking 1975 symposium, and *Meet Me at Infinity*, a posthumous collection of Tiptree's stories and essays.